Bad Dreams

ALSO BY KIM NEWMAN
AND AVAILABLE FROM TITAN BOOKS
Anno Dracula
Anno Dracula: The Bloody Red Baron
Anno Dracula: Dracula Cha Cha Cha
Anno Dracula: Johnny Alucard

Professor Moriarty: the Hound of the D'Urbervilles
Jago
The Quorum
Life's Lottery
An English Ghost Story

COMING SOON
The Night Mayor

KIM NEWMAN

Bad Dreams

TITAN BOOKS

Bad Dreams
Print edition ISBN: 9781781165614
E-book edition ISBN: 9781781165621

Published by Titan Books
A division of Titan Publishing Group Ltd
144 Southwark Street, London SE1 0UP

First edition: November 2014

1 3 5 7 9 10 8 6 4 2

Did you enjoy this book? We love to hear from our readers.
Please email us at readerfeedback@titanemail.com or write to us at
Reader Feedback at the above address.

To receive advance information, news, competitions, and exclusive offers online, please sign up for the Titan newsletter on our website: www.titanbooks.com

For The Peace and Love Corporation, Plc.

'First you dream, then you die.'

CORNELL WOOLRICH

THE MORNING BEFORE

1

Judi dreamed she was waking up. Without moving, she got out of the double bed, pulled a rough towel robe over the things she was still wearing, and searched the mess on the carpeted floor for her Camels. She found most of her clothes, relatively unspoiled, mixed up with Coral's. Also three empty Dom Pérignon bottles, a shredded Iris Murdoch paperback, some studded leather fripperies and a multi-coloured scattering of pills. Her head was an open wound, leaking steadily, and she had either vomited recently or would do so soon. She hauled her heavy black jacket out of the heap and patted its zippered pockets. No luck. She walked across the room, knees and ankles threatening to fail her, and became acutely aware of the sticky ache between her legs.

Sweet Jesus, did we get raped again?

Most of one wall was mirrored. On this side only, of course. The room beyond was dark. Even if she put her face close to the glass she couldn't see through. It was probably empty this early in the morning. The show was over. She sat at the dressing table and scratched her scalp. The spiky perm was well into its decay. She pulled her handbag open and went through it. The Camels were there, but someone had snapped her disposable lighter in half. Her money, credit cards, diary, hankies and address book were soaked. She stuck the least wet cigarette in her mouth, hoping she would not burn half her face off.

No matches. She would have to wake Coral.

The other girl was still in bed, comatose. She had been twisting and turning as if buried alive. A nylon sheet wound around her like a soiled blue boa constrictor. The bare mattress was missing several buttons, and patterned with old pee, blood and come stains. In the bruising on Coral's back, bottom and legs, Judi could see designs. The yellow and blue smudges were handsome faces with red welts for eyes. The faces coalesced, making a Japanese dragon with heaving shoulderblades for wings and penny-sized scales of ragged flesh.

The little green scorpion tattooed on Coral's wrist scuttled out from under her digital watch and took refuge in her armpit. Judi was back in the bed now, sinking into the mattress, soothing the ruffled dragon with practised massage. She had given up on Coral's matches, and spat the Camel out onto the pillow. The bed hugged her. The duvet slithered up over her bare legs. Judi's eyes turned inward, focusing on a white hot point three inches behind the bridge of her nose. The pain went away.

She was not dreaming she was awake any more. She opened her eyes and saw the skylight. The dingy grey looked about ready to fall. She had always thought Chicken Licken had a better grasp of cosmology than Galileo.

Really awake, she sat up in bed, wearily ready to go through it all again.

That was when she realized she was handcuffed to a severed arm.

2

The old, old man watched, his own reflection faintly superimposed on the dusty one-way glass. In his current condition, he was glad not to be looking at the silvered side of the mirror. He had lost a lot of weight recently. He did not like to be reminded of his flesh. It was turning into greasy lumps that shifted and shrank beneath his slackening skin. The fabric of his quilted dressing gown hung heavily on his arm as he raised a hand to the cold glass. His fingers were dead, the knuckles swollen with ersatz arthritis.

He was unaroused by the spectacle. Judi was thrashing around the room, unsuccessfully trying to rid herself of the dead weight hanging from her wrist. She was screaming, but he had chosen to switch off the intercom. He could still just hear the racket, but these Victorian walls had been built for privacy. Already, the girl was beginning to wear herself down. Already, he was beginning to feel the warmth.

He knew his face was filling out, settling comfortably again onto his skull. His hands grew fatter. The skin crept back over the half-moons of his fingernails. His fingers bent, knuckles cracking, he made a comfortable vice-grip fist. He felt himself expanding to fit his clothes. His dry mouth filled again with water. His teeth swelled, and sharpened, changing the shape of his jaw, making him grin.

Now, he was ready for Judi.

He used the connecting door. It had never been locked, but there was no handle on her side. Judi had finished with her hysterics, and was back in the bed. She was coiled in a foetal ball, with Coral's arm sticking out in place of an umbilical cord. The little green scorpion was resting. It had been neatly done. There was almost no blood. The room smelled musty. He caught the residues of spent lusts in his nostrils, and drew them into himself, tasting them as they went down.

The things he had watched last night were replayed inside his head. He smiled, new skin tight over his cheekbones. Judi, he remembered. And Coral. The clients. Pain and pleasure, locked together. And the almost pathetic pettiness of it all. It had barely been an appetizer for what he would do now. Coral, a pretty but dull girl, would have been a less substantial delight than Judi. Barely a morsel. But still, it was a shame she had been wasted. Her death had given him little sustenance.

He climbed into bed and cuddled Judi. He touched her fractured mind, feeling for the spots that would give first, sinking black fingers into her confusion. She was delicious. He stroked her side, his nails turned to bony scalpels. He opened her at the hip, and scraped the bone. She convulsed like an electro-shock patient. He clamped a passionless kiss over her shriek. He swallowed air, and her cries echoed inside, him.

He fed off her for hours, until her heart burst.

DAYTIME

1

Anne was waiting for The Call.

Every couple of days, she would telephone the old family home, and talk with Dad's nurse. She had never met the woman, and at the echoing end of the transatlantic line, she sounded like a little girl a long way away. Her father had had his second stroke back in September, and all the doctors were expecting the third soon. If not before the end of the year, then early in January. The first stroke, three years earlier, had just slowed him down and slurred his words. The second had put him in a chair and made talking a supreme effort. The third would kill him.

She had the Radio 4 early morning current affairs show on in the tiny kitchen, and the Channel 4 breakfast television service on in her front room, and was dividing her attention between them, following several stories as they broke. It was mostly international activity, in Central America and Eastern Europe, but there were a few local, London-based, items she was keeping an ear to. She had already done her two days in the newsroom this week, but she was scheduled to turn in a couple of pieces by Friday, to meet the deadline for the Christmas double issue. The Aziz inquest would be turning in a verdict in the next few days, and, depending on the degree of officially admitted police involvement in the youth's death, that would affect the conclusions she would draw in the last of her articles on racist attacks.

The old boiler rattled, and Anne checked the heating. The flame was going full inside, but the flat was not getting any warmer. She really ought to start looking for a new place in the New Year. When her father died, there would be some money from the estate. She shivered with the thought, and tried to unthink it, forcing it back into the blacks of her mind. She shivered again, only with the cold, and pulled her robe tighter over her nightie. It would be warmer when she had her clothes on.

There were tanks moving through rubble-strewn streets on television, and a foreign correspondent on the radio was making a report with the whoosh of anti-tank rockets in the background. Anne was not sure whether the coverages were of the same crisis. Usually, news wound down for Christmas; this year, events were speeding up as the holiday approached. Some governments were probably planning to spring nasty surprises over the Christmas break, purely to avoid publicity. TV programmers had already overloaded the airwaves with blockbuster movies, light entertainment specials and quiz-of-the-year features, and there was no room at the inn for states of emergency, covert activities or the odd execution.

She had a morning at home due, and the notes for her pieces were neatly piled by the word processor in the front room. That meant, since she did not have to struggle through the rush hour to get to Clerkenwell, she could take some care over breakfast. 'The most important meal of the day,' her British friends would tell her as her stomach somersaulted at the sight of grease-grilled bacon, runny eggs and a horror they called fried bread. In the kitchen, a cheerful vicar on 'Thought for the Day' was trying to draw some Biblical parallel between current events and those in Nazareth at the time of the Nativity. While her old-fashioned percolator dripped thick coffee, she mixed St Michael's 'Thick and Creamy' strawberry and mango yoghurt with Neal's Yard muesli, and added just a little milk. Two croissants were gently warming in the depths of the oven.

At eight o'clock, the radio and the TV hit news bulletins at the same time, and told the same stories in slightly varying ways. Anne did the remains of last night's washing-up. Two teacups, two wine-glasses, and the dug-out-from-somewhere ashtray. For a moment, she wondered if Mark had expected to stay the night with her. She thought that was not going to happen, but recently, he had been a bit broody around her at the office. He went all quiet and British when she was talking to anyone else, and was hearty with her in that slightly hollow way of his. She put the dripping cups and glasses up on the rack to dry. She was getting the impression that Mark was capable of a species of desperate devotion she would find stifling. For her, this year, turning thirty without having been married or had children had not been the stereotypical shock. The only thing she wished she had done was write a book, and there was plenty of time for that. Maybe she could fix up the racist attack series. It was an important subject.

She took the croissants out, welcoming the outrush of warm air from the oven. Outside the fire escape window, she could see frost-furred ironwork. It was cold, and the forecasters were saying it would get colder. She carried her breakfast tray through to the front room. The television was warning of a traffic snarl-up in North London. The trains were running intermittently because of the cold. Every year, winter caught London Regional Transport by surprise, as if they expected a dingy summer to stretch on until the year's end. Anne's fingers felt the chill, and she warmed them on the croissants. Sitting at the folding table she had pulled out for Mark and not put away, she ate the croissants and watched the television.

Usually, with her breakfast, she opened her mail and set aside letters that needed immediate replies, listed cheques in her account books and paid bills. She liked to get that out of the way before she started anything. Her father's lawyers were sending her a packet of legal documents federal express. But, thanks to the Christmas post, the mail was not arriving until late in the morning this week. She already had too many cards for her limited mantelpiece and shelf space, and was beginning to regret her decision not to bother this year. She took her first caffeine hit of the day, and considered the muesli and yoghurt.

At first, the expectation of The Call had been constant. Every time she heard a telephone ring, even if she was not in her flat or an office where she could be traced, she had been instantly certain that this was it, and felt her heart squeeze. Then, the dread had turned to a dull resignation, although she realized that, when it came, it would still surprise her.

Fathers died, she knew. Hers had written an entire play about the fact. And when the third seizure came, the film of the play would undoubtedly be pulled out of the vaults and shown on late-night television as a tribute. She had videoed *On the Graveyard Shift at Sam's Bar-B-Q and Grill* the last time it was on, but had not got around to watching it again. Produced on Broadway in 1954 and filmed in 1955, the property had been cited by the Nobel Prize Committee as a great achievement, but it had also dwarfed everything else Cameron Nielson ever did, including raise children. Anne still found it hard to associate the play, written before she was born, with the distant, kindly, disappointed man she had known all her life. In the big, last-act speech, where Maish Johnson – the role that proved Brando's Stanley Kowalski was not a one-off achievement – angrily expressed his grief at the death of Sam, the fatherly-wise owner of the all-night Bar-B-Q and Grill, and denounced everyone else's numbed reaction to the bad news, Anne knew that her father had written the cornerstone of his own obituary. He had been a young man when he wrote Maish's speech, fiercely identifying with his hero; how would he feel now that he had been pushed, presumably kicking and screaming inside his chairbound bone-and-flesh prison, into the Lee J. Cobb role of Sam?

She took a spoon to the muesli and yoghurt, and mixed them up more thoroughly. The news was starting to repeat, so she zapped from channel to channel, getting an early morning educational show about claw-feed grinding, a high-tech commercial for a bank, and three presenters on a pastel couch swapping mild innuendoes with a teenage pop star. The coffee was getting into her system, waking her up. She laced her cold fingers, and rubbed her palms together, generating some warmth. Back at the news, there was a thirty second blip on the Aziz incident: a black and white photograph, grainily enlarged, of the smiling Pakistani at his wedding; another, post-mortem, of his swollen face on a pillow; a brief, live, snippet of Constable Erskine, in uniform, being hustled out of the inquest, dodging microphones.

At the sight of Erskine's face, Anne felt a flash of cold anger. She had never met the policeman, but she had read the doctor's reports on Charlie Aziz, arrested for 'driving without due care and attention', breathalysed and proved not under the influence of alcohol, then battered to death by 'person or persons unknown' in a South London cell. The official version was that Charlie suffered a claustrophobic spell and injured himself fatally, but Anne knew that was not consistent with his all-round injuries and with the police force's unexplained suspension of Erskine, the arresting officer. Erskine, a blandly handsome young man, did not look like a monster, but then they never did. In his off hours, according to Anne's investigation, Erskine was a member of the English Liberation Front, a far right splinter group who alleged that immigrants from the Indian sub-continent and the Caribbean constitute an army of occupation and should be resisted with *maquis* tactics.

Aziz's parents were glimpsed, but they did not get to say anything. Over the last few weeks, attending meetings of the Charlie Aziz Memorial Committee to Stop the Attacks, Anne had got quite close to the boy's mother. She admired the woman's quiet determination, and her ability to cope with family tragedy while doing something concrete about it. Mrs Aziz, Anne believed, was quite capable of forcing answers from the police where years of investigating journalists would only get nothingy press hand-outs. And if that happened, there would definitely be a book in it. Perhaps even a television docu-drama. Perhaps…

She picked up her spoon, and the telephone rang. She dropped the spoon, and found herself shaking. It was only partly the cold. Using the remote control, she turned off the television. The ringing was needlessly loud.

Nerving herself for The Call, she picked up the telephone, and said 'hello'.

The line did not crackle. It was not from America. This was not The Call.

'Anne…' It was Mark. Her whole body tensed. She did not need an '…about last night…' conversation. 'Anne, I'm ringing from the office…'

He sounded edgy, urgent, like a conspirator during a crisis.

'Mark, I…'

'The police have been checking up on you, Anne…'

The doorbell rang.

'Mark, excuse me, someone at the door…'

She put the receiver down, and stabbed the entryphone buzzer. It would be the postman, and she did not want to miss him and have to take the trip to the sorting office to pick up the Federal Express packet. She unlatched her door, and stepped out onto the landing.

It was not the postman. Anne shrank back, mentally kicking herself for her lack of caution. In New York, that sort of mistake could get you killed; and London these days was not exactly a paradise of non-violence either.

'Good morning,' said the visitor. 'Anne Nielson?'

It was a civil service type in a grey topcoat, but the dread did not lift.

'Yes?'

He showed her a card, with his photograph under plastic. She looked at it, but could not focus on the words.

'I'm Inspector Joseph Hollis, from the Holborn Police Station.'

The name did not mean anything to her. She looked backwards, at the still off-the-hook telephone. She adopted a neutral expression, and did not invite the policeman into her flat. Any business they had could be done on the landing. She was not paranoid, but she had friends who had been harassed for what they wrote. She had not expected any official feedback on her Aziz pieces, but she was not surprised.

'Miss Nielson?'

The face was unreadable but vaguely sympathetic, the voice professionally expressionless.

She took a breath. 'Yes.'

'Anne *Veronica* Nielson?'

She expected to be told her rights. 'Uh-huh.'

'And do you have a sister, *Judith* Nielson?'

Judi! She always came out of left field, but today...

'Yes. What is this about?'

This time, the policeman drew breath. Whatever it was, she knew, it would be bad. With Judi, it was always bad.

'I'm sorry, miss, but I have to tell you that your sister is dead.'

2

The night before, Nina had been out with Rollo, one of her regulars. They had ended up at his maisonette in Hackney. She had tried her best, but just was not up to it. Afterwards, she had vomited biriani on his new duvet cover. It was decorated with ringlet-haired ancient Greeks kaleidoscopically demonstrating an assortment of lovemaking positions. It was supposed to be tasteful.

Rollo had kicked her off his futon and called for a minicab. He had given her less money than usual, and made her wait for the taxi outside his front door. She had got cold listening to him clatter about the house, tidying up, and had come even further down. Her toes were still frozen, without feeling, from the twenty minutes outside. She had had to pay the driver out of her earnings. Usually, Rollo would give the cabman ten pounds to cover it. He had not made a date to see her again. They had met in the first place through the 'Heartland' section of *City Limits*. He was 'in the music business', but did not have any records out at the moment. His sitting room was full of framed posters for concerts by bands she could barely remember.

Back in the flat, she hugged her Snoopy pyjama case, imagining a gentle and considerate lover. Someone like Jeremy Irons in *Brideshead Revisited*. A schoolfriend had once told her that all prostitutes were really lesbians. But, then again, Nina was not a real prostitute. She was... What was she? A party girl, she supposed. Like everyone else, she called herself a model on her tax returns.

Exhausted, she did not dream.

When she woke up, she felt ghastly. It was then that she decided to quit using smack. But smack was not ready to leave off using her.

Aware that she needed to build her strength again, she fixed up as substantial a breakfast as was possible with what she had left in the tiny fridge and the cupboard over the sink. Branflakes, six cheddar thins, grapefruit juice and a cup of jasmine tea.

She sat at the kitchen table, looking at the neatly laid breakfast for a quarter of an hour. The hot water in the teacup slowly darkened until she could no longer see the sachet in the bottom. She took the paper tab and hauled the teabag out on its length of cotton. She dangled it in front of her face, and took the soggy lump into her mouth. It was slightly scalding, but the flavour was good. She could taste the perfume.

She spat the bag out into a saucer, and began to nibble one of the biscuits. Her stomach contracted sharply. 'Soon,' she said, 'it's coming soon.' She kept the cheesy pulp in her mouth for minutes, squeezing it through her teeth. Finally, she swallowed. It hurt going down, but it hurt a lot more coming up.

She bent double, cracking the cereal bowl with her forehead. The spasms hit her again and again in the belly. She twisted off the stool and dived for the kitchen mat, curling up around her pain. Milk and bran dried on her face. She managed to control herself before the kicking started.

This had happened before. She could live through it.

After a while, she calmed down. She unwound herself, and lay face up on the floor, looking up at the Marvel comic covers pasted to the ceiling by a previous tenant. *Silver Surfer* and *Daredevil*, *Iron Man* and *The Avengers*. She had had a guy around for a party once who was a comic collector. He claimed that, unmutilated, several of the '60s issues that had been cut up for wallpaper were worth around fifty pounds. What a waste.

She sat up, and felt temporarily at peace with herself. It would not last. There was no smack in the place. She had hoped to be able to find the silver paper her last jab had come in, but it was lost. She had got a hit off that kind of minute residue before, by licking it. It felt like sherbert on the tongue, and a carnival in her brain. At least, it had once. More recently, she had been treading water, using the shot to stay even, not to get ahead. That was dangerous, but she was a strong person, she told herself, she could deal with it.

It took her a full minute to dial Clive's seven figure number. Apart from her own, it was the only one she knew. She had forgotten her mother's, and had a little book for regulars and friends.

Clive. Charming Clive. Well-spoken Clive. Cunning Clive. He was the one who had found the song with her name in it. Nina Kenyon. He had suggested she find a partner called Ina Carver. It was the first line of 'My Darling Clementine'. Ina Carver, Nina Kenyon. Excavating for a mine. Clive would have smack. He always had smack.

Clive's telephone rang four times, then his answering machine cut in. It told her in the kind of voice she usually only heard on *University Challenge* that Clive Broome was out right now and that she could leave a message after the bleeps if she wanted to. She did not.

She could not quite get her phone back on the hook. The tangled cord got in the way.

In any case, she knew Clive would only come across if she paid him for her last shot. He was her friend and he loved her, but he was a businessman like any other and he could not make that kind of exception. She barely had enough cash left over from last night to get her through the day.

Even from the other side of the room, she could hear the phone. The dialling tone buzzed, annoyingly loud, like a persistent insect.

She squandered a fifty pence coin on the electricity meter and turned the fire on full strength. Standing up, she felt pins and needles in her knees. The gilt-edged invitation that had come in yesterday's post was on top of a pile of newspapers, magazines and bills on the coffee table. Under the copperplate request for the pleasure of her company and the address, Amelia had written 'bring a friend'.

So, if she could get herself together, there was the prospect of earning some good money. Not in a terribly comfortable way, but good money was good money. She had been to Amelia's 'entertainments' before and survived.

And Clive would be at Amelia's 'entertainment'. And wherever Clive went, he did business.

'Bring a friend.' Nina had not known if Amelia was being graciously hospitable, or issuing an order. 'A friend'?

Nina had thought that had to mean Coral. The last time she had met Amelia, she had been with the skinny blonde in the Club Des Esseintes. The hostess could easily have been quite taken with Coral. The girl had certainly been exciting attention for as long as Nina had known her.

They had come from the same school in North London originally. At first, Nina had been the one to show Coral how to get along. They had worked as a sister act for a while, but had got on each other's nerves. They went back too far to be comfortable together these days. Coral could be a moody cow when she wanted to, and was ungenerous with her gear. She had stopped crashing most nights on Nina's floor a few months before, and found a place with the American girl, Judi. Once Coral moved out, Nina found she got on better with her friend. There were plenty of relationships that worked best that way.

Judi? Maybe Amelia meant Judi. Nina had introduced her to the hostess as well. The more she had thought about it yesterday, the less she had known whether to call Judi or Coral. In the end, it had hit her that she did not have to make a choice. Judi and Coral were still together, at the same address. If she phoned them, one would answer the phone. Today, she could not remember which she had spoken to. But she had arranged to meet with one of the girls at the Club. Judi or Coral. She wondered which.

In the cramped bathroom, it took Nina a while to get dressed. She kept being distracted by her face in the mirror. Even before she washed the bran off, she did not look like the girl in the old smack adverts. The ones that said it screws you up. Just because she did smack did not mean she could not wash and comb her hair – although soapy water did make her feel squirmy sometimes – and put a little make-up over the blue-ish crescents under her eyes.

She dressed for the party, mainly in her best black. She favoured forties styles, with padded shoulders and deep pleats. She always wore long sleeves. Nina posed like a model in front of the tall mirror. She looked so much better since she started losing weight. She did not have to suck her cheeks in to appear glamorous any more, and she had completely lost her stomach.

She still thought she could get by doing modelling, but she never had the money to assemble a decent portfolio and that was what you needed if you wanted to get into the big money. She only had one nice photo of herself, and that was years out of date now. One of her regulars had wanted her to model for him, but he turned out to be interested only in private camera sessions. She did not want any of *those* photos.

She brushed the tangles out of her hair, feeling the scratch of the tines on her scalp. There was nothing wrong with parties, really. They were probably easier than modelling jobs.

More in control now, she got back to the telephone. After putting the receiver properly in its cradle, she picked it up and, flipping her book open to the number, called Coral and Judi. Knowing what they were like, they probably needed reminding about the meet. Their phone rang and rang until she gave up. She tried Clive again, but put the phone down before his machine could finish.

There were hours to go before Amelia's 'entertainment', so she would have time to set something up with Coral and/or Judi, and to pull herself together.

3

While Anne waited for the policeman to come back, she listened to the hospital piped music. They were playing something strangled by a million strings. Irritated, she recognized 'I Saw Her Standing There' under the Mantovani massacre. Messages from administrators to doctors chirruped in the background like signals gone astray in deep space. The Synthesized Celestial Choir segued into 'Do You Want to Know a Secret?'

Even under normal circumstances, she could not comfortably listen to The Beatles any more. They had been so much a part of her pre-adolescence. The four chord melancholies and ecstasies had turned scary. It had been 'Helter Skelter'. They had gutted Sharon Tate in Hollywood, and shot John Lennon in New York. All that was left was musak.

Judi had been into groups with more honestly horrific names. Paranoid Realities, Skullflower, Coil, Bad Dreamings, The Manson Family Reunion, Three More Bullets and a Shovel. She would have spat on 'Love Me Do' and 'Please Please Me'.

Still, The Beatles had been with her all her life. Anne's first memory was of her father letting her stay up past her bedtime to watch them on *The Ed Sullivan Show*. Not the first time, but a re-run. Judi had not been born yet. Later, the *Double White* was the first album she had bought with her own money. She had played it over and over on the old phonograph in the cellar rumpus room of the summer house in New Hampshire. Cam had taken personal offence at 'Revolution No. 9', and so it automatically became her favourite track. Even so, she would lift the needle over it when he was not there.

Judi was around then, making her presence felt everywhere, all the time. She had been reading almost before she could put a real sentence together in her mouth, and father had taught her long division before she ever saw the inside of the school. There had been no doubt about it: Judi had been the clever child, the pretty child, the promising child. Cam was the first-born, and thus beloved of God (and his mother, Dad's ex-wife). That left Anne as the nondescript one in the middle.

Now, Cam was as rich and famous as it was possible for a self-styled *avant garde* composer to be, Anne was working her way up the ladder as a journalist, and Judi was dead.

'I'm sorry, miss, but I have to tell you that your sister is dead,' Inspector Hollis had said. No tactful build-up, no euphemisms. The policeman had simply established that he was talking to Anne Nielson, and told her what he had to. She could not help but wonder whether he was familiar with her Aziz pieces. They had not been calculated to endear her to the Metropolitan Police. But she knew really that this was how everybody got treated.

There are a million stories in the naked city, and not enough words to go around. What with government cuts, a copper's vocabulary would have to be pared down to the absolute minimum. No surplus circumlocutions, synonyms hoarded like golden acorns.

Back in November, Anne had interviewed an ex-marine who had written a good book about Vietnam. He never used the words 'kill' or 'dead', just 'waste' and 'wasted'. That was bluntly the best way of putting it. Wasted.

Anne saw the doctor who was supposed to have looked at

Judi when she was brought in. He was busy now, pulling apart the do-it-yourself mummy swathings wrapped around the head of a little West Indian boy. She glimpsed red cheeks, raw meat rather than blushes. This time, she was impressed by the doctor's performance as he kept up a non-stop stream of soothing chatter for the boy and his visibly anxious mother.

With Anne, he had been offhand, awkward. She wasn't his patient, just related to an inconvenient lump of deadness he could have nothing more to do with. Alive, you are a challenge; dead, you are an embarrassment.

There were uniformed soldiers, unarmed, in the corridor. With the ambulance drivers' dispute dragging on, many local authorities were calling in troops to man the emergency services. Two squaddies, berets folded and tucked into the epaulettes of their olive-drab jerseys, were sharing a cigarette and a joke in an alcove, trying to keep out of the way. Their presence in the hospital made the place not feel like mainland Britain. Anne assumed this was what combat zone first-aid centres were like, in Belfast or in Central America. Even this early in the day, the casualty reception was busy. With the holidays starting, it was a prime time for accidents. Anne had had to do the hospital ring-round when she was starting out as a journalist, fishing for stories. Now, that seemed a long time ago.

Anne had been at home that summer when Judi was fifteen. She was freshly graduated from journalism college, doing bits for the local paper and working on the novel she never did finish. She had been a witness to what their mother, in one of her infrequent bursts of British understatement, called 'Judi's turn for the worse'. It was as much her fault as father's, or Cam's, or anyone's. 'There are some days,' Judi had told her in a rare communicative mood, 'when I think that life is an unending Hell of misery and desolation, and others when it seems merely to be a purposeless punishment, unending in its monotony.' It was hard to come back with something like 'yes, but what will you be wearing to the junior prom, sis?'

That summer, Judi had realized that being clever was not getting her what she wanted out of life, and so she had decided to be stupid instead. She had stolen money from Cam's wallet and bought a Greyhound ticket to New York. In the city, it had not taken her long to find 42nd Street. On 42nd Street, it had taken her an absurdly, and probably mercifully, short time to find the undercover vice cop.

Father, the Great Man, had shrugged into a fit of inertia when the NYPD called, and so Anne had had to deal with it. Cameron Nielson Sr. came up with the bail, his agent kept it out of the papers, and Anne went to town to pull her little sister out of the pussy posse's holding cells.

The next time, Judi had used her one telephone call to get in touch with a stringer for a paper so yellow that a dog could piss on it without making a difference. He had to be told who Cameron Nielson was, but he came up with the headlines anyway. NOBEL PRIZE-WINNER'S DOPER DAUGHTER IN B'WAY BUST. BAR-B-Q MAN'S GIRL IN SEX FOR DRUGS RACKET. Shit, that had been bad for all of them.

Anne thought again about The Call. Father could not talk any more. He had not written anything much since the late '60s. But he had been the only Nobel laureate ever to write for Rock Hudson and Doris Day, and then have his script redone by a kid fresh from two episodes of *The Mod Squad* and some quickies for *Laugh-In*. Anne thought that humiliation had done more to Cameron Nielson than any of Judi's exploits. More even than Hugh Farnham and his Committee. His only substantial work in the last ten years was *The Rat Jacket,* an intensely personal one-acter about an informer committing suicide. Widely interpreted as autobiographical, the piece – Anne suspected – would eventually be seen as one of his most important. There was talk of Robert Altman doing it as a television play with Harry Dean Stanton.

'Miss Nielson,' said Hollis, not unkindly, 'we're ready for you now.'

The policeman escorted her to the lift. He took a gentle hold of her upper arm and steered her. She was too drained to be annoyed by the imposition. The lift was large enough to accommodate several six-foot stretchers, and smelled like a dentist's office.

'We've contacted your brother. He was at the Grafton, like you said.'

'That's where he usually stays when he's in London.'

'Cameron Nielson? That's a famous name.' He was trying to make conversation, keep her mind busy. 'Any relation?'

'We're his children. It's Cameron Nielson *Junior*.'

'*On the Graveyard Shift at Sam's Bar-B-Q and Grill*. It's a 20th century classic.'

'That's what they say.'

'I saw it at the National when Albert Finney did the revival. With Donald Pleasence as Sam. Of course, I've seen the film...'

'Elia Kazan directed that.'

'...with Marlon Brando, Lee J. Cobb, Therese Colt and Eli Wallach and... who was the girl? The English actress?'

'Victoria Page. My mother. And Judi's. Not Cam's. That was another actress, a woman who divorced Dad in the fifties.'

They were there.

It was not like morgues in the movies. They did not have walls with long drawers. The bodies were on gurneys like elongated tea trolleys, with green sheets over them. The air conditioning was breathing low, cooling the place even in December. The place could as easily have been a school kitchen.

Movie morgues were always antiseptic, as clean and dignified as chapels. This was dirty. The waste bins overflowed with plastic cups and used paper towels. Someone had left an oily car battery recharging on a wash stand, and the only attendant was a kid with an unstarched mohican. He wore a Cramps T-shirt under his soiled hospital whites and he was reading the Arts pages of *The Independent*.

'Of course,' said Hollis, 'we've already identified her from fingerprints…'

'Yes, this is just a formality, but it has to be done. Right? You have forms to fill in before you can forget her.'

She was immediately sorry for snapping at him. After all, he was not PC Erskine. Hollis continued without taking notice. He must be used to dealing with irrational people.

'You knew that your sister had a criminal record?'

'Oh yes.' Here and in New York. Possession, soliciting, resisting arrest, carrying a concealed weapon, whatever. Judi's Interpol file was probably more substantial than anything Anne had written.

Hollis lifted the sheet himself.

There had been a mistake. It was not Judi.

This woman was old. All the substance beneath her mottled skin had drained away. She looked like a life-size shrunken head. The hair was dyed a blotchy black, but the roots were the white-yellow colour of drought-killed grass.

'It's a mistake,' said Anne, disorientated. 'It's not her. She was…'

'Twenty-five. We know.'

'But…'

'Look again.'

The eyes were open, rolled up into the skull, whites red-veined. The dead old woman's mouth was shrunken, but still firm. She had all her teeth.

Not wanting to, Anne touched the face. There was a spot on the upper lip, where Bogart had a scar, where Judi had a mole.

'It can't be. How…?' She looked at Hollis, and answered her own question. 'Drugs. Heroin?'

Hollis gently eased the left arm out from under the sheet. He ran a finger over the extensive abrasions. Amid the bruises, Anne could see fresh and ancient pinpricks. And there was Judi's crescent scar over the inoculation marks. A childhood scrape with an electric lamp.

Anne wanted to cry, to break down, to give up.

Hollis was talking, almost lecturing.

'She was an addict. We know that. Recently, there have been some quantum leaps in the drugs industry. They don't need to import as much opium-derived heroin as they used to. The stuff can be synthesized in laboratories. Designer drugs, they're called. From California, originally. The stuff is cheaper, purer, more debilitating. Strictly, it's not even illegal yet. I've seen senile teenagers. It affects the metabolic rate. The processes that make you grow old... I don't really understand this... they get speeded up...'

Poor Judi. Wasted. Her whole life literally used up. Anne looked at the old woman's face and saw the child her sister had been. Judi had not died easily.

Hollis covered Judi again, tucking her in.

'Did she do this to herself?' Anne asked.

Hollis looked at the floor, not quite shrugging.

Anne did not say any more. She was too good a judge of her own character. She knew what she wanted. It was the same when their mother had left, and when the novel had not worked out, when she had first heard of Charlie Aziz, and when father had wound up mute in a chair. For her, it was only natural.

She wanted someone to blame.

4

Even the Kind dreamed. But with the passing of so many years, the old man had outlived his imagination. All his mind had left was the almost unbearable weight of memory. There was so much he could no longer consciously recollect. Yet all of it existed, untapped by his waking self, in his night thoughts…

By the standards of centuries he would live to see, it had hardly been a battle at all. A routine patrol of six or seven horsemen with maybe two lances between them had come upon the enemy encamped in a shallow valley and, against his orders, engaged them. The din had carried in the strong winds, and his own camp had been roused to the combat. His hand thus forced, he had committed his men to the skirmish. It had turned into a minor massacre.

Taking both armies into account, there were perhaps one hundred dead. But he was well pleased. The English captain had been taken, and he had spent a long, rewarding afternoon with him. The man had been a genuine soldier, not some royal cousin assigned a command to keep him out of treason and plotting at home. He was much more resilient than the children who were his frequent guests between wars, but, in the end, he had yielded as completely as the scrawniest peasant brat.

He was satisfied, glutted, complete. Beneath his helmet, the tangle of his hair, grey-streaked at dawn, was a match now for the purest sable. His lieutenants no longer remarked upon the changes in him. By now, they were used to his cycles and simply put his occasional youthful appearance down to sorcery. A few of them were given to boasting about their master's skill in the Black Arts, and that could be useful from time to time. Poor Sieur Barbe-Bleue, meticulously obsessive as ever, was even trying through atrocity and alchemy to ape him, searching in the ruined and abused flesh of small boys for an elusive immortality. But some of his other officers, an unfortunate number who would soon learn better, had almost forgotten to fear him. For them, the English captain should have been saved for a ransom, not wasted on pleasure.

He had his ragged cloth-of-gold pitched on the bloody grass, about where the fighting had been most concentrated. He looked forward to stretching out on the insanguinated ground and luxuriating in the residues as others would in a heated and perfumed bath.

After the Englishman was exhausted, and consigned to the bonfires with his followers and the dead horses, he paid a visit to the girl.

She was squatting between the fires, her face still streaked with blood, her hands clasped in prayer. Sometimes he wondered what she said to her saints. Did she apologize for the extra load of souls that were lining up outside the Gates of Heaven as a result of her conversations with dead divines?

He knelt before her, and took her young head in his hands. His fingers slid into her cropped, coarse hair. He picked out a hard-shelled parasite and popped it between thumb and forefinger.

He, the Monster, kissed her, the Saint.

That year, he favoured little boys. But his congress with the girl was different. Her skin was permanently marked with the weave of chain mail. During the physical act of love, she called him 'father' several times. Whether she meant her father in the village, a father at the church, or the Father in Heaven, he could not say.

The wind tore at the already tattered walls of the tent, detaching wisps of golden thread that floated over the camp. A detail was stripping the dead of their armour, and piling it up. The fires burned fiercely, roasting and consuming carcasses with much crackling and hissing. The soldiers sang, words about intercourse with goats set to sacred tunes.

Every so often, there was a gurgling cry. He had ordered the whores to comb the battlefield, cutting the throats of the wounded, no matter whose colours they wore.

Close to his already dwindling body, the girl slept, doubtless dreaming of the young king and the angelic voices that whispered inside her skull. He touched his head gently to hers and sadly tasted the emptiness within. Briefly, he thought there was something, but it was just a memory of the unending winds that forced this girl, and all like her, to and fro without regard.

Strangely, he did not feed off her.

5

There were Monsters, Anne knew. It was a secret she shared with Judi. Their father had met a Monster, and lost, before they were born. Anne knew all about it. She had seen the kinescopes. She knew the face of the Monster, and that their family bogeyman had once had a name, Hugh Farnham, but that was the least of it. He went on forever, revealed only by a tone of voice, a strident attitude, an indestructible set of mind, a few whistled bars of an old film theme tune.

'You have to stop thinking in absolutes,' her journalism tutor had told her. 'Life isn't a movie, with good guys and bad guys, heroes and monsters.'

She knew there were no heroes, but she could see the Monsters everywhere. Hugh Farnham was long gone, but there were others. PC Barry 'The Batterer' Erskine, the hate-consumed Ulster clergyman, the calf-faced girl on Page Three of *The Sun*, the presidential advisor, the Soviet chess grand master, the old hippie rock musician, the Middle Eastern mullah, the television quiz show MC, the political columnist in the downmarket Sunday paper, the science fiction writer hawking the fourth volume of his trilogy, and a thousand other, lesser, demons.

'Annie, did you know they had your old man on film in the

archives?' Pat, her college roommate, had asked. 'They've got his appearance before McCarthy.'

Strictly speaking, it had not been McCarthy. He had gone down with the astonishing hearings in 1954, when he had been crucified in court for daring to graduate from the easy pickings of Hollywood to try to detect traces of Communist infiltration in President Eisenhower's *Alma Mater,* the army. Father had been up before Hugh Farnham three years later, at the tail-end of the blacklist.

She had resisted the temptation for weeks, but finally she gave in. She had to scratch the itch, even if it turned into an open sore. Frankly pleading her special interest to the head of the Modern American History department, she was given access. She had to thread the projector herself, and confront the Monster in a draughty basement screening room with uncomfortable seats and a strict no smoking rule. In those days, she had been a smoker. In those days, like everyone else, she had even played around with drugs.

The kinescopes were not properly catalogued, so she had to watch until she found what she was looking for. Her father did not show up until the fourteenth of twenty half-hour reels, covering nearly ten years of different sessions, but she was still fascinated. It was Hugh Farnham, the Monster. Joe McCarthy had got all the contemporary press coverage and had an -ism named after him, and Richard Nixon had used the hearings as a springboard into grown-up politics. Even Roy Cohn, the legal *Eminence grise* who had died of AIDS a few years back, was comparatively well-remembered. But Farnham was Something Else. The others were in it for patriotism, self-advancement, megalomania, paranoid self-justification and financial gain. Half-way through his delicate dissection of Martin Ritt, Anne realized with a dizzying rush of vertigo that Farnham tormented people because it was his idea of fun. It met a need in him he could not slake any other way.

His eyes were nothing in particular in black and white, certainly not burning coals of melodramatic malevolence. And his voice was like a Broadway actor's in a Shakespeare play, unaccented but more British than American. He had always been something of a mystery man; in theory, Anne knew where he had come from and what he had done before the hearings, but, watching his smile, she found she had forgotten the precise details. His face was unforgettable, as if the skin of a pale cobra had been stretched over the bone structure of Montgomery Clift.

She wondered what had happened to him. Perhaps he had been badly burned in the War, and had had to be patched together by expensive teams of plastic surgeons intent on performing miracles. In the shadows of the courtroom, he looked older than Dracula, but, when he was firing questions at unfriendly witnesses like Kim Hunter or Zero Mostel, he was younger, more virile, more in control, than a matinée idol on a triumphant opening night.

'Are you now,' Farnham kept asking, always with the biting pause in the same place, 'or have you ever been, a member of the Communist Party?'

Unlike McCarthy, Farnham did not pronounce it 'commonest party'. The only thing her father had ever said about the Monster was that, at the height of the televised hearings, Hugh Farnham received more fan mail from women than Elvis.

Thirty-five years later, it was all clear. McCarthy was stupid – a blustering clown. It was incredible that he had got away with it for so long. The one indelible image of the period was of McCarthy whispering in Roy Cohn's ear like a school bully suddenly desperate for advice, and the lawyer looking shocked and shattered as he realizes just how doomed his buffoon boss is among all the smart lawyers. Nixon was a glowering, unshaven crook, a sweaty Boris Karloff in *Arsenic and Old Lace*. Anne understood why he had been God's gift to the protest movement, an Establishment villain who always looked and acted like one.

And the 'friendly' witnesses – Robert Taylor, Adolph Menjou, Therese Colt – embarrassed themselves and flushed lesser people down the toilet as they blurted out their hatred of anyone in Hollywood they thought might be communists even if they could not think of any actual proof of their left-leaning politics. But Congressman Hugh Farnham was John Wayne, Captain America, Parsifal and the young Jack Kennedy rolled into one.

Sweet Jesus, this man could have been *president*.

Waving a petition against the Committee signed by various Hollywood notables, Farnham even got chilling laughs with one speech. 'I want to read you some of these names,' he began, in a mildly sardonic manner, a brow arched. 'One of the names is June Havoc. We found out from the Motion Picture Almanac that her real name is June *Hovick*. Another one is Danny Kaye, and we find his real name is David Daniel *Kaminsky*. Then we have the case of Mr John Garfield, *né* Julius *Garfinkle*. Eddie Cantor, known to his mother as Eddie *Iskowitz*. The famous Edward G. Robinson, a.k.a. Emmanuel *Goldenberg*. A fellow who signs his autograph Melvyn Douglas, but who is really not a Douglas at all but a *Hesselberg*. A promising Broadway gent called Cameron Nielson whose birth certificate reads Comrade... pardon me, *Conrad* Nastase. There are others too numerous to mention. They are attacking this house for doing its duty to protect this country and save the American people from the horrible fate the communists have meted out to the unfortunate Christian people of Europe.'

When her father showed up, late in the day, she did not recognize him. It was a fluke that his hearing, which was officially an 'enquiry into the misuse of a United States passport' although the criminal charge hanging over him was actually Contempt of Congress, had been televised. By the time his name came up, everyone but the witchfinders had lost interest. It must have been a ratings-slow period. It was hard to connect the young man with the dark hair, quick grin and self-confident way with words to the person she had grown up around. All that was there were the horn-rimmed glasses and unearned Ivy League tie.

In the film, Cameron Nielson was confident that he could defeat the Monster. His daughter knew that he had been destroyed by it.

In 1957, the days of the blacklist were supposedly over, but her father was unemployable in Hollywood, his TV play *The Crunch* had been bounced without comment by all three networks, and his 'historical pageant' *Cochise and Geronimo* had closed after three weeks and two days on Broadway.

But he did not care. He had secret weapons. He was rich, he did not have to work. He had the example of his friend Arthur Miller, who had stood up straight at his hearing a year earlier and been treated leniently, his minimal sentence rapidly overturned. He had the Nobel Prize for Literature. That made it official: he was a national resource, like O'Neill, Faulkner or Hemingway. He did not have to prove anything. He had nothing to lose.

He did not even have to plead the fifth amendment. He simply did not have to answer the Question.

'Are you now,' said Farnham, 'or have you ever been, a member of the Communist Party?'

There was a long pause, long enough for the station to cut to a Kraft commercial if they had wanted to.

Cameron Nielson smiled, and hooked his thumbs into his vest pockets. If he had had a hat on, he would have tilted it to the back of his head. Suddenly, Anne realized how much her father had known about live television. He looked straight at the camera which must have had the orange operational light on, and answered the Question with another question.

'Well, Congressman Farnham, that depends...' His voice was full of New York shrewdness. 'That depends on who the fuck wants to know.'

There was commotion in the court. Someone – Sterling Hayden? – applauded loudly. The camera swivelled, and there was a brief shot of a director ripping off his earphones, unable to believe what he had heard. The camera calmed, and came to rest on the Congressman. Farnham did not show a flicker of emotion, but Anne could see his killer's smile.

'Mr Nielson,' he said, his eyes enlarging visibly, *I* want to know.'

Farnham simply looked at her father, and Cameron Nielson began to crack. The Congressman asked the Question again, calmly, and waited...

The camera held on her father, his smile twitching. He was sweating now, his one shot spent and useless. Finally, he made another move, shakily. 'Congressman, I believe the Constitution enshrines the right to freedom of...'

'Freedom?' interrupted Farnham, his teeth sharp in his grin. 'That's an awfully large word.'

Anne was sitting forward in her seat, sweaty hands on her knees. She had never really understood what had happened next. None of the accounts she had heard or read agreed. Her father never spoke about it, except perhaps for a few veiled hints in *The Rat Jacket*, in which the informer protagonist is grilled by a chess-playing genius policeman with a sadistic streak.

The film did not explain anything. By the end of the reel, her father had turned into the middle-aged man Anne had grown up with. Farnham kept asking questions, asking *the* Question, and then interrupting Cameron Nielson if he did not answer to the point. Evidence was produced – the membership lists of various Hollywood charitable organizations later proved to be Communist fronts, signatures on petitions in support of unionization, Sacco and Vanzetti, Soviet-American collaboration, supposedly propagandist passages in his plays. But the evidence was not important. This was a duel of character between Congressman Hugh Farnham and Nobel laureate Cameron Nielson, and, finally, her father caved in.

He did not go to prison like Hammett and the Hollywood Ten, he did not flee the country like Joseph Losey, Larry Adler or Carl Foreman, and he did not get away with it like Miller.

Cameron Nielson answered the Question. Of course, he named names. And, of course, careers were ruined, friendships broken, lives smashed...

She could not watch any more. It was the first and last time a movie made Anne cry.

6

Anne's relationship with her half-brother had always been, at best, considerably strained. They had not talked since she had described his *Orpheus to the Power of One Hundred* in print as 'music to cut your wrists by' and accused him of stealing most of his ideas from Karl-Heinz Stockhausen, John Cage and Spike Jones.

She knew he was in London for the premiere of his *Telemachus Symphony*, a piece he had been working on for eight years. He had not complained about the intrusion into his busy schedule of rehearsal, but Anne knew Cam well enough to realize how little he was interested in Judi's life and death.

As Cam talked on the in-house telephone, trying to get some breakfast sent up to his suite, Anne tried to remember how he had been with Judi. Cam had been away at school when Judi was born, and he had spent very few summers at their father's house. He was with his mother, or touring Europe with his octet.

To him, Judi was someone he saw once a year at Christmas and did not really like much in the first place. The last Christmas they were all together, seven years ago, Cam had given Judi a book about Beethoven, and she had given him three pairs of multi-coloured socks.

The only time Judi had ever affected him was when she was

a news item. The reviews of his first New York concert, even in the heavy papers, gave as much space to his half-sister's criminal record as his father's Broadway career.

'Success at last,' he announced. 'They stopped serving breakfast at ten, but they have some tea and scones left over.'

Anne looked at the smooth stranger. She understood only too well how he could think of tea and scones half an hour after looking at Judi dead on a collapsible table. She remembered her own breakfast, abandoned back in Kentish Town.

A discreet maid wheeled in the breakfast. They ate without much conversation. Anne scalded her tongue by drinking too soon the too hot, too weak tea. Cam showed her the cover design for his concert programme; a broken Greek mask, with white space for eyeholes.

They were interrupted by a telephone call. Anne was sure it would be more bad news, and felt a chill as Cam listened intently to a woman's tiny voice.

'Lex,' he said, 'precisely 7:35. Insist on it.'

It was Alexia, Cam's assistant at the concert hall. Cam was insisting the performance commence at 7:35 to the second because he had written in two minutes of minimal music between 7:59 and 8:01, during which he hoped his background chords would interact with the scattered beeping of the digital watches spread throughout the auditorium. He liked to include random factors in his pieces.

Alexia explained something, and Cam whistled unconsciously, an old habit. The crisis dealt with, he hung up.

'How's Dad?' she asked, wondering if he had heard more recently from the nurse.

'The same,' he said.

It cannot be much longer now, she thought.

He nodded, as if agreeing with her unspoken sentiment.

'Should we tell him?' she asked.

'I'm not sure he'd understand,' he said. 'You can't tell whether he hears or not. It might be best to leave him in peace.'

A pause. They were vacuum-cleaning the hallways outside. It sounded like one of Cam's bass lines.

'Cam, I'm not letting it go.'

'I know. I knew as soon as I heard. Annie, I know you won't listen but... Fuck it, you do not need to understand all this. It's not really anything to do with you or me. Judi is gone now...'

Wasted.

'...it was suicide really, you have to admit that...'

'Crap, Cam. Crap. You saw her. She was a hundred years old. And Hollis says it was not just drugs. She'd been beaten up. Lots of times. And she was torn open...'

The body had been found by dustbinmen, under some rubbish bags in a Soho alley. She had been dumped. The police thought the wounds on her hips and thighs were from rats.

'It was part of... part of the way she lived, Annie. She must have been beaten up and cut open every night. You know what kind of a whore she was. No wonder her heart gave out. Face it, she had been killing herself for a long time. This time, she finally managed to pull it off. Now, let's just leave her alone, please...'

Give him credit, she thought, he has not said anything about publicity, about his symphony, about his career.

He has not *said* anything.

He was whistling again, nervous and atonal. It was the signature sound that always insinuated itself into his work. Now, it struck a long-forgotten chord.

'Mr Whistle,' Anne said, startling Cam. Her brother stopped in mid-whine and closed his lips.

'I'm not scared of the bogeyman any more, Annie.'

Cam had been a strange kid, Anne remembered. How many other children had *scary* imaginary playmates? For a while, she had had bad dreams about Mr Whistle too. Now, she could not remember even what the nightmare child was supposed to look like.

'There are no bogeymen,' Cam said.

'No, but there *are* Monsters. We all know that.'

Anne picked up her shoulderbag, and the lumpy clear plastic carrier with Judi's personal effects.

'Monsters,' he shrugged. 'You shouldn't think like that. It's not helpful. There are only people. Don't people scare you enough?'

She walked to the door.

'Annie, where are you going?'

'Anywhere I have to.'

Five minutes after she was gone, Anne knew Cam would be on the telephone to the concert hall again, asking them to send a taxi over for him. He would be still worried about the two minutes' beeping.

She had tickets for tonight, but she doubted she would get to use them.

7

The immortal empire fell before it was born.

Even after so many years, he could still learn. In Shanghai, Tarr, Sniezawski and Baum had taught him to beware the complacency of the Kind. Life sometimes seems to slow like a river, almost coming to a comfortable rest. But there are always dangers. There are always dragonslayers, always Fearless Vampire Killers.

Although an orphan, he had always known he was not entirely alone. He had met his cousins at the sites of great plagues and disasters, and recognized in them the same unease he felt in himself. The Kind, he learned, were as old as humanity itself. Theirs was a secret history, never written in a living language, much of it concealed even from his questions. Comparatively young, he understood that the elders of the Kind had withdrawn entirely from the affairs of men and retreated to the shrinking white spaces on the map. He was impatient with such dainty cowardice, and, as if in the grip of a feeding frenzy, felt the zeal of a crusader as he set out to become King of the Cats.

There had been Kings before, Kings of the Kind, and Kind Kings who had ruled over the nations of humanity. The title, as he understood it, had been unused in centuries. Its last holders had abdicated or been overthrown. He had only to establish his Palace of Perpetuity and throw his court open to attract the others. The old ones, his uncles and aunts, maintained their loftiness and stayed in their seclusion, but their juniors, his cousins, were as eager as he to end the centuries of wandering. He was accepted as King by those to whom such things mattered. In Shanghai, he built his Palace and waited. Soon, its fame spread among the Kind. A mating pair arrived from the Dark Continent, no longer able to retreat from the explorers and the empires of Europe. Giselle, the exquisite child, slipped out of the darkness one night, cocooned in silver furs. It was she, thinking of a fairy tale, who had invented his title, the King of the Cats. Almost as old as he, she was still capable of seeming a genuine child. With each new member of the circle, he was able to piece together more of the history.

With Giselle, he shared the Dream, an experience he had rarely been able to approach, even with the dearest of his prey. Shaping everything within their perceptions, they had fused until their personalities could no longer be distinguished. They would reign, as King and Queen of the Cats, for an eternity.

The circle grew, but not as rapidly as he had expected. He was surprised to learn how reduced the numbers of the Kind were. Every newcomer seemed to bring the story of the death of another of the ancients. With each loss, irretrievable stretches of the history sank into oblivion like water in sand. Short-lived mankind might be, but it had multiplied insanely in the last few centuries. It was learning many new things, and forgetting its old fears.

He had taken more wives, had children. His cousins followed suit. The densely populated port, with its refugees, sailors and unnoticed masses, was perfect for the Kind. The international confusion of administration and corruption left many gaps that could be exploited. With several fortunes, aggregated down through the centuries in the world's great banking houses, at his disposal, he played by the rules of humanity for years. Officials in the service of the Dowager Empress and of the many foreign interests in the city were properly bribed. There were many willing to serve the King of the Cats, out of fear or desire. His strength, and the strength of his circle, surpassed itself.

Among so many robed orientals, he affected Western dress, importing black frock coats from England, satin-lined opera cloaks from Paris, linens from Holland. Giselle he dressed up like a doll, amusing her with each extravagant wardrobe. Always attuned to the pleasures of feeding, he took the time to appreciate other luxuries. Music, wine, art, literature, philosophy. With a dilettante's delight, he followed the threads of human endeavour, intrigued by their irrelevant attempts to chart their world, to map their fragile Dreams. He read his Darwin with interest. He could well appreciate the mastery of that which was best fit to survive.

But there never was an Immortal Empire. After one of the court's masques, a silky courtesan, the gift of the Empress who had provided the company with a pleasurable evening in the labyrinth beneath the Palace, was seen cast used and lifeless into the streets as her reward. The girl had had three devoted lovers, and they set about avenging her.

Philip Tarr, the British merchant skipper, Niall Baum, the Irish Jew spice trader, and Stefan Sniezawski, the much-decorated Polish mercenary. Practicality, mysticism and endeavour incarnate. The Kind had grown careless, had remained in the city long enough for their longevity to be noticed. The would-be avengers had heard all the stories about the creatures in the Palace. They consulted wise men and fools, and they framed their plans against the court.

During the celebration of the Chinese New Year, while the bulk of the company were amusing themselves with some guests in the maze, the Palace of Perpetuity was dynamited. He had been on the lowest level, feeding with Giselle. Their prey was a brother and sister who should have lasted for days. Buried alive, he had to transform himself drastically in order to get free. He burrowed upwards, insinuating himself through the loose rubble like a manta ray negotiating the complex cross-currents of the deep. He erupted into a courtyard, and found what was left of those who had escaped the initial explosion. Apart from Giselle, who followed his wormhole to the surface, none of the Kind had survived.

The three had brought a righteous mob with them, and applied the traditional remedies. Using ink-stringed cats' cradles, each of the courtiers had been trapped. Then, hawthorn and rosewood stakes had been pounded through their chests, pinning them to the ground. Finally, their heads had been lopped off with silver-coated scythes. Afterwards, some morbid wit had jumbled up the heads, matching them to the wrong bodies. The Kind did not give up life easily. He found impaled corpses pouring out blood hours after the initial butchery. Cloves of garlic had been shoved into slack mouths, and there were religious symbols everywhere, crosses, statues of the Buddha, icons, a Star of David. His eldest daughter's head lay in a shallow pool, its eyes still moving, a yellow prayer parchment pasted to its forehead.

The rage, the sorrow, the tangible residue of the recent slaughter. All these things made him stronger. The skin he had scraped off as he struggled to the surface grew back.

He spread the fires, lighting up an entire quarter of the city. Paper dragons caught easily, and flimsy houses burned like children's lanterns. He laid the company's remains where the flames would consume them totally. His duties done to the dead, he turned to revenge. With no especial joy, he destroyed his enemies.

Amid the holocaust, he found the Britisher, supervising a chain of bucket-passing coolies on the docks. He had embraced bluff Philip from behind, reaching up under his ribs and squeezing his heart with talons of ice. Giselle joined him, inflating her throat like a toad's to accommodate the gush of blood. With seven-inch fingers, she tore chunks of flesh from the dead, and chewed them like sweetmeats. She had not spoken since the explosions, but he could feel the emotion pouring out of her. He had to shut his mind to her silent screeching, lest her newfound madness carry him off, divert him from his purpose.

When Tarr was found, the other two followed them, blinded by idiocies about herbs and crucifixes and boxes of native earth. He fled inland with Giselle, leaving human carcasses and nightmare memories at every resting place along the way. Then, they reached the shunned temple in the hills, and turned around to wait for the Pole and the Irish Jew.

The Pole came first, clad in a lancer's greatcoat and carrying a new Winchester rifle. The least superstitious and most competent of the three, he was surprisingly easy. Afflicted with the sentimental streak of his people, he had lost much of his purpose with the death of his yellow harlot.

He took Sniezawski and changed him, pulling his neck out of true and crushing the rest of him into an eggshape. He fashioned a bony shell, like that of a Galapagos turtle, and slipped the Pole into it. The creature, its moustached head bobbing on an elongated stalk, its booted feet useless as flippers, made a spectacle of itself. Giselle howled with empty-headed laughter. In a moment of compassion, he lopped Sniezawski's head off.

The Irish Jew was more cunning, and more dangerous. His red hair shaven and in the robes of a monk, he came to the temple and was admitted as a pilgrim to the shrine. With the wooden daggers concealed in his habit, he killed Giselle. He used a silver-edged hatchet on her corpse, quartering her beyond repair. Then he sat on a mat, surrounded by fragments of the blessed bread, and waited for the Monster.

He found the last of his three enemies surrounded by the dead but shrieking body of his wife. Baum held up a consecrated wafer.

He leaned forwards, opening wide his mouth. The hinges of his jaw dislocated, and his neck vertebrae arched. The throat gaped, and extra rows of teeth sprouted. The walls rippled with the force of the changes, as he sucked Baum into the Dream.

With his first bite, he took Baum's arm off up to the elbow. The host disintegrated like wet paper in his gullet. He swallowed, and fingers relaxed in his belly.

Baum shrank within himself, and tried to run. But he was caught. This was not feeding. This was killing.

Then, King of the Cats no longer, he bit the Irish Jew's head off. And was done with it.

8

Anne phoned the offices from the Nellie Dean in Dean Street. She had to offload some of her responsibilities.

'Hello. Editorial,' said the voice she had hoped not to hear.

'Mark?'

'Anne. Hi,' a long pause. 'What happened to you? You never came back to the phone...'

She realized her receiver would be buzzing, still off the hook in the flat.

'The policeman? I was trying to tell you that that dopey Sharon gave out your home address.'

'It's all right.'

'You're not on the electoral roll? That's how they usually trace you.'

'No.' She had slipped through, three moves ago, and only now felt ashamed of it. She was committed, so she ought at least to be able to vote.

There was a fuss in the background.

'We've got a crisis right now,' Mark said before she could answer. 'We're trying to get the Central America thing into the Christmas issue. Can I call you back?'

'I'm on a pay phone. Listen, my sister has died. I need some time.'

'Lord...'

She could picture Mark not knowing what to say. She wished someone she knew less well had answered her call, someone who could take down her information like notes for a news item and tell everyone who needed to be told.

'What are you going to do?'

'Nothing stupid. Don't worry. But I need to ask some questions. I can't just let it drop, you know.'

'Okay. Well, I've got you down to write the Poll Tax vigil piece. Clare can do that. The homelessness feature is Nigel's baby, really. I'll do the sidebars myself.'

'My notes are on the computer. It's mostly done.'

'Fine. But there's the Aziz inquest. You've been on that story from the first.'

Anne had not thought of that. She felt she owed Mrs Aziz her continued support. And Erskine was still out there, waiting to get back on the beat.

'Don't worry,' Mark said, drawing in a breath, 'I was just thinking aloud. There's no blame involved. I'll deal with it.'

She imagined him juggling notes on his desk, trying to find room for what he wanted to say to her.

'Anne, about last night…'

'I know, Mark. Look, I'm sorry, but…'

She tried to picture his expression. It was hard to tell what he was thinking face to face. The telephone disguised him completely.

'Anne, I understand. This isn't a normal thing. Call in when you want to come out of the cold. Can I get you at the flat?'

'I don't know. Maybe not. I think I've got a week or so left over in holiday time. And it's Christmas the week after next, anyway.'

'Christ yes. I'm sure the collective can get its collective head around the concept of compassionate leave. I'll stamp it through the next magazine meeting.'

She thanked him, hearing the bustle of the newsroom in the background. Phones ringing, people laughing, typing, making tea. Life going on. She supposed she would not be at the office party this year. Just as well. It would only have meant another painfully circumspect hour or two with Mark. And she could do without the mistletoe and drunkenness jokes, or Clare trying to get everyone to dance to her old Abba records.

'Your sister?' he asked. 'The one who had the trouble?'

'Judi. Yes. Trouble.' The pips sounded. 'I don't have any more change. I'll be...'

Buzz.

She had lied; she did have two more twenty pence pieces. She dropped them in the slot, and punched the Aziz number. She owed Charlie's mother an explanation. She could talk to the woman. As she listened to the unanswered phone ringing, she wondered how alike she and Mrs Aziz were in their reactions to death. After a full minute, she assumed everyone was out, and gave up. She must call later. She did not want Mrs Aziz to hear from Mark that she was off the story for now.

Reclaiming her coins, she collected a Perrier water and an egg salad sandwich from the bar, and sat down alone. It was not twelve yet and the pub was practically empty. A fat alternative comedian Anne had seen on television was insulting the barmaid, and she was pretending he was hilarious. The bland Christmas record she hated – 'Christmas Caroline' – was playing through the speakers over the bar.

The largest of Judi's effects was a leather handbag. Anne had put all the other stuff in it and thrown away the plastic carrier the police had given her. Hollis had said that Judi's clothes would be released later, before the funeral.

Shit, the funeral. Anne did not even know how to go about arranging that. She supposed she would just have to look up 'Undertakers' in Yellow Pages and go with the Acme Funeral Company or whoever was at the top of the list. The Nielsons were third generation agnostics. A critic had once said their father spent his whole life looking for God, but Anne could not see that. She knew she would go for the simplest, most secular ceremony available. She was tempted to collapse, and play on Mark's British protectiveness to have him take care of the arrangements. He would know what to do, and be supremely efficient at it, sparing her as much of the strain as possible. But she could not do that. Anne Nielson did not use men as crutches. These were the '90s. Besides, Mark would use it as a way of getting closer to her, and he was too close already. This was family.

Judi's lighter had cracked, and the inside of her bag smelled flammable. There was not much to pick through, but she sorted all the items out and laid them on the table. Some plain rings; a skull earring; a studded leather armlet; a plastic bottle of codeine; a package of paper tissues; three shades of lipstick, scarlet, crimson and black; American Express and Visa cards; fifty pounds in fives; a purseful of loose change; a cardboard tube with a rocketship in it that contained two 'Invader' brand prophylactics, 'Launched by Automach Peterborough'; an imitation leather-bound diary/ address book; and a man's wallet.

Anne played with the wallet. It was stuffed with photographs and newspaper clippings. There was an old snapshot of the sisters, as children, with a pony, somewhere in New England; Anne was standing, smiling, holding the bridle while Judi, little more than a baby, perched fat and fed-up on the saddle, dress ridden up over her thighs. A photo booth strip of a young man Anne did not recognize. Judi grown up, with two other girls, caught in a flashbulb glare, trying to look deliriously abandoned in a nightclub. The last shot made Anne shiver.

The cuttings were an odd selection: a piece from *The Guardian* about father's stroke, a favourable review of one of Cam's concerts at the Pompidou Centre, a *Radio Times* listing for a late night screening of *On the Graveyard Shift at Sam's Bar-B-Q and Grill*, and samples of Anne's work from various papers and magazines. There was also an ancient anonymous letter Anne remembered arriving at the house and upsetting Dad. It called him a fink for informing on fellow travellers in '57. It had disappeared, and only now she realized Judi must have sent it herself, and that Dad must have known: over the years, there had been a steady trickle of abuse, but this one had really nettled their father. The only thing there that was about Judi was a report on a coroner's hearing she had given evidence at. Anne had not heard of the dead man, a stabbing victim, and could not work out what his connection with Judi had been.

'Checking the loot, eh, love?' said the comedian, laughing. 'Funny how the muggers get younger and prettier every day, innit?'

Anne looked up at the man. His chins were shaking, and he had a beerfoam moustache.

'Fuck off,' she said, her eyes fixed. His grin froze, and fell apart. He turned back to the barmaid, and made a remark Anne did not catch, laughing again.

Anne looked again at the items on the table, and tried in her mind to connect them with Judi.

As soon as Judi had arrived in London, she had telephoned her sister, but only to cadge some money. That had been two years ago. The sisters had not met since. Like Anne, Judi had right of residence thanks to their English mother. Two years was time enough to make a whole life. She picked up the armlet. The leather was cracked, and a few of the studs were missing, leaving tiny wounds. Not for the first time, Anne wondered how exactly her sister had lived.

And what was she looking for anyway? Keepsakes? Messages from the grave? Clues?

She had saved the book until last. It was such an obvious source of information. Under today's date was neatly printed 'N. Club D.E. 1.00'. N? A name? One o'clock? Morning or afternoon? Club D.E.? Going through the addresses at the back of the book, she found any number of people with N for a first or second initial, and addresses for several clubs, among them the Club Des Esseintes. That was in Brewer Street, just around the corner.

The Club Des Esseintes.

9

His haircut cost more than the average suit, and his suits individually cost more than the average good-condition second-hand car. Clive Broome had the Business sussed, and the first thing he had learned was the importance of always being well turned-out. If transactions needed to be made in venues where his style would be suspicious, he could always buy some spiky-haired lout to handle it. He preferred not to get too close to the retail end of the trade anyway. He was moving up the pyramid, and he wanted everyone he dealt with to know it.

Most nights of the week, Clive liked to screw somebody. But he insisted on sleeping alone. He hated the thought of waking up with a pair of alien elbows in his ribs and the sheets in a mess. After they had done the business, he had shifted last night's cunt into the spare room. By the time he was ready to get up, she was long gone. He also liked to sleep late.

As far as he could tell, nothing was missing. Gretchen, from Barnet, with a butterfly tattoo. She should not be hard to find. If any of his things had taken a walk, he would have the Sergeant Major cut one of her boobs off. Or give her to Mr Skinner.

He went cold, fast-forwarding through yesterday's business. The call from Mr Skinner, the deliveries, the white faces of the girls, the disposal. That was not over yet. One down, he told himself, one to go. He should not really get involved in deals like that. But they were useful. The Games Master was such a strange customer. It was well worth the risk of the disposal job to have Mr Skinner wrapped up and tied in with something messy. The man was monied enough to have some pull somewhere, and Clive could always use someone with pull. After the disposal, Mr Skinner owed him plenty. Still, Judi's face had been a frightener.

After dressing, he sat down in his work-room to go through the post and deal with the morning's telephone messages. Most of the letters were Christmas cards, from Business contacts and sentimental cunts, but there was also a whingeing note from his mother and his subscription copies of *Viz* and *The Economist*. Most of the people who had called him up had not left any sort of message, but Mink said that he had received the shipment of Brussels sprouts he had been expecting.

Clive still thought the vegetable talk was fucking stupid. He was supposed to be a wholesale produce importer, supplying his own chain of fashionably overpriced health food shops. Through design-oriented marketing, he had ridden the Green wave and successfully negated the duffel-coated hippie image of health foods to target the high disposable income of yuppies in high-stress jobs who would follow any dietary plan as long as it was expensive and minimal. The food business was even quite lucrative, but actually his real trade was drugs. The code-names just made Mink feel like he was in a spy film. It was a typical dopehead way of justifying habitual paranoia. It also suggested he thought he was just playing a game, and Clive was serious about what he did for a living. He was not thirty yet, but already he had been in the Business twice as long as most of the people he worked with. It was all about being careful.

But Mink's message was good news. Clive could now go down to the Hackney wholefood store and pick up the heroin his people were waiting for. New drug-of-the-month crazes like Ecstasy and crack might come along, and Clive was conscious that he had to keep such items in stock, while cocaine was capturing a more exclusive portion of the market but heroin was the white bread of the Business. There was always a market for the old staple diet of junkies. After a night in the space behind his airing cupboard, the gear would go to the Sergeant Major and be repackaged for his men in the marketplace. And he would be able to meet Mr Skinner's standing order.

Mr Skinner would be very pleased. Clive sometimes wondered what the man was up to. Obviously, the skag he bought wound up in someone or other's arm. His version was that heroin was much more convenient than cash. He was right there. Surely, the Games Master wasn't stuck on the H himself. He was not anyone's idea of normal, but he was not stupid. Clive was well aware of his position in the Business, at precisely that cusp where men in smart suits with career structures deal with deadbeats in tom jeans with minimal life expectancies. Mr Skinner was higher up the pyramid. When you got to where he was, it stopped being Business and started getting Political. Right now, it was down to Clive to make himself indispensible.

Clive started doing sums on his expensive pocket calculator. He had an upper second in business studies from the University of East Anglia. Most of the people he had known up there were working in the City, for the media or unemployed these days. Several of them were customers, although they saw the Sergeant Major's lads rather than him. He liked to think he was making more money and paying less tax than any of them. His calculator played the first eight notes of 'Money Makes the World Go Around'. That always gave him a giggle.

He was proud of the fact that he had three times voted for the best government the country had had in his lifetime. There was a picture of him shaking hands with Margaret Thatcher at a Young Entrepreneur of the Year dinner on his desk next to his Sinclair micro. He really admired her for the way she had opened up the economy to individual enterprise. He was a practised and popular after dinner speaker at local affairs, and his favourite address was entitled 'The Strength of a Nation Lies in its Human Resources'. For him, the Business was a business, not an amusement or an adjunct to a personal need. The drug trade was a consumer-led market, and he had got into it at the right time, meeting an increased demand and offering a better service than his competitors. The '80s had been a growth period, but he knew that bull markets always eventually swelled and burst. He could foresee the point when he would get out of drugs – at the right time, of course – and step up the pyramid.

Although the very nature of the Business brought him into contact with a load of moaning minnies and smackhead losers, he had started to employ only men who had proved themselves possessed of a decent amount of backbone. The Sergeant Major had been in Northern Ireland for a couple of years before they sent him to Pentonville, and he had brought some good new lads into the operation. One or two of the carriers had served in the Falklands. Clive did not employ users, and the Sergeant Major had standing orders to pay off with broken bones any of his lads caught with their fingers in the supply. Clive wanted long-term people who could be useful when he branched out.

Now, Clive telephoned the Sergeant Major. He would have been up since dawn, handling a couple of little things. He picked up the phone at the fourth ring.

'Sergeant Major.'

'Mr Broome?'

'How did things go?'

'Very nicely, sir. I've been to the bank, and I talked to the man you wanted seen to. There won't be any more trouble in Deptford, I don't think.'

Clive imagined the crack of fingerbones.

'That's excellent. I'd appreciate it if you'd drop by later.'

'Very good, sir.'

'Yes, we have another disposal job to do. A lot like the last one. No trouble at all.'

'Fine, sir.'

'Right. See you later. Take care.'

Clive thought for a moment about the other girl, Coral. And about Judi.

In his front room, Clive had a framed print of the Battle of Waterloo, a collection of imported pornographic magazines, a CD player and a VHS recorder and video tapes of all Torvill and Dean's greatest performances. In his kitchen, he had a case of expensive wine, a robot-chef and a microwave oven. In his lavatory, he had copies of *The Official Sloane Ranger Handbook*, *The Naff Sex Guide* and *How to Be a Wally*. In his work-room, he had a licensed handgun, five thousand pounds in small notes and a fax machine.

In his basement, he had a dead prostitute with her arm cut off.

10

As near death as he had ever been, he tried to slither over the beaten earth of the alley. His face hung off his skull in lumpy rags. One of the cuts had been high up and at the back of his head, and a torn curtain of skin and scalp had flapped forwards over his face. It hung over his eyes and nose like a wet scarf. Since his own pain had long since ceased to mean anything to him, he felt almost at peace in the red darkness.

The irony of it was that the men who had done this to him knew nothing about his real nature. They had killed him simply because they were paid to. He would kill them, but without true malice, or even true relish. If people habitually treated each other like this, who could blame the Kind for the way they treated the human race? Of course, it was really his own fault. He knew that he should never have got mixed up in politics.

He had tried to change when they assaulted him, but there had been eight or ten of them and they were very skilled in their profession. Using iron bars and sharp knives instead of crosses and cats' cradles, they had caught him efficiently before he could make himself more dangerous and ripped him apart. They had broken his arms and one leg, and his pelvis was twisted out of shape. Consequently, he could not roll himself over and had to try crawling face up. He grew horny talons, curving them into the hard ground. His hands clawed at the ground like scuttling crabs and pulled the heavy bulk of the rest of his body towards the mouth of the alley, assisted only by the occasional inchworm push of his good leg.

Arriving in Istanbul between the coming of talking pictures and the Wall Street Crash, he had drifted into the restaurant trade, turning a particularly vile brothel into a fashionable nightclub. He hired singers who actually could sing, rather than belly-dancers renowned only for their ability to pleasure simultaneously an inordinate number of patrons, and he replaced the group of criminals, cripples, degenerates and relics who had served as an orchestra with genuine musicians from Paris, London and New Orleans. Finally, he had struck an exclusive deal with Turkey's leading importer of American phonograph records, so that his club would introduce the latest Cole Porter or Irving Berlin song to Istanbul weeks before the Fred Astaire or Paul Whiteman versions became available.

It started to rain, and he began to feel as if vinegar were being pissed into his open wounds. Perhaps he had not outgrown pain after all. The entrails piled on his empty belly must be steaming. Somewhere above, but quite near, he heard music. It was Victor Young and His Orchestra with The Boswell Sisters, performing 'I Found a Million Dollar Baby in a Five and Ten Cent Store'. He stopped crawling, and feeling came back to his misaligned elbows. He tossed his head, and the bloody flap lifted from his face and fell more or less in its proper place. He looked down at himself. He was already covered with flies, and a scraggy monkey, a refugee from some street act, was picking at one of his ankles. It looked hungry enough to forget it was supposed to be a herbivore.

As usual, he had got bored with an easy life, and expanded his operations. He had never entirely taken his establishment out of the business of procuring, and he soon rekindled his taste for the marketing of human flesh. He imported girls, and boys, from Greece, Egypt, various Balkan pretend countries, India, China, even the Socialist Workers' Utopia across the Black Sea. Then, he found his acquaintances became useful in furthering a varied trade in foods, drugs, armaments, icons, rare books, general contraband and murder. Money had always bored him, but his interests also enabled him to build up a fortune in the simplest, least tangible, most negotiable currency in the world – information.

Stiffening his back for the purpose, he sat up suddenly. He dragged his arms from behind him and deposited his hands in his lap. He brushed the dirt and flies off his coiled bowels and pressed the functional mass back into his body. He reached for the cummerbund that had been torn off him during his murder, and wrapped it tightly about his midriff, easing shut the wound, that had disembowelled him. His insides realigned themselves, itching and burning by turns. He felt ready to use his arms again and reached for the monkey.

At first, he had dealt only with a mountain of a colonel in the Turkish Secret Police, supplying him with interesting tit-bits about the many foreign nationals who passed through his club. Then, he had delicately approached, in turn, the local representatives of Germany, Russia and Great Britain. There would be yet another war eventually, and Turkey was in such an odd spot on the map. Squeezed between three troubled continents and theoretically neutral, it was naturally at the centre of all manner of legitimate and illegitimate merchant and refugee activities, and the site of diplomacy and espionage on a scale he had not seen since his dealings with the papacy in the 14th century. It had eased the tedium to see the nations of humankind scheme and plot against one another, and to be able to take a hand in the shaping of the War that would change everything again.

The monkey's meagre meat and brief flare of dreamstuff helped, and he was able unsteadily to stand up. He smoothed his forehead and scalp over his skull, and tore away the dead tatters that clung to his cheekbones and neck. They had cut off his genitals and stamped them into the dirt. That was supposed to be a warning to his associates. It did not concern him much. Thorough his assailants might have been, but they had also shown a typically human lack of imagination in their treatment of him. After so many centuries of torture and violence, he would have thought that men would become practised in the artistry of feeding. But no, the race was still saddeningly small-minded.

He had been amused by the opportunity to juggle with the interests of so many nations and individuals, and had capriciously exploited the situation. Once he had denounced an innocent American tobacco trader as a dangerous enemy spy to the Nazis and the Soviets, and doubled his money by accepting two commissions to arrange his assassination. But someone or other had discovered one of his duplicities, or taken offence at one of his transactions, and had paid a gang of waterfront knifemen to drag him into this alley and ruin him.

Soon, he would be whole again. Then, his murderers would be his meat and drink. And he would find out who had employed them and feed off him. Then there would be the War, and wars were what he liked best of all. Europe would be a killing ground for a while, a banquet for the Kind. Then, he thought, he might go back to the United States. He had the feeling, listening to the torch songs of that nation on his Victrola, that America was about to become the most interesting country on the globe. The Old World was using itself up fast. There was life for the taking beyond the Atlantic, and a vitality which could feed him for decades.

In an upstairs window, a girl appeared. She was not beautiful, but she was not fat and disgusting either. She saw him as a stranger loitering in the dark alley below and routinely exposed her breasts to him.

He stepped into the light, and looked up at her. She did not scream. In her mind, she said she had seen worse.

'That's what you think,' he said out loud in the wrong language, one she did not understand. Through exposed and bloody teeth, he began to serenade her.

'Say it's only a paper moon,' he sang, 'Sailing over a cardboard sea, but it wouldn't be make believe if you believed in me...'

Fascinated, she remained in the window, waiting for him to come up to her. She was his instantly. He saw her entire life, from birth to this moment. Roumanian originally, Macha Igescu was seventeen years old, working for Demetrios Malacou. She loved him because he beat her less than her last protector, never more than once a week. She had had two babies – both sold by Malacou to strangers – and her dreams were befogged by the poppy smoke. She was nearing the end of her professional life. Malacou, she knew, would dump her for that plump-titted Arab bitch, and she would be sold on into some dark dormitory to do her work chained to a cot.

He promised himself that he would find Malacou and kill him for Macha. He would not feed off the pimp; he would just open his throat and let him empty. After all, he was going to owe Macha for his life.

Latching his fingerhooks into the crumbling stonework, he began his climb...

11

In Brewer Street, all the sex shops had identical notices up in their windows. A Merry Christmas to All Our Customers. The season of goodwill to all men gets everywhere. Anne wondered whether the girls in the Live Erotic Nude Bed Show had to wear Santa Claus hats and reindeer antlers. Weary shop assistants had been busy hanging paper lanterns from the rubberwear, and winding silvery tinsel through displays of sex aids. In a centrally-heated style shop, customers got to choose between purple and turquoise trenchcoats, assisted by young girls with cycle shorts and partially-shaven heads. A record store had a cardboard cut-out of Derek Douane, the teenage ex-choirboy who had inflicted 'Christmas Caroline' on the human race. Anne hurried past his fixed smile, trying not to think of the burbling, thought-destroying tune that could get into your brain and settle for hours. The traffic was snarled, and bike messengers were gleefully whizzing their way through the gridlocked maze of personalized numberplate limousines and delivery vans. In New York, this would occasion a din of honked horns, but the British drivers just sat and fumed in their tincans, waiting for the world to get better. Outside a Chinese take-away, three pigeons pecked determinedly at a splash of frozen sick.

A wino with black toes poking through his mangled trainers

aimed himself at her. He skittered through the Christmas-shopping crowds like a pinball, bouncing off walls, lampposts and people, his shaky eyes fixed on her. The grubby hand was already coming out, and the ritual phrase was working its way down from the speech centres of his brain to the spirits-slurred tongue.

'Excuse me,' she said, before he could get it out, 'Could you spare ten pence for a cup of coffee?'

Usually, derelicts retreated in astonishment at this tactic, but the Soho wino was a hardier breed.

'Fuck you, sister,' he coughed at her through black and broken teeth, 'and the horse you rode in on.'

She sidestepped him, and walked on rapidly. She was not happy with her behaviour. She had done pieces on homelessness. She ought to have more sympathy.

'I fought in three world wars for you,' the tramp shouted at her back. She wished Mace was legal in this country.

The capital was turning into a Third World city, she thought. At every central London subway station, there were begging kids, shivering in several layers of clothes, a pleading message printed in biro on a piece of cardboard. Less aggressive than the alky panhandlers, the kids were even more depressing, fiercely ashamed of their situation, never meeting the eyes of the passersby. The tramp she had dodged was one of the old-style bums, the last of the summer winos, and was most likely feeling the pinch. With younger, less stereotypically derelict, not obviously cracked people sleeping rough and trying to get into the spare change business, the old and alcoholic would be pushed out of their place in the begging order. The street population was expanding, as more and more people fell through the gaps in the welfare state's safety net. There were ways to get by, but none of them were pleasant, or safe. Soon, London would be just Tijuana, Bangkok or Casablanca with a lousy climate.

The Club Des Esseintes was difficult to find, but she guessed that it was supposed to be. There was a nostalgia shop at the address listed in Judi's diary, with a passport photographer's and a French model agency upstairs. The plaque was screwed to a wall papered many times over with posters for rock gigs and albums. A group called Faster Pussycat, frozen in mid-scream, dominated the pasted-and-torn collage. She had to look at the wall for a full minute before she found the sign. Someone had scraped a hole in Neneh Cherry's midriff so the words were still visible. Private Club – Walk Down. And in the corner, in little curlicue letters, Des Esseintes.

The shop was full of faded magazines displayed in racks, piles of movie posters and boxes of still photographs. The major display was a selection of one-sheets for films about Santa Claus. In one, the cheery old gentleman was brandishing a bloody hatchet over a naked girl. The ad line boasted 'it's a ho-ho-ho-horror!' You better watch out, Anne thought. Someone had driven a dagger smeared with stage blood through a smiling cut-out of Dudley Moore dressed as an elf. *Phil Spector's Christmas Album* was coming through the shop's speakers, 'Christmas (Baby Please Come Home)' by Darlene Love. At least that was an improvement on Derek Douane. 'Do you have any material on Caroline Munro,' a foreign customer was asking a bored attendant, 'or Rosanna Podesta?' Anne looked around the shop and found the stairwell behind an impressive array of Japanese warrior robots.

The spiral staircase was black, and the walls bright scarlet, but the well was lit only by one bare bulb at the top. Anne went down into the darkness. The stairs fed her into a corridor, dimly lit by imitation candles in electric sconces. The walls were blood red, the floor herringbone-tiled and polished. There were unrecognizable portraits of men in periwigs hanging between the candles. The Marquis de Sade, she supposed, and intimate friends.

A level below the street, she could no longer hear Darlene Love. Instead, there was the tinkle of musak. She recognized the tune and almost laughed. 'You Always Hurt the One You Love'.

The first serious obstacle stood at the end of the corridor, ominous in a black leather hood. His axe did not look like a prop, and there was a coiled bullwhip in his belt. He was wearing polished boots and lumpy tights, with his chest – muscle just running to meat – bare. Anne thought he was unlikely to be impressed by her NUJ card.

She wanted to go home and forget about the whole thing.

Suddenly, she was one of a crowd. Six or seven people had come down behind her, and she walked down the corridor with them, trying to seem at ease. They looked like an ordinary lunchtime group, office workers out for a Christmas drink. The executioner bowed and opened a pair of double doors, admitting them into a cellar bar. Evidently, he recognized some of the club's regular patrons. Anne was swept inside with them. She noticed one young businessman buckling a studded dog collar around his neck.

There had been a sign above the doors. The Inferno Lounge. She had expected a vaulted torture chamber in Hammer Films style, but, at first sight, the room was more impressive. Three walls and the ceiling were covered with a fairly expert mural in imitation of Hieronymus Bosch. Damned souls wriggled, turned in on themselves in the corners, pierced by water pipes near the ceiling.

The furnishings were black, with occasional silver and scarlet highlights. The only light came from a rank of glowing bar heaters and from the many television monitors, which were perched on high shelves above the bar and around the walls, or set into the tables like video games. Under the musak was the muted sound of whipping and slapping and yelping. There was also the rumble of something that sounded like vast underground machinery, grinding away behind the walls.

Anne climbed onto a stool at the bar, and looked around at the customers. There were a few young women in already-dated punk outfits, including one girl with green hair cat-napping upright a few stools down, but most of the people in the Inferno Lounge were conservatively-dressed men. Young to middle-aged white collar types, with briefcases and newspapers. The *Mail* and the *Telegraph*. Mostly, they sat alone, watching the televisions and ignoring their drinks.

Anne wondered which, if any, of these people, was N? She did not know whether Judi was meeting a friend, or a… she gulped mentally… or a customer. N could have been anyone, including someone on the staff rather than among the clientele.

Up on the monitors, Anne saw an array of sharp video images. An over-aged schoolgirl, complete with braids and ankle socks, taking her knickers down for a cane-brandishing headmaster. A WPC masturbating furiously with a truncheon. Two bored naked women ineptly flogging a tethered third party. An academic explaining the precise uses of a set of antique nipple clamps.

Anne tried to imagine Judi here, to imagine her talking with the other girls, or with the men. She had specialized in receiving pain, Anne knew, not in giving it. She would have had to determine which was any given client's preference. Looking at a thin blond young man in a business suit, while trying not to seem as if she was looking, she wondered whether he liked to hurt or be hurt. He had almost colourless eyes, and was ghost-pale in the videolight. He reminded her of Constable Barry Erskine, the Batterer. She imagined him making fists, and using them on a girl's face. On Judi's face. Again, Anne wanted to leave, but knew she had taken it too far to just go home…

'You can't just sit here, you know,' someone said, 'you'll have to buy a drink.'

The barman looked like a functionary of the Spanish Inquisition, in black robes, picked out with an assorted batch of mystical symbols. Otherwise, he could have been serving in any other unfriendly pub in town.

'Oh,' said Anne, 'Perrier.'

The barman exhumed a green bottle. When he unscrewed the cap, there was the faintest ghost of a carbonated fizz. He poured into a tall glass.

'Ice and lemon?'

'Please.'

He picked up the fruit slice and single lump with a wicked-looking pair of hooked tongs, and dropped them in her drink.

'Four pounds fifty,' he said. She hesitated. 'Remember, no one comes here to drink.'

She handed over a five, and received no change. She let the matter drop. She wished she had given the money to the wino out on the street. At least, he would be able to get drunk out of it.

Shit, what a hole.

Some of the young women were approaching the newcomers, pouting and trying to seem masterful. Even to Anne, it was obvious that the working girls were unable to take all this seriously. The thin blond dropped to his knees and licked a girl's creaking boot, his tongue probing the cracks in the leather. She had guessed wrong about him: he was into M, not S. When he looked up, the girl's face was set like a school pantomime version of the Wicked Stepmother, but otherwise she just looked ordinary and tired. The would-be slave kept dropping pound coins into her boot-tops. That must get uncomfortable.

Casually, Anne began her Nancy Drew act. 'Has Judi been in recently?'

'What's all this Judi stuff today?' asked the barman. 'Has she just won the Miss Popularity award?'

Anne pounced, a little too quickly.

'Has anyone else been looking for her?'

'Nina,' the barman said, looking around. It was difficult in the gloom to make anyone out.

Nina? N?

Anne looked around too. The barman had ignored the green-haired girl, so she was out. Which of the others could Nina be?

Anne turned back to the barman, and found that he was, for the first time, looking carefully at her. She knew he was realizing that he had never seen her before. She glanced at the doors. The executioner was standing by them.

'You're curious,' the barman told her. 'Open your handbag, love. Let's see your membership card.'

The executioner was coming over now. Nancy Drew had failed. She would have to start being Clint Eastwood instead, and she did not think she was really up to it.

'Eric,' the barman called the executioner, 'we have a trespasser who needs prosecuting.'

These people, she knew, were good at pain. That was how they made their living.

She dashed her Perrier into the barman's eyes, and snatched his ice tongs. Eric did not move too fast. She hoped he could not see a thing in his Batman cowl. At school, she had not been a quarterback, but she had not been a cheerleader either. She slammed painfully into the executioner, but he did not fall over.

She grabbed for his mask and pushed it. The eyeholes were now over his forehead. She backed off, but he still managed to hit her hand away before falling over his whip and sprawling on the floor.

She threw the tongs at the barman, and picked up a heavy metal and leather chair. The barman dodged the tongs, but did not try to come out and get her. The weight of the chair felt good.

Some of the businessmen were applauding, and calling for more. The blond was diverted from his ladylove's boot, and looking up at Anne, imploring with his watering eyes.

Everyone was staying out of the reach of Anne's chair. She jabbed it in the air a couple of times, like a lion-tamer. People cringed.

Anne felt the need to hit Eric with the chair. She brought it down on him with a log-chopping swing. He grunted and held his head, still trying to struggle out of the hood.

She threw the chair aside, and pushed through the doors. She did not know if Eric was after her or not.

She raced down the corridor.

She nearly lost a shoe on the staircase, but made it easily to the street. For the first time in years, she had a stitch.

Slowing down and trying to get her breath, she walked briskly through the shop and into the street. The cold wrapped around her. After the Inferno Lounge, which she now realized had been overheated, the outside chill was almost welcome.

As she tried to walk away, there was a tug at her smarting shoulder. Someone was pulling her handbag.

'Excuse me, miss…'

12

'Look,' said Tail Gunner Joe, 'isn't that Bogart?'

It was somebody else, but the observation helped the Monster understand the Junior Senator. Sitting in Romanoff's, an ill-fitting suit and a sweaty grin among so many tailcoats and panstick-smooth faces, the man was star-gazing, like any other gawk-eyed Mid-Westerner visiting Sin City – Hollywood, California. It almost made him endearing. Tail Gunner Joe was made for this town. Like the glove salesmen tycoons, the grease-monkey ape-men, the waitress demigoddesses and the bogus Russian royalty restaurateurs, the war hero witchfinder was a Great American Fraud. Even politics was not a big enough backdrop for his imagined autobiography. Tail Gunner Joe had to get into Showbiz, and rate more mentions in *Variety* than in *The New York Times*. His was an addictive personality, and the need for fame was as desperate in him as the need for his favoured stimulant, morphine. The Monster knew that the Junior Senator was on his crusade so someone would one day cast Spencer Tracy as him in a film of his heroic life from the dogfights of the war to the pit-bull tussles of the Senate. Like every crooked politician in the United States, he had seen *Mr Smith Goes to Washington* several times, and always identified more fiercely with Jimmy Stewart than Claude Rains. When he had got up in the Senate with his list of 'card-carrying Communists', he had been thinking of Mr Smith.

The Lawyer, a boyish mouse of a man with an intensity that frightened most, was irked by Tail Gunner Joe's lack of concentration. A quiet Jew, he was intent on his papers, and wanted to get the discussion back to the agenda. And the woman, creeping into middle-age with her bobbed hair and staring eyes, was just gaga. Russian originally, she was a prophet of Americanism, and had dignified her sloppy thinking with a neologism, styling herself as the avatar of Objectivism. Even Tail Gunner Joe, who was awed by her intellect, thought of her as a dingbat. The Monster knew there were only two people who counted at this meeting; him, and the Lawyer. They knew that Red-baiting was just a passing thing, and that there was a more important prize to be won through the Committee and its hearings. Between them, the Lawyer and he could own the dreams of America more thoroughly than Louis B. Mayer, Jack Warner or Sam Goldwyn.

'Mr Farnham,' said the Lawyer, 'as I am sure you are aware, we do not want to repeat the fiasco of Thomas and the Hollywood Ten.'

He nodded. Congressman J. Parnell Thomas had been the chairman of the House Un-American Activities Commission back in '47, the figurehead of the first anti-Communist purge in the film capital. Currently, he was serving an eighteen month sentence, for accepting bribes, in a prison in Danbury, Connecticut, where, by a nasty coincidence even the Monster found amusing, two of his fellow inmates were Ring Lardner Jr. and Lester Cole, doing a stretch for Contempt of Congress as a direct result of their appearances as 'unfriendly' witnesses before Thomas and the Committee.

'Thomas was a fool,' he said. 'You can't be St George and have your hand in the till.'

Tail Gunner Joe coughed, obviously not wanting to discuss graft and corruption. The Lawyer ticked off some point on his agenda, and the waiter returned with their drinks. The Junior Senator had obviously been hitting the sauce all afternoon, and was pleasantly squiffed. The Monster had arranged for the party to be taken on a tour of the Paramount lot this afternoon, and the Junior Senator was still excited at having met Cecil B. DeMille and Bing Crosby.

The *entrées* arrived, and Tail Gunner Joe attacked his seafood cocktail hungrily. The Objectivist picked at her salad, and the Lawyer stuck to his soft drink. They were an interesting contrast in repressions, the Objectivist trembling with her neurotic drives, the Lawyer locked tight up inside himself. They both wanted him, the Monster knew.

He sent back the soup to throw a scare into the chef. To him, something as invisible as power was a pleasure only if it *were* exercised at every opportunity. A new bowl, identically excellent, arrived instantly, along with the apologies of the management and an offer to tear up the bill for the whole meal. He graciously accepted, and lapped up a few spoons of bisque, savouring the taste.

Arriving in California shortly before Pearl Harbor, it had taken him a while to grow into Hugh Farnham. As always, when he remained in one place long enough, he adopted protective colouring. His face set, and he allowed it to change only to simulate the gradual process of ageing. Professional qualifications were easy to come by, and the false details of 'Hugh Farnham''s early life were almost absurdly easy to plant in various records. There were people who would swear to have known him as a young man, even as a child. Now, he was officially 'lawyer to the moguls' – sanctioned by both Hedda Hopper and Louella Parsons – and a big wheel in the motion picture industry, the California state legislature and the coming wave, Americanism. If he had actually been born in a log cabin on the prairies and grown up with the taste of Coca-Cola in his mouth and the prospect of a dignified old age on the White House lawn, he could not have been more American. After so many years of wandering, it did him good to put down roots. This was such a rich and stupid country. He had fed better here than he had for centuries.

The Lawyer still wanted to talk business, and the Objectivist wanted to talk philosophy, but, underlying their conversation, the Monster sensed their desire for him. He was amused that their preferences should be so similar, and relished the stag reels they were playing over and over in their brains. On a basic level they would never be able to articulate, they sensed some of what he was, and longed to submit to his feeding frenzy. The Lawyer, he knew, could never admit to his secret needs, and would even go so far into the closet as to link 'perversion' with the political doctrines he was intent upon helping the Junior Senator stamp out. The Objectivist, however, would sublimate her frenzies into her writing, turning out more and more turbulent, half-literate, half-blathering prose about the failures of altruism, the paramount rights of the individual and the tyranny of the common masses. It was so obvious that the hero of her most famous novel was her imagined version of Hugh Farnham that even one or two of the reviewers had noticed it.

A movie star came into the restaurant, weighed down by furs and diamonds, and trailed by her mother and a discreet entourage. The Monster waved, and the mother, one of the friendliest of the friendlies, beamed a grotesque smile at him. Tail Gunner Joe was impressed that he knew such legendary screen figures, and insisted on being introduced.

'Ginger,' the Monster said, 'this is the Senator from Wisconsin you've been hearing so much about.'

The dancer put on a smiling face as the plump, rumpled politician kissed her hand. The Junior Senator was as sincere as if he were soliciting votes.

'You were wonderful in *The Groom Wore Spurs*,' Tail Gunner Joe, the undiscriminating picture fan, said. The star's smile froze solid, and the Monster tried and failed to remember what her last good film had been.

'I hope you'll be kicking the Reds in the ass,' said the star's mother, claiming the Junior Senator's attention with expansive gestures. She was expensively made up to look like her daughter's bloated twin.

Tail Gunner Joe grinned, even as the Lawyer was wincing, and made a meaty fist. 'Sure will, ma'am,' he said, 'anything to please a lady.'

The star and her entourage swept past. Tail Gunner Joe was warmed with a glow he would retain all evening. He had met real movie stars, and had something to boast about to the folks back home.

'The real problem is in the content,' the Objectivist said, trying to impress him. 'All too often industrialists, bankers and businessmen are presented on the screen as villains, crooks, chisellers or exploiters. The Communists want to put over the message that personal success is somehow achieved at the expense of others, and that every man has hurt somebody by becoming successful. It's pernicious nonsense, of course. The Reds say they want to destroy men like Hitler and Mussolini, but what they really want to destroy are men like Shakespeare, Chopin and Edison.'

It was a neat little speech, and the Junior Senator was pleased with it, nodding as if he understood. The Lawyer had an 'all very well, but…' expression, and was holding up his papers again. He was impatient for names, dates and times. The Monster was reminded of a first-time director trying to wrestle a pair of recalcitrant stars into following his script. For him, the Objectivist was just window dressing, of no real interest except for her intellectual credentials. For too long, all the thinkers and artists had been on the left; the crusade had to take the eggheads it could get, no matter how scrambled. The Lawyer was perceptive enough to realize how sham the Objectivist was, and cynical enough to know that, even if he had not been able to finish her last book, there were a million Americans who had and swallowed her bombast as deep thought. If it were not for his cowardice and self-denial, the Monster would have quite admired the Lawyer. Quite.

The dance band was playing 'Mona Lisa', an Oscar-winner the

year before for *Captain Carey, USA*. The Monster enjoyed the Academy Awards, and always made sure he got the best seats for the ceremony. The tangle of emotions was so delicious. Winners and losers were meat and drink to him. These days, he just tapped his meals, disdaining to drain them completely, sampling the dreamstuff but sparing the flesh. It was a revelation, how much he could enjoy feeding without killing. In a sense, there was more delight in leaving his broken prey alive.

'Let's talk names,' said Tail Gunner Joe, belching.

The Objectivist's claws came out. 'Yes, let'ssss. You should squeeze Trumbo, Lawson, Dmytryk and Hammett some more.' Her face was tightened as she spoke, her elaborately-applied make-up cracking. 'A spell in prison will have jolted them. They should be ready to turn on their fellow Reds.'

The Junior Senator looked contemptuous. 'Hah. Trumbull, Dimitri and Hackett are nobodies. Who cares about directors...'

'Writers,' the Objectivist said, with a little moue. 'They are writers.'

'Writers, then.' The Junior Senator signalled for another drink. The armpits of his lightweight suit were getting alcoholically dark. 'Writers are chickenshit.'

The best-selling novelist knitted her fingers and shut up. The Lawyer enjoyed her discomfiture. And the Monster rolled the little tangle of emotions around in his mouth, like brandy. He had a slight rush.

'What the Senator means to say,' the Lawyer interpreted, 'is that the Committee should make every effort to secure high-profile witnesses. We must not underestimate the importance of the public recognition factor in these hearings.'

'Nobody gives a fuck about who writes pictures,' the Junior Senator growled. 'What we want, dollface, is *stars*. Am I right, Hugh?'

The Monster nodded.

'We gotta get out of this business with Joe Shmoe from Kokomo, author of *Andy Hardy Goes to Leningrad*, or Sammy

Kikestein, assistant trainee camera operator on *Pinkos of the South Sea Islands*.'

The Lawyer's face did not move when Tail Gunner Joe mentioned the mythical 'Sammy Kikestein', but he winced inside. Anti-Semitism, the man knew, was a two-edged sword.

'If those writers are Commies,' Tail Gunner Joe blustered, 'they should just be taken out and put against a wall. We could all care less about them... them...'

'Anonymous masses,' the Objectivist suggested.

'Yeah, anonymous. Now, if Clark Gable was a Red...'

'...not that we have any reason to suspect he is,' the Lawyer put in, addressing his footnote to the Monster.

'No, but if he were, if Katharine Hepburn or William Holden or Kirk Douglas were pinkos. Then that would be *news*. You gotta gimme stars.'

'Gale Sondegaard,' the Objectivist stammered.

'Who?' asked the Senator, spitting pugnaciously.

'An Academy Award winner.'

'Best Supporting Actress. Nothing. Gimme before-the-title stars.'

'John Garfield.'

'A has-been.'

The Monster sat back, and watched them squabble. There was a great nexus of power forming around these people, he knew, and, as Hugh Farnham, he would have to be in the centre of it. But they were such petty tyrants, schoolchildren playing domination games. The Objectivist was squirming, trying to swallow her distaste for the Junior Senator, and to suppress the pictures she was making in her mind of herself spreadeagled naked and bleeding over a rockface as Hugh Farnham savagely drilled her from the rear, the flesh of his body merged with oily quarrying equipment. A founder member of the Motion Picture Alliance for the Preservation of American Ideals, the Objectivist had spun her suppressed kinks into a successful novel and a travesty of a film, and the Monster found it strange to see himself distorted through the broken lens of her mind into the masterful brute played so stiffly in the movie by Gary Cooper. The veins in his cheeks and neck swelled as the Objectivist worked herself up to a crazed interior climax, while trying to pay attention to the Junior Senator. A drop of sweat dribbled from her hairline like a tear. The Monster breathed in her flood of feelings, and was nourished by them.

Here, in Romanoff's, surrounded by fools and knaves, he felt again like the King of the Cats.

'Say,' the Junior Senator asked, 'would you think Ginger would mind if I asked her for a dance?'

The Monster was amused. Tail Gunner Joe was no replacement for Fred Astaire. The Junior Senator was taken with the idea, and rolled it around his mind for a while, forgetting the Committee and the purpose of this meeting.

In dreams, Tail Gunner Joe was top-hatted, white-tied and tailed, swirling gracefully with the movie star; the Lawyer was in the dark with a wet-mouthed Japanese boy, nervously certain he was being watched by invisible eyes; the Objectivist was grovelling in the mud, Hugh Farnham's huge hands pressing her shoulders down, his pile-driver penis thrusting brutally into her.

In dreams...

In the 20th century, Hollywood was the capital of the Dreamworld. It was the perfect place for him.

Then, *she* walked in...

13

The flat in Old Compton Street had a Yale lock and a Chubb, and Nina was not quite up to the relatively simple set of motions necessary to deal with them. She kept her keys in her handbag, and had to root about for a while. Then, she rattled the long Chubb key in its hole, struggling with a rusted mechanism. Her hands started shaking and she could not insert the Yale key properly without putting her bag down and using both hands. She had really not stopped crying yet, and occasionally added yelps of frustration to her strangled whining. She made a hell of a racket.

A door across the hall opened a crack. Anne was acutely uncomfortable in the dingy corridor, fully aware what the invisible neighbour would think. At least Nina lived in Soho, within easy distance of the place where she had accosted Anne. Otherwise, Anne would never have been able to steer her to a safe place and do what had to be done. Come to that, Anne wished she knew precisely what did have to be done.

Finally, Nina got into the flat. Anne noticed a formidable array of extra locks and chains on the inside of the door. If it was hard for the girl to get in, it would be impossible for anyone else. A sensible precaution in her line of business, Anne supposed.

Nina crumpled up and fell into a balding armchair. Anne had

to pull the keys out of their holes, pick up Nina's handbag, and lock the door behind them. Anne wondered again how she was going to handle this.

She could not help but find the young girl unnerving. At first, Anne had thought her a shade too chic for the Club Des Esseintes. Her dress looked like the sort of thing Lauren Bacall used to wear to a gangster-owned casino, and her face could have been put together for a *Vogue* fashion shoot. Now, with tear-tracks in the pancake on her cheeks, and her hair turned ratty as she ploughed fingers through it, she looked much more like what Anne realized she was. A junkie and a hooker. Exactly like…

…exactly like Judi. Nina might be able to pull herself together and make herself presentable when she went out, but Anne suspected that she was finding it increasingly hard to assemble a desirable face. She looked about the slightly messy flat. There had been no card thumbtacked to the door-jamb downstairs and the most expensive appliance in the living room was an Ansafone, so she guessed that Nina was a call girl rather than a streetwalker. By the standards of her profession, she was probably doing quite well. For the moment. Judi must have lived out her last years in rooms like this. Also, she must have been as near the edge as this girl was now.

'Do you know Judi Nielson?' Nina had asked on the street. 'I'm looking for Coral and her.'

Anne had not known any easy way to break the news, and she had not been ready for such a complete crack-up. It was odd, having to comfort a stranger for her own bereavement. And embarrassing, hugging a crying girl in the middle of the pavement, with cursing shoppers flowing around them. Also, Anne was worried that the Club Des Esseintes might send someone after her. The executioner could hardly dash out onto the street in his leather outfit, waving an axe, but he must have street clothes somewhere.

Somehow, she had coaxed the girl's name out of her, and

where she lived. Now, she was going to ask her questions. She asked strangers questions every day of her life. Usually, they did not want to give straight replies, but she tried to get them anyway. In this case, she knew she was going to hate hearing the answers as much as Nina was going to hate telling them.

'I'll make some tea, shall I?'

Nina didn't exactly say yes, but Anne went into the tiny kitchen anyway. There was no milk, except for an inch of sludgy cream in a carton, so she used the last sachets of jasmine tea, which she found loose on a table top next to the carton. There was a couple of days' worth of washing-up in the bowl, and she had to fish out, rinse and wipe off a pair of mugs. They both had Royal Wedding pictures on them. There was a disassembled coffee percolator on the draining board. Anne realized that Nina's kitchen looked a lot like her own. They even had the same spice chart blu-takked to a cupboard door.

Looking for clean teaspoons, she opened the drawer by the sink. It was full of sex aids. Grossly outsized rubber penises, a tangle of leather and rubber belts, a dildo with a small model of a leaping dolphin attached to the shaft, vibrating electric eggs, an electrically-operated plastic tongue, various large rings with peculiar attachments and an assortment of unidentifiable objects that might have been instruments of torture. And a plastic case full of little scalpels. Plus several bubble-packs of batteries.

It occurred to Anne that Nina had probably slept with more men in the last month than she had in her entire life. And so had Judi.

She slid the drawer shut, and probed in cold and scummy water, coming up at last with a spoon. She wiped it dry on a kitchen cloth, rubbing the greasy wetness off her hand at the same time. The spoon's underside was discoloured where it had been held over a flame. She wiped it again, very thoroughly. Her knuckles ached, and she rubbed her hand back to life in the dishcloth. She poured the old water out of the bowl, being careful not to dump any of the crockery into the sink, and turned on the hot tap. The pipes coughed and ran. Eventually, steam rose from the washing-up as it was again submerged.

She dumped the teabags in a wastebin shaped like a pair of buttocks, and carried the mugs of tea into the other room. It was not mainly a living room, she realized. It was a bedroom.

Nina still hadn't pulled herself together, but she took the tea easily. She warmed her hands on the mug.

Anne turned on an electric fire. The dust on the elements started to singe and smell. She sat opposite Nina, on the edge of a low chair, leaning forward, elbows on knees, taking regular sips of the still-too-hot tea. She scalded her tongue.

She had conducted plenty of difficult interviews. Her first session with Mrs Aziz had been especially nervous, as she tried to show some balance, probing for details of any criminal history her dead son might have had. She also remembered the Home Counties councillor who had been placing compulsory purchase orders on private houses he had then sold at a huge profit through his girlfriend's estate agency, the famous writer who had nothing to say about his current book but plenty of comments on attractive young lady interviewers in tight jeans, and the Christian Crusade leader who had been using starvation, regular beatings and harsh punishments to keep his young followers in line.

'My sister,' she began, 'did you know her well?'

Nina swallowed some tea, and shook her head. Anne could not tell if the gesture meant yes or no. Nina put the tea down, clawed her hair again, and tried very hard.

'She was my friend's flatmate. We... we worked together sometimes.' Worked together?

'Do you mind me asking questions?'

Nina nodded, 'No, I want to... I need to talk. I'm close to the end.'

'What do you mean?'

'It's nearly over, isn't it? Judi's dead. I think Coral is too. We're just girls. Just tarts. No one cares. I wish... I wish...'

Nina trailed off, hands over her face. Her nails were chewed, old varnish flaked away, and there were prominent blue veins between her knuckles.

'Yes?' encouraged Anne.

'I wish I'd never grown up. I wish I'd stayed at school. I wish I'd stayed with my Mum. I'm only nineteen. I've always been fucked up.'

'Did you know if Judi was… was using any kind of drugs?'

'Smack?'

'Heroin, yes?'

'Once, I think so. I don't know.'

'A special kind of heroin?'

'I don't know. Clive would know.'

'Who's Clive?'

Nina halted. Anne knew she did not want to go on. Apart from anything else, the girl was scared.

'Remember, I've nothing to do with the police, Nina. Right now, believe me, they probably like me a lot less than you. Now, who is Clive?'

Nina decided to talk. 'A dealer.'

'Drugs? Does he get heroin for you?'

'Smack, yes.'

'And for Judi?'

'I think he did. He does other things. Judi was with him for a while, but they had a big row and split up. She says he's scary, but…'

'Is Clive a pimp?'

Nina was almost indignant. 'We don't have pimps any more. That's stupid. We get beaten up and fucked over enough as it is. We had a girls' co-operative for a while, but now we just freelance on our own. The game isn't like that now. It's mostly just the girls.'

'And you're self-employed?'

'Yes. I'm on Schedule D. I do my own accounts. I've never gone on supplementary benefit.'

'What about Clive then?'

'He fixes us up sometimes.'

'For a commission?'

'No. Well, yes. He has expenses, he says. He puts work my way sometimes. And he did a lot for Judi before they broke up. He's more a friend than a work person. He sent me a Christmas card. It's the only one I've had so far.'

Anne wanted to cry for Nina, to do something for the girl. It was too late for Judi. But maybe she could do something here, something for her sister's memory.

'What did Clive do for Judi?'

'He set her up with some people. Rich people. Weird, if you know what I mean. But we all got paid.'

'You *and* Judi were with these people?'

'Yes. We only went together once. This woman in St John's Wood had a party. She called it an "entertainment". Coral was with us too.'

'Do you remember any names?'

'Well, I shouldn't… but… this woman was Amelia Something. The last name isn't English. German maybe. Dorf. And there was one really creepy guy. I didn't like him at all. He was called Skinner. Mr Skinner, no Christian name. They called him the Games Master.'

'Games?'

'Do you really want to know? I mean, Judi was your sister and all, but…'

'No, I suppose not. You're a nice girl aren't you, Nina?'

'Yeah, so what am I doing like this? I know, I know. It's not easy.'

'It never is.'

Nina looked at her, shrugging. She had a strand of her hair in her mouth, and was chewing nervously. The flat was warming up, but Nina was still shivering.

'Did you know anything about us? Judi's family?'

'Not much. We were watching a film on telly once and she said her Dad had written it or something. It was an old film in black and white. Marlon Brando and Therese Colt were in it. We didn't believe her, and Coral teased her about it. She shut up. I suppose it was true, wasn't it?'

'Mmmm, yes.'

'I knew it really. She pointed out some things you had written sometimes. You're a good writer.'

'Thanks. Judi would have been good too. At something.'

Nina tried to smile, and showed too much of her skull. Her cheeks were too tight over the bones, and there were hollows above her temples. Her eyes were still young, but the rest of her body was ageing fast. Anne remembered Judi's withered look.

'Amelia Dorf is having one of her "entertainments" later this afternoon,' Nina said.

'Are you going?'

'I may have to.'

'Why?'

'Because I'm broke, Anne.'

'I can give you money.'

'Not enough. I need to do some smack. I'm not an addict, but I need it to work sometimes. I'm gradually cutting it out, like Judi, but you can't do it all at once. Clive will be there. He always has good smack. And he's straight with it.'

Anne felt an icy calm. Seizing on what Nina had said, she casually asked the next question, knowing it was the key to the story. 'You say Judi was off heroin?'

'Yes. As far as I know, she had been straight for over a year. She was never a big user. Just a jab once in a while.'

'How did she look?'

'Uh, you mean how did she *look*? Good, I suppose. Pretty. She's a pretty girl. Much prettier than me. As good as Coral sometimes. And Coral is amazing.'

'So, the heroin hadn't affected her in any… permanent way?'

'Not really. She lost some weight, but she was looking better lately. When she broke up with Clive, she tried to talk me out of smack. She said I was being stupid.'

'And...?'

'Well, she was right, wasn't she. I've always been stupid.'

Nina was looking at Anne and seeing a social worker, a schoolteacher, a Mum. 'Thick, that's me. But I'm not an addict. I'm not. I just need a shot sometimes. Just sometimes.'

'Like now?'

'Yes, 'fraid so.'

'Would you do something for me if I gave you some money?'

'What?'

Nina was alert now.

'The rich people this afternoon? The "entertainment"?'

'Ye-e-es?'

'I'd like you to help me meet them.'

14

She was with a thin, angular young man, who was wearing a slightly too large sports jacket and horn-rimmed glasses. Nobody noticed *him*, but everybody, including the homosexual Lawyer and phallus-worshipping Objectivist, was compelled to stare at *her*. Some fought the urge and carried on talking or eating, intent upon their tableware while their dinner companions' eyes expanded, but most gave in. Even in a crowd sprinkled with authentic movie stars and frequently pinned-up starlets, she drew glances like a magnet draws iron filings. Without needing to look at the dancing star's table, he knew that she must be fuming hatred at the new beauty. All movie stars feared their juniors. He was amused again. Nobody in Romanoff's, himself included, qualified as the woman's junior.

She was, he knew instantly, one of the Kind.

Her hair, so blonde it seemed in this light to be white, was worn unfashionably long, and her evening dress, off the shoulder and floor-length, simple enough to pass in almost any century. Like him, she wore little jewellery. Like him, she excited attention wherever she went. No matter how hard the Kind might try to camouflage themselves among men, they could not suppress the glamour.

Mike Romanoff himself seated her, and her protégé, removing

a 'Reserved' sign from a prime table. For an unknown, she was rating unprecedented treatment.

Tail Gunner Joe and the Objectivist were still trading names. She was suggesting Communists and fellow travellers from the Screen Writers' Guild, and he was huffily claiming he had never heard of them. The Junior Senator was greedy for big fish. The Lawyer, he realized, was looking at him and trying to figure something out. It would be impossible for him to even guess at the truth. Compartmentalized and secret-filled the Lawyer's life might be, but he had few dreams, and he could never hope to tap in to the Big Dream he sought to control. The Lawyer's questions about Hugh Farnham were entirely practical, and entirely irrelevant: how much could the man be trusted, how could he be controlled, what could be used to leash him?

She was looking across the room at him, a catlike smile on her lips, her eyes seeming to swell in her face. She had known him at once, as he had known her.

It had been sixty years since the End of the Immortal Empire. Since Giselle's death, he had not encountered another of the Kind. He had heard nothing of the Elders, and wondered occasionally whether he was the last of the family. It would have been so easy, amid the chaotic bloodletting of two world wars and innumerable revolutions, colonial disputes and massacres, for the Kind to die out, and pass from history as unnoticed as ever, its Fall eventually percolating through into the myth-echoes that were all they ever left behind.

Evidently, this was not so.

'King of the Cats,' she said, inside his head, amused at his surprise.

He controlled himself, and nodded minutely, raising his glass to her.

Her protégé was trying to get her attention, and she was brushing him aside. Waiters were flocking to their table, and the young man, left on his own, was awkwardly ordering wine and food for the both of them. The Monster sensed in the young man the seeds of the extraordinary. It could hardly have been otherwise, if this creature were interested in him.

'Outside,' the words formed in his mind, 'on the terrace.'

He was excited by the meeting. He noticed his nails had changed, growing hard and pointed, sharp enough to part the tablecloth. And teeth were swelling in his cheeks, tearing the inside of his mouth. He subdued his body, and excused himself, reaching for his cigarette case like a Noel Coward character.

The Objectivist looked at him as he walked towards the terrace, gliding through the dancing couples. The orchestra was playing 'A Dream is a Wish Your Heart Makes'. He felt the tendrils of her desire snapping back at her as they broke, as he slipped out of the crowded restaurant.

Beyond the curtains he was alone, looking out at the lights of Hollywood. There were premieres out there, and searchlights stabbed the velvety sky. In the darkness, the Dreams sparkled.

'Your Majesty,' she said, appearing through the curtains like a leading lady, 'I am honoured.'

She was mocking him.

'The Kingdom of the Cats is over,' he said. 'I'm Hugh Farnham, now.'

'Hugh. Very well. You change your names with your skins, nephew.'

'We all do.'

She made no noise as she came near him, her dress catching the lights of the city.

'Not all. I'm Ariadne.'

He had heard of her, but not much. Giselle had met her in Portugal, after the Lisbon earthquake. And, he realized, he had seen her credits on motion pictures.

'Of "Gowns by Ariadne"?'

She smiled. She was supposed to be one of the Elders, but she was not above being flattered by recognition.

'I am pleased to meet you,' he said.

'No, you aren't. You were enjoying your uniqueness, imagining yourself the last of the Kind.'

He said nothing. She was more beautiful even than Giselle, and stronger even than he.

'We've flourished since your little kingdom fell, you know. We've changed our ways, while you've stayed the same.'

'Am I to be punished, then?'

She laughed, musically. 'Oh no, Hugh. You may follow your own road. Perhaps there'll be another Kingdom of the Cats. You can always rejoin when you get tired of playing with all this...'

She extended her arms, including the city in her gesture.

He reached out to her, drawn to her burning ice centre. Feeding was one thing, but this desire was different. The way he felt for Ariadne was not so different from the way the Objectivist or the Lawyer felt for him.

'No,' she said, holding his hand, 'I don't think so. I have other business to...'

'Who is he?'

She was taller than she had been, her cheekbones more prominent, her eyes brighter.

'My date?'

He nodded.

'A man of genius, nephew. A lamb among wolves just now, I admit, but a remarkable man. Cameron Nielson.'

He knew of the young man. A playwright, his first works – a two-handed drama about a prisoner and his psychiatrist, and a family saga called *Father, Son and Holy Terror* – had been successful on Broadway, netting two successive Drama Critics Circle Awards, and were optioned by Mark Hellinger at Universal. Along with Arthur Miller and Tennessee Williams, he was expected to shake up the American theatre a little.

The Monster had a taste for geniuses. In his mind, he saw Ariadne opening Nielson's head, and scooping his genius out in grey lumps.

'Not yet,' Ariadne said. 'Later, maybe. But not yet. He has things to do.'

'Why do you care?'

She smiled again. 'I'm a patron of the arts.'

A wind blew by, bringing a chill. Ariadne's dress clung where the wind pressed, and stirred, flapping on her other side. In the starlight, her skin was as dead white as her hair, but her eyes shone, red under green. She was the adult Giselle might have become in a thousand more years. 'And you,' she said, 'will you ride your crusade?'

He nodded. She laughed.

'It'll be interesting. But it'll be the end of you.'

It was like a blow. The Elders were always like that, secure in their survival, contemptuous of the rest of the Kind, treating them like children playing at the edge of the precipice, knowing better but doing nothing.

'I don't think so.'

'Well, maybe not. Maybe you'll last. But your friends in there are a poor lot.'

'They don't matter.'

'That's a dangerous thought. You should be careful about the people you mix with. I prefer the brilliant...'

'So do I, they taste better.'

'Not just for that, nephew. They're less prone to envy us. Among humans, the brilliant are freaks and sports. It's mediocrities you should watch. Like your friends back there, arguing about movie stars. When they've finished with the Reds, they'll want to see your head on a pole. Have you read that woman's books?'

He was embarrassed, and shrugged.

'I trust you've not fed off her. She would be such a feeble meal.'

They had nothing more to say to each other, but they stayed on the terrace, politely sampling each other's memories. There were great parts of her experience that she successfully kept him away from. She was much older, much stronger. It was not really new to him, being powerless, but it was hardly relishable.

All she gave him were a few pictures of the world as it had been for her. And yet, she exhausted him in a single draught. All his ghosts were conjured up for her. It was a wrenching, unpleasant experience, but he submitted to it, hoping to impress her. When it was over, she looked at him with an expression he would never be able to wipe from his memory. There was a nannyish kindliness in it, but also disappointment, and – intolerably – pity. She shrugged, her dress rippling from her shoulders, and smiled.

'No,' she said again, 'I don't think so.'

His question was only a thought. Some day?

Her answer was not even that. Maybe, who knows, never…

She gave him her hand to be kissed – the Kind always found it hard to dispense with the old manners – and left him, the curtains closing after her. On the balcony, he was alone again.

His fingernails, he realized, were two inches long, and curled into bony barbs. And his mouth was full of blood.

Inside, he was shaking. She had left something of herself in him, perhaps out of tenderness. He hated her for that gesture, and tried to force the images she had spilled into him out of his mind, erasing the centuries with a burning fury.

A girl came out. She had a short black dress, red hair and pale freckles the assistant director who had supervised her screen test thought would not show in Technicolor. She was lighting a cigarette, and shivering. She was here with the assistant director, and was not sure whether she should go to bed with him tonight. He was important, but maybe not that important. Daphne had told her to get an agent, and sleep with him.

'Oh,' she said, 'I'm sorry… I thought there was no one out here.'

He laid his hands on her shoulders, and looked into her face. Her eyes moved from side to side, trying to take all of him in. His nails pinched her bare skin, drawing points of blood.

Still trying to wash Ariadne out of his mind, he bent his neck and kissed the girl – Therese Colt – on the mouth, forcing his long tongue into her throat, latching suckerlike to her tonsils.

Therese did not struggle, melting in his embrace as she had done during the screen test with the iron-jawed desert sheik.

He sucked part of her in, finding the Mary Teresa Garrity beneath Therese Colt, and gulped it down. She tasted bitter. After Ariadne, they would all, for a while, taste bitter. He sucked back his tongue, pulling it out of the girl with a rasping slurp, and pushed her away.

He wiped his bleeding mouth with the back of his hand, scraping away skin, then pulled out a silk handkerchief from the top pocket of his dinner jacket, balled it, and used it to mop up the mess. Therese was looking at him with concern, unheeding the part of her that had just been torn loose. Blood was seeping from one of her nostrils, and his nailpoints had opened three twin vents in the side of her dress, exposing more freckles.

'Mister,' she said, 'are you all right?'

He ignored her. She stepped closer, reaching out, but then her knees gave way and she slumped to the floor in a faint.

The Monster grabbed the rail, and took control of himself. Gripping tight, he watched his hands as the nails shrank. He smoothed his hair, and tugged at his clothes, sharpening his appearance.

Therese would recover. She had warmed him, helped him survive Ariadne's indifference. He had taken something from her, but had also left something inside her. Perhaps he had chilled her heart where it needed to be chilled. She would not sleep with the assistant director, but she would become a star.

He left her there, and went back into the restaurant. Ariadne had rejoined Cameron Nielson, and was listening intently as he talked to her. The Monster knew he was talking about his work, for he could feel the young man's burning intensity from across the room. Ariadne had her hand lightly on his arm. The Monster was still shivering. Ariadne gave him the briefest of smiles, and returned her attention to the playwright.

They would never speak again, the Monster and Ariadne,

although they would occasionally be in the same city and sense each other's presence. If there were, as she had implied, others of the Kind still surviving, then he never encountered any.

Tail Gunner Joe was drunk and getting abusive, calling the waiters 'kikes' and 'Commies'. He was itching for an injection, the Monster could tell. The Lawyer was making inscrutable little notes. And the Objectivist, deprived of his presence, had gone to the powder room to repair herself.

'And when we've finished hammering the fuckin' Reds,' Tail Gunner Joe told the Lawyer, 'we're gonna go after the fuckin' queers.'

The Monster watched Ariadne lean over to Nielson, and saw the playwright's face rise to meet her kiss.

'Fuckin' asshole bandits oughta be strung up,' the Junior Senator grumbled. The Lawyer was shut up tight, his face not registering everything, but the Monster could sniff his funk.

Ariadne broke the embrace, and nipped playfully at Nielson's ear. He smiled, an odd expression on so serious a young man, crinkling his face like a comedian's. He called the waiter for more drinks.

If he could not have Ariadne, the Monster swore, he would have her protégé. Not now, but when she was through with him.

He would have Cameron Nielson drained and drunk dry, and he would then turn his attention to anything, or anyone, that came from the man. His women would weep blood.

When he was through, it would be as if the playwright had never walked the Earth.

15

In the taxi, on the way to St John's Wood, Nina fell asleep on Anne's shoulder. The creosoty smell of the girl's hair dye was pleasant in a roundabout way. Anne almost relaxed.

Nina had lent her an outfit – a short, tight skirt, black tights, a black jacket not designed to fasten up – and helped make her up. She had suddenly turned into a teacher, gently ridiculing Anne's idea of a tarty face, and subtly rearranging and highlighting her make-up. Anne had to admit she did not look bad, and hoped she could pass for one of Nina's workmates. She had tried a pair of Nina's spike heels, but they had pinched painfully, and she had to hope her comfortable flats would pass. They were black, highly polished and matched the rest of her get-up.

It was a dingy afternoon, and slate grey slabs of cloud had brought the already early sunset forward. The chilly, heavily padded interior of the cab was comfortably gloomy, lit only by the orange numbers adding up on the meter as the fare increased.

Anne found that Nina had, in her sleep, reached out and taken hold of her hand. Nina's own was cold, but she squeezed gently. The unconscious intimacy surprised and comforted Anne. She wished that she could express her feelings in such a simple, honest manner.

Of course, a cynical footnote inevitably came to mind.

Doubtless, Nina was habitually intimate with strangers in ways far more involved and far less innocent than hand-holding.

Anne could not help thinking of Judi.

For the first twelve years of the dead girl's life, Anne had seen her sister, been with her, talked to her, spent time with her, almost every day. And yet, her images of Judi as a baby, as a little girl, as an elementary school pupil, as a young teenager were alternately fuzzy and artificial, like the photographs she had collected in a folder somewhere. Anne was not sure whether her memories were first hand, or had been impressed upon her by the familiarity with those snapshots and the reminiscences of relatives.

Everything else about that period of her life was still vivid – arguing with Cam about trivial things like who should sit in the front seat of the car, being taken for the first time to the theatre for one of Dad's plays and not understanding what was going on in the dark auditorium or the remote stage, being taken by her mother on a holiday for two in the desert where the cowboys had lived and getting bored after a few days with the heat and the sand. But Judi, dead Judi, was quietly fading from her memory like a disgracefully dissolute pharaoh being rubbed out of the history books by unforgiving high priests.

In that folder, there were a number of photographs of babies and little girls, usually caught by the sun among the greens of the garden in New Hampshire, that Anne could not identify. They might be of Judi, but they could as easily be of her younger self. Not until they reached school age, apparently, had the sisters developed any distinctive characteristics of their own.

Much clearer in her mind were the scenes from later life.

Now, it seemed to Anne as if the first time she had really noticed Judi was during the summer after she returned from college. During the three years the sisters had mainly lived apart, Judi had grown into an intelligent, difficult, uncomfortable teenager, chain-smoking at fifteen, reading her way through every book in the house, from *Peyton Place* to *The Romantic Agony*. She had been interested in Anne only in that she would have liked to know the blow-by-blow details of her sister's sex life as a student. She had lost her own virginity, she boasted (confessed?), to one of the local stupids, and was just getting over her initial disappointment with sex by casting around for less conventional ways of annoying her family. Now, Anne suspected that at twenty-one, with two whole neatly-over-and-done-with love affairs to her credit, she must have been unbearably priggish and self-obsessed. Love Affair Number Two was going to be her first novel, but that had worked out less well even than the real life episode. Judi had read some of her draft chapters, and gone uncharacteristically quiet, refusing to offer criticisms or comments. Shortly afterwards, Anne had abandoned fiction altogether.

Three years later, when Anne had already decided to move to London and visits to Judi in police stations were no novelty, she had seen Judi squatting in a New York City cell with five other prostitutes, dressed in glittery tatters, with a face like a painted and bruised punk madonna, and dried blood on her neck and upper breasts. Anne, brought up with liberal folk myths of the Chicago Democratic Convention, Paris *soixante-huit* and Attica, had seen the red badge of courage and threatened the polite lieutenant with a hard-hitting exposé of police brutality.

'What you don't understand,' she had been told, 'is that your sister is a specialist.' The policeman, displaying no relish for it, had tactfully and patiently explained that Judi had come by her bruises at the hands of clients who had bought her and paid for the privilege of using her as a punching bag. This was worse than Anne had been prepared for. Prostitution, she could just about understand; the rest was beyond her fantasies, beyond her experience.

She had argued with Judi for hours in an interrogation room, overseen by a police matron who read *Cosmopolitan* and looked like a more dangerous Angie Dickinson. Anne had tried to get Judi to name names and swear out complaints against the men who had gotten their rocks off beating up on her. Judi had calmly insisted on protecting her sources of income. Unlike their father, she did not want a 'rat jacket', a reputation as an informer. Of course, the NYPD did not sic Hugh Farnham on her, so she never found out just how tough she was.

Now, Anne realized how typical Judi was of the family. Their father had a Nobel prize, Cam was supposed to be the best in his field and she was herself acknowledged as on the rise. Judi had chosen to be sado-masochist hooker, but she was determined to be the best, most professional sado-masochist hooker in the world. Given a few more years, she would probably have made more money than any of them.

Anne felt a warm, wet touch at her throat. Still asleep, Nina was trying to kiss her neck, licking at a patch of skin with catlike absent-mindedness.

Embarrassed, Anne lifted the girl's head. Nina woke up just as the taxi driver found the address he had been given.

'I was dreaming…'

EVENING

1

It was the kind of quietly well-off residential street where mass murderers live, unnoticed behind the Neighbourhood Watch stickers, until someone turns up a toenail in the rosebeds. The houses were well-maintained, nineteenth-century and 1930s flourishes kept in good nick by careful owners, but there was an overwhelming drabness to the buildings. In the twilight, the only real colour came from the bright estate agents' notice boards posted outside almost every home. The whole street was for sale. This was an expensive part of town – upper upper middle and lower upper – and even the family cars parked in drives were high performance models. But the cracks were beginning to show. There was a stream of rubbish clogging the gutters, as if a parade had passed by with waste-paper substituting for tickertape. A few years ago, that would have been the mark of the scruffy Camden council, but now the rot was creeping into well-heeled Westminster. Even prosperity was not what it had been.

It was not Belgravia, but it was certainly well-off, thank you very much. Quite apart from the usual expenses, mortgages and service charges would be punitive around here. The media and entrepreneur types attracted to the district were unlikely to be rich enough long enough to buy a permanent stake in the prestigious postcode. Anne knew; she had lived in a street like this for a few months, sharing her flat with that psychopath from the BBC, and had had to move on when the *Newsweek* commissions petered out.

Amelia Dorf's house was different. Nina knew it right away, and led Anne across the road to it. It was set apart from its neighbours, like the manorhouse of a village. Built as a home for a large and prosperous mid-Victorian family, the five-storey pile had not, like all of its neighbours, been converted into almost affordable small units. The already formidable garden wall was topped with spear-tipped railings that were probably sharpened every day. The wrought-iron gates might have been expressly designed to keep out the most determined and well-equipped lynch mob.

Anne knew that all this meant money, and in an inexhaustible supply. Bank balances like international telephone numbers. Amelia Dorf. She would look through the files when she was in the office. Anyone rich enough to live in this house must have made the news some time in her life.

Nina dealt-with the entryphone that had replaced the bell-pull. A snake-neck swivelled above, and a closed circuit camera peered down. A green light winked, and the gates rattled mechanically. Nina pushed them inwards, and they were through before the buzzing stopped. The gates locked behind them.

In front of the house there was a lawn. The centrepiece was an eight-foot tall evergreen topiary dildo.

The front door was open by the time they got to it. Nina and Anne were let into the house by a large and solid man who looked slightly Scandinavian. Anne guessed that he spent most of his days in a gymnasium and knew all the correct Latin names for the muscles he had developed. He wore a quilted floor-length dressing gown that could have passed for a formal ball dress in old St Petersburg. Nina knew him.

'Hello, Anders,' she said, chucking her shiny black coat into his hands, 'this is Anne.'

Anders ignored Anne, but carefully folded Nina's coat with

the casual reverence usually found in dry-cleaners or the very best restaurants.

'You're early.'

'It said five on the invitation Amelia sent out. It must be past that now.'

'Typical of you, Nina. No one comes at the time on the card. That's why we always invite for two hours early.'

'I'm sorry, but it's not my fault.'

'It's hardly considerate, you know. We're not really ready.'

Anne took off her own coat, which he took willingly and hung up. She kept her handbag though. Turning from the coat racks, he stared into her eyes in the manner recommended by most 'How to Impress Girls' handbooks. Anne almost laughed.

'Anne,' he said, lowering his glance to her chest, 'you have startled eyes.'

Anne raised an eyebrow.

'You've lived many times, I can tell. We've met before. In the French Revolution.'

Nina chipped in, 'Anders was the Marquis de la Somewhere-or-Other.'

Anders took her hand, and kissed her middle knuckles.

'Of course,' Anne said, pulling her fingers free. 'How could I forget? How is that pain in your neck, citizen?'

He looked up, and really looked at her this time. There was a tracery of little scars under his jawline, as if someone had scooped out a pouch of flesh with sharp fingers. He looked too young for plastic surgery, but Anne suspected he was just vain enough to take self-perfection to expensive lengths.

'Now whose eyes are startled?' she asked.

He started ignoring her again. Nina pulled at his heavy sleeve, perhaps harder than she had meant to. His collar shifted, and Anne saw thick muscles with more scars.

'Clive?' said Nina. 'Is he here yet?'

'I told you. You're early.'

'But doesn't he stay over sometimes?'

'Sometimes, but not now. I'm staying here now. And a few others. Daeve Pope is here. Clive is with Mr Skinner on business. They'll both be along at tea-time. Do you mind? This is expensive, antique.'

He shook his arm free of her hold, and hugged himself. Anne caught a look of nausea under his patina of health and vigour, as if he could not bear to be touched by another human being.

'Ciao, Nina,' said a short young man, stepping out from a room, 'who's your friend?'

He came into the light, grinning. Anne put his age at about thirty, but he was wearing the striped blazer and straw hat of a public school prefect, and his slightly fuzzy chin suggested he had not started shaving yet.

'Anne,' Nina said, 'this is Daeve Pope. He's a writer...' Nina had been about to say 'he's a writer too,' but Daeve cut her off. 'Perhaps you've seen my work,' he said, 'I do essays for *Kerrang* and *Metal Hammer*. I'm interested in thrash metal.'

Daeve had a cigarette case out. He offered it around too quickly for anyone to accept, and stuck a fag in the corner of his mouth. The cigarettes were a brand Anne did not know, but they must be extra king-size because they were disproportionate, like props from a science fiction film about shrinking people. As he lit up, Daeve looked like a nearly adult-sized child.

'Just thrash, of course. I do not tolerate glam in any way, shape or form. It's the only thing left in rock and roll with the balls to blast and the dick to come through.'

'He's a good writer,' Nina said. 'You can tell.'

Daeve puffed a cloud of smoke, and hung his head on one side, posing. 'Remember,' he said to Anne, suddenly shaking his head up and down so that his boot-black hair flopped over his face and pumping the air with an angry milkmaid's fist, 'just thrash.'

He grinned, tossing his hair back, and took another drag, slipping back into his room like a jack in the box.

Nina looked at the door Daeve had closed behind him, then at Anne. She shrugged. Anders, who had frozen like a stone lion while Daeve was in the passage, came back to life and turned into the sinister butler from an old Boris Karloff movie.

Anders led them down the sparsely furnished hallway, and ushered them into a large room. It was a windowless den, decorated with paper chains and Chinese lanterns. There was a fully dressed Christmas tree, with baubles, lights and presents, and an open fire in an alcove the size of an upright piano.

Behind a glass-topped desk sat an elegant woman in her forties, with purple-streaked hair coiled in a psyche knot and Morticia Addams make-up. She was wearing surgeon's gloves and delicately shaping a Paramount mountain of white powder in front of her. It looked like flour, but a fistful would be worth what Anne had earned in the last year.

There was a naked child squatting by the fire, looking like a tattooed savage in the echt-psychedelic light from the tree and the blaze. He was playing with a pile of expensive toys. He flew a foot-long, perfectly detailed model of Concorde in his hand, and gingerly crash-landed it among the burning logs. He pulled his hand out of the flames quickly and sucked his slightly singed fingers.

The plane's wings melted first, dripping gobbets of molten plastic. Then the beaked body bent downwards and flopped onto the logs. The boy thumped the floor and crooned in ecstasy. He reached for the starship *Enterprise*.

Anne recognized him. It was Derek Douane, the twelve-year-old ex-choirboy of 'Christmas Caroline' fame. He had his face on the cover of every girls' magazine on the stands. Not since Little Jimmy Osmond had Anne been so personally sickened by a pop singer. Before 'Christmas Caroline', he had had a big hit with a vomitous reggae cover version of 'Puff the Magic Dragon'.

'Ahh, Nina,' said the woman at the desk, Amelia, 'thank you for coming. And, as requested, you brought a friend.'

She got up and shook Anne's hand. Her glove was talcum-powdered with cocaine. Foreign surname or not, she sounded as Anne had once imagined all English women sounded, like Jenny Agutter or Julie Andrews.

'This is Anne.'

'Anne. You'll find us amusing, I hope. And rewarding.' Wrinkles of perturbation appeared on her white forehead. 'Do I know you?'

'I don't think so.'

…Anne knew her now. Amelia Dorf. She had seen her before at a press conference. She was on a women's committee formed to oppose the Campaign for Nuclear Disarmament. The GPA. The Global Peace Something. Alliance? Agency? Activists? They wanted the West to stockpile as many atomic weapons as the East, and had, in the Gorbachev era, been darkly muttering about the increasing threat of Third World nations with a nuclear capability. Amelia would not remember her. She was just one of an audience of journalists. No, Anne knew that Amelia thought she was a familiar face (and voice?) because she had known Judi…

'Ahh, you're American?'

'Canadian,' she lied.

'Canada, right. Where the Mounties come from. Do make yourself comfortable. We won't really be starting for a while, so we can get to know each other better before the others arrive. Nina, you know where the drinks are kept. Get us all something would you.'

Amelia sat Anne down on a giant cloth marshmallow, and sunk cross-legged on the carpet next to Derek. She wore a leotard that showed off her concentration camp figure, and knee-length alligator-skin boots.

'This is Derek. He's staying for Christmas because he can't be with his Mummy and Daddy.'

The child star turned and looked at Anne with Neanderthal hostility. His pupils were shrunk to pinpoints, and half his face was red from being too close to the fire. Amelia plucked a paper napkin from one of the several cardboard dispensers scattered around the room and wiped the spittle from his chin. She threw the napkin into the fire, where it flared like a meteor next to the softening spaceship.

'You know, bitch,' said Derek in his not-quite broken voice, 'your tits aren't big enough.'

Amelia slapped him with an open hand.

'Don't be vulgar, Derek. Anne is our guest. We must make her feel at home.'

Derek didn't mind being slapped at all. He hugged Amelia, and whispered in her ear. She giggled indulgently, and pushed him away.

Embarrassed, Anne looked into the fire. The bridge of the *Enterprise* was distorting, pulled out of shape by weights inside the model.

'Can you hear the screams?' asked Derek, baring his teeth like the fly-eating madman in the old *Dracula* movie. 'That's what I like the most. The screams. At my concerts, I make girls scream.'

'I'll bet you do.'

The model in the fire fell apart with a hiss and some plops. Parts of it sizzled, and the logs spat like burning sausages. The stench of burning plastic stung Anne's nostrils.

'That scream there,' said Derek, reaching out to catch the unheard shriek. 'That's Captain Kirk. When the *Enterprise* caught fire, he knew he was going to die and wanted to do all the things they wouldn't let him do on television. He slashed up his captain seat, and whacked Mr Sulu in the belly and shat on Chekhov's face. He was going to fuck Lieutenant Uhura, but his cock caught fire and dropped off. It was plastic like the rest of him. He's melting down into a puddle with the rest of his crew. The blob there is Kirk's cock, and Spock's ears, and Uhura's twat, and Dr McCoy's left leg, and bits of ground-up dilithium crystal. All the crew are just a screaming glob of burning plastic now. Just the same as their starship...'

During his rant, Derek had been getting more excited. He reached down and started fingering his stubby penis. Amelia slapped his hand away from his bald genitals and pinched his foreskin. He squeaked and shut up.

'That's enough playing for today, Derek. You've run out of toys. I'll have to ask Santa for some more. Now, go and put some clothes on.'

Derek padded over to a pile of colourful clothes, and obediently started to wrestle with them. Anne wondered what Amelia had the kid high on. His hand-eye coordination was way off, and getting dressed was too much of a struggle for him to accomplish alone. Amelia, treating him like a toddler, helped him with the difficult moves, fussing with buttons, and preventing him from strangling himself with rainbow-striped braces.

Nina came back with a tray of liqueurs. Anne took a glass, but only sipped the thick orange liquid once or twice. The heat from the fire was already getting to her head, and she knew that she needed, above all else, to remain in control. Amelia developed a sudden craving for Christmas cookies, and told Nina where to find them. The girl left again. If she had curtseyed, she would have been just like one of the maidservants on *Upstairs, Downstairs*.

Amelia got back to the cocaine, and went to work on it with a gold razor-blade. She cut it into white slug-trails that striped the reflective desktop.

'Would you care to indulge?'

'No thank you,' Anne said. 'Sinus trouble.'

'Ahhh, yes. There's a lot of 'flu going around. It's best to save it for later, anyway. We don't want people to think we're piggish, do we?'

Nevertheless, she took a tiny pinch and snuffed it, throwing her head back. She was like a cook, Anne thought, unable to resist a lick of the icing.

'There,' said Amelia, seeming not at all dizzy, 'that's better.' She picked up the blade again, but gripped the wrong edge. 'Ouch, I'm opened…'

She held up a gloved hand. It looked like a jewellery store replica for displaying rings. There was a seeping red line on the tip of her forefinger. Droplets fell on the desk, rolling like mercury on the glass, soaking into the cocaine like piss in snow.

Amelia waved her hand. 'Derek, come here...'

The child was at her side instantly. He took Amelia's hand and professionally peeled back the glove. It came off with a snap. He stroked her palm, as if playing 'round and round the garden', and bent his head over. He took the wounded finger into his mouth and sucked quietly. Amelia ran her free hand through his bleached blond hair.

'Anne, isn't he lovely?'

'Oh yes, lovely.'

'And he's so talented. He's a singer, you know.'

'I know.'

'And such a nice smile, don't you think. It's no wonder he has such a following.'

'On the radio, they don't seem to play anyone else.'

'No, that's right. But then again, why should they? He's so much better than all the others. What's his song called? "Christmas Caroline". Such a clever title. Once you've heard it, it goes round and round your mind forever. You keep thinking of it at the most unlikely moments. You never forget it...'

'Oh no, never...'
'"Tell me, Christmas Caroline,
When you say you'll be mine,
You raise a round of loud applause
From old Mr Santa Claus.
We walk down the lane, dear,
Just us and the reindeer,
It's such a jaunt,
And you're the only Christmas present I want."'

In Anne's opinion, Amelia's rendition of the song was superior musically to Derek's recorded version, but unfortunate in that it made audible the lyrics that were incomprehensible in the original. She wondered what Mr Thrash Metal would think of it. Or Cam, who was often said to be interested in the fine dividing line between music and pain. Maybe that was Derek's major achievement, uniting people of such different tastes in their single opinion of him.

'Look at these eyes,' she tilted Derek's head upwards, 'so darling, so knowing. Such a warm little mouth he has.'

At that point, Anne realized that her hostess was certifiably deranged. She was getting fed up with sick people.

'Anne,' Amelia said seriously, almost dangerously, 'don't just agree with me all the time. If you think I'm a fruitcake, please do say so. I hate persons who don't speak their minds.'

She smiled sweetly, and suddenly wasn't as out-of-touch and fuzzy-minded as Anne had thought. She had come down off her mental space shuttle and become disturbingly lucid. Anne realized she would have to work harder, conceal more about herself, if she were to get through this.

'Have you ever read *Lolita*?' Amelia asked.

Did Amelia suspect that Anne was not just another disposable tart like Judi and Nina? Was the question a clever trap to find out what kind of person she really was? If so, Amelia had misjudged her tarts. Anne had not read Nabokov, but knew her sister had. She hesitated, and told the truth,

'No, but I saw the film. With James Mason.'

Amelia seemed surprised at even that trace of a cultural background. Anne would have to watch herself, try to seem more like Nina. She tried to pout, and felt silly.

'That's right.' Amelia was too intent on patronizing her to notice the face-pulling. 'With James Mason. Humbert Humbert, the James Mason character, is wrong about little girls, I think. They're so boring, so unimaginative. Not sensual at all. Not like little boys.'

Amelia pulled her finger out of Derek's mouth, and rubbed it dry. The bleeding had stopped. She put an arm around the boy. Derek looked at Anne, smiling innocently. With his eyes shut, he looked like a happy imbecile.

Whatever Anne thought of Derek Douane, this was child abuse and an obscenity. Her crusading instincts were aroused.

'No, not at all like Derek,' Amelia continued. 'He's so promising, you know. He'll be quite passionate, I think. A fatal man. They'll all want him. To use him and be used by him.'

Anne was excluded. Amelia's words were directed at her, but she was talking to the boy.

'Wouldn't you just *luh*-love…' Amelia caught her voice on the word and had to start again. 'Wouldn't you just love to slit his little throat, and watch the *fuh*-fucking little toad *buh*-bleed to death…'

Derek snuggled against Amelia's flat breasts. Anne tried not to look as if she wanted to be sick.

'That, I think, would be quite an experience,' said Amelia. 'That, I think, would make me *cuh*-climax like an alley cat.'

She took another pinch of cocaine, and snorted it with a rattle of phlegm. Derek began to hum 'Christmas Caroline', and Amelia joined in on the chorus.

2

On the way to the pantry to get the Christmas cookies, Nina got lost. The house was big and old, with a lot more corridors and rooms and unexpected turns than seemed necessary, but she had done enough of these 'entertainments' to be familiar with the lower storeys. The route from the den to the pantry was quite simple, she thought. She had to take a walk down a short corridor from the main hallway, go down a few steps to the kitchen. The pantry was just a walk-in alcove off the kitchen. Easy. But somehow, she found herself in a large, empty room. There were wall-sized French windows through which she would in daylight have been able to see the back garden. Now, it was in darkness. There was the vague suggestion of orange light beyond the high wall that marked the rear boundary of Amelia's property; the streetlamps were already on.

Nina sat on the floor and cried. She was in a state. Why was Clive not here yet?

The stomach cramps had been coming back, off and on, all day, but so far she had been able to keep them under control. In her flat with Anne, and in the taxi, she had been able to conceal her pain from the older woman. Now, the spasms were worse than ever.

She was shaking with the cold, but the fire in the den had

been irritating and overbearing. Under her heavy clothes, she felt filthy, as if there were a layer of vermin-ridden earth between her naked skin and the fabric.

Things were moving all over her. She scratched and pulled, but could never find the leeches under her blouse or the spiders crawling inside her tights.

She doubled up in pain, and rested her forehead on the carpeted floor. She willed the pains to recede, and gradually they did.

She needed to eat, to shower, to rest, to sleep. Most of all, she needed some smack. She needed Clive. She needed help.

When Amelia had had her serve the drinks, Nina realized just how far gone she was. She had found it difficult to read the labels on the bottles. The delicate glasses had felt thick and awkward in her hands, soft as putty but covered in cutting edges. When pouring, it had been impossible to line up the bottles with the glasses, no matter how close she held the neck of a bottle to the rim of a glass. She had soaked her hand and cuff with *crème de menthe,* and the sticky liquid seemed to have crept up her arm. Her fingers felt as if they were encased in cool wax.

Where was Clive? Good old Clive? Clive the dealer. Clive the healer. Where was Clive?

She scratched her arm; but could not find the stickiness. Her needle tracks were not that bad. Yet. Really, she could wear sleeveless dresses if she wanted to. But not in winter.

Of course, she would have to get off smack in the long run. Or else she *would* look like that girl in the adverts. But she could handle that later. Right now, she needed a fix. Just one more fix, perhaps, then she would stay away forever.

Maybe she would have to do it gradually, taking less each time, taking more time between each time. Perhaps she could get something on the NHS? 'Lady, how about two packs of your old heroin for one of your new improved biological methadone?'

But right now, she needed Clive.

Her stomach clenched like a fist, but there was nothing in

there to come up. Her bowels opened like a tulip, but there was nothing there to come out. Her head throbbed like a burst boil, but there was nothing there...

Nothing.

She was empty, and only Clive could fill her up. Where was Clive?

Eventually – after how long? – the pains passed, and she was able to stand up. She could feel nothing, as if her entire body were mummified in thick wads of flavourless chewing gum. Moving was difficult, but at least it did not hurt.

Like one of the shambling dead, she left the room and returned to the main hall. Then, without thinking, she found the right corridor. She floated down the steps and opened the door into the kitchen.

Anders was there, supposedly supervising the preparation of an assortment of mixed salads for the buffet. A lumpish Belgian girl called Lise who did menial tasks about the house but hardly ever spoke was grating cheese over a rice dish.

Anders was playing with Daeve.

He had the writer laid out, face down with his baggy trousers around his knees, on a marble-topped kitchen table, and was anally violating him with a large, unwashed carrot.

Anders held Daeve down with a clever grip on the back of his neck. Nina now knew what the expression 'squealing like a stuck pig' really meant.

Anders looked up at Nina and laughed. He was stripped to the waist, and she could see the lunar map of dead skin and fresh scars that was stretched tautly over his Schwarzenegger musculature.

The squealing stopped as Anders plucked out the carrot. Nina knew, as her stomach hit her again, that he was going to take a bite out of it.

'Nyaaah,' he said, chewing, 'what's up, doc?'

3

It was all rather pathetic really, not at all the orgy of degradation she had half-imagined. Amelia had left off quoting from the wit and wisdom of her favourite mass murderers, done a few lines of cocaine, and started to whizz around the room. She was demonstrating aerobic movements and hostessing for her guests as they arrived.

Anne was sort of expecting blubbery cabinet ministers and worn clergymen, slavering and ready to practise their secret vices, but the guests turned out to be unidentifiable nobodies. For a while, she thought she could have been at any moderately boring Christmas party.

The women wore Laura Ashley or Ghost dresses, the men wore expensive jeans. Anne realized that the younger, prettier members of both sexes had been bought and paid for. She was supposed to blend in with that group. There were no obvious freaks, transvestites, monsters or exotic creatures. Well, not any more than usual.

The guests greedily snuffed cocaine, ate platefuls of designer salad, listened to Amelia's Jean-Michel Jarre CDs, smoked ordinary cigarettes and weedy joints, and talked about cars and mortgage rates and money and dry rot and Eastern Europe and computers and their weight and Christmas and sex. It was all very '80s, the young, rich and shallow turning middle-aged, tax-assessed and empty. None of this had anything to do with Judi.

Derek Douane was being cooed over by a pair of predatory women in their fifties, not minding their tanned fingers in his hair, on his face or twanging his braces. Daeve was lecturing a bank manager on the stylistic differences between Bolt Thrower, Odin and Meat Market. Anders was playing major-domo outside.

She was trapped, pinned to a bookcase by two smoothly stupid, slightly drunk young men. One, Toby Farrar, was a career army officer out of uniform, the other, Baz Something, was a cricket-playing travel agent. Farrar was short with livery lips and thick black eyebrows, and Something was prematurely bald and thought he was really cool. They were both assholes, and they were both boasting about their early sex lives. Anne stopped listening while they were comparing their masturbatory records, and watched for new arrivals.

'Six times a day,' said Something, 'that was my personal best.'

'Piss on that,' said Farrar, 'that was my mean average.'

Nina seemed to have lost contact with Planet Earth. Earlier, she had taken Anne aside to ask her if she knew when Clive was coming. The girl had not quite forgotten who she was, but had got her mixed up with her sister. Now, she was out in the hallway, stationed eagerly near the front door.

A veiled woman, with scarlet fingernails, was challenging every man in the room.

'You want to arm wrestle?' she kept saying. 'Beat me and you can do whatever you like to my body.'

Anne was surprised that nobody was taking her up on it. The woman had a figure like the young Jane Russell.

Farrar was surprised too. When the challenge got through to him, he disobeyed the first rule of the services and volunteered.

'This is his first time here,' said Something. 'He doesn't know any better, the daft bollock. Watch this.'

Farrar and the woman – whose name, funnily enough, was

Jeane Russell – were seated either side of a small desk. Someone put a paper hat on Farrar's head, and he straightened it. She unpinned her veil, and Anne saw she had different-coloured eyes, one blue, one hazel. Everyone crowded around. Something put his hand on Anne's bottom, but did not seem to mind too much when she peeled it off and gave it back to him. Everyone quietened and Amelia turned off Jean-Michel.

In the hallway, Nina was asking someone about Clive.

Jeane Russell held her hand, dainty but thick-wristed, up, and flexed her fingers. She put her elbow down firmly on the desk and leaned forwards.

'Hold on,' said a computer-designing nonentity, 'the final touch...' He put two ashtrays full of smouldering butts either side of the field of combat, and sprinkled a few drops of fuel from his lighter on each. Little flames grew. Burning cellophane crackled.

Farrar did not look too happy. Jeane Russell flexed her fingers again.

Farrar drained half a glass of vodka and orange, and grasped Jeane Russell's hand.

Someone said 'go for it' and was promptly ignored.

Farrar and Jeane Russell looked at each other. Jeane Russell smiled, and crushed the man's hand as if it were an eggshell.

Farrar yelped at the sound of grinding bones, and looked around in dazed fury. Jeane Russell brought his arm down as easily as a barmaid pulling a pint and dropped his hand into a burning ashtray.

Someone who knew what she was doing produced a pitcher of iced water for Farrar's hand. She also used it to put the fires out.

'Shit,' said Farrar, 'you bitch!' He tried to slap Jeane Russell with his left hand, but she backed out of the way and just laughed at him.

'Anyone else?' she asked. No one came forward.

'How does she do that?' Anne asked Something.

'I don't know,' he said, holding up his own once-ruined hand, 'she just does.'

Farrar came after his friend. 'You bastard, you could have warned me. Look at this…'

The officer held up his wedding ring between thumb and forefinger. It was a squeezed oval, and cracked top and bottom.

'Cathy will do her fucking nut…'

4

Clive did not like the idea of spending the early evening with Amelia Dorf's crowd of goat rapists and rich sickies, but as an entrepreneur he knew the importance of maintaining a personal relationship with his best customers. Besides, there was a good chance of turning up tonight's cunt at Amelia's 'entertainment'. Then he could leave early, and get on with the Business.

He was listening to electro-funk on the car stereo. He liked music with a rhythm.

The Sergeant Major had handled Coral pretty well. Since it was two-in-a-row time, he had taken a lot more precautions with this one. By the time she showed up in that rubbish dump on the Isle of Dogs, there would be little left that was recognizable. With luck, she might be buried forever under the wet newspapers, stinking food remnants and empty cornflake packets. Mr Skinner would be very pleased. This job was one of his 'specials'. He had certainly got his money's worth.

Later, Clive had to go to a club and watch the Sergeant Major and some of his army mates. They were very well organized. They would pretend to get pissed and start a fight. There would be a lot of damage and a few people would get hurt, but the lads would be away by the time the police could get round to the place.

The manager had been trying to set himself up in the Business when he knew full well that Clive had the franchise. He needed to be reminded of the way the world was arranged.

Also, it would be a thrill for the cunt. 'Want to go to a club and see some damage done?' That would be a good pick-up line. Very good.

Clive wanted to see the manager with a broken nose, blood on his dicky bow and frilly shirt front. Maybe the Sergeant Major would go in for some Greek dancing, and smash all the house DJ's records instead of plates.

He was buzzed through the gates, and parked neatly in front of the house. There were quite a few cars ranked in the drive. Someone with safe sex on the brain had draped a pillow-case over the glans of Amelia's silly dick-shaped bush. He set the car alarm, and went up to the door.

Before he was even inside Amelia's hallway, some harridan was leaping him, kissing his face with dry lips, pulling at his lapels. Her breath was foul.

'Clive. Oh God, Clive, it's been so long… it's so good to see you. Clive, you've got to… I need… I can pay… Clive, I…'

It was Coral's old flatmate, Nina Kenyon. Luckily for him, Amelia's bodybuilding freak had been handling the entryphone and was there to pull her off him. He put her down.

'It's all right, Anders,' Nina said, 'I'm sorry. I just need to… could we be alone, please?'

'Clive?' he asked, obviously awaiting orders to hurt someone.

'It's okay, Anders. I can deal with this.'

'Fine.' The muscle mutant waddled off. Nina was all over him again, but more ingratiating this time, controlling her desperation, soothing the wrinkles she had put in his coat, unwrapping his scarf.

'Clive, I'm sorry. I didn't mean to come on so… I need you… I need a hit… please, Clive…'

He had dealt to her fairly steadily. When she was flush, she had been stupid enough to pay over the odds. When she was broke, she had been stupid enough to plead for credit. She used to be a good cunt, now she was a dressful of dead fishmeat.

'Let me get my coat off, for fuck's sake. It's expensive. Used to walk around on a camel's hump.'

She pulled his topcoat off, and took the scarf. She fumbled, dropping them on the floor and picking them up, sorrying wildly, before shoving them onto the rack with the others. Clive reckoned she was well past skin-popping. She was up to two or three needles a week, and had gone without for maybe forty-eight hours. She would cut off her right arm and give it to him if he came over with as much as a single bag.

'I can't do business here,' he said. 'It's a party.'

'Clive, come on. Clive, please. I need some smack. Not much, just enough. It's the last time. Please... *please*...'

'Nina, fuck off. You still owe me from the last time. Remember. You don't have a tab any more, it's all used. You have to clear that before I can even think about transacting with you again. Now, leave me alone...'

She had dragged him into a room that turned out to be empty. At least she had the sense not to do her grovelling and pleading in front of other people. She would not let him go. She opened her purse.

'I've got money. Look. Anne gave it to me. Here...'

'I don't know any Annes.'

'Here, look...'

She held out two freshly crumpled ten pound notes, one in either fist. He prised them free, smoothed them, and pocketed them.

'Fine, Nina. Now we're even. I'm glad to see you're learning a little responsibility. It's important...'

'No, Clive,' she screeched at him, 'it's not for last time. You don't understand. It's for this time. Now. Clive, please...'

'No, Nina, that was for last time. *The* last time. I should never have extended credit to you then, and I won't do it again.'

'I don't have any more.'

'Then I don't make a sale.'

'You don't understand, Clive...'

'I think I do, Nina.'

'Clive, what about if I were to...'

'No, that won't do. It'll have to be cash. You've depreciated recently, gone down against sterling.'

'Clive, I...'

He left her babbling and crossed the hall to the party. He kissed Amelia and gave her a Christmas card. It was a privately printed cartoon of Santa Claus having sex with Rudolf the Red-Nosed Reindeer. Amelia tore the envelope open and laughed.

In the den, Clive calmed down and practised his charm again. He exchanged a few pleasantries with Jeane the Amazon, and collected on a small cocaine deal with a Senior Lecturer in Romance Languages. There were some people you could trust, after all.

Cocaine. There was another staple seller. Like Moët et Chandon or Chanel No. 5. The preferred drug of old money, and, by extension, of the *nouveau* mob. His most loyal cocaine customers were in the City, Whitehall and the Palace of Westminster.

Nina came in soon after, flapping her arms like pterodactyl wings, and pounced on a girl he had never seen before. Anne? She looked like a good cunt. Nina had her hand in the other girl's handbag, and was begging her for money in exactly the same terms she had used on him while begging for heroin.

Even if she came up with the money, Clive was not about to hand over a bag in the open. She was so far gone she had got seriously stupid. But it was all his own fault really.

Now, he had the Sergeant Major and his sales force to deal in person with small customers like Nina. She was a hangover from the old days, when he had had to hustle the stuff himself. He had several like her and they were very nearly impossible to ditch. Of course they died from time to time, so there was a light at the end of the tunnel.

'We got totally wrecked yesterday,' said one of his old-fashioned die-hard dope customers, 'and rented out *Santa Claus – the Movie* on video. It was the most moving experience I ever had. They ought to hand out gear instead of ice cream to the kids.'

'Yeah,' said his Tonto-hairstyled girlfriend, 'we had a megalaugh.'

A deep-voiced character with five o'clock shadow all over his face and fists like Popeye the Sailor grabbed the girl by her Indian beads and slammed her up against the mantelpiece.

'I just hate it,' he growled, drooling between yellow teeth, 'when people misuse the suffix mega.'

He banged her head backwards, knocking down a domino row of Christmas cards.

'It denotes quantity, not size,' he growled, dropping the girl. He stumped off, in search of split infinitives and incorrect usages of the adverb 'hopefully', and the Last of the Hippies picked up his Moonchild or Starbeam or whatever, and calmed her down.

Nina was back, with a fiver and some change.

'Clive, I'm really sorry about earlier…'

He would not take the money. She put it in his lap. He picked it up and dropped it in a bowl of fruit punch. The coins sank between the bananas, apples and mushrooms.

'Nina, just fuck off will you.'

'Clive, I need you. I'll do anything. Please…'

He stood up and slapped her. Hard. Everyone shut up and looked at them.

'Now look what you've done, you stupid cunt. You've spoiled the party.'

'Yeah,' said somebody drunk who just wanted to be nasty, 'you tell her. Break the cow's arm.'

This, thought Clive, might be fun.

He took a double handful of Nina's jacket, above her breasts, and tore. Tiny buttons flew, and she clutched herself. She shook her head wildly. Her hair was a frightful mess. Her make-up was streaked.

The man who had agreed with Clive grabbed Nina's jacket collar and tried to rip down her back. Someone else pulled her necklace, and imitation pearls spread underfoot. There was a lot of screaming and laughing.

Nina was passed from person to person. Everybody tried to take something – a scrap of clothing, a lock of hair, a false eyelash, a brooch. They pinched and kissed and cuddled and laughed and swore.

Nina was beyond hysterics. Her mouth opened and closed, but Clive could not tell whether she was making any noises. Everyone else sounded pained and crazy enough.

He stood back and watched. Someone started singing 'Oranges and Lemons', and everybody joined in. Clive was surprised that he remembered the words. All those years of *Listen With Mother* must have sunk in.

> 'Oranges and lemons,
> Say the bells of St Clements,
> I owe you five farthings,
> Say the bells of St Martins…'

Amelia was in there, jostling and tugging with the worst of them. And Anders, showing off his strength by tearing only at the thick material of Nina's suit. Only Nina's friend, Anne, stayed out of the game, and she was not doing anything to stop it. Clive looked at her, and she looked at him.

He poured a drink. Châteauneuf-du-Pape. It was supposed to be very good, but all wine tasted alike to him.

Nina was on the floor now, sobbing, and the others had a rugby scrum over her. Already, there was blood. The girl had had her hands over her face and was rolling from side to side. She could do little to protect herself.

Soon it would get out of hand. But it had got out of hand before, and Clive had coped with it.

Judi and Coral. Now, *that* was out of hand. And Clive had coped with that.

He would ask for even more money this time.

One of the men had his fly open and his dick out. He was going to take a leak on the girl, but Amelia pulled him out of the circle with a cry of 'not on my carpet'.

Everybody backed off now. It was the last verse of the song. Jeane the Amazon picked Nina up. The girl was a mess.

'Here comes a candle
To light you to bed,
And here comes a chopper…

Then Mr Skinner came down.

5

'To...'

This was sick, sick. Anne knew she ought to do something, ought to intervene. But...

'...chop...'

She looked at the young man, Clive. He was anonymously handsome, studiously calm and trying to be detached. He wanted to be apart from the humiliation he had engineered. Men like this, a man like this, had taken Judi apart...

'...off...'

Was this man to blame? Judi's ex-. Ex-what? Boyfriend? Pimp? Drug pusher? Here he was, enjoying the party, watching the games. And Judi was dead. She could see him sweating. She guessed he was almost bursting with pleasure...

'...your...'

Then, he came into the room. The Monster. But he could not be the Monster. He could not...

'...HEAD!'

The Monster parted the circle of people, and took Nina from Jeane Russell. No, not the Monster. Just a man. He held Nina. Everyone shut up, except the girl. The man stroked her face and hair, soothed her whimpering, kissed her bruises, shushed in her ear. No one interfered.

'Mr Skinner…' Amelia's sentence trailed off into empty air. The man had looked at her, and shut her up.

Skinner. Anne had heard of him, and not just from Nina. One of the guests had been talking about him. He was supposed to be someone you were afraid of. She could understand that.

Of course, he was not the Monster. He was not Hugh Farnham.

Actually, the resemblance was minimal. He was a big man too, and his face had that same patched-together lizardy look. But that didn't make him Hugh Farnham. He was conservatively dressed, in a dark, three-piece business suit. He wore a tarnished gold watch chain across his waistcoat. He had a dark, fur-collared coat draped like a cloak over his shoulders.

He included Nina in his coat, an angel wrapping a child in its wings. He looked at Anne, smiling slightly, then at everyone else. He spoke, in accentless English.

'A specimen, I suppose. Of what, though? Vice unrewarded?'

'Mr Skinner,' said Clive, 'we…'

'Yes. I know. You were playing. Just playing. You know I don't like you to play games without me, but you went ahead regardless. You know you need your Games Master. Without me, you do crude, unimaginative things like this…'

He showed them Nina's face, lowering his fur collar away from it. She was empty, used up.

'You don't understand pain. You can't appreciate it. You let nasty little personal grudges creep in, and you taint the experience. You have to go beyond that, transcend revenge and pique and cruelty and cowardice. Pain is of and for itself alone. I've told you this before, but you are a small-minded lot, really. I despair of you.'

Anne looked around her. The guests were completely cowed, like golden calf worshippers contemplating shards of Moses' broken tablets. This was astonishing. Skinner released Nina from his protection and set her down in an armchair. She allowed herself to be posed like a mannequin, but drew in on herself when he let her go.

Anne had met presidents without a tenth of what Skinner was using. And she knew that he was barely stretching himself. These were just make-believe decadents.

'She was bothering us,' said Clive, almost whining. 'She wanted…'

'Yes.' Skinner paused. 'What did she want? What did she want that you have but wouldn't give her?'

Clive did not want to answer.

'The drug?'

Clive swallowed. 'Yes, she never paid…'

'Never. I think not, Clive, but let that pass. Heroin is interesting stuff. You supply only the finest, don't you…'

Someone made a joke Anne did not get, '…only the best, because graded grains make finer flour…'

And Daeve said, 'Heroin, it's what your right arm's for.'

There was only one sceptic in the crowd. Toby Farrar. It was his first 'entertainment', Anne remembered. He had not learned the applicable procedures yet. He stepped forward.

'Who the fuck are you, fruitbat?'

He pulled at Skinner's empty coat sleeve. The expensive item slithered off his back like a shed snakeskin. It fell to the floor. Skinner's shoulders expanded. He grew taller.

The circle reformed, around Skinner and Farrar. Anne was part of it now, with Derek Douane on one side, and Jeane Russell on the other. Should they join hands?

Farrar knew what he had got into now, and stood to attention. He was still holding the coat sleeve. Skinner prowled around the man, his head in close like a drill sergeant chewing out a quivering private.

'Who the fuck am I, friend? I'm just another fruitbat, Major Farrar.' His head bobbed independent of his body. 'No one at all really.'

Skinner raised his hand to Farrar's face, and put his thumb in the officer's left eye. He pressed, just hard enough, and drew back from the falling man.

Farrar swore, and got up, holding his hand over his face like an eyepatch. Red tears stained his cheek. The hand came away bloody. He had not lost the eye, but the upper lid was neatly sliced. Toby Farrar's wife would think he had been in the wars.

'Clive, what is your complaint against this girl?'

'Credit… she wanted credit…'

'And?'

'…and that's not the way… not the way I do business.'

'Of course not. You all know Clive Broome, don't you? He's an honest businessman. His terms are hard, but equitable. Cash for drugs.' Clive winced. 'Or cash for sex. Cash for pain. Cash for anything, really. Anything you want. He provides quite a service.'

Someone muttered, '…the swindling bastard!' It was the man who had first joined in when Clive started on Nina. Obviously, he wanted to see blood, and didn't much care whose it was.

Now Clive was in the circle with Skinner. Farrar was back with the rest, holding a handkerchief to his eye. He had been converted.

Anne did not like Clive, did not care what happened to him. If he had had anything to do with the way Judi died, then she wanted him to suffer as much as possible. Did that make her the same as Amelia as the others?

'What's wrong?'

'I told you, Clive. I'm disappointed. You are promising. But you don't have a philosophy. You don't have purity.'

Skinner put a hand on Clive's shoulder. Anne knew he was not disappointed or annoyed or anything. He was just playing. He was just hurting people for his own amusement.

Or maybe there was more to it?

'What do you want from me?' Skinner asked everyone. 'What do you want from your Games Master?'

There was quiet.

'Do you want to be entertained? Do you want to be hurt? Or do you want to learn? Do you even know what you want? You must want something, or else you are nothing. Nothing at all.'

He stood by Nina. She was curled up in her chair, head down, coughing a little.

'This girl, Nina. You want to see this girl suffer? You want to see this girl hurt? To see this girl hurt herself? You want to see… to feel… what?'

It was Amelia who came forward. She was the representative.

'Yes, Mr Skinner,' she said, 'take her. Then show us something. Show us something we will never forget. Help us know ourselves.'

'Very well. Clive?'

'Yes.'

'Give me some heroin please.'

'What?'

'Heroin.'

'But…'

'I think you can trust everyone here. They all know what you do for a living.'

Clive searched his pockets, as if looking for a train ticket. Someone laughed. It was obvious he did not have pockets full of drugs.

'You have some, of course?'

'My car…'

'Yes. The compartment under the passenger seat in the front, right? Very clever. The keys please.'

Clive fished them out of a pocket, and handed them over. Skinner looked around, and picked his man.

'Major Farrar?'

Farrar came forward. He was not in pain now, but he still had a red tear of blood on one cheek. He looked like a lopsided clown.

'It's the BMW. You'll have to peel back the carpet. It should be easy. Clive?'

'It's in a Malteser box.'

'Good. You understand, Major? Bring the heroin here.'

Farrar knew how to obey an order. Skinner crouched in front of Nina.

'Now you'll get what you want. I'll look after you.'

She shrank in her seat. Again, Anne felt she ought to do something but could not think of anything.

They all stood around in silence. The computer salesman suggested they play 'Twenty Questions' or 'I Spy', but a glance from Skinner shut him up.

Farrar came back with a small boxful of heroin. Skinner picked out three sachets.

'That's too much,' said Clive, 'she might…'

'So?'

The dealer almost smiled, and visibly relaxed. He was out of the circle. Nina was in it again.

Skinner gave Nina's handbag to Amelia. She emptied it on the floor, and picked out the junkie kit. Bent sugar spoon, a length of rubber tubing, and hypodermic needle. She dumped them on the arm of Nina's chair. The syringe was a proper hospital model, not a disposable pipette.

Skinner laid out the sachets in a row next to the kit. Nina was too far gone, too traumatized, to pay any attention. Even heroin could not reach her.

'Clive,' said Skinner, 'do the honours.'

'I'm not very good at this. I just sell it, I don't use it.'

'Very wise, I'm sure. But you must be familiar with the business end.'

'Yes. I'll need a bigger spoon.'

Amelia handed him something from a silver service. He examined it. It was unusual, a dinner-size replica of a teaspoon, with a carved apostle at the end of the handle.

Clive spilled some of the powder as he heaped it in the spoon, and could not hold it steady over his lighter flame, but finally he got it liquefied. The spoon would be ruined.

'It's a good idea to mix it with citric acid,' he said. Nobody offered him a lemon slice from their Perrier.

Amelia rolled up Nina's torn sleeve and tied the tourniquet

tight around her upper arm. Veins stood out bluish against pale skin. Anne saw the beginnings of tracks. Nina was still pliable, uninterested in her situation. Clive drew the heroin into the syringe, filling it to capacity.

'She'll overdose,' he warned.

'Not if she's strong enough,' said Skinner. 'Give it to her. She doesn't have to use it. The decision is hers.' Nina bent and unbent her bare arm. She looked around. She was coming back.

'Clive…'

'I'm here, Nina. Here's your smack. It's all right now, all right.'

'Uh?'

'You don't have to pay. It's all been taken care of. Now, be a good girl and take your medicine.'

He put the syringe in her hand. It rolled in her fingers, but she quickly got a hold on it. She smiled.

'Nina, it's up to you,' said Skinner.

'Nina,' said Anne, 'don't…'

Skinner swivelled to look at her. His eyes were nothing special, but he was fearsome. Perhaps he was the Monster?

'Don't what?' he said, smiling.

'…don't…' Anne tried to say.

'Don't *die*?'

'…no… yes…'

'It's up to her, isn't it?'

Anne could not say anything. Skinner was looking at her, and she felt a caress of terror. Was she to be next in the circle? The Games Master was taking an elaborately casual interest in her. After a long moment, he turned away, and paid attention to the current victim.

Nina held the syringe properly now. A drop appeared at the tip of the needle. No air bubbles. She looked at the others, she looked at the syringe, she looked at Anne.

'Don't… please.'

Nina broke. She erupted out of her chair, yelling, and charged for the door. She shouldered her way between Anne and Derek. The child, laughing, fell over. Anne was jolted, but Jeane Russell held her up with a painful grip.

Nina was out of the door, and the syringe gone with her. The cry receded, and her clattering footsteps became distant. She had gone upstairs. Nobody moved.

It was a big house. Anne knew Nina could easily find a place to kill herself in private. Poor thing.

'Clive,' said Skinner, 'you, and this girl – Anne, isn't it? – you go and bring Nina back. Stop her from wasting herself if you can. It's important. We'll keep the party going while you're gone.'

Clive knew enough to do what he was told. He took Anne's arm and dragged her out into the hallway, towards the stairs. She did not fight.

Inside, she was cold.

The Games Master knew her name. Skinner knew who she was.

6

He did not know why but, upstairs, Amelia's house reminded him of a jungle. It was remarkably clean and well-maintained, and all the lights worked but Clive felt as if he ought to be wearing a pith helmet, and carrying a hunting rifle that could bring down a charging rhino at fifty paces. With the American girl as a bearer, and that dopey cunt Nina as rogue quarry, this was a skew-whiff safari.

Every time he had been led through the house previously, it had been different. The mix of the original architect's unusual commitment to the concept of asymmetry, the previous inhabitants' rabid fetish for amassing ridiculous quantities of Victorian bric-à-brac and '30s kitsch, and Amelia's own declared desire to keep her environment in a state of constant flux had turned the place into a confused and confusing labyrinth.

'We'll never find her,' he told the girl, Anne. 'Let's just hang about out of earshot for a few minutes and go back.'

She looked at him in a queer, incisive way he did not like at all. He wondered who the fuck she was.

'I don't think that guy Skinner would like that.'

'So?'

'So you're scared of him. All of you are.'

'That's not true.'

It was not true. Was it? Mr Skinner was weird, unpredictably dangerous, even, but he was just...

Just what?

If anything, Mr Skinner should be scared of him. After what Clive had done for him, he would be forever in his debt. In his power.

'I can handle Mr Skinner.'

'Yeah,' she said, unconvinced, 'right.'

'Let's try and find the second floor. The lights are on up there.'

'This is the second floor.'

'Not in England.'

'Oh yes, you people have to have a nothingth floor.'

There was something about the girl. She was not a loser, like Nina, or a sickie, like Amelia. She was sharp. Clive had got so used to being able to fool everyone in this circle that he was unnerved by her obvious clear-sightedness. The rest were wrapped up in a fog, from drugs or cracked minds, but Anne knew exactly what was going on.

Of course, there were some things she could not know about.

She had got him on Mr Skinner, though. Really, he had to admit that the man scared him. Clive liked to hurt people as much as the next person, felt the need to confirm his power over others, but Mr Skinner was a specialist, an expert. He could hurt capriciously, pointlessly, even against his own interests...

Like now. Mr Skinner needed Clive, and yet he was punishing him, making a great show of his obsolescence. This search party was crazy.

'Why you?' Anne asked him as they climbed the stairs. 'You're not his type.'

Christ, did she know *everything* he was thinking? He suppressed the urge to respond, to tease an answer to the question out of himself. He did not want to think about it.

For what was he being punished?

The second floor landing was spacious, a gallery almost, but much less cluttered than the lower parts of the house. Passages fed off left and right. As far as they could see, the walls were plain white, with evenly spaced-out black doors. It all looked like an enlarged version of those laboratory mazes they let rats loose in.

He decided that Anne was probably a very good cunt. Americans were all easy. Except Judi. She had been difficult. Perhaps this expedition did not have to be a total waste. He had screwed girls who hated him before, and had always got something out of it.

He stepped near the girl, and put an exploratory hand on her hip. He tried his nicest smile, and prepared to whisper his suavest come-on line.

'You have a lovely smile,' he said, 'may I taste it?'

She took his wrist between thumb and forefinger, and held his hand up between them as if gripping a putrid fish by the tail. She turned her thumb- and fingernails in and pinched, probing for painful pulses between the bones. She let go.

'Look, Clive, I don't like what you do for a living, I don't like the way you treat girls at parties, I don't like your taste in shirts and I don't like the way you look. Therefore, I suggest we concentrate on finding Nina.'

He could not help asking himself: what was wrong with his shirt?

'What's the point?' he said, rubbing his cuff over the place she had gored him.

'Maybe we can stop her hurting herself.'

'It's too late for that. I know a lot of smackheads. She's got to have stuck it in her arm by now. She's dead, only she'll be able to move around for a bit longer. Not much longer.'

'You kill many this way?'

'Fuck off,' he said, suddenly angry. 'Who do you think you are, Joan of Arc? I'm just like anyone else. I sell people what they want.'

'But you have to make them want it first. You have to make them want to die.'

What was this girl doing at one of Amelia's dos? She certainly did not blend it with the crowd. Clive thought she might be a rare type of pervert who gets off on vociferously condemning all the vices she actually practises. He had heard of that brand of peculiarity before. But she did not strike him as a girl who would get much pleasure out of flagellating herself with self-loathing and trembling hypocrisy. She was more the grit in the cream type, born to be a pain in the backside, always getting at you.

'Okay,' he said. 'Let's stop arguing and find the girl. I still think she's on this floor. She'd want the lights on.'

'Fine. But the corridor is lit up both ways. Which did she take?'

'It doesn't matter. She'll be in one of the rooms. We can go through them easily. I reckon they only have one door apiece, so she'll be trapped. Not that she'll be able to do much about running away. She'll be on a bed somewhere, out of her skull.'

They took a passage to the left, opening each door in turn and flicking on the interior light-switches for each room. This floor apparently was a private gallery of some sort. The first room was hung with explicit 18th century paintings, depicting the classical rapes of chubbily nubile girls by an assortment of animal and half-animal deities. The second was a showroom for garish '50s jukeboxes.

'Have you noticed,' said Anne. 'There are no windows.'

'Amelia is nutty. She's always having the builders in to fiddle around with something or other. She must have had this whole floor bricked up from the outside.'

'Why?'

'I told you, she's nutty.'

The next room was full of mounted animals. They were stuffed and posed in all manner of positions, demonstrating sexual unions between incompatible species. It was supposed to be funny, but Clive thought Amelia's kinkiness could get monotonous after a while. Anne did not pass comment, and he shut the door.

'What is it with this Skinner?' asked Anne. 'What does he do?'

'He's just… just rich, I suppose. Rich and twisted.'

'There's a lot of that about.'

'I know.' Clive wanted to go on. He had never had anyone to whom he could talk about Mr Skinner. Not even the Sergeant Major. Not even Judi. There was no one he could really trust. 'But he's different…'

'What do you mean?'

'Amelia and the others. They're just playing. Mr Skinner is serious. With him, all this… all this stuff is important, almost as important as being alive…'

'And you? Do you like these games?'

She was good at asking questions, he realized, good at getting answers. Just like Judi. He did not like that.

Judi had always tried to rub his nose in parts of his life he just wanted to let lie there and be profitable. He was glad he had got rid of her. Admittedly, she had been the one who left, but, in the end, he had been the one to do the getting-rid-of. Poor Judi. Poor old, dead Judi.

He opened a door.

'Jesus Christ!'

The room was a walk-in freezer. Hanging from ceiling hooks were butchered human carcasses. The opened door jarred one, and they swung to and fro, bumping into each other like the elements of an executive toy. Lifeless knuckles scraped the floor.

Anne reached in and turned on the lights. The fridge was not as cold as it ought to have been.

'Bacon, I suppose,' she said.

She touched a corpse. He could see now that it was a distorted papier-mâché sculpture, luridly coloured in red. The ribs were wooden struts, thinly papered over. The cooling coils on the walls and the spreading stains on the floor were painted.

'Francis Bacon, I mean.'

'It's fucking sick!'

Clive had thought it would be Judi and Coral again, on a much larger scale. Even the Sergeant Major would have problems with this much cuntmeat.

Actually, after the first shock, the sculpture did not look real at all. The limbs were out of proportion, and you could read the newspaper headlines under the thin red paint. But, somehow, it was worse than real.

Who the hell had Amelia got to make this anyway?

'Nina,' Anne shouted. 'It's Anne. I want to help you. It's all right.'

Her voice did not even echo in the passages.

Around the next bend was darkness. The lights were not burning.

'She must have stopped here,' Anne said, 'or doubled back.'

'No, we'd have run into her.'

'Maybe.'

Anne called out again. There was no answer of any kind. Clive wondered why they had not heard anything from downstairs. It was odd that the party should get so quiet. There was no music, even.

Then, he felt the world shift on its axis, and knew that a new reality had slotted into its place. New physical laws, new moral dictates, new topographical patterns. It would be a major adjustment, and he did not know how to cope with it yet.

'There's something wrong here,' he said.

'She could be on another floor.'

'I don't think so... Let's give up and go back downstairs.'

He turned his back on the darkness to argue with Anne. That was when, with a glass-cracking shriek, the harpy brought him down from behind. A talon punctured the flesh under his chin, and tore...

7

Clive spun around and collapsed at the same time, heaving from his shoulders in a spasm which threw Nina off his back. Anne tried to catch the girl, hoping to embrace her from behind and pin her arms, but missed getting a sure hold on her. She was slammed into a wall by Nina's weight and momentum, and felt the shock of the impact in her teeth. Knots of pain throbbed in her spine.

Nina was still screeching. It was an inhuman, continuous sound, containing hatred, rage and triumph beyond expression in words. It was a horrible sound. Anne remembered her brother's premiere. Cam's concert should have started by now.

She reached for the back of Nina's ripped jacket, but only managed to get a handful of hair. Nina stood up, and the hair was pulled through Anne's fist. It was as if a steel rope had been scraped across her palm.

She looked up at Nina and could see that the girl did not recognize her. She was completely feral, a tie-dye splash of blood across her front, her fingers bent into claws. She turned away, and ducked into the darkness. Out of the light, she shut up. Anne heard rapid, birdlike footsteps. Then nothing.

She looked across the passage at Clive. He was half-sitting, half-slumped against the wall, vainly trying to move.

Nina had stabbed him with the syringe. It hung unpleasantly from his ruined throat, broken. The glass was cracked, the handle loose, and the needle bent. It had been emptied, but was more than half full now. With blood. Clive's jacket and shirt were stained, and little squirts rose and fell from his wound with each heartbeat.

Anne guessed that he had a severed artery. She got up, steadying herself against the wall, and took a few experimental steps. Her back did not ache that much. She had not been damaged.

Clive rolled his eyes, and tried to speak. Blood leaked out of his mouth, but nothing else.

It had happened too quickly to be absorbed. Anne knew that Nina had stabbed Clive, but she was not sure whether she had doped him as well.

He was an ugly mess, and he was still alive, but Anne could find no emotion to feel for him. She had seen her sister ancient and dead on a stretcher this morning, probably because of Clive or someone like him. She did not even have any squeamishness left over.

He moved feebly, trying to lift a hand to probe his wound.

She felt uncomfortable, watching him die and unable to care about him. She did not know what, if anything, to do for him. So she left, and went after Nina.

She did not want to think about him any more.

8

It did not hurt, so he knew it must be serious.

He saw Anne look away from him and leave his field of vision. He could not turn his head. A light came on, banishing the darkness around the corner. She was following Nina, the stupid...

Everything was clear. He was trapped in his body, as surely as a crashed motorist could be held in a wrecked car by a locked seat belt. Unless he got himself free soon, he would die...

He concentrated on trying to stand up. There was some feeling, not much, in his knees and upper thighs. He pulled, and managed to bend forward at the waist like an oarsman. He could touch his toes. He got hold of the polished tip of one of his shoes, and tried to pull himself away from the wall. His head was between his knees and he could smell the blood. The wetness was pooling in his lap.

Then, for a moment, his back and shoulders were working properly. He achieved some sort of upright position, although his treacherous legs deserted him immediately. He staggered through the open doorway, into the painted freezer, feeling his knees giving out with each inept step. To steady himself, he hugged a sculptured torso. An arm came loose and fell off, revealing scrunched up newsprint where there should have been ligament, bone and muscle. He knew he was bleeding all over the work of art.

Someone else came into the room and sat down on a plain wooden chair to watch him struggle. It was Mr Skinner, calm and hungry. The man's face gave nothing away. He was neutral. He was not going to help Clive out of his crumpled BMW, but he was not going to kick the bent door shut on him either.

He knew Nina had poisoned him as well. He had never had heroin before, but he knew enough junkies to recognize the effects. Although the pins and needles in his legs could perhaps have been from loss of blood. Purple lines floated on the surfaces of his eyes, coming briefly into focus, then retreating into vague smudges.

Purple haze, he thought.

Finally, the pain came.

First it hit him where Nina had, just below his jaw. From this nucleus, it swiftly spread throughout his head and trunk, leaving only his limbs in an unfeeling limbo. He almost passed out, but his eyes would not close. He kept on fighting…

Fighting for what?

…kept on fighting to stay upright. The lumpy statue in his arms was crumbling. Large chunks fell around his feet. Something gave way like the bottom of a carrier bag, and the bulk of the papier-mâché was squeezed out. He realized that in the centre of the soft fake torso was a hard real butcher's hook. The remains of the sculpture slipped through his arms, and he sank onto the sharp iron prong.

It went into his upper belly, and caught under his ribcage. He felt himself pulled out of shape, his innards adopting new alignments.

The hook was a curved icicle. It was uncomfortable rather than agonizing. The ice spread through his chest, forming around his beating heart.

His hand and arms were free, but his knees and ankles had long since given out. He could feel nothing at all below the hook's point of entry. He jerked downwards, his entire weight on the hook and chain. It held. He did not fall.

He swung his left arm up in a reverse backstroke, and grasped the chain. He felt the links pressing into his palm. He hauled, taking some of the weight off the hook, but not enough.

Then he felt for the pain in his neck. His hand seemed like a flesh mitten, fingerless and clumsy. He wrapped it around the syringe, ignoring the jagged glass which tore his skin.

Mr Skinner had come closer. Now, his face was only inches away from Clive's own. He was as near as a lover or a parent could ever come. Clive felt delicate feelers worming through his mind, draining his pain, his fear. It was a great relief. He felt arms around him, lifting his body up, easing him off the hook.

He pulled the syringe out, and weakly flung it away. The bottom half of Mr Skinner's face was suddenly reddened. Clive heard the fountain, and knew that he had torn something important. He saw an arc of blood, and knew that it came from his own neck. It was oddly like going cross-eyed and seeing the bridge of your nose. Then, the blood got in his eyes.

Clive shook his head, and cleared his vision. Mr Skinner was smiling an impossibly wide smile. Fifty or sixty perfect, pointed teeth gleamed between his parted lips. Then his face faded until, at last, only his smile was left behind.

9

'Nina!'

The girl had darted into a dark stretch of the corridor, and could not be found easily. Anne trailed her fingers along the wall at shoulder height, but there were no switches or dangling cords. She could still see, dimly, which meant that there must be a light source somewhere near. Somewhere.

'Nina!'

She went forwards, step by step. The floor proved untrustworthy. She had already found a few unexpected steps, up or down, and slammed a toe against a new level. It was all fairly pointless, like the needless ha-has of a carnival funhouse.

She stopped and listened. The house was silent. It was as if the whole place were deserted and derelict.

What were Amelia and her guests doing? She hoped that they had not dispersed from their downstairs room. Could they be playing some Sadeian variation on hide and seek? Could they be in the dark, waiting for her?

'Nina, it's me. Anne.'

The girl must have calmed down. She must be within earshot, but she was keeping quiet. She had been hysterical, now she was probably close to catatonia. Anne thought Nina had found a hiding place and was lying low. She could imagine the girl curled up in a cupboard, trying to breathe noiselessly, willing her heartbeat to be less loud.

God, the house was quiet! Admittedly, this was a placid residential district, but there should be some exterior noise: occasional traffic, water dripping from the eaves, distant carol singers, murmuring electrical appliances. There was nothing. The walls must be ten feet thick.

She found the light. It came from a tributary passage that lead off from the main corridor at a curious angle. The rooms must be not quite square. A funnel of light fell from a circular ceiling hole, drawing attention to the skeleton of an ornate spiral staircase. It was a rickety old piece of work; presumably intended for servants banished from the regular stairs. It could not have been easy to hump awkward loads up and down the wobbly death trap. There were grinning gnomes worked into the iron filigree, running downwards helter-skelter.

Nina would have been drawn to the light, just as Anne had been. She must have gone upstairs. Anne started upwards on the shaking staircase, but had to stop abruptly. The hole extended a foot or so above the level of the ceiling, and then ended. There was a dim fluorescent tube in the recess. She could not go up, only down. The floors below were dark. Carefully, she descended into an unknown, unlit room.

She stepped off the bottom stair onto a carpeted floor. The light above her was remote and useless, blocked off by the triangular edges of the staircase. In the dark, she took little steps, her hands out before her. She found a wall, and hugged it. She edged sideways, clockwise. After getting into and out of three corners between stretches of flat wall, she found a door. And by it there was a switch. She turned on the light.

The room was bare, except for the staircase, and a pair of indifferent watercolours of dead flowers that hung on the wall opposite the door. The paintings were at eye level. Why had she not jostled them while feeling her way around?

It did not make sense, so she gave up thinking about it.

The door was not locked. The passage outside was unlike the ones on the floor above. It was as wide as a small room, but there were bulky pieces of old furniture against the walls between the doors, and Anne was forced to squeeze through a narrow and irregular middle path. Hard wooden angles pressed into her.

'Nina.'

On the floor, she found a scattering of porcelain shards. Several ornaments from a displayed collection of unpleasant little figurines had been swept off a small table. The girl had come this way, she was sure. Again, Anne started looking into every room for Nina. All the doors were unlocked. The rooms beyond were filled with more forgotten furniture. This must be where Amelia shifted everything when she was having building done. A few of the pieces were properly stored, with dustsheets and numbered tags, but most of the stuff was just crammed in every which way.

Progress was slower than it had been upstairs. Welsh dressers and tallboys kept getting in her way. And she was alone.

Would Clive die? Could she have helped him?

This was not much of a party. Anne knew she had to expose Amelia and her friends. The magazine would not go for it; they could not afford the lawsuits. But she had friends on the tabloids, the *News of the World*, the *Daily Mirror*. Pop stars and society hostesses in S and M games that led to death. Deaths? She could keep Judi out of it, but ruin a good few careers, businesses and marriages. There would probably be multiple prosecutions. The Global Peace Whatever would lose a lot of credibility, she reflected. Maybe not: those far right moralists had plenty of ways of surviving nasty revelations and expelling offenders from their ranks. She now believed that her sister had died, if not through the direct actions of the people downstairs, then at least through her unhealthy associations with them. What she had seen done to Nina would have wrecked anybody.

Scum. Scum. Scum.

The rooms were like the passage, packed with antiques. Most of them were in states of disrepair. Crippled chairs with missing feet and tufts of stuffing coming through the cracks; dead, useless grandfather clocks with faces but no hands; embroidered hangings eaten with mould patches that made hunt scenes resemble maps of unknown worlds. But there was no dust, no dirt, no cobwebs. All this was looked after, preserved in its current state of decay.

She opened a door, and found herself in the Bacon room.

...but surely that was upstairs. No, she must have invisibly ascended through those upwards-sloping corridors and irritating little steps, and come down again on the spiral staircase. For the last few minutes, she had been travelling in parallel to her previous route. The junk rooms alternated with the gallery chambers like the opposing teeth of a zip-fastener. Only the Bacon room interconnected both strata of the house. It had two doors. Clive would be beyond the other. Dead?

Despite everything, she had to see him. She could not immediately do anything for Nina. Perhaps she would be able to stop the bleeding. Maybe even save his life. Save him for the Old Bailey and whichever penal dustbin they locked dope peddlers in.

Anne had once written a piece about prison conditions. After a tour and a few interviews with convicts, she was in favour of sweeping reforms. But she wanted Clive to get dumped into a *Grand Guignol* Devil's Island with whip-wielding guards, running filth in the cells and Neanderthal yard bosses. She hoped he would be gang-raped in the showers every night. A liberal, she remembered someone saying, is just a reactionary who has not been mugged yet. Tomorrow, she realized, she would be socially conscious again. Tonight, she would have elected Dirty Harry as chief of police. Shit, she wanted out of this mess.

She opened the other door...

'Clive?'

...and found herself in a part of the house she had never seen before. It was either a passage or a long, thin room, a stone-walled storage space lined with gunpowder plot-style wooden barrels. It was more like some sort of cellar than an upstairs room.

Obviously, there was more than one Bacon room.

She looked around, carefully this time. One of the dummies was fully dressed. She should have noticed it earlier. It was not at all like the others in the room, like all the ones in the other room. They were all dismembered portions, with exposed ribs and piglike pink hides.

It was the figure of an old, dead man. She was reminded of Dorian Gray at the end of the book, unrecognizably decrepit, identifiable only by the rings sunk into the fleshy fingers. This statue was shrivelled inside its suit, hanging from a hook in its chest.

She did not want to touch it, but she had to.

She had expected it to be weighted, to feel cold and heavy. But it was an obvious fake, papier-mâché light. The wrinkled skin, while rubberized to lend some semblance of naturalism, was dry and fragile.

It was a repulsive piece of work, but paradoxical. The concept was violently unpleasant, extravagantly horrible. But there was a bland expression worked into the prune-like face. It was like a sentimental 19th century vision of peaceful repose after protracted suffering, the miserable on Earth rewarded in Heaven.

Of course, the statue was in modern dress. A suspiciously stained smart dark suit, just like Clive's. In fact, the costume was exactly like Clive's, down to the horrible shirt and expensive shoes. It was another of Amelia's bad taste jokes. And now the effort would be wasted, since its subject was in no condition to be either offended or amused.

Anne was tired, and fed up. It could only be about eight o'clock – her old-fashioned watch, unwound this morning, had stopped – but she felt as if she had been up all night, working to meet an insane deadline. All she wanted was to get this whole thing over with, so she could go home to Kentish Town and sleep in her own bed.

It would be cold though. There was no one in the apartment to turn on the electric blanket.

Downstairs. She would go downstairs and tell Amelia what had happened to Clive. She knew what would happen. Skinner would take over. The guests would disperse. Ambulances and doctors would be called, the right people would all be bribed, and the sordid mess would be efficiently covered up. She would never be able to prove a thing. Whatever. She did not care.

Leaving the Bacon room, she made her way through the junkyard corridor. She thought the spiral staircase would lead her down to the party.

…but she could not find the room. It had been distinct from the others. It was comparatively empty. She turned corners she was sure she had never encountered before. Had she taken the wrong route? Every room she looked into was the same. She came full circle around the house, and opened a door to find herself looking up again at the dangling corpse statue.

Now, she could see that it even *looked* like Clive. Or rather, as Clive would look if he were to live to the age of one hundred and fifty and then die. It really was a wretched thing.

She tried to picture the door of the room with the stairs. Had it been disguised to blend into the wall? Could she have missed it by mistaking it for one of the panelled wardrobes? Did it have an exterior handle? She could remember nothing.

Anne felt an urge to throw the kind of temper tantrum she had been able to get away with when she was six years old. She wanted to whimper in frustration and break something. But there was no one around to be made uncomfortable, or be coerced into helping her out. She was on her own. Anyway, her father and Cam had invariably known when she was faking. The Nielsons had always been a family of know-it-alls.

She walked through the Bacon room again, avoiding the central figure, deciding to try the place with the barrels.

…but now here was a main passage beyond the door, spacious

and well-lit. A few yards down, the passage broadened out and became a mezzanine. There was the main staircase she had climbed with Clive a while – how long? – ago.

Could there be Bacon rooms, more or less the same, dotted throughout the house in order to create confusion? If so, then Amelia Dorf was an incredibly subtle and sadistic bitch. But, of course, she had known about the sadistic part. As for the subtlety, that seemed quite alien to the woman who coochy-cooed over children she wanted to mutilate. It was now obvious that Amelia had never been in charge.

Anne knew exactly whose fault this, all of this, was. She remembered his unremarkable eyes. And she remembered that he had known immediately who she was. Whatever game was being played now, it was between them, between her and Skinner.

Now, the walkabout was over. The rest of the party was just a flight of stairs away, in the room off the main hall. She heard a tinny phonograph. The record was 'Mr Sandman' by The Chordettes. It always gave Anne goosebumps, especially when the unidentified male voice answered the girls' plea for Mr Sandman to bring them a dream with a drawn-out, ever-so-slightly creepy 'ye-e-es?'

…but the main hall was not one flight of stairs down. Peering over the balustrade of the mezzanine, Anne saw a huge conservatory, thronged with man-sized plants. The far wall was a large expanse of ornamented glass, with pitch blackness beyond. Heat rose from the depths, and every smooth cold surface was damp with condensation.

Shit, this house was crazy! Anne realized now how jumbled up and contrived the interior was. The architect must have been an opium fiend.

The Chordettes finished. Something rustled in the undergrowth. Anne cautiously went down the stairs.

'Nina?'

Tropical blossoms turned towards her, stamens quivering. It

was some species of voice-activated flytrap she had never heard of. There was a crackle of static, like a public address system at a church social, then another record started. Mama Cass crooning 'Dream a Little Dream of Me'.

Anne was annoyed.

'Stop playing stupid games, assholes!' There was no answer, just the song. 'Clive is hurt. He might be dead.'

She knew it was not a game any more. She wished she had a gun, the more powerful the better. She would have been happiest with a flamethrower.

Something clattered on the tile floor, behind a frothing bed of shrubs. The flesh of the plants was waxy, with green highlights from the directional lamps. The whole place was artistically lit. Anne glimpsed a different shade of green, moving among the vegetation.

She looked around for a blunt instrument. Something heavy and barefoot was padding around the conservatory. Something not human.

Then, the foliage parted. A giant cat's head poked out. Its eyes gleamed as if the irises were neon rings. It was a tiger, dyed green. Its fur was arranged in punkish spikes.

She made it to the staircase, and dashed at random back into the bulk of the house.

This could not be happening. Could not, could not, could *not*!

10

After Clive, he was full but unsatisfied. And he knew in his bones what that meant. This had all happened before. It was time to make a new start. He would need to feed beyond the point of gluttony, and then retreat to await the change. He would have to build himself up, because the change would take it all out of him.

There had not been much to Clive. But he had been young and in good condition. His physical substance had been a tonic, but already the hunger was coming back.

His clothes were too small now, pinching him at the neck, the waist and the crotch, stretched tight over the shoulders, the chest and his muscled limbs. It would not last. The feeding he had had from Clive was only a momentary boost. Already, he felt himself dwindling in his suit. Soon, he would be completely spent.

As for the rest of it, Clive had been a disappointment. At the moment of extinction, he had held the young man's mind up like a pierced coconut and let all the thin milk trickle out. Compared with Judi, there had been almost no yield. Down deep, Clive was unimaginative, inactive, petty, unquestioning. Judi was still with him, still struggling against the dark. Clive was already less than a ghost, less than a memory.

Still, the surges of animal strength pleased him. He scooped a handful of marble out of a bannister as if it were plasticine, and briefly enjoyed the traces of the many fingers that had brushed over this patch of cold stone down the years. He dropped it, and it bounced down the stairs. Someone was coming up.

'Mr Skinner?'

It was Amelia, looking eager. She was forever busily seeking out new gratifications, forever unaware of the weasel he always discerned nestling in her skull.

'Amelia. I asked you to stay downstairs with the guests. There are rules, you know. It would be much simpler if you obeyed them.'

'But...'

'I know I don't always explain myself, but you must always do what I say. I have reasons. These things are vitally important.'

She stepped over the marble chunk, and walked up to him. Even standing on the same broad step as him, she seemed pitifully small.

'Clive and the girl. It's been at least an hour. And Nina...'

'I found Clive. He's gone. Anne is lost, but I know where she is.'

'Nina?'

'She'll turn up.'

'Shouldn't we...?'

'No. There is no point now.'

'You look flushed. Have you been overexerting yourself?'

She reached up and touched his cheek. He felt a slight tickling as his old skin blistered. There was no pain, but he flinched from the contact. Amelia's unsubtle lust for him darted out of her like static electricity. He was repulsed by the scramble of images in her mind. She reminded him of the Objectivist.

They were standing on the main staircase, two flights up from the party room. He could hear the nervous chatter of the guests. He could make out all the separate conversations. Other sounds caught in between the meaningless words. Drinks being poured, a plastic cup crumpling, someone beating a fingertip tattoo on a table.

He had them all fixed in his mind. There were sixteen people in that room, standing, sitting, lying. Anne was getting out of the conservatory. Nina was curled up under a bed upstairs. Amelia was with him. Clive was used. There was no one else. The nearest house was empty. No cars or people moved in the street outside. Beyond the garden was a fairly busy road, but all the passing drivers were wrapped up in their tincans, insulated by Christmas drinks and trivial pursuits.

It was perfect.

He held up his right hand, stretching his fingers, and took Amelia's face in his grip. Her puzzled expression was covered. The thumb hooked under her chin, and the fingers pressed the top of her head an inch above the hairline. His nails grew, curving into her.

She could not speak, but he saw her panicked eyes staring from the spaces between his long fingers. Her cold nose pressed into his palm. Muffled sounds came from her throat.

'Shhh, Amelia. It's over. You'll always be with me now. Isn't that what you've wanted?'

He squeezed and pulled, taking off the front half of her head. He ignored the raw, splintered mess, and leaned forward as if to kiss where her lips had been. He caught the weasel escaping as an insubstantial wisp, and inhaled it in through his nostrils.

He was not interested in the meat, just the flavour.

She was sour, but strong. Not as nourishing as Judi, but an excellent appetizer for what was to come. She had always been ruled by her desires. He savoured the weasel on his palate for seconds, and then breathed her into his lungs. She was still startled, but almost comfortable. She had been easy to incorporate.

He threw the face away, and went downstairs to join the party. He was ready now. Ready to give in to his feeding frenzy.

11

*H*ere be Tygers. In St John's Wood? She had seen it, but she did not believe it. On the mezzanine again, she turned and looked back, down into the conservatory. There was no animal that she could see. The shrubs were not even disturbed. The song finished, and the loudspeakers just hissed. The place was completely undisturbed, if not completely undisturbing.

Anne wondered. Had she somehow been drugged? She had drunk only Perrier at the party, and eaten nothing. But she could have been slipped something somewhere, through a pinprick. Had Clive done anything? And what kind of dope produced that kind of idiotic but vivid hallucination? She did not want to think about it; that would only make her more disorientated.

The time is out of joint, she thought. 'Oh cursèd spite,' she said aloud, 'that ever I was born to set it right.' There was nothing awry in her mind now. She could remember *Hamlet* and the dates of important battles in the Revolutionary War and the names of Disney's Seven Dwarfs and the telephone numbers of old boyfriends and the faces of people she had known in college but not seen in years and the deadlines for the three pieces she had been working on...

Millions and millions of bits of information were still in her head, correctly labelled and neatly stored, but she could not work out the geography of this house, she was seeing green tigers and she was afraid in a way she had not been since childhood.

She was afraid that the Monster was going to get her.

In another part of the house, the screaming started. She could not work out how far away it was, but the shrill was enough to hammer into her skull like nails. There were many voices, screaming differently, loudly raised in a badly orchestrated cantata. Somewhere, violence was being done. If there was a tiger, it was loose now among the party guests. Loose and hungry.

It was time to get out. She could call the police – call Inspector Hollis – make a fool of herself, level hysterical accusations, have a breakdown, go to bed for weeks, miss Christmas. But first, she had to get out. She had to get out of this house.

The main staircase must be near, somewhere in the centre of the house. If she could get to the main hall, she could automatically open the gates from the instrument panel by the front door.

That would mean getting past the party, getting past whatever was happening to the guests.

The screaming was dying now. A few stragglers kept it up for a few seconds, then there was nothing. Just quiet.

She had not been able to work out where the noise had been coming from. It might even have been just another sound effect. Presumably…

She stopped thinking, and turned away from the mezzanine, plunging back into the corridor maze.

12

Under the four-poster bed, Nina was safe, curtained from the nightmare by the bedspread. The monsters could not get her here.

But, cling as she might to the bolster she had taken with her to stop her screams, she could not stop shaking.

She did not know whether she had used the smack. She remembered the needle going into flesh, but she was not sure that it had been her own. Her right arm had gone to sleep below the tourniquet.

In the dark, she imagined red-eyed rats scurrying around her, lashing her with their tails.

She heard her own heartbeat, alarmingly rapid, and she heard the sea in her ears.

She was crying like a baby, sobbing for her Mum. The monsters were prowling in the bedroom, searching for her. She heard their hissing breaths, and the hard, sharp noise of their hooves on the polished floorboards. She prayed they would not think of looking under the bed.

Mr Skinner was inside her mind, whispering, alternately cajoling and scolding her. He held his coat open, and called her to him. He had everything she needed. If she got to him, she would never have to worry again, never have to want again.

She tried not to listen to Mr Skinner. She tried.

But he was persuasive, kindly, paternal…

The rats nipped at her flesh, biting through her ripped clothes, sinking sharp little teeth into her skin. The monsters argued among themselves in monster language, tails lashing.

Mr Skinner was calling for her.

Her heartbeat was still quickening in a crescendo. Soon, it must peak, and stop…

Mr Skinner's coat was warm, welcoming. Wrapped in it, she would be able to sleep again, to dream sweet dreams, to wake up refreshed between clean sheets.

The rats got to her face, and she screamed inside herself, pressing her face to the bolster. The vermin were inside the pillow, biting outwards, clawing at her tight-shut eyes, scratching her tear-tracked cheeks, forcing their furry heads into her mouth.

One monster wanted to lift the bedspread, but his friends were contemptuous. They locked grinding horns, and scuffled.

Mr Skinner was singing, old songs from the '30s and '40s. He was like the bandleaders her Gran remembered, in a crisp collar, soothing through a megaphone.

Nina wanted to go to him.

'Yes,' she said aloud, 'yes, yes, yes!'

Mr Skinner finished his song, and bowed. Flashbulbs went off from the audience.

She was his. As soon as she got to him, she would be his.

She tried to get up on all fours, and bumped her head on the underside of the bed.

Her heartbeats were like a constant patter now, and she felt pains inside her chest and head.

The curtains parted, and light gushed into the dark space. Under the bed, Nina realized, was where the monsters lived. They were not afraid to come in after her.

Her heart stopped. For an eternal moment, she waited for its next beat…

13

Anne had given up the rational approach, and picked a passage at random. When she came to an intersection, she had ignored it or taken a new direction without bothering to think about it. She had passed through a few rooms. Now that she was looking closely, she realized that most of the rooms in the house had two doors. Each was a fat little passage in itself. She had not found any more Bacon rooms. Most of the decor in this part of the house was modelled after Hollywood's idea of elaborate period furnishings. Nobody real seemed to live here.

In a Versailles bed-chamber, attended by dressmaker's dummies in brocade jackets and periwigs, she found Nina. She had unconsciously put into practice the Winnie the Pooh principle, which rules that the most effective method of searching for a lost person or object is to get lost oneself on the assumption that some force of nature brings all forgotten things together in ignored niches and unfrequented locales. Of course, now they were both lost.

Nina was half-hidden under a four-poster bed, trailing silk sheets behind her like a bridal train. She was sprawled, hugging a sausage-shaped pillow like Linus' comforter. Anne could see that she was biting deeply into the pillow. Earlier, Nina had been stretched a good many notches too tight; now, she had snapped, and was flapping limply.

Her cuff was still undone, and the tourniquet had made her hand and lower arm into white marble, but Anne could see no new puncture. She guessed Nina had been too overwrought to shoot up. Maybe, she had successfully fought the need.

'Nina...'

The girl cringed at Anne's voice, and chewed the pillow. She had been crying, and was still shaking badly. It was difficult to tell whether she was retching or sobbing. She rocked back and forth.

Anne crouched, and gently tried to pull the pillow away. Nina was reluctant to give it up. Anne coaxed, and stroked her hard jaw. Finally, the girl let her teeth unclench, and relinquished a wet mouthful of cotton.

She put the pillow down, and hugged Nina. The girl responded, gripping Anne in a desperate embrace. It was like a wrestling hold. She tried to soothe the girl, and Nina relaxed. Anne unknotted the rubber tubing from her arm, and pulled the tourniquet loose. Nina's upper arm was ringed with red, but she bent her elbow and wriggled her fingers, getting the circulation going again. They stood up, and Nina half-sat on the edge of the bed. She stretched and lay back. She was nearly asleep.

'No,' Anne said. 'We have to get out of the house. We can't stay.'

'I'm tired.'

'I know. So am I. But we can't stay. This is a bad place.' Anne knew she was treating Nina like a four-year-old, but could see no other way to cope with her. 'I think something's happened downstairs. Did you hear the noise? I don't think we're safe here.'

'Then... let's... go home...'

'Yes, let's. Home. Come on, get up. I'll help. Here...'

She lifted Nina, getting the girl upright. Anne made sure the girl was not hurt. Nina had given up completely. She did not protest when she was led towards the door.

'This house,' said Anne, 'it doesn't seem to make sense. Where is the main staircase? Do you know?'

Nina smiled wanly. 'Through that door, turn left...'

'Are you sure?'

Nina was waking up. For a moment, she was supremely confident. 'Of course. Come on, don't be a slowcoach.'

Anne found herself being led. Nina was right. The main staircase was there, and two flights down, so was the main hall. The place was empty, quiet and normal.

'That's crazy,' Anne said, 'I'm sure I came this way...'

'Crazy? How?'

'It's nothing. Nothing really. I just got lost.'

They went downstairs, carefully and without incident.

'Anne?'

'Yes?'

'Hold my hand.'

'Sure.'

They touched fingers, and got them entwined. Anne kissed Nina on the cheek.

'Eugh,' the girl croaked, 'don't get soppy.'

'I won't.'

They were downstairs now, in the hall. It was not a fake. Anne saw her own coat hanging up on the rack with the others. There was no noise of any kind from the party room. The door was closed.

She knew she would have to take a look.

'Stay here,' she told Nina, letting her hand go, 'this will be over in a moment.'

She held the doorhandle, took a deep breath, and opened the door.

...the room was a mess, but there were no people there. Drinks stood abandoned. The Christmas tree was broken, having shed a layer of needles and broken baubles onto the presents. Food and cigarette butts had been trodden into the precious carpet. The open fire had practically died. The lights were still on, and a cassette was clicking in a tape deck.

Nina took her hand again, and tugged her away from the open door. 'Has everyone gone?' she asked.

'I think so.'

'Should we find someone to say goodbye to?'

Anne turned away from the party room. 'Let's not bother. Let's go.'

'Amelia usually pays. A hundred pounds. Sometimes more, if you've been...'

'We'll bill her later, okay?'

'Okay.'

They got their coats. Nina wanted to keep holding hands, and hurried the sleeves over her arms so they would not be out of contact for long. It was a bit embarrassing but Anne was glad of it.

The instrument panel looked complicated, but all the switches were neatly marked. The monitor showed the street outside in snowy black and white. There was no one about. Anne flipped the switch that opened the front gate, and the ironwork brushed the bottom of the video image. 'There,' she said. 'Easy.'

Nina opened the front door by hand and stepped outside, pulling Anne after her...

It was very dark, and Anne felt something slap into her face and stay there. She lifted it aside – it felt like a heavy curtain – and still could not see anything. Nina's grip tightened. The door had shut behind them.

'Anne, where are we?'

She did not know.

In her coat pocket, she had a pen with a little light in it, for taking notes in theatres and other dark places. She felt for it, and brought it out.

The glowworm lit up both their faces. Nina was frightened again. There were mobile shadows above her nose and eyebrows. They were in a large wardrobe. The curtain had been a crinoline, hanging from one of two rails that ran just above their heads.

'This...'

'...doesn't make sense. I know.'

There was no handle on this side of the door. Anne tried to

get her fingers into the jamb, but could not. It appeared to have locked itself.

'We'll suffocate,' said Nina.

'I don't think so.' Anne pushed aside an armload of dresses, finding only another rank of old clothes. 'I don't think this is a regular closet. It's deep. More like a passage...'

'There's a way out?'

'At the other end. Right.'

On Anne's side, there were women's clothes – elaborate ball gowns with mock jewels sewn into the bodices and rustling, puffy sleeves and skirts. Nina faced a succession of sombre gentleman's wear – black evening suits, heavy overcoats. A few brass and silver buttons gleamed in the minimal light.

There was not much space. They could not go side by side. Anne took the lead, and dragged Nina. The girl's hand was cold now, although it was quite stuffy in the passage. It was not an easy progress. The clothes had not been disturbed for a long time and were as thick and tangled as jungle foliage. There would be untold vermin nesting in the folds of material.

Anne would have had good use for a machete.

A few of the wooden hangers had rusted wire hooks which bent and broke as they passed. Bundles fell down, stirring up dust. Nina had a coughing fit. The fallen clothes were as difficult to wade through as thick mud.

They must have penetrated twenty feet into the passage, and there was still no hint of an end within reach.

Anne felt the wind knocked out of her. She had blundered into a suit that was much more solid than most. She staggered back, and had to be steadied by Nina. A dark, hanging shape blocked the way. Holding up her light, Anne saw a cavernous opera cape with a Mephistophelean magician's tailcoat hanging inside it. And inside both was a large corpse.

Nina had a minor convulsion. Anne's hand felt crushed.

'Anders!'

It was, but, for all his weight, he looked hollow. Anne touched his dead white face, and felt nothing that had been alive.

'No,' she said, 'it's a sculpture. I've seen them before. Look, it's supposed to be Anders grown old…'

The hair was white, the neck muscles flabby. The face was minutely wrinkled, the flesh beneath semi-liquid.

'Let's go on.'

Nina was hesitant.

'You don't have to touch it.'

They ducked, and squeezed past. There were others. Some were unrecognizably altered or mutilated, but most were obvious caricatures of people Anne had seen at the party. Not only were they made to look lifeless and tormented, but they were crammed into mouldering fancy dress costumes. Toby Farrar wore the braided tunic of a Hussar, and even had a jaunty helmet perched on his head. Jeane Russell was an unsuitably voluptuous fairy queen with gossamer wings and golden spangles on her bare, withered arms. Derek Douane was got up as a Dickensian urchin, with a broken neck and a dirty face. Daeve was a knobbly-kneed schoolgirl in a navy blue pinafore, with red spot freckles on his cheeks and straw-coloured ropes attached to his beret.

It was hot in the thin corridor, and the hanging husks made going forward practically impossible. The two girls paused, grimy and breathless, in the middle of the sick display. Nina tugged Anne back, towards the way they had come from.

'We can't give up now,' Anne said. 'Try to ignore these things. They're not real.'

'There's a thing in here with us.'

'What?'

'A thing.'

Anne listened, but there was no noise at all.

'It's an animal,' said Nina.

A tiger?

'I don't think so,' said Anne. 'Let's go on. It can't be much longer. We must be nearly there.'

They struggled a little further. Baz Something dangled absurdly, in the ballooning pants, curly-toed slippers, tiny waistcoat and bulbous turban of an Arabian Nights eunuch. His paunch bulged over a sash. At the end of the line was the computer salesman, dressed up as the Queen of Hearts. His death was supposed to have been messy, and there was a lot of realistic blood all over his costume. In the centre of his chest, where there was a heart motif on his tunic, there was a ragged hole disclosing his real heart, which looked to have been squeezed by an iron fist.

Nina screamed, horribly loud in the confined space.

'One of them touched me,' she said. 'Touched my hair.'

She tried to put her arms around Anne, but could not. A body got in the way. Anne banged her elbow on a solid wood wall.

'They're just statues.'

Anne pulled Nina along. They left the bodies behind them. The passage was wider now, with room for four racks. There were enough costumes here to keep the Paris Opera going for five successive seasons. But it was easier to move forward.

'They're after us. They're not dead.'

Nina was whining. Anne wanted to slap her. She was at the end of her patience. None of this was helping.

Her light was carried forward. It picked out a face, and they stopped. Nina's hand-grip was painful again. The face smiled.

'Good evening, Anne.'

It was Skinner. He looked more like Hugh Farnham now. There was some scarring on his cheek. Anne thought it was growing as she stared at it. She had nothing to say.

'I knew your sister, you know.' The bastard did not even look evil. 'Intimately.'

She could not look away from him. He smiled blandly again, without much enthusiasm. He was as tired as she felt.

'Skinner, what the fuck are you playing at?'

'Playing?'

She remembered it was not a game any more.

'Playing? That's for imbeciles like Amelia Dorf. You and me, Anne, we don't play games.'

'Yeah, right.'

Nina yanked her arm hard, pulling Anne's shoulder painfully. She turned away from Skinner. The other girl had plunged behind a curtain of fur coats. Anne was pulled into the clothes and lost her balance. Then she was down, and Nina was on top of her. The pen-light rolled away. Nina let go of her hand. Anne felt fingers in her throat, squeezing hard. She reached for Nina's hands, and grabbed what she hoped were her little fingers. She bent the fingers back. There was a squeal, and she was released.

Anne tried to get up, pulling on a coat, but Nina was still pinning her to the floor. There was still some light. Looking up at Nina, Anne saw a dead face. Just like the other effigies.

The scuffle at the Club Des Esseintes aside, she had not been in a fight since elementary school. The trick with the little fingers was the only thing she remembered from a piece she had once written on self-defence courses for women. She was no good at this. She rolled from side to side, trying to get the Nina Thing off her chest.

She got hold of a fallen ulster and stuffed it into Nina's face. It wrapped around her head. The Nina Thing tore at it, but Anne was released. She pushed the girl hard, and heard her fall over.

The struggle had been silent. Neither girl had grunted or sworn. There had only been a few sharp yelps of pain. Skinner might not even have been there.

Skinner?

Free of Nina, Anne got her head down and charged. She did not connect with Skinner as she had expected, and fell down. She scrambled along on leftover momentum, using her hands and knees more than her feet.

It was dark, and the passage was narrower now. She brushed

the walls with both shoulders, and even banged her head when she tried to stand up.

There was something behind her, coming after her, coming to get her. The Nina Thing. And it was not alone. The others, the guests, were there too, in a pack. They were not alive, but they were not dead enough either.

She considered lying down on the floor, covered with fallen dresses, and waiting for their touch on her neck. But she could not make herself give up. She kept on.

She kept on until she ran into a wall of loose boards. They fell apart, wood splintering, nails wrenching, and she burst out of the side of a building.

She stumbled and fell, her palms striking wet, dirty concrete. She felt cold night air on her face.

ENTRE'ACTE

1

In his dream, Cameron Nielson Jr saw life as a motion picture, unspooling steadily in the white-hot gaze of the bulb, the past piling up like celluloid string on the projection booth floor. CAMERON NIELSON in *The Cameron Nielson Story*. A Cameron Nielson Film. From the Cradle to the Grave with CAMERON NIELSON. 'It'll run and run,' Cameron Nielson.

His early years had been mainly montage. The young composer practises his scales while waiting for a big break. The young composer at odds with his family, who want him to follow a less daring course. The young composer working late into the night, notes flowing from his stylo. Women, leaving. Landlords knocking on doors, demanding money. Dishes piling up in a sink. Fingers in close-up, struggling with a recalcitrant piano. Electrical equipment accumulating around the traditional musical instrument. The reflection of a soldering iron in protective goggles as the musical weapons are forged.

Variety headlines spin out of the papier-mâché mist and chart the rise of a career. Fatherly, distinguished men scoffing at the hero's genius in smoke-filled clubs, plotting his come-uppance, but ultimately being swept away by the rollercoaster force of his obsessive talent. Early successes are built upon, as different audiences are superimposed, each clapping a little louder than the last, a crescendo rising. The young composer called out of his electronic cocoon after a performance and taking his bows with the other musicians, a rare grin on his sweating face. A devoted woman, her face a blur, clapping from the wings.

And throughout it all the music, first heard as an eerie sketch inside the hero's head, skeletally indistinct and bone china fragile. Then, as the young composer experiments at his consoles and keyboards, taking on some meat, becoming stronger, deeper. Finally, in a triumphant climax, bursting forth strong and unforgettable, exploding from his mind into reality, in THX sound, blasting at the acoustics of every concert hall in the world.

Then, amid the frenzy of music and applause, a clinch with the devoted woman and a fade to a painless old age. The composer, with talcum powder-white hair and a young face, dying content in his bed, surrounded by adoring and grieving children, his music living on. Under the end title, a pan across a series of busts in some Elysian hall of music. Palestrina. Bach. Beethoven. Mozart. Brahms. Wagner. Mahler. Stravinsky. Schoenberg. Stockhausen. CAMERON NIELSON. *The End,* in curlicue letters. A CAMERON NIELSON PRODUCTION.

'Cam?'

'Uh?' He jumped a little as Alexia slipped the *boutonnière* into the lapel of his tailcoat.

'You were dreaming,' she said.

He concentrated. He was calm. Before a concert, some people went to pieces, chain-smoking, hands trembling, shaking whisky out of the bottle. Cameron Nielson Jr became the still centre of a hurricane, as collected and single-minded as a great neurosurgeon before an operation.

'I'm sorry. I have to carry the whole piece in my head.'

Alexia smiled. His *boutonnière* matched her corsage. She had been his personal assistant throughout the preparation for the performance of the *Telemachus Symphony,* and they had slept together, three times. He was beginning to find the sex interesting, and had already started to wonder whether he should try to make her position permanent. The English girl was efficient and brought him just the right touch of warmth. He knew that he could be an ice-cube at times – God knows, Beethoven, Mozart and Wagner had not been easy to live with either – and Alexia took the chill off him.

She patted his lapel, straightening the flower, and kissed him like a little girl.

She was very English. His father had married an English girl, after divorcing Cameron's mother. The Nielsons were all drawn to this country. Perhaps it was a genetic thing. In all likelihood, Anne would settle for an Englishman. And Judi…

He drove his family out of his head, and let the music flood back. As a boy, he had been certain that he was adopted, or that his mother had taken a lover. Once, well after her marriage to his father was over, he had even asked her, but she just laughed at him. He remembered the red-cheeked embarrassment, and his subsequent determination never to let it show again. For a while, he had even resisted his name, scratching out the Jr on any documents with his full name on them, and signing himself C. Eugene Nielson. Now, that seemed cowardly. He simply had to stake his claim and fight for it, making sure by his works that everybody knew who Cameron Nielson *really* was. The brilliant young composer, not the burned-out playwright.

'Not long now.'

'No.'

'Nervous?'

Alexia did not know him well, he realized. 'Of course not. It's too late for that.'

Performing this piece was as complicated as launching a space shuttle, involving synchronized computer systems, traditional orchestral instruments, African drums and as many technicians as trained musicians. Cameron was not merely the composer and conductor, but a theremin soloist and the director of operations.

There were human elements involved, and that would give the piece an immediacy, but so much of it was pre-programmed, with tapes played and sounds conjured by infallible computers, that most of the work was already done. The performance itself was important, but it was almost of academic interest. *Telemachus* was already a thoroughly achieved work. Presenting it to the public was like unveiling a finished sculpture.

'Then why are you whistling?'

He realized he had been, and clamped his lips. It was a habit he had had as a child. A bad habit. His nanny had scolded him over and over, but he had never been able to stop. She conjured up a bogeyman, Mr Whistle, who pulled out the voices of little boys who whistled, leaving them only with their whistles. That had been before Dr Spock. He had been terrified, but still unable to stop. He had dreamed about Mr Whistle, picturing him as a child-sized man in a Little Lord Fauntleroy outfit, with floppy velvet bows and knickerbockers, his head a white eggshape, featureless but for a shark's gash of a mouth. He knew that he still whistled sometimes, but the bogeyman could not scare him any more.

'It's an old thing with me, Alexia, I'm sorry.'

'Don't be,' she said, smiling. 'I think it's cute.'

'Cute? That's not an English expression.'

The girl stepped back, away from him. 'Obviously I'm being polluted by an American.'

There were good luck cards on the dressing room table, from tutors, colleagues, a few friends. There was nothing from Dad, of course, nor Anne. He could not expect their interest. But there was a note, heart-stoppingly cheerful in its brevity, from Judi. It must have been mailed a few days ago, with a second class stamp. It had stopped him dead, for a moment.

'Here's another one,' Alexia said, producing a square envelope, 'delivered by hand. Sorry it's a bit bent.'

He slit it open with his finger, and glanced at it.

'Best wishes for your career,' it read, 'from...' Mr Scribble?

'Mr… I can't make this out, Lex. What do you think?'

'Begins with a W,' she laughed. 'Looks like Whistle.'

Before he could stop himself, a piercing howl was forced through his teeth.

'Sounds like Whistle too.'

He suffered a flashback, an out-of-place reel from an old dark house horror movie, or maybe a nightmare being offered for psychoanalysis to Ingrid Bergman. The young composer wanders through a haunted mansion, trying to exorcise the spirits of his tyrannical father and castrating sisters. Molten watches tumble out of wardrobes, cellos sprout spider-legs and scuttle musically in the shadows, faceless conductors lash out with scorpion-tailed batons. All very symbolic, with theremins on the soundtrack. And also in the house is the Monster, Mr Whistle, obscene drool leaking onto his embroidered vest.

He dispelled the images, and hugged the girl, almost desperately.

'That was a surprise,' she said. 'I knew you weren't the composing machine they say you are.'

They? Who were they? Who had been talking?

'I'm sorry,' he said, embarrassed.

'It's all right. This is a big night. You have a right to be nervous. What with your father, and your sister. No one could blame you.'

Was she already making excuses? Did she know something about the performance he did not?

He let her go, and walked to the mirror. As always he wore the traditional evening clothes. He liked the reference to the classical tradition. His white tie was perfectly tied, his shirt-front stiff with starch and studded properly.

Alexia whistled this time, off-key. A wolf whistle. Cameron forced a smile.

The digital clock was counting down towards the performance. On the closed-circuit monitors, he saw the technicians taking their places at the instrument banks. The stage was dominated by a cracked mask with blank, blind eyes. Telemachus, himself. Cameron thought the face looked like his father. The instrument monitors were reading normal as the equipment started up. Alexia brought him his headset, which he slipped on like a minimalist space helmet. He was becoming part of the machinery of the piece. He checked his watch against the clock, and mentally ticked off the functions as they were performed.

7:31.

'It's nearly time,' Alexia said, needlessly.

The orchestral musicians were filing out, also formally dressed. Minerva Beaton, the cellist, had resisted *Telemachus* at first, refusing to become part of the machinery of the piece, but those arguments, hateful to Cameron's memory, were over now. She had had to be converted, but now she was a true believer. She would serve the symphony.

'Who's that?'

Alexia pointed to a shape moving on one of the monitors, just behind Minerva. It was shadowed, and small.

'There shouldn't be any children backstage.'

There was a gleam in the dark, as if reflected off a large eggshell. Then the shape was gone.

'There's no one there,' Cameron said quietly. 'No one at all.'

'No,' she said. 'There was...'

'It was just a glitch,' he said, too forcefully. Alexia held his glance for a few moments, a furrow between her eyebrows, and dropped the subject.

7:33.

Light was flooding the monitors as the curtains rose. There was polite applause as the mask came into view, and the performers settled.

'Ready?'

He nodded, and left the room, Alexia a few steps behind. The door was held open for him, and he threaded his way through all the backstage equipment. Alexia took her canvas chair in the wings, her bug in her ear so she could relay if necessary his almost subaudial commands to the technical people.

7:34.

Cameron Nielson Jr stepped out on the stage just as the initial applause was dying, and climbed the dais with leisurely ease, settling down behind the theremin stand. He nodded to each of the performers. There was a flicker of applause for his appearance, but it faded away on schedule, leaving him three seconds of silence by the clock on the theremin before the first tonalities sounded out.

Then at precisely 7:35, the nightmare began.

2

In his nightmare, the device with the beeping alarms misfired because, by 7:59, the audience was laughing too loud for their watches to be heard. The tittering started during the first five minutes of the piece, and grew.

The music was his, and emerged as written from the apparatus he had designed for it, but it was changed. The effects he had carefully measured were misjudged, comical, obscene, absurd. Minerva Beaton could hardly keep her long face straight as she sawed her cello. The eerie, longing notes of his Telemachus theme sounded like whoopee cushions.

Beyond the lights, Cameron got the impression of audience members thronging the exits, trying to get out of the concert hall. He tried to keep going, his hands wringing sounds from the theremin. Painful feedback boomed from the amplifiers, and he realized he was whistling again, the sound dreadfully enlarged by his headset and hurled out into the auditorium.

Telemachus looked down blindly on his humiliation. And the childsized intruder shifted in the shadows around the stage, mocking him from the darkness.

He started coughing, and blood spatted across the note-dotted creaminess of his score.

Somehow, he made it through to the end.

There was no crescendo of applause, just a lone volley of claps. Alexia was trying to make him feel better.

He wrenched off his headset and fled the spotlit stage, pushing past the girl, hiding his red face in the dark.

When the last resonances of the symphony had died, all that was left was an electronic whine. It sounded like an idiot child whistling. Somebody turned it off.

The film sped up as Cameron ran out of the building, still in his tailcoat, and tried to lose himself in the streets around the Barbican. His shiny shoes pounded the sidewalks, and neon signs flashed the names of increasingly seedy nightclubs at him. It started raining in sparkling sheets, the technicians pouring water down from above his eyeline onto him. Rich, orchestral music, a kitschy concerto in the style of Erich Wolfgang Korngold, thundered on the soundtrack, vibrating his teeth.

Mr Whistle was still dogging him, not pursuing but just keeping up. The bogeyman did not need to do anything more to him. His fate was complete. In the space of a few cuts, he had a thick growth of stubble, his shirtfront was soiled with liquor, his hair was wild and his tails were tattered. He had a bottle of cheap booze in his hand, and was swigging from it.

He was in a flophouse, his coatsleeve wrinkled up above his left elbow and his shirtsleeve ripped away. The vein pulsed in his arm as the makeshift tourniquet drew tighter. Judi, her face white with Gothic make-up, handed him the glowing syringe. As the needle slid into him, he whistled sharply, hurting his ears. Rain washed Judi's face away.

Then, the sun came up and the nightmare shifted gears. He was in a gutter, cold clean water running around him, washing the grime and sleep from his face. A figure loomed over him, haloed by the sunlight, and picked him up, her arms slipping tight around his chest. Her blonde hair shone gold.

'Lex?'

She did not try to soothe him, but she took him away from

Skid Row, pulling him into a kingsize bed with freshly-laundered sheets. He was naked and clean again, his pains salved. The music came back. Things were not as bad as they seemed…

In the long run, they were much worse.

The night before the wedding, Cameron Nielson Jr burned his manuscripts, one by one. Alexia stood by and watched him do it. Acting as his agent, she had got him a commission to score a 15-minute TV documentary about autumn leaves. He thought he could do it. A sub-Elgar theme was whistling in his mind. In the burning pages, he imagined his electro-acoustic instruments sparking and self-destructing like a spaceship set at the end of a low-budget science fiction film. He reached for a more conventional musical palette, strings and woodwinds.

They were married in church, in the West Country village where Alexia had grown up. Her parents were delighted. Anne was there, representing his family, and his Dad, his spirits lifted by his recent turn for the better, sent a cable of congratulations to the groom and a mash note to the bride. Turning from the altar, Cameron could not see Mr Whistle among the congregation, but did think he glimpsed Judi, loitering embarrassed near the back.

After the ceremony, Alexia kissed him and loved him. He was enfolded by warm feelings. There was gentle applause, and flashbulbs popped. The orchestra played only harmonic music. Everything was easy.

After the honeymoon, Alexia was pregnant and he was progressing well on the film score. His work proved acceptable, and further commissions resulted. No one knew his name, but people hummed his tunes. He wrote the theme music for a British television serial adapted from a Barbara Cartland novel. He wrote a thirty-second piece for a shampoo commercial that enabled him to buy a house in the country. With his wife and Cameron Nielson III, he had a comfortable life, cocooned by money and anonymity. He never thought of performing again, or of serious music. If there was something lacking in his life, he did not know what it was.

Meanwhile, thanks to a series of startling medical breakthroughs, his father was recovering from his debilitating strokes. He almost literally returned from the dead, and his personal memoir, *Facing Death,* was the strongest thing he had written since the '50s. A seventy-five-page essay, it climbed the *New York Tunes* bestseller list and was *the* talking-point book of the year. Following that, there was a revival of interest in Cameron Nielson Sr, and most of his theatrical works were staged in New York and London. *The Rat Jacket* broke box office records on Broadway with Dustin Hoffman and Al Pacino, *The Crunch* was directed by Peter Hall on Shaftesbury Avenue, and *On the Graveyard Shift at Sam's Bar-B-Q and Grill* was remade by Steven Spielberg with Marlon Brando as Sam, Robert DeNiro in Brando's old role and Meryl Streep as Angela. Cameron's father began writing plays again, and managements competed for the rights to stage each new mature masterpiece. He was pleased for his Dad, and things were better between them. When Martin Scorsese filmed *The Rat Jacket,* Cameron Nielson Sr tried to get his son the job of writing the score, but the deal fell through. Cameron did not mind about that, even when Harvey Broadribb, who had been at Juilliard with him, won the Academy Award for his work on the movie.

Anne sent him a signed copy of her first book, *Remembering Judi.* A non-fiction account of their sister's last years, *Remembering Judi* won the Pulitzer Prize and was a hardback bestseller. It was turned into the highest-rated Made-for-TV movie ever produced, catapulting Nina Kenyon, the young unknown cast in the lead, to multiple awards and international stardom. After that, Anne became a novelist, won the Booker and the Whitbread in the same year with different books, and was given her own television show. He wrote the opening and closing signature tunes for the programme, but they were dumped after the first season and replaced with 'something a little more distinctive'. He wrote more shampoo, hairspray, deodorant and sliced bread commercials.

On a visit to England, Cameron's Dad met Minerva Beaton at a dinner party arranged by Alexia and wound up marrying the cellist. She reminded him of someone he had known as a young man. At the age of forty, Cameron was presented with a baby brother, Todd Nielson, upon whom everybody doted. When his own son was old enough to go to school, Alexia took up painting, working her way away from representational landscapes into suggestive abstracts based on the British countryside. Her work was too unconventional for immediate popular acceptance, but Cameron could tell how good she was, and was supportive even when she was discouraged. Anne and Dad both bought her paintings and displayed them prominently, and Cameron used his fee from a sanitary napkin commercial to finance an exhibition in London. Alexia was critically acclaimed, and several major galleries purchased her, but she did not become immediately collectible. She joked that she would only make money fifty years after she was dead, and he told her that money did not matter.

Cameron went to a lot of receptions, private views, book launches, first night parties, movie premieres and testimonials. His father, sister, wife and stepmother – Minerva became a much-in-demand soloist and had a big-selling jazz-classical crossover album – were always being honoured, and he always tried to turn out to support them. He got used to people asking him 'and what do *you* do?' He needed less and less to work, his commercial and film scores earning him a steady residual income. He did not miss his music, and could barely remember his performing days. Alexia and Cameron III gently chided him for his whistling habit, and he developed an aversion to his own work. Even when Alexia, who remained a young woman even as her hair silvered, tried to point out the strengths of his pieces he mentally tuned out. He had spent his life designing inoffensive wallpaper, he realized, and he was not really ashamed of that.

Cameron III asked for a guitar for his thirteenth birthday.

Cameron wanted to give him a computer, but Alexia prevailed and soon the house was full of twangs and scales again. His son was obsessive about music, mastering classical, folk and rock modes with alarming rapidity. At sixteen, he put together his first group and, with a cash present from his grandfather, put out a record of his own songs. It got a lot of airplay from John Peel, and was written up extensively by the music press. A major company signed him up, and he had a series of top ten hits while building a serious reputation. Elvis Costello called him a genius, and Jonathan Demme made an in-concert film of his appearance at the Hollywood Bowl. Cameron III was embarrassed by the *Smash Hits* following and tried not to be a teen idol, whereupon he was celebrated all the more. Cameron knew how good his son really was, and encouraged him to break free of the pop straitjacket. Cameron III recorded duets with Stevie Wonder, David Byrne, Frank Sinatra and Kiri Te Kanawa. Then, he wrote a West End musical based on his aunt's *Remembering Judi* and it transferred to Broadway, with Nina Kenyon making an impressive singing debut in her original role, finally outgrossing everything written by Andrew Lloyd Webber. On *The Tonight Show,* Johnny Carson did a whole monologue on the theme of, 'yes, but who is Cameron Nielson *the Second*?'

Todd Nielson became a medical researcher, and finally did something about the ageing process. Their father was one of the first beneficiaries, and the whole family was able to gather at his 100th birthday party. Cameron talked with Minerva, who was being magnanimously tolerant of her husband's much-publicized affair with Nina Kenyon, and with Anne, who was well into the tertiary stage of her fourth marriage (to Didier Bishopric, a society restaurateur) and just back from the Betty Ford clinic after a spell of amphetamine dependency. The family had asked him to compose a tune for the party, but he had declined. He did not do that any more. Finally, his son stepped in and wrote a song, 'Not Out', that would become an anthem for the new generation of active centenarians. However, thanks to a nervous disorder, Cameron Nielson III was unable to play at the party and, at the last minute, Cameron agreed to step in. After his son's band, joined for the occasion by Minerva, played 'Not Out', with Nina handling the vocal, Cameron sat at the piano. Everybody sang 'Happy Birthday to You', drowning him out. It was a great occasion.

Cameron III's condition got worse, and his uncle Todd recommended specialists. Alexia was tormented, and poured her feelings out on canvas, producing some of her best work. Cameron spent a lot of time sitting at his piano with the lid down, his fingers resting on the wood, whistling unconsciously. The specialists tried increasingly radical treatments, but his son did not recover. In the nursing home, Cameron III wrote an album's worth of his very best material, railing against the darkness that was crowding in on him. At the funeral, Cameron's stepmother played the cello while he stood with his arm around Alexia, feeling drained and empty.

Anne overdosed alone in her penthouse, describing herself in her last note as 'just another dead junkie'. Their father wrote a tragic play about his daughters, and Nina, grown old enough, played 'Amy', the character based on Anne. There were characters equivalent to Victoria Page, Judi and Todd, but no one in *An American Family* resembled Cameron. There were new arts by now, shared dreams that could be shaped by the skilled. Susan, Anne's daughter by Didier, became one of the first geniuses of the form, moulding her night fantasies into unforgettably affecting tapestries of emotion and narrative.

The Museum of Modern Art in New York held a major retrospective of Alexia Nielson's paintings, but his wife did not live to see it. She succumbed to an unexpected cerebral haemorrhage at the easel two weeks before the opening. Her last, unfinished work was uncharacteristic: a portrait of her husband, prepared as a birthday surprise. He insisted it be exhibited, although it lacked a face. Several journalists who covered the event assumed that

Alexia was Cameron Nielson's daughter and that he, despite his name, had married into the family.

Hugh Farnham was discovered in a retirement home in Florida, living under an assumed identity, obsessively chewing on his rusks. He agreed to a televised debate, hosted by Dan Rather, with Cameron Nielson Sr. Farnham was still feisty on the show, but Cameron Nielson, looking younger now than his son, was as skilled as a great matador, and finally evened the score with his former tormentor, driving him to tearful contrition. Waving a fist at the camera, Cameron Nielson recited the names of those blacklist casualties he had avenged at last. At the reception after the show, Todd, learning for the first time of the ancient history of his family, spat in Hugh Farnham's face. The old inquisitor slunk into the night, spittle still dripping from his cheek.

Cameron, needing nothing, sat around the house, surrounded by other people's books and music and art. A journalist interviewed him for a book about his family, and when *The Nielsons* appeared, it made no mention at all of his professional life. He did not mind.

He whistled, tunelessly. Alone, with no worries, he whistled. The whistling became louder, more piercing, more painful.

Sitting at his piano, he howled. He looked down and saw he had battered his fingers bloody against the wooden lid.

He was coughing.

The whistling sounded like feedback, and his hammering on the piano became a dying round of applause. He was in the light, but there was darkness all around.

One of the perils of dreaming too much was that you got flashbacks afterwards. He tried to clear the phantoms from his head and grasp reality.

He looked up and saw Minerva at her cello, and Alexia, young and alive again, in the wings.

He was not sitting at a piano. It was a theremin.

The whistling stopped, and the music began.

3

His hands hovered above the instrument, refusing to move, but the opening notes of the symphony came from the theremin.

Nobody noticed that he was not contributing. Tapes cut in and overlaid the unearthly siren-call of the electroacoustic instrument, and Minerva's cello answered the melodic tonality with a delicately offhand echo.

Cameron was sweating. His hands were stuck in space, a foot away from the theremin. He felt as if he were pressing against a strong, polarized magnetic force.

But the theremin played its part by itself, as if it were programmed to.

The *Telemachus Symphony* swelled. The audience were hypnotized by the piece, each member, even those cynical about 'so-called "modern" music', knew they were present at a historic event. This was a première that would be remembered forever.

It was for Judi, Cameron decided. He must make that clear to the press. And for Dad.

Now, perhaps, they would understand.

His wrists began to ache, and his nails were empurpled with blood.

Anne. He must tell Anne.

He was not a total ice-cube. This music proved that.

The symphony continued, greater than anything he had ever done. It was greater than him. He was not needed any more.

His hands were released, and he dropped them to his lap. The theremin was playing itself with passion, with feeling. For the first time, he understood his own work. His face was wet with tears.

Minerva's solo came and went. The trick with the watches was more than a technical stunt, it actually worked in the context of the piece, sucking the audience even further into the spell.

Quietly, humbly, Cameron took off his headset and set it down on the floor. He slipped off his stool and backed away from the theremin stand. No one noticed. The music had them all.

He turned. A single globular tear crept from the white blank of Telemachus' eye and ran down the giant mask.

Alexia was sobbing gently in the wings, stifling herself into silence. The music went on, and on.

Cameron left the stage, unremarked, and stepped into a carpeted, brightly-lit corridor. He could still hear his music, as if it were very far away.

He needed a cigarette.

He felt light-headed, as if he had been awake for days on end.

Looking for a concession stand, he turned a corner. The bogeyman was waiting for him.

It was a long time since he had seen Mr Whistle. They had both grown up. Mr Whistle's clothes had grown in size with him. He was a tall, broad man now, but he still wore knickerbockers and velvet. His face was different, almost human, but he still had a shark's mouth.

'Hello, Cam,' he whistled. 'Long time, no see…'

Cameron felt small again. The music was fading. Mr Whistle seemed to be growing to giant size, his huge head scraping the ceiling. He was forced to bend at the waist, looming over him.

'You have such an interesting family,' he said. 'So varied, so talented…'

Cameron remembered his dream, remembered the thickly-populated nightmare life he had led, trailing off into a bland and dusty future.

Mr Whistle smiled, teeth cutting his lips. He wiped his mouth with the back of his hand and tore away a ragged stretch of skin.

'Just think of me as the Ghost of Cameron Yet to Come…'

Could he hear laughter from the auditorium? He was clutched by dread.

Was it all coming true?

'We stand at a crossroads, Cam,' Mr Whistle said. 'You, and your entire family. You know how I served your father, and let him live. You know how I loved your sister, and made her die. They each had a choice. As do you…' He was held fast again, his whole body wrapped in an invisible field.

'And Anne?' he asked.

'Her too. I'm dealing with her even as we speak. As a ghost, I'm not really here. I could tear you in two, but I'm not really here. It's one of my many talents.'

Cameron did not doubt his old bogeyman. He remembered Mr Whistle's ways.

'You're whistling, little boy,' the Monster told him.

He was. He could not stop himself.

His half-heard symphony was a background for his tuneless whistle.

'You know what I do to little boys who whistle?' Cameron was a child again, the hell of life before him. Growing up, exams, acne, practice, arguments, girls, alienation, scales. He could not go through it all again.

'I take their voices!'

The whistle died in Cameron's throat.

'That's better. You won't need to speak. This is a yes or no question. You can nod or shake your head.'

Cameron realized that Mr Whistle looked a little like Hugh Farnham. He was a bogeyman for all the family.

'Consider yourself lucky. I've given you all a choice, but you're the only one who is getting it straight, all cards on the table. There are no subtle, metaphorical struggles here. This is a simple deal.'

Cameron tried to hear his symphony, strained his ears for it. The music was there, but very faint.

'You've seen a possible future, stretching out from this evening. I can't guarantee it will be exactly like that, but you must have got the picture. You can expect a long and happy life if you give up serious music. Simple, isn't it? Which would you rather died, you or your music? You know how your father chose. He has had the benefit of a fine son and beautiful daughters, but there have been no more great plays.'

The music was growing louder. It was inside his head, but throughout the building too. He tried to get a fix on it. It was strong and clean. It expressed the feelings he had never allowed himself. He could not let it go.

'So, let's get this clear. Nod your head if you want to live, without music...'

Cameron held still.

'Live? Die? Music? Happiness? It doesn't mean much to me. I get mine either way.'

Mr Whistle rested a large hand on Cameron's shirtfront. He flexed his fingers. Cameron felt an electrical tingle.

He had decided. Not until now had he really known how much it all meant to him. He was older now than Mozart had been when he died. He still had a lot more to write but, considering that he was bowing out with *Telemachus,* he thought that he would not leave a negligible *oeuvre* behind him.

'Well, Mr Ice-cube...? What can I do?'

Cameron's throat started working. It was agony, but he got the words out.

'You...'

Mr Whistle knew what his decision had been. Static

crackled between his fingers, and Cameron felt the bolts charging into his heart.

'...can...'

The killing force came. It exploded inside him just as the last notes of his symphony died away. As he fell, a smoking black handprint on his chest, he heard the standing ovation building. They were calling for him, whistling shrilly, stamping their feet.

He smiled as the life went out in him, looking up at the already transparent Monster.

'...you can *whistle*!'

NIGHT

1

'**B**A-ba-bomp-ba-ba. '

Anne tried to stand up. It was not easy. She nearly lost a shoe pulling her foot out of the hole behind her.

'BA-ba-bomp-ba-ba. '

It was dark in front, but there were indistinct swirls of painfully bright colours to the left and right. Stained glass and neon, Technicolor and Dayglo, fireworks and foil-embossed paperback covers.

'BA-ba-bomp-ba-ba.'

The scat-singing was loud, but it was fighting several other pieces of music in an arrangement that was less contrapuntal than cacophonous. It was merely the nearest and loudest of five or six clashing noises. The scum skimmed off the top of an ocean of din.

'Ba-ding-a-dang-ding. '

This was not St John's Wood.

'Ba-ding-a-dong-ding. '

This was somewhere in the centre of town. The West End. Soho. It did not make sense.

'Blue *MOOOOONNN!*'

Her eyes hurt. She covered them, blinking purposefully.

'Dib-da-dib-da-dib-dib.'

It was dark inside her head.

'…moon, moon, moon… blue moon…'

Each 'moon' from the backing vocalists was a needle pushed through the bridge of her nose, probing for the forepart of her brain. It did not hurt as much as it should have.

She took her hands away from her eyes, and looked again. The world got clearer, as if someone were twiddling the focus of her retinae. Her eyes tuned in, but her mind could not match them.

She leaned against a rough, damp wall, feeling an icy draught on her ankles. It was very cold, and she was very tired. She felt hung over, and a million miles from the bed she wanted to be asleep in.

How the hell had she got here?

And where was here?

She was in a narrow passage that crookedly connected two busy streets. It was irregularly paved, and lit only by an open window a few storeys above. There were no doors in the walls, but she could tell from the noise that the building she thought she had come out of was a pub. The boards she had broken through were an entrance to the cellar. She tried to superimpose this place on Amelia Dorf's house, but could not make the images jibe.

There was nothing coming after her any more. She thought that the cellar was empty. It was dark down below, but she could make out the shapes of beer kegs. No monsters, no people. They had given up.

But it had all been real. She could still feel the points in her throat where the Nina Thing's fingers had fastened. She must have plenty of other scrapes and bruises.

She got out of the passage, and found herself somewhere she recognized. She was back in Brewer Street. There were crowds of people about. Ordinary, real, non-monstrous people. The pubs had not let out yet, so it must be not be later than eleven. She had thought it must be well into the small hours. The streets were not exactly reassuring, but they were safer than the old dark house, or the wardrobe of death.

Next to the pub was a loud strip club. Bare coloured bulbs flashed on and off around a come-on sign. 'Beautiful Girls XXXXXXX Totally Naked.' There were black and white posters under glass, just a shade more indecent than allowed by the law. So much for the Clean-Up Soho Campaign. The silver paper stars pasted over nipples had peeled and slipped to the bottom of the case, leaving the pouting, overdeveloped girls with gluey smudges on their breasts.

'Come in and slobber over our fat ugly bimbos,' bawled a fat ugly young man in jeans and a windbreaker, standing in the middle of a yellow-lit foyer. His breath was steaming in clouds, and he stamped his feet in a crooked little tap-dance step to keep his doubtless numb toes warm. 'Get your rocks off as they get their clothes off. Sex, sex, sex. Get your lovely, steaming, thirst-quenching, piping hot, country-fresh sex here! You can't get things like this in Russia, you know. It's a free country here. Sex, sex, sex. God save the Queen, and all who sail in her...'

The bored black woman in the club's ticket booth looked up from her knitting magazine and laughed. Nobody was being lured in. The spieler noticed Anne.

'Fuck off back to your own turf, lovey,' he shouted, 'you're putting the shits up the punters. You've got a look on you like Dracula's bleeding daughter!'

He raised his hands, crossing his fingers to make a crucifix.

'Back! Back, I thay!' he adopted a Karloffian lisp. 'Begone hellthpawn!'

Anne retreated, and was jostled along the pavement by a group of colourfully-dressed Chinese kids with '70s punk haircuts. They chattered and laughed, being rude about Western passersby who could not understand their language. Anne knew she was being discussed, anatomized as a freak.

She wondered just how awful she did look. She did not feel all right inside. She realized that she had not eaten properly in twenty-four hours. Just half a breakfast and a sandwich in the Nellie Dean ages ago.

The Chinese kids piled into a pub, pushing and kicking each other. A gust of beery hot air hit her. She wanted to be sick. A young man in a smartly hideous jacket tried to come out while the kids were trying to go in. He was buffeted from side to side, and swore in what Anne thought was an Australian accent. He pushed her, and headed off on a determined course for somewhere.

She tripped, and tottered at the edge of the kerb. She stepped into the gutter and got her balance. A McDonald's carton crumpled lousily under her shoe, and her heel squelched into a half-eaten Egg McMuffin.

The music mix was more offensive out in the open. Anne could pick out random snatches of disco, Derek Douane, reggae, acid house, rhythm and blues, funk, Kylie Minogue and '60s oldies. The result was a sweaty medley, harsh and brittle on the surface, but cheesy and rotten underneath.

Every shop in sight was open, selling sex. She walked towards Wardour Street. That would be quieter, calmer. She could get her bearings. There were a few clubs at the lower end of the street, but it was mostly owned by monolithic movie companies. She went past displays of posters and stills for upcoming films, gradually calming herself. Heroes posed with guns: Sylvester Stallone, Kurt Russell, Rutger Hauer, Clint Eastwood. If she could get to Tottenham Court Road tube station, she could get home almost on automatic pilot.

First, she needed to make herself human again. She crossed the road, dodging a limousine with a personalized numberplate, and squeezed into a long, thin pub called The Ship. It was full of leather- and PVC-clothed young people, banging their heads in time to the music. This was one of the overspill places for The Marquee, just down the road. Daeve Pope would have been in heavy metal heaven.

A battered man in a woollen hat, one eye almost closed by a bruise, was appealing to the drinkers.

'Are there any East End boys here?'

He was ignored. Anne tried to get past.

'Come on now. East End boys. I need some help. One of our own's been done over. Gimme some help. Come on.'

Some of the patrons were getting annoyed. The would-be lynch mob leader grabbed an arm and was shaken off. 'Where's the old East End? I need some fucking help.'

'Listen,' said a cockatoo-plumed girl, 'we wouldn't fight for our country. I don't see why we should go to war for our fucking post code.'

'Bitch. One of our own is bleeding…'

Anne got out of the mini-drama and went upstairs to the Ladies. It was empty and relatively clean. She locked herself into a cubicle and took a leak. It was good just to sit down, and she was tempted to rest her head against the partition and get some sleep. It would be so easy just to give up for a while.

She pulled herself back together again, and hauled herself out of the cubicle to make full use of the facilities. A girl with a superheroine costume was holding her face up to the mirror, tracing a cobweb pattern on her pale cheeks. Anne looked at her own face. It was pretty ghastly. She washed. The dirt and the make-up came off easily, and there were no obvious bruises underneath. Even her neck, which still hurt, was unmarked. She had lost her handbag somewhere, but her wallet was still in her inside jacket pocket, and she had some make-up things in her coat. The coat, mercifully, was large enough to cover the clothes she had borrowed from Nina. She lipsticked in her usual modest mouth and combed her hair. Her reflection looked like her again. She even practised smiling.

Walking to the station, past the brightly-lit boutiques, cinemas, remainder bookshops and tatty souvenir stalls, all decorated for Christmas and building up to the January sales, she found herself having to think about what had happened to her.

Drugs. It was something to do with drugs. Maybe they had doped her Perrier at Amelia's, with LSD or some other hallucinogen. Then, after she had taken her tour of Nightmare City, they had brought her into the middle of town and dumped her.

But it did not feel like drugs. She had done acid once, at college, and it had not been anything like this evening's entertainment. What she had just been through was insane and illogical, but also unambiguous and actual. It felt real.

Not LSD, then. Maybe something a good deal weirder. Something expensive and experimental, like Inspector Hollis' designer dope.

Hollis. She must call him in the morning, give him all the names she had found, and let the police handle any investigation. This evening had proved her incompetence as Philip Marlowe.

A taxicab cruised by with its light on, and she decided to signal it. It would be faster than the underground. But, as she pulled her hand out of her pocket, she remembered. She had given Nina all her cash, and the girl had thrown it at Clive. If she wanted to get home in comfort, she would have to find a cashpoint. The taxi was gone. There was no point in bothering. She turned her back on the street and descended into the underground station.

Underground. The tube. That was how she thought of it. Not as the subway. She was turning British. Writing a piece a few weeks ago, she had had to think very hard before remembering the American expression for council housing.

It was still quite busy. She found her travel pass in her top pocket, and slipped it into the automatic gate, muttering 'open fucking sesame' to the machine. It refused to accept the bent card, and she had to find a barrier run by a human being. The robots were doing a lot of turning people back, and the guard-manned point was thronged with a wedge-shaped queue of complaining travellers. Anne hung back, but got past in a minute or so.

She would take the Northern line to Kentish Town. It was only six stops. Her flat was only a few minutes' walk away from the station. Then, she would sleep.

She was underground. Going down. Please mind the gap.

As she descended the escalator towards the platforms, she noticed the digital clock in the ceiling. In the station, the time was 10:37.

She did not have to wait long for a train.

2

The man opposite her was nodding, muttering to himself, just this side of being asleep. There were dusty stains on the lapels of his suit jacket, and his too-small cloth cap was creeping backwards on his scalp with each roll of his head. He had a bald spot, under a straggle of brown hair, and a ratty Fu-Manchu moustache. His arms were wrapped around a full carrier bag on his lap. Anne could see bottle-necks and wrapped sandwiches. A stick of French bread stuck up, resting against his head like the neck of a cello. He did not look well at all.

There was no one else in the carriage; unusual on this part of this line and at this time in the evening. In Central London, this was a peak travel hour. The restaurants and movies and theatres would be starting to turn people out. A lot of service workers would be clocking off. The train should be at least half full. She should still have been able to get a seat, but she should not have a carriage practically to herself. It was unusual, strange; but unusual and strange were not words she was prepared to apply to anything short of a surreal Hell on Earth after her day.

Tomorrow, it would all seem crazy. Next week, she would have talked it through with three or four different people. Hollis, Mark, Nigel and Clare at the office, maybe even Cam. She would prod them, and they would rationalize things, give explanations, make jokes, suggest she calm down. It would all start to seem more like a bad trip, a bad dream. Now, she knew that it had not been a hallucination, it had been real. Soon, she knew she would be thinking in terms of shock, stress, guilt reaction, grief, anxiety, a clouded mind. Eventually, she would convince herself.

But…

At the next stop, Goodge Street, a young couple and an old man got on. The girl wore tiny earphones, and had a Sony Walkman slung in a holster from her belt. Anne heard the tinny thrash of muted music. A demon drum solo was turned into the nagging p'tum-chk p'tum-chk of a dripping tap. The two kids stayed by the doors, necking. The boy stroked the girl's side, twisting the Walkman lead around his fingers in a one-handed cat's cradle.

The old man, shabby and bearded, sat one seat away from her. He stank of paint-stripper. She knew she was about to be hassled.

'Excuse me…'

She was too tired. She ignored him.

''scuse *me!*'

She really did not need this. She looked up at the advertisements above the windows. A faded bra ad was dotted with circular orange 'this poster degrades women' stickers. Right on. This city degrades women. The old man touched her sleeve. He had spider-shaped scabs on his knuckles, and several beercan tab-pulls bunched on his ring finger.

'Miss?'

She gave up, and turned to him. He smiled. His beard was grey-white, but discoloured yellow around his mouth as if he had been drooling thin custard. He had ill-fitting false teeth like the Civil War issue dentures Walter Brennan used to wear in Westerns where he was the feisty old-timer.

Walter Brennan never pissed in his pants, though. Walter Brennan never gargled with methylated spirits, or wore the same ragged T-shirts for months on end, or slept in a cardboard cocoon in a condemned house, or bothered young women on the subway.

'Miss?'

'Yes,' she said, non-committally.

'Miss, do you have…'

His voice did not quite work properly. His beard and teeth got in the way. He hawked phlegm, and started again.

'Do you have a sister at home… *just like you*?'

She did not understand. 'I'm sorry?'

'A sister.'

She tried to make out an expression on his creased face. There were lines of dirt embedded in his skin. His nose was red. He was a clown, a bum. But there was something almost intelligent in him somewhere, something deliberate and malicious.

She had to get rid of him.

'Fuck off, creep!'

'Ssssssissster!'

The train stopped again, Warren Street. There was a pause, the automatic doors unclenched. More people got on. The wino looked away from her. There was quite a crowd.

Please, she thought, let someone sit between me and him, let someone sit next to me.

Someone did, but it was no relief.

The new man was young and huge. He smelled of stale faeces and tomato sauce. He wore an army greatcoat, not big enough to cover his blubbery belly although it was buttoned across his chest. He was a skinhead, and had a line of swastikas tattooed around his neck. His hand was deep in a damp newspaper parcel.

'Want one, darling?' he said, shoving a bundle of vinegary chips up to her face. The stodgy strands were long and thick and twisted, spotted with mobile gobbets of ketchup. Looking at the food was like staring into an abdominal incision.

'No thanks.'

'Go on. You could do with some building up.'

'It's okay, thanks.'

'You'll need all your strength.'

She had heard that the British ate fish and chips out of old newspapers, had seen it in films about the blitz. But that was a long time ago. Now, fish and chips came in plain white paper. But the skinhead's food was wrapped up old-style.

The wino leaned and leered at her from behind the cover of the chip man's mighty stomach. The rails were bumpier than usual this evening. She was being shaken thoroughly. The strap-hangers were swaying unsteadily, as if the metal floor were running in wavelets. The wino chuckled silently. She realized that the strange thing about him was that he was not drunk.

Anne looked away. The carriage was pretty much full now. Almost every seat was taken, and there were plenty of standees. The necking kids had gone. Most of the passengers looked down-and-out, or rowdy, or indefinably depraved.

By the doors, where the couple had been, three teenage boys were scuffling and messing around. One swung from a chromed pole like an ape. They had rosettes and long tartan scarves. One wore an oversize silk jockey's cap with a little teddy bear pinned to it. She thought they were Scots.

Football fans, she supposed. Football hooligans, they called them over here. Dear old staid, conservative, non-violent Britain. Soccer fans were its contribution to the global tradition of random violence. Back home in the States, sports followers were fanatics, exercising an insane competitiveness on the stands, pouring out aggression through their team's performance. But outside the stadium, the hostility evaporated. Over here, 'what team do you support?' was tantamount to a declaration of war. This sceptre'd isle, this happy breed, this bunch of foul-mouthed assholes…

One of the kids started winding his scarf around his head, mummifying himself. His mates laughed, and helped him tie the topknot. The teenage monster lurched and bounced a beercan off his head. One of his mates took the dented tube away from him and opened it, splashing froth over a window. The mummy staggered stiff-kneed down the aisle, arms outstretched in a drunken monster impression. He was laughing.

The man opposite woke up suddenly. His cap fell off. The mummy tripped over his legs, and only saved himself from falling by grabbing one of the row of dangling blackjacks above the seats.

'Mind my bloody chips,' shouted the NF paratrooper, hugging his food. The man opposite was holding on tight to his groceries. His bag was ripped, and tins fell out.

The mummy clawed blindly with his free hand, groping for the chip man's voice. He clutched air in front of Anne's face. She tried to recede into her seat, to keep out of it.

'You a fucking bloody Nazi boy, Jummie?' burped the mummy in an unmistakable Glaswegian accent. 'You a pansy for Hitler, Jummie?'

'He bends over for the SS,' said the mummy's cap-wearing friend, making an obscene fist, 'you can tell. He's a glove puppet. It's official.'

The mummy tottered over her. His scarf was loose at the chin. He took the flapping, tasselled end and slowly unwound. Anne looked up to see his face. The scarf came away and fell on the floor, twisted in a multiple S.

His face was dead. He was a noseless, lipless, leathercheeked horror-comic-from-the-'50s dead person. Eyes like red poached eggs rolled in their hollows. A pink, healthy tongue stuck out between the exposed teeth.

'Hey, you, Jummie,' he said to her. 'Gissa kiss, love.'

Anne knew she was back on the Nightmare Express.

She tried to stand up, but the chip man held her arm, pinning it to the seat rest. He had the face of a potato now, coarsely vegetable with pitted depressions instead of features. Something pressed her right shoulder down. She was completely stuck.

She looked, and found that the shoulder-holder was Jeane Russell from Amelia's party. She had a belted trench coat over her fairy queen outfit. Her face was full and red now, almost bursting. She was evenly speckled with silver glitter.

The zombie hooligan leaned over her.

'Gissssa kissss!'

The tongue was impossibly extended, pointed and wet and more alive than the rest of the thing. It poked out and wriggled like a slug. He bent to kiss her. She squirmed.

The train stopped again. Mornington Crescent. The doors opened and closed impersonally.

The hooligan froze, and withdrew. The holds on her arm and shoulder eased.

'Gissa kiss?' It was whining now, pathetic.

'Uh-huh,' she said, 'not on a first date.'

From now on, she had decided, she would fight back. She did not like being a victim. She was going to take back the night. At least, she was going to try.

The station was not Mornington Crescent. As the train pulled out, she saw gleaming white, bare walls slide past the windows. No movie posters, no multi-lingual Telecom ads, no London Transport signs.

More passengers had got on. Her travelling companions had quietened, as if someone in authority had arrived. Anne knew that she was the only live person in the carriage. She recognized a few faces from Amelia's party, but most of the dead people were strangers. One startling apparition a few seats away was masked, and got up like a Chinese mandarin, with clacking claws for hands emerging from generous silk sleeves.

There were plenty of vile smells, and the train was colder than it ought to be.

The wino pulled his clothes apart, exposing old wounds.

'See,' he said, 'stigmata!'

The chip man kept lifting handfuls of soggy potato to his head, but instead of shoving them into a mouth he was plastering them onto the featureless mass, sculpting himself a parrot nose, acromegalic brows and a Kirk Douglas chin.

But it was still a tube train, grubby and battered. Those advertisements were still there, plugging temp agencies, breath fresheners, computer dating, a lurid paperback about anthropophagous slugs, holiday firms...

'Okay,' she said, looking about at the others, 'what comes next?'

At the other end of the carriage someone started moving, coming towards her, weaving past the standing dead, eyes fixed on her. It was a girl, in a better state than the others. She could almost pass for human. Almost.

Anne stood up.

'Judi?'

3

Anne started forwards, to hug her sister. She thought better of it, and held back. She felt awkward. Judi smiled.

'I know what you mean, Annie.'

Judi looked better than she had in the morgue. Actually, she looked better than the last time Anne had seen her alive. She had been on drugs then. Now, she did not need them.

'The only thing I shoot into my veins these days is formaldehyde, Annie,' she said.

Anne stepped backwards, the train rocking under her feet, making her unsteady. Judi had always tended to know what she was thinking, but now she knew her sister really could read her mind.

'You don't know the half of it, Annie,' Judi said. Her ironic smile and quizzically raised eyebrows excluded the rest of the dead people. The sisters had instantly re-established their old understanding and intimacy. 'It's weirder than you think.'

Anne could have laughed, but did not.

'I don't fucking believe it, Ju.'

'You'd fucking better try, because there's a lot more coming your way. I'd hate to spoil it for you.'

'Skinner?'

'Yeah, Skinner. It all comes down to him really, but I guess you knew that already.'

'I suppose so. How...'

'...did I get into this? Don't ask, Annie, don't ask. It's a shitty story.'

Judi had her young face back again, and it looked good. Her punk/kabuki make-up was professionally applied and striking; her black short hairstyle was stylish and street chic. She was ready for a dusk-to-dawn party, self-possessed and poised enough to appear in a hairspray commercial.

'I had your bag,' Anne said, 'but I left it somewhere. At that club, or at Nina's flat. I don't remember.'

'That's okay. I don't need those things any more.'

She was perfectly turned out: patterned black tights, black pointed ballet shoes, snug black mini dress, and an expensive Marlon Brando black leather jacket with the arms hacked off to turn it into a waistcoat. Her arms looked pink and strong. She wasn't feeling the cold.

'It's a shame about Nina,' Judi said. 'She was a good kid. Dumb as hell, but a good kid.'

The waistcoat was slashed with unnecessary zips that glistened like moist scars. The shoulders were padded like a flak jacket, with fringed epaulettes. Useless straps hung undone. Peace signs and Anarchy symbols were picked out in steel studs. Judi's hands were in Kangaroo pouch pockets over her stomach. Her fists pushed the leather out. Anne could make out the ridges of her sister's knuckles.

'Annie, did we have a good childhood?'

Anne looked away exasperated. Only Judi could get to her so quickly, and only this discussion could push her over the edge. It always came up at the very worst of times. They had last gone through the pointless business in the visitors' room of a police station. Now they were practically in the afterlife, and here it all was again...

'On a scale of one to ten, how would you rate our parents? Individually and as a combination? With regards to each other, to us as a combination, to us as individuals, and to society as a whole? Could they have been any worse, do you think?'

'Ju,' Anne realized they were back to their little kid names now, 'Ju, I don't really think it matters any more.'

'Maybe not, but it's interesting. Do you think we would have been better off if Dad had been a small-time failure? As opposed to that special big-time type of failure who looks like a success until the last reel and then turns yellow and runs?'

It was embarrassing, having this talk again, and in public. The dead were listening intently, enjoying the psychodrama. Any moment now, Judi would be turning them into a jury, appealing for their verdict on the Nielsen family. What a ridiculous way to behave.

'Ju, I'm sorry.'

'What for?'

'All of it. Dad, Cam, me, Vicky. I'm sorry. We should've...'

'It's too late for should've, Annie. Should've, could've, would've. It was all so complicated, you know. Even before Skinner. We came into it all too late to make any difference. Dad could never write it out, you could never think it out...'

Anne was crying now; not just politely staining her cheeks, but leaking profusely from her eyes and nose. She got a handkerchief from somewhere, and wiped herself, but it did little good.

'You know who we should have had as a father, Annie. I thought it out once. Ibsen. Old Henrik wouldn't have fallen apart in front of Farnham's Witchfinders, Annie. Or screwed up his kids like we were screwed up. Or written that fucking awful *Graveyard Shift* thing.'

Judi was crying too. Little, disciplined tears that ran beautifully over her make-up mask without ruining it. The death-faced hooligan had his arm around her now, comforting her, consoling her. He looked reproachfully at Anne, huge eyes moving in their orbits.

'We should stick with our own kind, Annie. Stick to your own kind.' Judi accepted the hooligan's chaste cheek-touch of a kiss. 'And you can see what my own kind is these days...'

Jeane Russell also cuddled up to Judi, patting a shoulder with a diaphanously gloved hand. The whole carriage was behind Judi. Anne was alone.

'Ju...'

Judi gently shrugged free of her attendants, and came towards her. Anne realized that she had backed against the end of the carriage, against the door to the driver's cabin. Judi came to her, smiling with closed lips.

'Annie,' she breathed, 'let's give up and go with it. Get it over with.'

Judi took her hands out of her pockets, and brushed her fingers up and down the front of her waistcoat. She tugged at her zips, opening little pouches in the leather. Some of the zips crept open by themselves, tooth by tooth. Silver-edged lips twisted slightly, and opened. Things were moving inside the waistcoat, pushing outwards, distending the leather, reaching for the air.

The first one came out of a mouth just under the right epaulette. It was a tongue, then it was a crooked finger, then a snake-headed tentacle. The lump at the end was shaped, but featureless. The tentacles were blind and probing. They were not part of Judi, but they came from her. Judi diminished, as her substance flowed into the protuberances. Anne could see the blobs of unformed flesh moving down the tentacles through peristalsis.

'You have to go with it, Annie.'

Judi's face was shrinking again. She was starting to look as she had done in death. Old and unidentifiable. The bulbs were swollen now, turning a fleshy red. Trails of yellowish fluid dribbled from the pockets, and ran down the waistcoat. Judi was leaking badly.

'Come on, Annie. Let's make up.'

Judi was feeble now, unsteady. She was not up to coping with the motion of the train. Tentacles from the region of her waist wrapped around poles, and she stayed upright. The new growth looked strong. They had the power of constriction, and Anne guessed they would be sticky to the touch.

A tentacle waved towards her. It was like a bloated anemone frond. The train was slowing down, coming to a station.

Anne grabbed the tentacle, and yanked hard. It was warm and unpleasant in her grip, but it did not slide free. She felt a mild nettle sting. Judi gasped, and bent double. The tentacle came out of her body as easily and unendingly as a roll tape measure. Anne swallowed the gulp of hot bile that came up in the back of her mouth.

Judi was coming apart inside her waistcoat. Anne pushed the thing that had been her sister away. It went into the crowd, deflated and insubstantial, and was caught as they surged forwards.

'Annie!'

The shout died as Judi's emptying clothes fell on the floor. Rivulets of yellow filled the grooves in the floor.

The dead were coming for her. She kicked out in imitation of martial arts movies, putting her hip behind the blow and landing her foot sideways into the hooligan's stomach. It did not give, but bones broke like sticks somewhere inside him. He was in the way of the rest of them.

The train was in a station. The single door beside her slid open, and she pushed herself out of the carriage. She stumbled on the steady stone of the platform, and put a hand out to stop herself slamming into the curved wall. She took the impact on her wrist.

'Mind the gap,' said an automated voice, 'mind the gap.'

The train moved out, its doors still open. She saw hateful faces pressed to the windows. Judi looked lost among so many dead people. Sparks flashed under the wheels. The noise of the train receded and went away.

She had stopped crying.

4

In the darkness of the Dream, he floated. His feeding frenzy exhausted, he was torpid, unable to pay attention to the rat in her maze. For the moment, he was the shaper of her world, the worker of her destinies; but he was too tired, too caught up in his own changes, to follow her progress as conscientiously as he should have done.

A swarm of ghosts gyred around him in a multiple helix, allowed some measure of self-determination by his preoccupation, furtively snatching their existence from his body and his mind. The strongest of Amelia Dorf's guests had already been processed and were settling into their new shapes, raw recruits in his army of phantoms. The lesser personalities – Clive, Anders, Amelia – were completely absorbed, gone forever unless he should choose to make the effort to reassemble them. They would do his bidding, more or less, and for the present they would have to cope with Anne.

Of course, she had her own ghosts, as she must almost be ready to realize. She would hardly have been able to get as far as she had already without a very strong image of the outlines of the world, of her own personal dream. She had even been able to effect an imperfect superimposition of her reality upon his own. He had come across very few others not of the Kind, with that strength of vision. He wondered whether it was a hereditary factor, passed down from her father, gained by him through osmosis. After all, he had been one of Ariadne's protégés.

Anne Nielson was an extraordinary woman, as he had known for years. Her father, when he came up before the Farnham Commission, had proved extraordinarily resilient, but he had still caved in, and then he had proved richly satisfying. More recently, the lesson had been reinforced by delicious, dangerous Judi. Even the son had had a tang to him, although he had proved surprisingly hard to digest at the end. It was a varied and satisfying meal, but the last dish would be the most exquisite, the most sustaining. He would need to fast, to recuperate, to change, before he would be ready to take her.

He had sifted through Judi's memory, had scooped into Anne's mind, but could find no traces of Ariadne. The girls had never met their father's one-time patron, had never even heard of her. Cam had a vague memory of a glamorous 'aunt', who had once taken a remote interest in his father, but it was no more than a shadow. He was disappointed somehow. Perhaps he should seek out Ariadne. By the standards of the Kind, their sole meeting had been almost yesterday. It was probably too soon to see if she had changed in her opinions of him. No, the best he could do was to fortify himself with the Nielson family, and wait a century or two. Everything would change in time. Things changed faster as time progressed, he had noticed in this dizzying century. He would meet Ariadne again. Things would be different between them.

Like an Elizabethan tickling the back of his throat with a peacock feather to induce vomiting so he would be able to face the next enormous course, he brought up another cloud of ghosts. Insignificant, meagre, thin and tasteless presences who could safely be ignored, who could safely be set free. Most of them came apart like butterflies in a whirlwind and were dispersed; some struggled for infinite moments, trying to summon up enough reserves of strength to achieve reality, before they were spent. A few tried vainly to coalesce into a hardier entity. Amelia fluttered against his lips, entreating to be let back in. He blew her away.

He had only sampled Cameron Nielson Sr during the hearings, then let the man live out a diminished, unproductive life. There were no more prizes for Cameron, no more Pulitzers, Critics' Circles, Nobels. And he had never taken home a statuette on Oscar night. He had had the playwright in his power, and been tempted to astonish the court and the television audiences by sucking him dry on the stand. But, rather than feed, he had just taken away Nielson's reputation, his genius, his worldly stature. He had even been rather touched by *The Rat Jacket,* that last flare of Cameron's talent, and had been amused by the author's recreation of his Hugh Farnham persona as the intellectual, bullying cop. Had he known that the man should be allowed to father his children? Or had he been too cautious, too frightened of his increasing visibility?

This was a strange century. He could no longer run his course in one place, and simply leave a continent to start again. The faces, manners and origins of notable men were too highly publicized. He could change his appearance, but not enough to become immediately unrecognizable. From now on, he would have to devote himself to private achievements. That would limit his amusements, but nevertheless he was confident in his ability to find purposes to suit him, enthusiasms to pursue, people to relish… It would be a long while before he turned into one of the Elders, hiding away in a living death, nurturing their effete Dreams, too fastidious to get involved with the tumult of humanity.

A wraith approached him, and latched on like a bat, suckling greedily from his surplus, desperate for a shape, for an identity. It was Judi; she had been seriously ruptured. He let her have her fill. She was important to him, a link with Anne, a shared ghost. He touched Judi's conscious memory, curious about the meeting on the train. She put up a token resistance, but, knowing that she only existed on his sufferance, opened her mind to him and let him prowl.

The train scene was fresh and painful inside Judi. His admiration was excited by Anne. She was picking up the knack. It was such a simple thing, to go against the consensus reality, but so few human beings could work up the willpower. Given time, she could learn to shape the Dream to her will. But, of course, he would not give her time. Hers would be an untried talent, an unfulfilled potential. Even in its protean state, however, it would make the business of feeding off her protracted and tiring. But incomparable.

He twisted, and descended in his dream.

He delved deeper in Judi's memories. He considered Anne as a child, as a schoolgirl, as a college student, as a would-be parent substitute, as a journalist. Judi had read practically everything her sister had ever written, including an uncharacteristic series of pieces on tin toy collecting, sofa beds and other arcane subjects published under a pseudonym (Angela Buonfiglia) taken from one of their father's plays. Further back, Judi had envied Anne her college boyfriend, had always tried to impress and amuse the older girl, had briefly tried to copy her clothes and food preferences, had longed to be asked to share her toys so that she could express her devotion through generosity. He tried to dilute Judi's images of her sister with objectivity, with his own observations, with Cam's tightly-guarded feelings, with the pathetic and stupid judgements of Clive, Amelia and a few of Amelia's guests, and with the slight tastes of her he had sampled at the entrance to the maze. He had less than a tenth of the jigsaw puzzle pieces, but even the fragments of a picture he was able to put together made him ache for Anne. He was motivated, he would have to exert himself…

His feet settled on the concrete of the tube platform. He reined in his multitudes, incorporating them. Even Judi. He was alone. He had seldom been more powerful this close to a change.

Anne had gone. There were no egresses in the featureless white tile walls. The tunnel was the only way out. She had chanced the darkness. She was a clever girl, to realize that there would never be another train in this station.

Already, the rails were softening, the circular tube was becoming ovoid. His presence froze the decay, but it would start again when he followed Anne into the tunnel. In time, the station would resolve itself, healing as invisibly as a wound in the deep of his brain. The overhead lights started going out, but that did not matter to him.

He stepped off the edge of the platform, onto the track. He knew which way his rat had bolted. Balancing on the dead third rail, he tightrope-walked after her, into the tunnel.

5

She knew she was not in a tube tunnel any more. The wall she had been feeling her way along in the dark had given out. There were no longer regularly spaced Christmas emergency lights to give an outline of her surroundings. The narrow path she was walking was not bordered by a shiny track. If she stopped to sit and rest, she could feel cold earth and a few scrubby patches of grass either side of the rough strip of asphalt.

Above her, around her, was total darkness. There was no ceiling, there were no walls. The darkness was infinite. She was out in the open somewhere, but there was no trace of light. No stars, no fireflies, no streetlamps, no fires.

There was no wind, but the still air was freezing. She wished she was wearing thick trousers rather than a skirt and tights. Preferably arctic survival gear. Walking through the chilly night was like wading through pampas grass. The cold was as sharp as a straight razor. She could not feel her toes. Her hands were deep in her coat pockets, fingering the last patches of warmth near her body. There was probably ice on her cheeks where she had been crying.

She kept on walking, picking up her feet and putting them down. Going somewhere.

It had not been Judi on the train. At least, it had not been all of Judi. Just as it had not been all of Nina in the wardrobe. Just ghosts.

But no one believes in ghosts really. Not M.R. James/Jacob Marley/white sheet-type ghosts. Ibsen-type ghosts, maybe. Not that she had ever actually read old Henryk, or seen *Ghosts*. Judi had one-upped her in the literacy game again.

Then there was a light ahead. Three indistinct lines, shaped like a soccer goal, silhouetting an oblong. It was some kind of a building, with the light source squarely behind it. She could make out the hard black edges, and see how the light diffused around them.

It was obvious that she would not like what she found there. That much she had picked up from the way things were going. But she was glad to have proof that she had not gone blind in the dark.

The building was further away, and bigger than she had guessed. She could not measure time that well any more, but it took a considerable while to get there.

This side of the building, there was a single, small light. It was above a door, above a weathered sign she could not read.

Knowing she would regret it, but knowing she had no choice, she took the door handle and turned…

Something sizzled above her, and hissed. She really was blinded, by the light this time. She turned away, into the darkness, electric blue and orange lines imprinted on her eyes. They faded quickly.

She looked upwards. There was a neon sign, flashing on and off, crackling slightly. It was familiar.

SAM'S, it said in big letters, BAR-B-Q AND GRILL.

She pushed the door open, and went in.

6

Worlds away, across an ocean, it was late afternoon, time to take hot chocolate to an invalid. Outside, it was just dark, and there was thick, Christmassy snow on the ground. She had put up decorations all over the house, although the invalid could only get to two or three rooms. The tree was in his bedroom, and she had made paper angels for the bathroom. She had put fake snow and a silver star on the mirrored door of the medicine cupboard. She had finally arranged with the agency for a substitute nurse, a single girl who needed the triple overtime, to take her place over the holiday. But she would be back before the New Year, doing her best to make the old man's last months mess-free and painless. Tonight, she would sit up with her patient in his study and watch *It's a Wonderful Life* on television. It was on every Christmas, and was one of her favourite films. She remembered seeing it many times as a child, and was looking forward, after several years, to rediscovering its pleasures. She found it hard to believe that her patient had ever worked in Hollywood, had known people like Jimmy Stewart and Gloria Grahame. There were signed and dedicated photographs of them in his collection, unframed and unsorted after some long-ago house-moving. Also, photographs and letters from names she knew: Lauren Bacall, Tennessee Williams, Alistair

Cooke, Arthur Kennedy, Paul Robeson, Jean-Paul Sartre, Cole Porter (another invalid), Lee Strasberg, Adlai Stevenson, Elia Kazan. She wondered whether they all had letters and pictures signed by him. As soon as she entered the study, she knew that he had given up. He was slumped into his chair, his blanket on the floor, a paperback book by his foot, spine-broken, pages down. She tried to find a pulse. Nothing. He was gone.

7

It was the original Broadway production, with most of the cast that had gone on to be in the film. She had walked on somewhere in the third act, after Sam's stroke. Lee J. Cobb would be sitting the rest of the play out in his dressing room while the other characters revolved around the void left in their lives, in the centre of the play, behind the bar. His passing out of the drama on the graveyard shift was so complete that Cobb never even came back to take a curtain call.

Anne slipped into a booth, and sat as far away from the action as possible. A waitress brought her a cup of coffee. She was practically an extra, having already chipped in with her five lines, and was just trying to create an illusion of a real Bar-B-Q and Grill by looking busy in the background. She was young, and pretty in a lipsticky '50s way, but made up to look sluttish and bedraggled. Up close, Anne could see the panstick make-up and exaggerated black patches under her eyes. The coffee was cold tea, tart and nasty, but Anne sipped it anyway. She wanted to remain inconspicuous.

Downstage, Sam's World War Two buddy and sidekick, played by Eli Wallach, was trying and failing to dispense Sam-style worldly wisdom and advice to the bar-owner's son-in-law. He, played by a young Martin Landau, was a shell-shocked, psychologically impotent Korean War veteran who had just discovered that his wife (Kim Hunter) had been shacked up with Maish (Marlon Brando) while he was in a prisoner-of-war camp. In an earlier scene, he had shown off the automatic he had brought home with him from the army, lovingly unwrapping it from its oily cloth, caressing it like the woman who was lost, seeking a response from its cold metal that he could never get from his flesh. Without Sam to calm him down, the Landau character was going to shoot someone. He was already working himself up to the boil.

Landau had his back to the black space that replaced the fourth wall of the bar, and was taking a rest. His face had gone blank, while Wallach did the acting for both of them. Anne wondered whether Stella Adler would have approved.

'It ain't so bad, Johnny,' said Wallach. 'Broads. Who can figure 'em? Maish ain't such a bad guy.'

'He wuz draft-exempted. Me an' my brudder goes to Korea, an' get tortured by the slants, an' good ol' Maish sits on his ass in a gas station.'

In the movie, Maish had sat on his 'setter' in a gas station.

'Only 'cause of his leg, Johnny,' said Wallach. 'Maish got a bum leg from when he was a kid. You don't notice it so much 'cause he got a special kind of way of walking that covers up, but he couldn't pass no army physical. You want a shot?'

'Yeah. A shot.'

Anne's father had written several different endings. She had seen the manuscripts. Landau could shoot Maish, his wife Angie, Wallach by mistake or himself. In the out-of-town try-outs, he shot Maish; on Broadway, he shot Angie; and in the movie, he shot Wallach and himself. The movie ending was a compromise. The Breen Office and the Catholic Legion of Decency had not really wanted Landau to shoot anyone: they liked Bing Crosby films about singing priests, not modern American tragedies. Warner Brothers had stood up to the censors, forcing them to back down by waving a fistful of Broadway reviews in their faces, and then told Dad he could not shoot the girl at the end. Therese Colt, the politically acceptable substitute for Kim Hunter, had to be alive to go off with Brando at the fade-out.

A stage manager put a cool jazz record on the jukebox, and everyone settled down to wait for Brando to come on again. Maish had good news; he had just sold his first story to *Atlantic Monthly* and quit his grease monkey job. Everyone else had bad news; Sam, Maish's surrogate father and everybody's favourite wailing post, was in the hospital with his third heart attack. He had not bothered to mention the first two to anyone; he had been too busy serving up advice and worldly wisdom between his steak specials and famous salads. This was the big scene, Brando's big scene, the one she had heard about all her life.

The jazz was a slow, sexy trumpet solo, high and piercing. Betty, the waitress with higher billing, began to dance alone, trying to distract everyone from their worries in her own way. She had been hired by Sam in the first act, even though he knew all about her backstreet abortion (jailbird ex-husband, in the film). Betty was played with a wobbly New York accent, from Rottingdean to the Bronx via Beverly Hills, by Victoria Page.

Anne had not seen her mother in three years; and she had only seen her as she was here in old movies and photographs. She was the Hollywood Star going legitimate on Broadway, with a terminated contract back at Paramount and an egghead boyfriend. She was married to the Mayor of some Californian retirement colony these days, and still occasionally did guest appearances on television shows about geriatric detectives. She always played the private eye's old flame who was in trouble, and she still paused for applause every time she made an entrance.

But here was Vicky, her mother, younger than she was. She looked a lot like Judi. Under the arc lights, she was even made up like Judi. She moved sensuously, showing off her dance training, carried away by the music, caressing herself in a way that would have to be toned down for the movie. She started to hum – the critics had been ready to pounce, but Dad had not written a song in for his then-fiancée – muttering under the tune. Anne was close enough to realize that she was just counting time, 'one-two-three-four, one-two-three-four', but to someone in the auditorium, she seemed to be expressing the inexpressible, summing up the hopeless yearnings of all the night people…

Then Brando came on.

He had worked himself up in the wings. One night, he had got himself into such a state while thinking through the offstage bit where he quit his dead-end job that he had laid out a stagehand who had spoken to him. It was just the sort of thing Maish Johnson would have done. He shouldered his way through the door, and almost danced across the stage, giving the impression of a limp but also covering it up. Every part of his body was in motion. He never just stood still on the stage. He was a pinball, bouncing off the fixed actors, lighting up the beacons in Dad's text. Anne was astonished. She forgot herself, and felt, for the first time, the full power of her father at the height of his talent. She wished she could talk to him again, tell him that he had not lived pointlessly, that he had set down something which would last…

Brando grabbed Anne's mother by the waist from behind, and waltzed with her as the solo peaked and died. Then, she was dismissed from centre stage and the star was left to his scene. From the elation of his entrance he segued into puzzlement, as Maish was unable to believe that Sam was not at his usual spot behind the bar. Wallach tried to tell him about Sam, but Brando would not listen. He had to tell his news to someone. He hopped from stool to stool (Anne could see the legendary sweat pouring off him) and finally settled next to Landau.

'I guess old Sam meant a lot to all of us,' said Wallach deliberately, aware that no one was watching him. 'More than we ever counted on.'

'Yeah,' said Landau, back still to the darkness, 'I hope he pulls through.'

'Oh sure he'll pull through, Johnny. Whaddya say, Maish? Sam, he's indestructible. Like Superman. Back there at Anzio...'

'Can it,' snapped Brando, slipping into his big speech like Glenn Miller going into a trombone solo. 'Sam was just a guy like the rest of us. He hadda take a shit...' (it had been a 'crap' in the movie, and that had been a Hollywood first) '...he hadda wash his face. He drank cups of coffee like Brazil was goin' outta business. He was...'

...and so it went on. One critic had compared the speech to Mark Antony's eulogy, but even Dad thought that was too strong. The extra waitress, unnoticed, broke into tears as she did every night. She lost her part completely, but everyone was focused on Brando. He was talking about Sam, but he was also talking about God. Her father was talking about gods and leaders and heroes and politicians, sermonizing on their greatness but saying that he did not need them any more. Brooks Atkinson, the *New York Times* drama critic, wrote that it was about Franklin D. Roosevelt. Arthur Miller said it was about Eugene O'Neill, whose bar was just down the street from Sam's. The Farnham Commission had called it the 'throw away your crutches' speech, and suggested that it was about Lenin or Trotsky (they were not sure which). Anne found it easy to forget the missing wall, the cold tea, the painted faces. This was reality. More real than anything that had happened to her since Nina fell asleep on her shoulder in the taxi on the way to St John's Wood.

A jangle cut through Brando's tirade, and he left off. There was a pause. Audiences were too awed even to applaud. The ringing was not at all like a real telephone. It was just a sound effect. Wallach, also in tears but concealing them like a professional, scooped up the receiver from behind the bar.

'Sam's Bar-B-Q and Grill,' he said. Then, he nodded and 'uh-huhed' for thirty seconds. Brando stepped back into a shadow, forcibly diverting audience attention to the other actor.

Wallach put the phone down. He looked at everybody. It could have been the longest pause in American theatrical history. People who saw the play on its first run remembered it as lasting for a full minute. No one ever managed to wrest enough attention off the stage to time it. No one breathed.

'It's Sam,' said Wallach. 'He just bought the farm.'

Anne's mother started sobbing uncontrollably, and had to be comforted by Jed (Howard Da Silva), the stammering vacuum cleaner salesman. It was a fine display of histrionic hysteria, but Brando topped it, stepped on it, destroyed it, by knocking back the shot Wallach had poured for Landau and pulling apart a stale doughnut.

Anne realized that she had misheard Wallach's line. He had not said that Sam had just bought the farm, he had said that *Cam* had just bought the farm.

Cam? He would have been only two years old. In the '50s, Cam had been her father's name.

'He made this place, I guess,' said Wallach. 'It won't seem the same going on without him. I guess I'll sell up. I could move to Florida.'

'No,' shouted Brando, hitting the bar so hard that all the props on it shook. 'No. When a guy gets a Nobel Prize, it means something. There ain't no committee that can take that away from him.'

Landau got up. Everybody had forgotten him. He had been working himself back into his part. His eyes gleamed with Satanic fury, his slicked hair was mussed into horn shapes. Cuckold's horns, Devil's horns. It was a neat trick. He had his gun out.

Mother screamed again – the Betty role really was a drag, Anne realized – and Da Silva hugged her.

'Yeah,' sneered Landau, 'and nobody's takin' Angie away from me. Specially not you, Mr Draft-Exempt-Gas-Jockey Hemingway!'

Wallach leaned over the bar, trying to dampen Landau's anger, but it was no good. He was spitting his lines out, his still-sharp

Brooklyn accent cutting into Brando's tortured presence. He waved the gun wildly.

'You and Angie thought you were God-damned smart, huh? Poor old Johnny Boy was havin' his toenails pulled by the slants, an' you had it real easy. You gotta way with words, Maish, but you don't know what dyin' is like. You seen it in the movies, you read it in books. Well, here it is happenin' to you. Dyin'. Cam died. He was a fink and a squealer, and he died. Now, you…'

It was time for Kim Hunter's spectacularly unfortunate entrance. Landau's safety catch was off. The door Anne had come through opened. She leaned out of her booth to see Angie come in. There was no one.

'Angie!'

She turned back to the action. Landau was talking to her.

'Get outta here, Angie,' shouted Brando, 'he's drunk.'

She was standing up, alone in her part of the stage. She did not have any lines. Everyone else had got out of the way. She looked at Landau's gun – it was not a prop – and then at his face. He had turned into Skinner.

'Angie,' he said in Landau's voice. 'This is what dyin' is like.'

Then he fired.

8

It had been a long night for Maish. A lifetime ago, he had shambled into Sam's for a cup of mocha java and a cruller. He had been newly-born then, but with a set of memories as deceitful as Eve's belly button. He had talked, many times, about a previous life, but he had no pictures in his head to go with the words in his mouth. His stories about Angie and the gas station owner and his ambitions as a writer could have been second-hand, alibis learned by rote to cover up someone else's crimes. He thought he might have lived before, he kept being haunted by that queer sensation Sam called *déjà vu*, but he was aware that his previous lives were identical, or almost identical, to his current experiences. It was a whole lot weirder than flying saucers or the search for Bridey Murphy.

He was supposed to be a gas station attendant, but he could not imagine what a gas pump or even an automobile looked like. He was a writer, but his vocabulary was limited to the comparatively few words he had been given to speak. In his mind, he felt uncomfortable even using the phrases he could pick up from the others in the bar. He knew that he was supposed to have badly broken his leg when he was a kid, to have made love to Angie and Betty and many other nameless girls, to have written an as-yet unpublished autobiographical novel about his time with a streetgang. He knew these things, but only as simple facts. The mass of tiny details he could recall about the bar and the people he met there accounted for the only rounded, complete, satisfying experiences he had ever had.

It was just like Jed's speech. Sam's was the only real place in the world, the only place where anything counted. Everything else was a shadowland where life was dreamed not lived. 'Th-th-this is where you puh-pay for your sins,' Jed always said, 'not in church, in Sam's Bar-B-Q and Grill.'

A minute or so ago he had said that even Sam had to take a shit. So how come he had eaten doughnuts and drank coffee all evening without having to use the Men's Room? Deep down, Maish knew there was something wrong with his life.

He had been caught in this place forever, only coming to life in the well-lit arena of the Bar-B-Q and Grill. Everything else was dark and skeletal, like an unremembered dream. Everything that had happened this evening, that would happen in the next few minutes, was familiar, planned, tedious. He knew that this world had been abandoned by its Creator, but he was still following the vagrant god's orders.

Somehow, it was different this time. The old man was dead, really dead. He had not just been carried out of the door into the darkness never to be seen again. Somewhere outside the bar, outside the world, the man had really died.

When he had been talking about Sam, he had not been thinking about what he was saying, the words came automatically. But he had been thinking, sensing how different it was this time. There was no more *déjà vu*. He was free. He did not know what freedom meant yet, but it was marvellous and frightening. Maybe being free was the same as being dead.

It was clear now. He had seen Johnny shoot Angie many times, an impossible number of times. He had taken the still-hot gun away from the man, had cradled the dying woman, had spoken the speech given him, had paused for the darkness to fall on them all. There had been variations – slight differences of placing, of phrasing, of feeling – but each time the actions had been basically identical.

This time it was different. There was no tyrant god to make him stand by and watch Angie, the woman he loved but had never really met, be killed. Things could be changed.

'Angie,' said Johnny, taking a shaky aim, 'this is what dyin' is like.'

As Johnny pulled the trigger, Maish heaved himself forwards. His bum leg gave out, but he fell into the line of fire. He felt the push of the bullet going into his chest before he heard the amazingly loud crack of the gunshot. His shin hurt more than his broken ribs, his punctured heart.

There was no one to overpower Johnny, to take the gun away from him, but the young man seized up as soon as he had fired, falling into a statue state rather than go against the script. On his knees, real blood soaking his shirt, Maish looked up at Angie. It was not Angie, it was some other woman, but that did not matter. He did not know what to say. He opened his mouth, but only blood came out.

Never again.

Never again would he limp, dance, dream aloud, drink, eat, hit Jed, lean on the bar, listen to Sam's advice, play with his switchblade, try to get a game of cards together, burst out his good news, be shattered by the bad news, watch Angie get shot, talk to the darkness, start all over again.

This was what dying was like.

9

For Angela Buonfiglia, the next five years started badly. But things got better.

The homicide lieutenant, Joe Hollis, took an immediate dislike to Johnny. He had been in Korea too, and knew that Johnny was one of the GIs who had admitted under torture that the United Nations forces had been involved in war crimes. He dug up the spurious confession that Johnny had put his name to. Hollis pursued the case with a ferocity that surprised his jaded colleagues and unearthed a witness – a patron of Sam's who had gone unnoticed that evening – who testified against Johnny. He had overheard the young veteran swear to get even with Maish Johnson, and claimed to have seen Johnny take a deliberate aim before gunning the man down.

Angela managed to get her divorce through before Johnny's execution, but felt obliged to visit her ex-husband on Death Row. He just sat grinning from behind the bars, playing solitaire but never winning. She went to too many funerals. Her father's brought out the whole neighbourhood for an extravagant Italian-Irish-Jewish wake that went on for days, while Johnny and Maish were laid to rest in scarily similar, sparsely attended grey-day ceremonies, one inside a prison, one outside. Aside from her, the only person at all three ceremonies was Joe Hollis, who shook her hand at Johnny's burial and vanished from her life.

Angela made enough out of the sale of Sam's Bar-B-Q and Grill to set herself up in a small business in the garment centre. At first, she simply busied herself with the accounting and retail side and bought in stock from Europe, but gradually she discovered a talent for designing patterned scarves and blouses. Her signature became a brand name, and she was able to put her prices up. 'Design by Angela' began to mean as much as 'Gowns by Ariadne'. Audrey Hepburn wore 'Angela' clothes, and Princess Grace, Peggy Lee and Jacqueline Bouvier Sinatra. When Elvis Presley and John Wayne turned up on *The Tonight Show* with identical 'Angela' ties, male adornment suddenly ceased to be considered unmanly.

She opened an 'Angela's' in Washington DC, then San Francisco, then Chicago, then everywhere. Her designs were featured in *Vogue*, exhibited at art galleries, imitated by others. She had a small love affair, with C.D. Broome – a college graduate who thought he wanted to be a novelist – but it ended messily. Tired of New York and its ghosts, and buoyed by a ridiculously large fee from a Hollywood studio that had used her designs under the titles of a glossy romantic comedy, she took a year off to travel around the United States. At the end of that, she settled in New Orleans.

She did a quarter as many designs, and sold them for four times as much. During Mardi Gras, she had a cliché meeting cute with a French-speaking aristocrat, the owner of a prestigious but popular restaurant. On the night that they made love for the first time, she told him about Johnny and Maish, and he told her about the homosexual experiences he had had as a younger man. She understood about him, he understood about her, and, three weeks later, they agreed to marry...

9

For Angela Buonfiglia, the next five years started badly. And things got worse.

The homicide lieutenant, Barry Erskine, took an immediate liking to Johnny. He had been in Korea too, and while he was overseas his-own wife had divorced him to marry her piano teacher. He had often thought of shooting them and trying to get away with it. Erskine pursued the case with a ferocity that surprised his jaded colleagues, and unearthed a witness – a patron of Sam's who had gone unnoticed that evening – who testified for Johnny. He had overheard Maish threaten the young veteran, and claimed to have seen the dead man pull out a switchblade before Johnny drew his gun.

Johnny stayed in jail for three weeks. No charges against him were ever brought. He was even given his gun back, with a note to remind him that he would have to renew his permit in the next few months. Angela went alone to Maish's pauper's funeral, and with Johnny to Sam's. She was surprised how few of her father's friends and patrons bothered to turn out for that dismal day. Fortunately, she was able to wear a thick veil. When Johnny had found out she had been to Maish's funeral, he had worked her face over. Erskine turned up at the wake and exchanged nasty jokes with Johnny. He looked her over, grinning like a fiend, before leaving, and warned her to stay out of trouble.

It turned out that Sam's habitual generosity had got him into debt, and the Bar-B-Q and Grill had to be sold off to settle up with his many creditors. The first night that Angela spent with Johnny in their walk-up apartment after he got out of jail ended up with him breaking three of her ribs. She was grateful that he was unable to rape her, but knew he would think of something to do to make her sorry. Eventually, he found out how sickened she was by his nailless toes, and started forcing her to massage his feet. He liked to reminisce about his time as a POW, and made up ever more elaborate stories of torture and degradation.

The couple could not get by on Johnny's disability pension, and Angela had to get a job as a waitress. Of course, the owner of the diner that had replaced Sam's took her on, and she put up with ridiculous hours, sweatshop wages, groping patrons, and an infernally filthy kitchen with all the resignation of the justifiably damned. She had a nasty little affair with Nino Kenyon, one of the cooks, that broke up when someone told him about what Johnny had done to Maish. After a while, the patrons did not even bother to grope her.

Johnny's feet got worse, and she suspected him of opening old wounds with broken beer bottles while she was at work. He cultivated new scabs and scars, and had to hobble around the apartment on crutches. He rarely went out, but followed the televised HUAC hearings avidly. Korea had not been enough for him. He often talked about how much he would like to go out to Hollywood and shoot some Commies. When the news came through that Orson Welles had hanged himself rather than name names for Hugh Farnham, Johnny celebrated with a three bottle binge. He wrote to newspapers and politicians, naming prominent and obscure citizens as card-carrying Reds. He received a thank you letter from the desk of Hugh Farnham, but eventually Detective Erskine came round and told him to lay off.

Erskine told Angela that Johnny was becoming an

embarrassment, and ought to get some sort of psychoanalysis. Angela barely made enough to feed the both of them and pay the rent, and federal subsidies for veterans' medical care had just been slashed by the McCarran administration, so she had to ignore the advice. Often, she wondered what her father would have said. One morning, after work, she came home and found that Johnny had taken his gun out of its drawer and shot off three of his toes.

10

Angela dreamed. Even tucked in comfortably next to Didier in the big old safe bed in the big old safe house she could only think of as a mansion, Angela dreamed. In the morning, she could never remember where her night thoughts had taken her. Didier could extemporize forever his dreams, their amusing quirkiness, their disorientating surrealism, but she suffered from instant amnesia. But she knew that she did dream, of Something, of Somewhere, of Someone…

'Perhaps, Angel,' Didier said one morning, 'it is you who are dreamed of…'

That kind of pseudo-insight was not at all like Didier. It was the sort of thing she would expect from one of Rod Serling's *Twilight Zone* introductions. Immediately, her husband slipped back into character, and started pressing exactly the right buttons. She was won over, and, their elaborate breakfast forgotten, they decided that Didier did have an hour or two to spare before he was needed in his office…

Later, alone in the newly-unmade bed, Angela thought again about her dreams. Several of her friends were in analysis, and she knew from them that dreams could be important as a key to your character. Of course, she did not need analysis. Everybody she knew would cite her as an absolute model of fulfilment and balance. Perhaps, she thought, she was not very good at being happy. Perhaps that was why she needed to dream, to fulfil a deep-seated and perfectly natural desire to have some misery in her life.

Her husband, former homosexual or not, was as flawless a part of her world as a robot designed to act like Rossano Brazzi or Gregory Peck. He accorded her all the reverence due to a Victorian angel in the kitchen, and never disapproved of her need to have compartments of her life separate from him. Her career was important to her, and she had kept it going after the marriage. And yet, it did seem strange that doodles which came out of her unconscious when her mind was at its emptiest magically turned into unimaginable amounts of money.

In her sunken marble bath – a marvellously stupid luxury she was almost ashamed of – she thought about the symmetries of her life. She was entering middle-age with the body she had had as a twenty-year-old. Her financial security was assured for a lifetime. Their doctor saw no reason why they could not have children if they did not put it off too long, and she was tempted by the prospect of motherhood. She was never alone, except when she wanted to be; she was never bored, except when she wanted to be.

…and who could ask for anything more.

Later that summer, they started going to the movies like teenagers. The film that made the most impression on her was *North by Northwest,* a chocolate box-coloured romantic thriller with Cary Grant and Eva Marie Saint. She had found other Alfred Hitchcock films boring and cynical, but this was, on the whole, lovely. Grant was charming, but she was also attracted to James Mason, who was a civilized villain and had many of the qualities she liked in Didier. In one scene, she had a delightful buzz of recognition, realizing that she had designed one of the scarves worn by Saint. But there was a snake in Eden, a disturbing presence among the thrills and comedy. One actor – the man who played the villain's male secretary (and former lover?), the man who trod on Grant's hand as he dangled off the faces of Mount

Rushmore in the climax – frightened her more than any monster in any horror movie she had ever seen.

If there was a cast list at the end of the film, the projectionist closed the theatre curtains over it, and so Angela did not get the actor's name. Didier, a film addict who often sneaked out of his business in the afternoons to catch matinees of war films and Westerns she did not want to see, could not remember the name of the actor who played the secretary, but thought he had been in *Pork Chop Hill*, playing a soldier in Korea.

Korea. Of course. That was who the actor reminded her of. Johnny. He was older, smoother, less explosive, but the wide, sneering lips and scarily glowing eyes were the same.

Oddly, unnervingly, the actor turned up again within a week. On a summer re-run of *The Twilight Zone*. Angela did not really like the Serling show, but found it affected her, unlike a lot of the network pap television had been churning out since the industry switched from live television in New York to filmed series from Hollywood. The episode was a weird Western, 'Mr Denton on Doomsday', with Dan Duryea as a drunk given miraculous gunslinging abilities by a travelling salesman. The scary actor loitered around the cramped studio barroom in sinister black leather outfits, sadistically tormenting Duryea. In the inevitable shoot-out, the man who frightened her was shot in the hand by the suddenly superskilled Duryea, but she could not watch any more and had Didier turn off their receiver. While he was brushing his teeth, she got out the *TV Guide* and found out the actor's name.

It was Martin Landau, and that did not mean anything to her.

There was another face that bothered her whenever it turned up on TV or in the newspapers. Hugh Farnham's. But half of America was frightened of Hugh Farnham. She had signed a few petitions against HUAC once, at the prompting of Maish Johnson, but had not really followed the hearings. However, like everyone else, she had been shocked when the stories about Farnham came out. The papers called him 'The Modern Bluebeard' and were loudly asking why the FBI had not tracked him down yet. The scandal sheets reckoned he was in South America with all the Nazis. The father of one of his young victims had become something of a celebrity by devoting huge sums to the search for Hugh Farnham. Even President Stevenson had spoken out against his former opponent, and made an unprecedented top level intervention in law enforcement to hurry up the capture of this vicious killer. Farnham was a Monster, everyone agreed.

Martin Landau, Hugh Farnham, and Johnny. They all had something to do with her somehow.

That night, while Didier slept, she thought of that evening in Sam's Bar-B-Q and Grill. The evening that Johnny shot Maish, the evening that her father died. It was the most vivid memory she had. Sometimes, she thought it was the only evening she had ever truly lived through. Since then, she had been only half the woman she used to be. Perhaps less than half.

As summer turned into fall, she started to remember her dreams. Johnny was in them, and Maish, and her father. And her sister. But Angela did not have a sister, much less a sister with clothes and hair like an alien princess from a cheap science fiction film. She dreamed of London, a city she could recognize but had never been to. And there was a man in her dreams who frightened her more than Martin Landau, Hugh Farnham and Johnny rolled into one. He had scaled skin, and a lizard's tongue. Inside, he was a dragon and she had to kill him before he consumed her.

Suddenly, she dropped her design career. She decided it was flimsy and insubstantial. She found herself talking less and less, even to Didier. Her husband remained attentive, and even left her alone when she was in a terminally uncommunicative mood. Sometimes, she tried to annoy him, to hurt him. But he could not be moved. He was too perfect.

One morning, alone in the mansion, she decided that living the shadow of a life was not enough. She was well into the second bottle of pills, washing them down with tasteless vodka, before sleep enveloped her.

She had not bothered to leave a note, realizing that there was really no one left behind to read it.

It had been a nice dream, but only that…

10

Angela dreamed. Even exhausted next to Johnny in the sick-smelling bed in the sick-smelling walk-up she could only think of as her purgatory, Angela dreamed. In the morning, she could never remember where her night thoughts had taken her. She only knew that she woke up as worn-out and tired as when she went to sleep. But she knew that she did dream, of Something, of Somewhere, of Someone...

When she got out of bed, Angela felt like something the cat had sicked up. As usual after the graveyard shift, she had slept well into the afternoon. Last night had been a bad one; *another* bad one. She had a waitress' ache lodged permanently in the small of her back, and a couple of its children were budding under her shoulder blades. According to Betty, who delighted in everybody's afflictions, her knees and ankles would be next. She hated working all night, but the extra twelve cents an hour helped her keep treading water. It was less immediately strenuous than the three-to-ten shift, but a good deal more soul-eroding. Nobody happy eats after midnight.

Johnny was sleeping too, in front of the tiny television set, his ruined feet up on their special stool. She saw that he had been punishing himself again, and bled in his bandages. Orange and brown discolourations marred the linen that had been pristine white when she left for work. On the mantel over the bricked-up fireplace was the jam jar in which he kept his pickled toes. He still claimed that had been an accident. In her tatty robe, she tidied up around him, emptying ashtrays, clearing up glasses.

He had had his friend the cop over last night. They had bitched and griped and watched television together. Johnny liked to threaten her with Barry Erskine. 'Angel,' he would say, 'if you leave, I'll have Erskine shoot you down just like I shot down your boyfriend.' The cop had tried to feel her ass a couple of times, but he did not have the balls to do anything with Johnny around. After all, everybody remembered who was the killer in this apartment.

The TV was still on, a news show. Hugh Farnham sat in a studio talking about Cuba with a fawning woman. Johnny still had a letter from his desk. When Pat McCarran stepped down and Nixon moved up, Farnham would be in line for the Vice-Presidential ticket. Nixon and Farnham. Angela did not think she would bother to vote. There was film of Havana, with US Marines on the streets, peasants in the fields and Battista waving on a balcony. The commentator talked about the hanging of Ernesto Guevara, and the trial of Fidel Castro.

'Yeah,' grunted Johnny, waking up, 'stick it to the Reds!'

After the piece on Cuba, Farnham talked about the new HUAC hearings, under the chairmanship of virgin Congressman Cohn. He would not be taking part this time, but he was lending his full support to 'those who would help our nation purify itself'. Johnny opened a bottle of beer with his teeth, and cheered as the froth bubbled over. 'Oughta be hung like dogs,' he snarled, 'goddamn pinkos!' The commentator read out a list of actors, soldiers, directors, writers, state officials and sportsmen who would be subpoenaed. One of them was Marlon Brando, whom Angela had always liked.

'Lousy commies! Oughta line 'em up outside the Kremlin an' open up on 'em with tommy guns. Lousy Ivans oughta be put down like *roaches*!'

Angela felt woozy, and nauseous. She backed away from Johnny and wrestled with the bathroom door.

'Whassamatter, Angel?'

Johnny never used to call her 'Angel'. It had been 'Angie' once. She thought of herself as 'Angela', but nobody ever called her that.

'I feel...'

How did she feel? Sick, but not quite. She cramped into the closet-sized bathroom, and crouched by the bath. Clothes hung around her from ropes stretched across the room. She had spasms in her stomach.

There was a Frankenstein Monster clumping about outside. Johnny had got up, and was moving around the room. Things fell over. Johnny swore.

Angela pushed aside a curtain of drying nylon hose and was sick in the bath. She heaved up what looked like orange frogspawn. It was like spitting a cloud of tiny pebbles that rattled on the backs of her teeth on the way out. They were pills. She could read an unfamiliar brand name on the less-dissolved ones.

For a moment, she thought she was going crazy. Then, she realized it was the other way around. Crazy was going her. Her crazy was going. It was coming together in her head.

'Angel,' shouted Johnny, banging on the door with a crutch. Everything shook. 'Lemme in!'

She did not ache any more. Despite her recent vomiting spell, she did not feel empty any more.

Looking in the freckled mirror, she found herself changed. She was not younger or healthier or better-looking, but she was at least herself again.

'Angel, you wanna keep some teeth? Open up!'

The apartment was not next to the elevated railway, but it shook as if a train were going by. Bottles fell out of the cabinet over the sink. Talcum powder rose from a smashed jar like tear-gas from a canister. Damp clothes flopped on the floor. The bathroom, always small, appeared to shrink to the size of a coffin.

She stood up and wiped her face on a towel.

'Angel?' Johnny was whining now, pathetic rather than threatening. She knew she could take him.

'Angela!' His voice was changing. It was darker, deeper, nastier.

'In a minute,' she said.

She found her clothes on a chair. Her real clothes. She got dressed. Johnny had stopped banging.

There was a frosted glass window in the bathroom. If you opened it, you could see the vacant lot next door and the building beyond it. Now, she knew, there was none of that there.

'Angela!' He was seriously annoyed.

She opened the bathroom door.

'Angela?'

'That's not my name.'

'Of course,' he said, straightening up, 'and Johnny is not mine.'

Skinner did not need the crutches.

11

There were still leftover bits and pieces of the walk-up apartment dotted about the place, but it was a strip-lit open-plan office now. On Skinner's desk was a presentation case containing Johnny's Korean medals, and one of the GI issue Mickey Spillane paperbacks he had got his kicks out of. Perched on the central heating unit, Anne saw the jar with Johnny's three missing toes floating in it, and a framed picture of Sam and his daughter outside the Bar-B-Q and Grill. The photograph was fading fast, like an Instamatic snapshot in reverse. The faces had already gone. Behind her, there was no bathroom, just a rank of filing cabinets.

The office had no windows, and the only door was fifty yards away on the other side of the room. To reach it, she would have to negotiate a maze of partitioned-off desks, potted plants and photocopiers. A few of the magazines she did work for had places like this, and she tried to avoid spending time in them. Apart from the Monster and her, the office was empty. There were Christmas cards hanging on a clothesline on the wall, and a few perishing balloons huddled in a corner.

The desk was between her and Skinner, but he was tall enough to step over it. He looked no more dangerous than a typical editor.

'You know what they say about werewolves,' she said, 'there's always a tree between you and it, but never a tree between it and you.'

'I'm not a werewolf.'

'No, but you are a Monster, right?'

'I suppose so.' He smiled with his mouth, just faintly. His face was anaesthetized. He could have been wearing a tissue paper death mask. It was like the old *Mission: Impossible* show; she expected him to peel off his face to reveal Martin Landau underneath.

'Anne,' he said, 'may I call you by your first name?'

'Sure.'

'Angela?'

The name was like a slap in the face. But she rolled with it, and came back, still sure of who she was.

'No, not Angela. A nice try, though.'

'You mustn't hold it against me.' He sat down in a swivel chair, and pushed himself back from the desk. He knitted his fingers behind his neck, and looked up at her. He was totally relaxed, which she knew was supposed to make her nervous. She looked down at him, not flinching.

'Don't you feel bad about Angela?'

'How do you mean?'

'Well, in a very real sense, you are responsible for wasting her. You took the pills.'

'Oh, *that* Angela. Well, it wasn't real…'

'I doubt if that argument would go down very well with her. She had a great deal of self-determination, you know. She was independent of you.'

'What about the other Angela?'

'Just the same. A little less aware, perhaps, but just as valid a personality. Incidentally, what makes you think that were only two Angelas?'

'Skinner, there wasn't even one. We both know that. My Dad made her up. And he didn't give her that much. A big scene in the first act, a walk-on in the second, and getting shot in the end.

She's supposed to be having this big affair with Maish, but they're only on stage together when she's being killed. All the rest comes from you...'

'And you. Don't underestimate yourself. I've never been to New Orleans.'

'Okay, and me too. A bit of Dad, a bit of you, a bit of me, a bit of Kim Hunter, a bit of Therese Colt, a bit of Angela Pleasence. That doesn't make a real person.'

'Why not?'

'Because they don't, that's why. They should have kept Kim Hunter for the movie, though. But she was blacklisted by then.'

'What's that got to do with anything?'

'You're the blacklist expert aren't you?'

The skin around his eyes crinkled, and set in little folds. She knew he had not expected her to figure it out.

'You don't change that much, Skinner.'

'You're sharp.'

'And you were Hugh Farnham?'

'Once.'

'Before that?'

'Oh, you don't really want to know. Lots of names. I can't be expected to remember all of them.'

'Any famous ones?'

'A few.'

'Going back a long way?'

'That's right.'

'You're a vampire?'

'No,' he chuckled to himself. 'Well, not very often.'

She was fed up with hanging around exchanging small talk with an inhuman mass murderer. But Skinner was enjoying himself.

'Do sit down,' he said. 'Would you like some coffee?'

'Sure. If there's any going.'

She sat in a chair and wheeled it up to the desk. It was not really comfortable, and she experimented, sitting with her legs crossed, uncrossed, sprawled apart. The backrest and the arms were too low. She settled for a relatively painless perching position.

'Black with sugar?'

'Do you know everything?'

'Not everything. Just enough to get by. Judi has a good memory. She knows how you drink your coffee.'

'She did. I've cut out sugar for the last two years.'

'Okay, so I look like an idiot. I won't try that kind of Win Friends and Influence People trick again.'

He pressed a buzzer on his desk, leaned forward, and said something in an unrecognizable, sibilant language into the intercom. Seconds later, a bell like a microwave oven went off behind Anne. She turned in her seat, and saw a blinking red light above a cupboard door.

'It's a dumb waiter.'

She opened the door, and reached in to bring out a paper cup of coffee. It was instant, but hot and tasty. The first swallow scalded her tongue, and she was careful after that.

'It's been a long time, Anne. A long time since I came across anyone as self-possessed as you are. You've held out much longer than I expected.'

'Thank you.'

'I don't pay compliments, I make statements of fact. You are a most capable young woman.'

'I know how to fix a plug.'

'I don't doubt it. Judi was good too. Not as good as you, but way above average. Still, in the long run, she wasn't good enough. Which is why she is where she is today.'

'Which is, exactly, where?'

'That's a good question. She's with me. Always.'

'*All* of her?'

'No, not all. But enough of her, Anne. Enough.'

'You bastard.'

'Judi wasn't good enough to walk away from me. And you

aren't good enough, Anne. Don't feel insulted. Maybe once, twice in a thousand years does someone like that turn up. I'm old. Maybe I'll never meet anyone that good again. You have no idea how depressing I find that thought, how boring my life can get...'

He was doling his words out carefully now, putting an actorish emphasis on them. If a politician talked to her like this, she would campaign vigorously against him.

Skinner trailed off, his face a mask of wistful resignation. He reached below the horizon of the desktop, and she heard a drawer being pulled open. He dipped a hand into it like a smooth gangster reaching for a concealed gun. He held up a purple lizard, gripping its tail in his fingers but letting it settle in his palm. The little reptile looked around, blinking spirally.

'Pretty, isn't he?'

'Oh sure, he's adorable.'

He held the lizard up to his eyeline, and examined it. He kissed it on its minutely horned snout, then bit its head off. He dropped the cleanly decapitated thing on the desk blotter. It bled very little, but twisted and thrashed like a loose power cable. Skinner chewed for a few seconds, then spat over his shoulder. Anne heard the pulped skull plop into an 1880s barbershop spittoon.

Skinner produced another lizard, smaller and greener, with a frilly collar.

'Want one?'

'No thanks.'

'I thought not.'

He bit again, spat again. Anne sat, hands idle in her lap, coffee abandoned, watching this polite Monster indulge his vice. Kicking bodies wound down like clockwork toys on the blotter.

'Well, Anne, here we are...'

'So?'

'So what are you going to do about it?'

'You tell me.'

'Um, well, the natural course of things would involve me pinning you down – and you know I could do that – and feeding off you. Everything up till now had just been an entertainment, like silly Amelia's party games. Feeding is serious. You don't understand what that means, but you must have some idea by now.'

'And if you feed off me?'

'You'll be with Judi. You'll be just like Judi, in fact. Not that that is entirely a bad thing, but I think it might be wasteful...'

He leaned forward, shading his kills, supporting his head on a bridge of his interlaced fingers. He had mismatched cufflinks.

'You have qualities, Anne. I could make you like me.'

She was annoyed. 'You could never make me like you.'

'No, not like, *like*. You could be one of the Kind.'

'You mean I could live forever, see the world, torture people and bite the heads off lizards? That's an awfully tempting offer, but...'

He raised a little finger and silenced her.

'Yes,' he said, 'you have qualities. You're not actually that witty, but very few people would even try to make jokes in a situation like this. Irony is a much underrated attitude.'

'And how do people get to be like you, Skinner?'

'I've always been one of the Kind. You can never have that, of course, but I can teach you things, do things for you. It's not common, but it's not unprecedented either...'

'Would I be right in assuming that there aren't any lady monsters running around these years?'

He paused after that one, thinking carefully. He was slower than he used to be.

'You are very perceptive,' he said, finally. 'To answer your implied rather than your actual question, yes. I would welcome the company of an equal. Not that you could be my equal without a substantial investment of time and effort. As for whether there are others of the Kind left... well... as far as I know, there are not...'

Suddenly, with a squirt of creepy excitement, Anne realized Skinner was lying.

'I am the last,' he said.

'There ought to be a protection order out on you. You don't want to wind up like the dodo or the passenger pigeon.'

She was shaking now, not with fear but with rage. She wanted to take him apart. She tried not to explode. Skinner was crazy but calm.

'Passenger pigeons,' he mused. 'I saw them, you know. You've heard how they used to flock. They could blot out the sun for hours. Your country was a marvel until recently, and you covered it in concrete...'

'Me personally?'

'Yes, you. And Judi. And people just like you.'

'So we paved paradise and put up a parking lot?'

'Ha! I hate America very much, Anne. More, even, than Egypt. I can't even go there any more. I was at Antietam, you know, in your War Between the States...'

'I got through high school, thank you very much.'

'I'm sorry. During the ten years of your country's ill-advised involvement in Indochina, some 50,000 Americans were killed in action. At the Battle of Antietam, 40,000 fell in one afternoon.'

'And those were the good old days?'

There was something weird in his eyes now. '1862 isn't my old days, Anne. It's not even my yesterday. It's my this morning.'

'What put you off the States then?'

He shrugged, a ribbon of skin peeling from his cheek as his grin relaxed. 'Shall we say, a loss of vision?'

'So, if I marry you, we can't go visit with Mom and Dad?'

'I don't want to marry you.'

'What kind of a girl do you think I am?'

'A stupider one than you seem. Like your sister...'

His left eye had drooped shut, covered with dead skin. Skinner was tired, sleepy, worn out. He was still arguing, but she could sense that his heart was not in it any more.

She knew that she could get out of this.

'By the way,' he said spitefully, 'you'll never visit your father again. I heard on the world service news just now that…'

With a Bruce Lee yell, she burst out of her chair and threw herself against his desk. It turned on its side, and she grabbed hold of the two upper legs. Skinner's chair rolled backwards against the featureless wall. Her knees were bruised, and she was not really strong enough to heft the whole piece of furniture, but she pushed with her entire body. A drawer came free and crunched up like a matchbox. Lizards scampered beneath her feet, dispersing with unbelievable speed.

All she could see of Skinner was one pale hand, gripping the top edge of the desk, and his weakly kicking, grey-trousered legs. She slammed the desk against the wall. A desk leg came off. She drew back, and slammed again. Skinner grunted and ruptured. There was a burp of foul air. Inside Skinner, a gurgling started and stopped.

She heaved the desk aside. A partition fell over. Skinner was hunched up, arms over his head. She kicked him viciously about the shins, and battered his head and torso with the broken leg. She prised his arms apart, and smashed in his face. It dented easily. His hair came off in one piece like a wig. His chest fell in.

She stopped hitting him, and stepped back. There was no noise now, except the whir of a concealed extractor fan. She bent over Skinner and picked up his face. It was like a crumpled linen handkerchief. It tore and she had to wipe her hand on the wall to get the cobwebby scum off her fingers.

All that was left was an empty skin.

12

Naked, he woke up. His long body had a reddish tinge, and he was tender all over. Even the soles of his feet were soft. His skin was young and tight, unshrivelled. He felt his face. The nose was a little flat, but the flesh was firm. The change had been relatively painless, and he thought he would be satisfied with the results.

Still a little light-headed, he stood up. There was a kimono hung on a hook nearby. He clothed himself. He rubbed the clear gum away from his eyes. He had not bled anywhere.

Anne was standing at the other side of the office, holding bits of his old skin. He was between her and the door.

He was not sorry she had turned him down, but, newly reborn, he was not ready to feed on her yet. He was still overnourished from his pre-change gluttony, and he had to reestablish control over the ghosts he already had before he could take on another one. Especially a ghost who was liable to be doing a lot of struggling.

'Anne,' he shouted, 'over here.' His voice had an unfamiliar, boyish sound in his ears. He liked it.

She turned to look at him, the bitch.

He grinned. His teeth were sharper now. With simian agility, he leaped on a desk. While he was in this state, he wanted to stretch himself a little. His backbone was elongating, making use of his extra ribs. His fingers developed an extra knuckle apiece. His toes turned to fingers. He flattened his hair to his almost oval skull, slicking it down with natural juices. He wanted to sing.

She was scared. Perhaps for the first time, she was really scared. He could taste it, and he was aroused.

'Keep young and beautiful,' he crooned to her, 'if you want to be *loved*...'

She came for him, for the door. He twisted on himself, gripping the desk with his handclaws, and flipped his lower body around. He took a semi-orgasmic pleasure from his own muscle strength.

He was going to let her go again; for a while. She could not get far. There was only the Dream out there. He had his lines into her head. He could reel her in and land her any time he wanted. First, he had to give her a few more jolts, tire her out, take the fight out of her...

He reared up on his hind legs, and sprang in front of the door. Her way was barred. He shrilled one of the old songs, in the language he never got to use these days. In the song, he boasted of his ghosts.

Then he stepped aside, opened the door, and mimed an 'after you'.

She was past him faster than one of the lizards and in the hallway. She looked at the lift doors and – clever girl! – decided to take the stairs.

Pausing in the stairwell, she turned to look back at him. Was that supposed to be a come-on? Was she enjoying the chase? In any case, he was not ready to follow yet.

She stuck her middle finger up in the empty air, and said, 'suck on that salamander!'

Then she was gone.

13

The business of getting out of the building was straightforward. She had been expecting everdescending stairs, windowless walls and doorless lobbies. Exposure to Skinner's worldview had led her to assume his office would be the only inhabitable portion of a skyscraping concrete coffin.

She was wrong. They had not even been more than five or six storeys above the street. And, on every floor, the stairwell was outfitted with a picture window. The eternity lighting made dark mirrors of the plateglass oblongs, but she could make out the outlines of a world beyond. There were points of light out in the night, and dark shapes, moving things, people, ghosts...

All of which worried her; it meant that he was saving up for something special. 'Snake-hearted bastard!' she spat.

The lobby was spacious, flavourlessly modernist and empty. The stand-up ashtrays were empty, and the continent-shaped patches of fading damp on the tiled floor testified to the fairly recent presence of the after-hours cleaners. There was a revolving door cylinder, but Anne chose to push against one of the sets of conventional swing doors. That seemed less risky. She stepped outside. The swing doors swished shut behind her, sucking back the bubble of warmth that had been protecting her.

Back in the night, it was bloody cold. Her breath frosted

around her in a cloud, and she pushed her ungloved hands into her coat pockets before the chill bit into her fingers. She was on a flat expanse of concrete twenty feet off the ground. Wide, apparently free-floating slabs stepped downward from either end of the terrace. Beneath her was a shallow, well-lit pond. The dirty blue bottom was covered by yard-round scallops of coconut glacé. Ice hung off the tricorn fountains like drapes of frozen tripe.

She knew exactly where she was, for the first time since... Since when? New York, New Orleans, Sam's Bar-B-Q and Grill, the tube train, the station, Soho, Amelia Dorf's house, the taxi, Soho again, Nina's flat, the Club Des Esseintes, the Nellie Dean, Cam's hotel, the hospital, her flat, her bed? When this was over, where would she be? In bed, waiting to be woken up by Inspector Hollis' phone, call? Or in Skinner, waiting to be conjured back into some kind of half-life?

Right now, she was on the plaza outside Centre Point. The reinforced concrete and glass erection stabbing the empty sky above her was at the intersection of Charing Cross Road, Oxford Street, Tottenham Court Road and New Oxford Street. From where she was, she could see the large yellow flag outside Foyle's, the famous bookshop where she had always found it impossible to find anything. The view was all very detailed and realistic.

She had heard that most of Centre Point was untenanted, because London W1 rents were too high for even the wealthiest businesses. There was, or perhaps had been, a hostel for the homeless on one of the floors. For her, the white elephant was one of the city's best investments. When she had first come to London, it was the first useful landmark to impress itself upon her – unlike most touristy places, it was in the middle of the area where most of her business meetings had to take place – and she still used it often as a point of reference when in the centre of town. Furthermore, it was perched on top of the tube station she had to use most often, and the 134 bus, which went right past her flat, terminated underneath it.

The familiarity was not comforting, although she knew that she had something to do with the selection and recreation of this particular plot as part of the Dream. It must be about four o'clock in the morning, after the departure of the latest of the late night people and before the arrival of the earliest of the early morning men. A single car circled the building and vanished into a side street, carefully negotiating a one-way system designed to cope with the heaviest traffic in the country even though it made incredibly complicated the process of making a simple right turn.

Everything was given a pale blue illumination by the street lighting. A few Christmas displays winked. It all looked real, but Anne knew better by now.

She looked up at the building, trying to read an expression on its long tall face. She thought she could make out a gameshow host grin, barracuda-toothed and insincere. Skinner's eyes were somewhere up there. She smiled herself as she backed away, realizing the mistake. Somehow, Centre Point had wound up with the Empire State Building's dirigible mooring mast.

'When does the gorilla show up, old man?'

A venomous frost had spread like lichen across many of the upper windows. A sheet of ice the size of a large Vermeer detached itself and slid free. Anne's heart clutched like a fist as the glassy mass shattered ten feet away from her. Cracked ice spread towards her shoes like a flood of marbles. Skinner was reminding her to keep running.

She hit the steps and got off the plaza. The usually impossible intersection was easy to cross against the lights. The car, a boxy '30s model, had gone. There were no people at all in sight, which proved she was still in Skinner's wonderland. Even in the deadest of the dead hours, this place was populated. Not as thickly as nearby Soho or the West End clubland, perhaps, but these were still 24-hour streets.

So, what next?

Running had done her no good so far, but she was getting the idea that it was expected of her. Putting up a stiff resistance might not help her win, but it got her a few bonus points. However, she also knew that nothing was going to persuade Skinner to let her off the forfeits. She even got the feeling that the more she inconvenienced him in the short term, the more he would get out of feeding off her in the end.

Feeding off her? What exactly did that mean? Doubtless, something unbelievably nasty.

Of the four main avenues, she chose Oxford Street. She started to walk towards Marble Arch, then turned left, heading back into Soho. The place seemed to be in the middle of this business. It was like Skinner's secret lair. Somewhere in the vice heart of town, the Monster was waiting for her.

She had no crucifix or wooden stake or pistol-load of silver bullets or flaming torch or hammer and sickle or bell, book and candle. That stuff would have comforted her less than an M-16, or one of those skeleton-handled Uzi sub-machine guns, or an anti-personnel rocket launcher. Preferably, she would like the Air Force to lay down some pretty heavy napalm around Skinner, then send in the Green Berets led by John Wayne, Sylvester Stallone, Arnold Schwarzenegger, the Incredible Hulk and Godzilla. After that, and only after that, she would ask the President to fall back on their country's thermonuclear resources. Even then, she figured her chances at about twenty-eighty against. All she was going into Hell with was her mind. Christ, that had better be enough...

Gradually, she became aware of the ghosts. Not used to them, exactly, but alert to their presence. She had them pegged as a sideshow, and did not want to expend any energy worrying about that sort of thing. She would need everything for the Main Event. They were in shadows, behind shop windows, in pedestrian subways, congregated in car parks. She did not want to look too closely, half-aware that concentrating on them would give them more substance. Then, they might get in her way. So far, they were not bothering her like the things on the train had, but they could easily be provoked.

In a lamp halo, standing at a shelterless bus stop, she found a man from the past, dressed in a white tropical suit and panama hat out of *A Night in Casablanca.* He had spats, and a wing collar, knife-edge trouser pleats, and no face. The cigarette in his holder was burning to ash without any help from him. He had no mouth, so there was no point to his habit. Otherwise, he was placid and unfrightening.

Likewise, the gaggle of gypsies in Soho Square, huddled under the eaves of the gardener's hut, nursing their wind-whipped fires, quaking with superstitious fear. Their horses whinnied and shifted between the shafts of their gingerbread-decorated caravans. They made signs at her like Transylvanian peasants in a Dracula movie, warning her not to go to Borgo Pass on Walpurgis Night. Were they trying to help her? Grandfather Nastase, dead long before her birth, had been from the Carpathians. Or was she being misled? She waved to them, trying to be jaunty, and kept on walking.

The next apparitions, which she encountered in a passage between Dean Street and Wardour Street, were a little more hostile. She was only a few doors away from the place where Nina's flat had been when two men in vaguely piratical costumes stepped out. Had they been visiting Tina – Teenage Model One Flight Up – or just waiting to ambush her? They had headscarves, baggy pants and cutlasses. One of them touched a cigarette lighter's flame to the oiled and pleated ends of his beard and moustache, setting them to burn slowly. They snarled and showed their claws like threatened cats, but stayed away from her.

The samurai in Wardour Street was not so timid, and his sword was definitely not ornamental. He waved the three-foot razor within an inch of her face, slicing loudly through the cold-thickened air. He yelled, and made a series of dazzling passes in front of her, like Sergeant Troy in *Far From the Madding Crowd.*

She had no doubt that he could have chopped her thin like salami if he had been allowed to. She stood still as a mannequin, flinching only when the flashing light from the sword got in her eyes. He was a dirty, pockmarked man with bad teeth and an elaborate topknot. Like the other ghosts, he was a bit faint; not see-through exactly, but a little lighter than a living person ought to be.

'Tell me, Toshiro, how much of your life can you call your own?'

He seized up in mid-slice, stared into her face as if pondering the question, and relaxed out of his stance. His sword drooped, and became a bow handle as its point pressed the ground. In a fluid move, he sheathed his weapon, saluted her, and was running off. His sandals flapped against the sidewalk. He turned right at the end of the passage, and was gone. Behind him, he had left a perfect white camellia. She picked it up and found that it was a paper thing that came apart in her hands. He really had looked like Toshiro Mifune.

'I suppose that was supposed to be a warning, old man,' she said aloud, as if addressing a God who was hard-of-hearing. 'Go no further, right? Well, I think you're bluffing. I figure all this shit is putting a strain on you. I reckon you're slipping...'

She walked Southwards, deeper into Soho, towards the lights.

'...those last couple were pathetic, Skinner. Not your standard at all. If you watch too many old movies, you cripple your imagination. Yours is gone, old man, atrophied. You're hobbling right now...'

A sign above a closed sex shop on the other side of the street came on: YOU WISH, ANNE, YOU WISH.

She turned to the storefront – a modest expanse of crushed red velvet littered with lacy corsets and studded leather – and talked back to the sign.

'...and wishing makes it so, right? Piss on that, old man. This is my dream too, and I can wish you out of it.'

The bulbs darkened and came on again in a different pattern, in different colours. I WON'T BE A BEDPOST FOR YOU, ANNE.

She got it at once.

'Very seasonal, old man. But that doesn't win you any gold stars. Even I've read *A Christmas Carol*. Here's one for you: you're nothing but a piece of undigested beef!'

A pause, then: ANGELA, WHERE'S JOHNNY?

'You still playing that game? I'm out of that forever, and you know it. You haven't got one tenth the creativity my Dad has, you can't do a sequel to *On the Graveyard Shift*. That's like Harold Robbins writing *The Brothers Karamazov Ride Again*.'

ANGELA.

'There is no Angela any more. Just me, Anne…'

ANGELA, SAM'S DEAD.

'Dead and in a play, Skinner. That doesn't count.'

ANNE, YOUR FATHER IS DEAD.

She did not let him hear the sob in the back of her throat. She swallowed it, and went on. 'I know. I suppose you want the credit, old man. It wasn't you. It was just old age. You ought to know something about that. How are the arteries, then? Hardening nicely? How many more skins can you get rid of before there's nothing left of you?'

ANNE, I'M FOREVER.

'Like Hell…'

YES, LIKE HELL.

He took her from behind, like they had trained him to take North Korean soldiers. Armlock around the neck, punch to the kidney. She turned in his grip, so the blow thumped into her spine. It hurt, but did not make her crumple like a Raggedy Ann doll. She tried to get a knee round to slam into his groin, but she could not turn that far. Hot breath condensed on the back of her neck and in her hair.

It was Johnny, of course. He did not look like the Martin Landau of *On the Graveyard Shift*. This was a post-*Mission: Impossible* caricature, with an overemphasized satanic cast to its features. Landau was made up as Johnny turning into a demon. He had reptile eyes, several rows of tiny teeth and a lashing adder's fork. He nuzzled her, licking her cheek with the wet, sandpapery tongue.

'Angel, Angel,' he slobbered, 'never leave me again...'

She pincered her elbows behind her, as if doing the Turkey Trot, and slammed into his ribs. It did not do much good. He did not have a proper hold on her any more, but she was not free either. He let go her neck and grabbed her elbows.

'Angel, let's get back together...'

'No way, Skinner. That's all over!'

She knew what to do now. She brought her knee up towards her stomach, tensed her thigh and belly, and smashed her heel down on the thing's instep. It yowled in agony and let go of her. She whirled away from him, turning to face him. The rubbery thing was hopping comically, holding its throbbing foot like Deputy Dawg (*'oh my toe bone!'*) and spitting wildly. Maliciously, she stepped forward and stamped on the other foot. It took a few tries, as the thing dodged her shoes, but she got it in the end. It screamed again, and went down on its knees. Johnny was a liquid image for a moment, held together by a soap-bubble skin. Then, it collapsed on the pavement, and ran through the cracks between the paving stones. Not even clothes were left. Only a set of Korean War issue US Army dogtags.

Breathless, laughing, hurting inside, Anne shouted, 'Hah! That wasn't even a nice *try*, Skinner. Give up and go home!'

The next one was just *sick*. It was Clive, dead, hanging in an old-fashioned red telephone box. Up close, she realized he was not suspended, he was floating. The box was full of something as thick as milk, but as transparent as water. An eerie light filtered down through the liquid. The body gently shifted. The jacket was spread out like folds of skin and muscle during open-heart surgery. By Clive's ankles, the telephone receiver floated like a too-light anchor.

His neck was ripped open, as it had been the last time she saw him alive, and there was a dark stain on his torn shirt. The liquid and the distilled light rendered him in black and white, but she could tell it was blood on Clive's shirt. His face had shrunken onto his skull, and then been bloated by the water. The result was not normality.

Clive opened his dead-as-coins eyes, and tried to outstare her. Like Johnny, he was horribly funny. She would have left him to pickle, but she wanted to see what came next. After all, in his position, what could he *do* to hurt her? He was moving now. It must have been an effort to bring those arms down, fighting against the thick liquid and clogged clothes, especially considering that he was dead in the first place. His mouth was like a goldfish's, opening and closing. The wound in his neck pulsed like a sphincter. It was either a makeshift gill or a revolutionary new design for an asshole.

His swollen palms flattened against glass panels, and his back wedged against the other side of the box. He looked angry, although his lips had been soaked too long to be able to recede over his teeth in a snarl. It was not funny any more. A shoe scrabbled against one of the lower panels. Then, he started to exert some pressure, bending and straightening his body as best he could. He was still quite strong.

She got out of the way. The door came open. For an instant, the mass of liquid retained the shape of the telephone box. Surface tension or something, she supposed. But even in this world, there was no miniscus that could do the job of a plate glass fishtank. The level of water fell, and a torrent emerged from the lower quarter of the box. It spread into the street. The Clive Thing came out in a sitting position, and landed on his ass. He did not flap like a fish. Words and water spouted from his mouth and neck.

'You cunt, you cunt, you cunt, you're going to die, you...'

He pushed against the paving stones and launched himself upright, then stumbled for her, arms outstretched. His sleeves were splitting at the seams as his arms pulsed and grew. She backed away from him. His fingers were winding together, making a point, the nails fusing into a needle-barb. His hands were becoming obscene organic syringes.

'You cunt, you cuntface bitch, you know you want it, you know you neeeeed it...'

His jacket burst at the armpits, and swelling sacs, rough-skinned with sparse hairs, descended. His arms were transparent now, a spiral tracery of clear plastic veins laid around the white bones, bunching together at the wrists.

He was frothing purple at the mouth. His underarm testicles pulsated, spurting fluid into his arm-tubes.

Anne knew what it would be. Nina had shot him fully of it. It would probably be high-grade, unpolluted heroin. The best death money could buy.

'The first jab,' he said, his words distorted by his misshapen mouth, 'is free.'

A pearl of smoky white liquid grew at the tip of his right syringe, and dribbled down the glans-like swelling that had been his hand.

'The rest, you have to pay for.'

She ducked under his thrust, and punched away his second, left-handed, attack.

'Hey, cunt, want to go to a club,' he said, 'and see some damage done...'

He was awkward, finding it difficult to move. He was full of heroin now, bursting to get rid of it. He shot a jet in an arc, and it splattered against the window of a stylish fashion shop, dripping like soapy water. The veins in his neck were throbbing purple, and water was still pouring out of his clothes.

She wrenched a waste-bin off a lamp-post, and held it in front of her, blocking his darting syringe stabs.

She threw the bin at him, and dented his forehead. He slipped, his heels working against the wet sidewalk, making scuffmarks. Overbalanced, he went down again. His left arm shattered like a dropped glass, and he screamed as brown-streaked fluid exploded out of him.

She took a careful, malicious, aim and kicked the sac under his right arm, feeling the satisfying give of weak flesh under her toepoint. The Clive Thing's screech cut through the cold night and filled her ears with his pain. He writhed, falling apart in the slippery mess. She got her foot under the thing, and easily rolled it over onto its stomach. He moved as if attempting the breast stroke, his ruined left arm flapping. She brought one of her killer feet down on his spine, snapping it in several places. The crack was like a rifle shot.

She walked away. The Clive Thing tried to swim/crawl after her, dragging its sodden lower limbs. It gave up quickly. When she looked back, it was just a man-shaped smear on the road, kicking feebly.

She was in Old Compton Street now, but not the Old Compton Street she had been in that afternoon. And she knew she was hurting him.

The city was less realistic now. The sky above was solid black, like a tent canopy, and the street was closed off at either end like a film set. Most of the buildings were probably false fronts or backdrops. Patisserie Valerie was painted on loose-hanging canvas, not very well, as if it were supposed to register as realistic from the back of the Royal Circle rather than up close. It had been painted for the daytime, with frozen patrons clogging the place and white and red pastries in the windows, and looked wrong in this night scene. The dream was fraying around the edges.

She brushed by a pillar box, and stopped to examine it. The thing had not felt right. The slot for letters was a strip of black pasted onto the red. There was a poster for a rock gig slapped on the side of the box, but it did not have real writing on it, just a series of squiggles. The whole thing was as soft as a pencil eraser. Soon it would be foam rubber, then gelatine, then ice cream, then candyfloss. Then, just a smudge.

'I think you're spread too thin, Skinner. You're rushing things, getting careless. It's time to turn in, old man, time to go to sleep...'

Another set of lights came on, above an amusement arcade this time.

I'LL GET YOU YET, MY PRETTY.

'Uh huh? You wish, old man, you wish!'

14

In her dream, Judi was being neglected.

She did not know where she was exactly, but it looked mainly like her father's house in New Hampshire, although her room was like the bedroom of the flat she shared with Coral in the Elephant and Castle. Looking at the walls, covered with pinned-up pictures and news items from magazines and papers, she saw a collage of her entire life. There were a few posters from her brief infatuation – now a shameful, much-suppressed memory – with John Travolta in the era of *Saturday Night Fever*, and an overlapping series of book-covers, neatly torn from paperbacks like hunter's trophies, marking her absorption of the matter that had been in the volume. Then, there were magazine illustrations that had caught her fancy at some time in her life – the craggy face of W. H. Auden in black and white, socialites in bow ties grinning in nightclubs, a *Spitting Image* Ronald Reagan as Rambo, a pleasure boat sunk in the Thames, a poster for *Blue Velvet*. There was Cam at a concert, Clive shaking hands with the Prime Minister, Anne trying to get an answer out of a police constable who did not want to be interviewed, her mother and William Conrad in a TV movie, her father in Stockholm accepting his damned prize.

There were other people in the house, but they did not see it as she did. They had their own Dreams. Some of the other ghosts she had known in life. Jeane Russell, who had been a professional swimmer, came in wearing a navy blue one-piece bathing suit, her dark hair dripping. She was friendly, but offhand, refusing to acknowledge that this was not normal. She had a gymnasium somewhere, and was obsessively working on her body. In her father's study, among the comforting books and signed photographs, she found Coral, one arm stiff at her side, her free hand clamped over her eyes. Judi could not communicate with her either. In the music room, she found Cam, whistling tunelessly. Clive had drifted past once or twice, and tried to catch her attention, but he was strangely shrunken – perfectly-proportioned but only three feet tall, wearing a miniature version of one of his usual smart suits. She was tempted to hit him, but let it go.

On the front lawn, where the children had been allowed to play croquet only if they promised not to argue and always ended up in tearful fights, Judi found Amelia Dorf, a used-up husk in a line of similar remains, some of them dressed in the style of remote historical periods.

There was one ghost who frightened Judi, and who would occasionally loiter around. She was called Giselle and seemed to be a lost little girl, but her face was ancient. She could usually be found on the lawn, playing with the remnants, crooning madly to herself. She was spiteful, and could pinch and nip if she got close enough. Feelings were deadened in the Dream, but there was still pain.

The Dream did not extend far beyond the boundaries of the Nielson property. Judi would sometimes sit in the driveway and look out into the white mists that hung immobile just a few yards down the drive. The road disappeared into them, and the hedges just faded out. Nothing came out of the limbo, and no one ever ventured into it. But Judi knew that, just beyond sight, there was someone. A woman, young and strong, with nearly white hair. She was not in the Dream, but she could tune into the dead channel if she chose. A name formed in her mind: Ariadne. It was a seductive name. She rolled its syllables around her mouth, imagining the name's owner.

Judi tried to remember the village as it had been when she had been living at home. She and Anne, blessed and cursed with the sophistication due to the offspring of the smart and famous, had never had much to do with the local kids. They had had a private name for them, the stupids.

There had been a point in her life when Judi would have done anything to be a stupid. But you cannot unlearn anything, cannot regurgitate knowledge, experience and aptitudes like an undigested meal. Still, she had tried hard.

She wondered what had happened to Trey, the nineteen-year-old bar-helper she had gone with when she was fourteen. He had been a major stupid. His idea of success was becoming a cop or a rock singer. His first ambition had been out because of his string of juvie beefs, and he had dumped her, after a beating, when she had told him he could never make it in music because he was too white.

Most of the time, it was just boring. She tried the television and the radio, but could only get dead static. The appliances all worked, but the records in their perfect sleeves were all smooth and uncut. She realized that she had read all the books in the house, and wondered if this was Hell…

Sometimes, she was let out. Skinner put her to sleep and woke her up somewhere else, to have her appear to someone…

She could still remember the subway train, and Anne.

But most of the time she was left on her own, to her own devices. She lay in her bed, and tried to practise total recall, seeing how much of her life she could put together in perspective.

She thought a lot about Anne. She wished she had tried harder to get on with her sister, had tried harder not to disrupt the already shaky peace of the family. With a father who was a walking open wound, a mother who flitted by on occasional whims and a half-brother who wandered about like an army officer in a POW camp, thinking only of his hidden escape tunnel and an eventual release, the Nielsons had not been anything like the families she remembered on television, *The Brady Bunch*, *The Partridge Family*, *The Waltons*...

She had never had a chance with Cam, but she could have had a real relationship with Anne. But now, it was too late...

At first, she had been sure she was dead. Now, she knew better. Her body was dead, but she was still around, as part of the Dream. The Dream was somewhere out of space and time, carried around in Skinner and yet immeasurably vaster than him. It was possible to die out of the Dream – Amelia and the corpses proved that – and she sometimes wondered whether she should try to finish herself off and get it over with.

There were already enough zombies in her family.

She could not do it, though. Even at her lowest, she had never wanted just to die.

Remembering, she found more lows than she would have liked. There was a temptation to dwell only on the better moments, but the lows were as much a part of the pattern, and she felt obliged to summon them up.

She did not know whether she had been conscious when Skinner killed Coral, but she saw it replayed over and again as if she had been. Of course, Coral had been there, and Amelia and Clive had been involved. Perhaps Judi could now sample the memories of everyone in the Dream. It had been upstairs in Amelia's house, in one of the old bedrooms, with the two-way mirror on the wall. Even Amelia had been shocked, and had run for her cocaine stash as a way of handling it. After Coral, came Judi. She remembered the Monster feeding off her, remembered the bursting of her own heart, remembered the struggle that had come afterwards. Skinner had called in Clive to handle the bodies, and from him Judi could see herself propped up in a Soho alley in the early hours, swiftly dumped like a bundle of newspapers for collection. Coral was buried deeper, on a rubbish dump in some to-be-redeveloped wasteland.

Eventually, she went out onto the croquet lawn and found what was left of Coral, her arm separate from her, lying with Amelia and the others. Giselle was sitting next to her, breaking her fingers, trying to feed off the girl but tasting only dry ashes which made her sick. Giselle coughed up grey matter, and crawled away, disgusted. Judi touched Coral, and the remains fell apart completely. The girl was gone. So, it was possible to die more. She wondered if she would miss Coral.

The girl had been fun. Once, giggly drunk in the flat and surprised at themselves, they had made love. It had been pleasant, but they had never repeated the experiment. Very few of Judi's good memories had to do with sex or love, and so that once was precious. She had never really enjoyed hurting or giving hurt, but that was the way it had all too often worked out.

She slept and ate, or at least pretended to, and changed her clothes regularly. She had a lot of clothes. Everything she had ever owned was in the house, and it all, back to her smallest baby-dresses, still fitted her.

She learned the names of some of the other ghosts. She had long conversations with an Irishman named Niall Baum who thought he was in a Dublin boarding house in the 1870s, and learned from him a little more about the Monster. From him she learned that Giselle was of the Monster's kind, and that she had been his wife – a thing beyond imagining – until an end was put to her. Too many of the others spoke and thought only in languages she had no way of understanding.

Bored, she tried to kiss Niall, and he disappeared. She felt strange after that, and could remember Shanghai, a series of explosions, and a bloody struggle in a temple in the hills. She felt some of her fuzziness disappear, and was not sure what had happened.

The ghosts were becoming fewer in number, and she was feeling more solid. It took her a while to realize that she was taking them all into herself. It was bizarre, not entirely comfortable, and – she suspected – dangerous.

How could she hope to stay Judi if she were taking all these others on board?

She could understand Mandarin now, and Turkish and mediaeval French, and other useless tongues. She had died in battles from before the time of Christ down to Khe Sanh, and in numberless squalid, fundamentally unchanging, beds down through the centuries. She felt especially close to Macha Igescu, who had died for the first time in Istanbul in 1938; they had both been whores, both been wasted in a city across the sea from the land of their birth, had both excited and touched the Monster... Digging deep, she was surprised to discover a thinned relationship: Macha's cousin in Bucharest had been married to a Nastase whose uncle had emigrated to America and changed his name to Nielson.

Judi had seen the Clive ghost with a similarly shrunken young man, whose perfumed curls and thin greased moustache made him a childish dandy, and learned from Macha that this was Demetrios, who had been her pimp and protector. After feeding off her, the Monster had killed Demetrios as a favour. It was one of his many capricious gestures.

Eventually, Nina Kenyon turned up. She was wearing torn clothes, and her make-up had streaked. Judi was glad to see her, and they hugged.

'Judi,' the other girl said, 'I'm so tired.'

'Sleep, then.'

'I will.'

Judi stroked Nina's hair, and the frail ghost became faint in her embrace. Macha joined them, more hair, more hands, and Judi felt the Roumanian girl's cheek sinking through her own.

Suddenly, she was alone, remembering Coral smoking at school and a boat trip across the Bosphorus.

She was still Judi, but she was Nina and Macha too.

She saw Clive and Demetrios, but they were the size of housecats, and scurried away.

She remembered shaving her head, surrounded by religious relics, and vowing to bring down the King of the Cats.

Then, she knew that was Niall Baum's memory.

As an experiment, she seduced a ghost. A tiny Indian girl with an elaborate pearl ornament shaped like a snail's shell in one nostril. Judi took her, and absorbed her. There was a rush of unfamiliar experience, and a sense of gratitude at being no longer alone. Kanchi was by far the oldest of the ghosts she had come across, and Judi was startled by the vividness of her memories.

The Monster, whom she thought of as Guillaume of Oswestry, had accepted her in marriage as a gift, and fed off her a little at a time over a period of months. There was nothing in Kanchi's experience which jibed with any history Judi knew, and so she could not even guess how long the girl had been a ghost.

The house changed with each of her absorptions. She found new rooms, fabulously unfamiliar and yet homely. She lived memories, fantasies and illusions. The Dream expanded, the mists receding, and the New Hampshire house became a higgledy-piggledy palace.

She collected ghosts, absorbed and became them all. She swam with Jeane Russell, and was exhilarated by the self-image of a healthy, perfectly-tuned body. She fought with Stefan Snieszawski, and was astounded by her sword-wielding courage in battle. She crept up on Cam and finally put things right between them, absorbing him gently. She was surprised at what she found within her half-brother, and a little shamed by his turbulent depths.

From Nina, Judi learned about Anne. She saw, and was delighted by, her sister in the Club Des Esseintes, hitting Eric Wardle with a chair. It was strange, as Anne threaded herself into pictures Judi knew intimately but could not associate with her sister. Here was Anne in the Club, in Nina's flat, at one of Amelia's 'entertainments'...

She found a dried-up doll on the lawn, and knew that it was both Clive and Demetrios Malacou, gone forever. They resembled a pickled set of Siamese twins in a freak show. She tried to suck them in, but there was nothing left.

She was almost alone in the Dream. She was all the ghosts in one. She remembered being Niall Baum, Kanchi, Nina, Macha Igescu, Cam, and the others, but she was still herself, still Judi.

Giselle hid from her, but she saw her handiwork everywhere. Rooms were vandalized, and the remains violated.

Finally, on the lawn, she caught the ancient little girl and, shutting her ears to the shrieked pleas, ate her all up.

As Giselle gave up the struggle, Judi felt a sudden vertigo. The palace, the lawn, the mists beyond. They all collapsed, leaving only a limitless darkness.

Judi was the Dream.

15

The Club Des Esseintes was not hidden now. A fiery, twisted sign burned above the window of the nostalgia shop, casting a hellish glow on the display of comics. All the covers stuck to a formula – the superhero in trouble. There was Superman OD'd on Kryptonite, Iron Man rusting away to nothing, Swamp Thing falling victim to a Deep South drainage and reclamation scheme, the X-Men Xed out by the League of Evil Mutants. Anne knew that, in the end, these super-guys would win. She was not super, but she was in trouble, and she thought that she could win too. She had to think that. She had to.

The amusement arcade next door was a joke, with clanking, clattering and bleeping sound effects but no moving parts. Crude tailor's dummies posed over the pinball tables and video games, their stiff hands unfit for the tasks they were supposed to be performing. The music was wrong too – big band jazz, not hip-hop loudness. Skinner was giving up on the street.

He was in the Club Des Esseintes, and he wanted her to come for him. Fair enough. Then, he would not have to bother dreaming the city properly. They would have it out, and one of them could go home to sleep. Anne was tired, but she would be okay for the big finale. She was sure.

The nostalgia shop was locked up, the sign on the door said

'open'. So in she went, knowing the way now. The shop was empty of people, but there was a whirring and clicking in one corner. The collection of Japanese warrior robots was swinging into action. Eyes flicked on and off, mighty plastic arms lifted, jet planes became miniature android colossi, death rays warmed up. She took a lightsaber from a *Star Wars* display and swept the robots off their stand. Designed to take the aggressive play of even the most creatively destructive child, the robots were unharmed and dangerous.

She stamped on a hawk-faced humanoid with buzz-saw bracelets. She had been doing a lot of damage with her feet recently. This time, all she did was hurt her ankle. One of the little bastards pinched her calf with blunt metal claws. She kicked it away. The plastic light sabre was proving useless, so she exchanged it for the centrepiece of a display promoting a video-only splatter movie, *The Cincinnati Flamethrower Holocaust.*

She wished it were for real, and so it was. She adjusted the nozzle like the one on the weedkiller spray back home in New Hampshire, and turned the flames on. A spurt of fire came out of the hose attachment. She swept the flame in a scythe-swath in front of her, aiming low. The robots went up instantly, and fell aside. They became little mounds of bubbling plastic and twisted tin. The stench was ghastly. The fire spread to some early *Howard the Ducks,* and died out suddenly. She dropped the toy on the floor, and stepped over the burned patch.

The spiral staircase was still there. The burning smells were stronger, and some were coming up from below. She had never come across brimstone, but this was what she would have guessed it was like. Also, there were waves of heat coming up from the Club.

She went downstairs.

The corridor was the same as it had been this morning, but the portrait frames on the wall were untenanted, containing either sheets of blank coloured canvas or meticulously dull paintings of chairs and curtains. She expected that the Marquis de Sade and his intimate friends were wandering around.

There was no executioner-suited bouncer guarding the doors. Eric must only work the day shift. She was glad of that. He would have been sure to remember her and hold a grudge. This time, the musak was reworking an old Everly Brothers song, 'Love Hurts'.

Again, she went into the Inferno Lounge. Inside, it was Hell.

16

In the place that had been the Inferno Lounge, but was now simply an Inferno, he waited for her. He had put her image up on the television monitors, and watched her coming for him. In his freshly-stolen youth, he was impatient for it all to be over. The expectation of pleasure coursed through his body. There was an electric tingling in his venom glands, in the flesh under his fingernails and in the tip of his penis. All the self-control he had learned was needed now. His mind kept his body on straining leashes.

The change had made him himself again, but he would have to discharge some of his surplus energy before the build-up literally tore him apart. He watched Anne on the monitors. The ghosts he had sent after her, to signpost the way to his lair, were pussycats compared with the ghosts forming in the red shadows of this room. He cheered and hooted as she overcame the weaklings he put in her way. He was glad to lose them. Once out of Anne's sight, he knew they would cease clinging to existence. They were gone forever. He sensed her growing confidence in her ability to survive this game, and the muscles in his arms spasmed in delight. She would be a feast, an unparalleled feast.

Although he was paying most attention to the monitors, he had other things to take care of. With a splurge of raw thought, he reshaped his environment, tearing down and building upon the banal Dante-and-Bosch conception of Hell that had been fostered by the decorators of the Club Des Esseintes. In the murals, damned souls began to wriggle in their torment, snake-tongued devils prodded them with tridents, vats of blood and excrement came to the boil, the Vices cavorted in a sinful jubilee. Every scream he had ever heard was replayed in a choral symphony of terror that Anne's brother would have sold his soul to have written. At the bar, a former Pope of the Black Church set up a line of fire and ice cocktails.

The best of his ghosts were still with him, the ones who had been as vital as Anne, the ones who had kept him alive well into his third millennium. Judi was there, and the three from China, and those who had come against him earlier. They had given him a hard time once, but they were his now, his utterly, to do with as he wished.

He called Judi out of the Dream, and bound her with fire. Surprised at the strength he still sensed in her, he threaded iron through the fire to make sure. She rattled her manacles, but was held fast.

Manacles would have many memories for her, he was sure.

He fashioned a throne of twisted corpses from the mural, and sat regally upon it. His ghosts stood like attendants. On the screens, Anne burned a horde of dolls. He liked playing the Devil, but it was just a game.

'I'm just a thing of nature, like you,' he told his unlistening ghosts. 'I'm no more the Devil than an alligator or a trap-door spider is. All this…' he gestured to the fiery lakes and the infernal landscapes '…is your Dream. I'm only borrowing it for a while.'

Anne was outside now, in the corridor. Her television image flickered with its soon-to-be-released ghost. How sad, he thought, that she would never appreciate how special she was. At least, not until she had lost the qualities that made her so.

Anne came into the Inferno Lounge. The doors banged behind her, and became a part of the gargoyle-sprouting rock wall.

'Gotcha!' he shouted.

17

At the centre of his Pit, he was sprawled casually in a high-backed chair wrought from a tangle of living limbs and torsos. Bones had been broken and reset during its manufacture, and the component people still suffered the pains. A face stared out from between his elegant ankles, silently screaming. Its eyeballs burst like lanced boils, spattering the backs of his trousers with steaming humours. Skinner did not mind. He could walk through a downpour of burning filth and stay as well-turned out as Fred Astaire. To her surprise, he had some of Astaire's loose-limbed vitality. Even as he relaxed, she could see the agility and expertise of his movements. He was younger than she had ever seen him, but the youth of his body was coupled with the skills and experience of an immortal genius. The ridges of his multiply healed scars lit up like orange neon veins under his skin. He was laughing at her. It was the least human sound she had ever heard. In this light, his hundreds of teeth were ruby-red and shark-sharp.

She did not believe in the Devil, she did not believe in the Devil, she did not believe in the Devil...

'My world, and welcome to it, Anne.'

...but the Devil believed in her.

'You look like a dream,' he purred.

Standing behind his throne like Satan's lady-in-waiting was

Judi. She was whole again, and wholly his creature, wrapped in chains. He held out a hand, palm up. She took it, and stroked it, the links of her handcuffs polished and shining. Her studs and chains and zippers held a million reflected fires. Her face was as dead and beautiful as that of a make-up-masked magazine model.

As usual, Anne could expect no help from her sister.

She stepped towards him, fingers hooked into claws. She was going to open his face like a pair of thick curtains. She did not get very far.

She could not see them, but they came from everywhere – out of the walls, swimming up through a floor that was solid to her but liquid to them, from under the Club Des Esseintes' bolted-down tables, out from their perches on ceiling fans and light fixtures. Horny hands grabbed her, and held her like leather straps. Her elbows, hands, knees, feet, hips, neck and head were held fast. She was forced to look ahead, at Skinner. Something with damp fingers was pulling her hair. Something with fingertips that stung like nettles had a hand in her clothes, and was painfully tickling her stomach, circling her navel with mosquito bites. Barely audible obscenities were cooed into her ear.

This, she knew, was nothing.

Skinner got out of his throne, and strolled towards her. He did not dance, but his walk had the pantherlike litheness of the very best professional golfers. He put his huge face near hers. Clamped down, unable to look anywhere but into his eyes, at his teeth or up his nose, she felt like the victim of a skilfully sadistic dentist. If she looked to her extreme left, rolling her eyes so far that her optic muscles ached, she could see a black and red blur. Judi was standing back, watching the operation without interest, like a dental assistant who has seen all the bridgework she ever wants to but knows that she has a better job than all her friends who are waitresses.

He did not need a drill or a probe or a hammer and chisel. He extended an impossibly long finger and began to trace lines on her face. When the tip came near her mouth, she clenched her teeth, determined to resist any oral rape. Even when the sheathed but sharp nail caressed the soft swell of her eyelids, she kept her eyes open, looking fixedly up at him. His breath was sweet, like cinnamon. There was something about him that reminded her of every lover she had ever had.

He unconsciously licked his lips, and kept on touching her face. She knew he was getting off on it somehow. Unusual little muscles in his throat, cheeks and temples were twitching slightly. He had closed his eyes, and was transported with pleasure. She felt the fight going out of her, as if it were draining into him through pinprick pores that opened wherever his fingernail pressed.

Not pinned down, but embraced. Not dying, but living. She wanted to go to sleep.

Her face cooled as he massaged it. She relaxed, became absurdly comfortable. The stinging on her stomach faded away. All sensations went away…

…she dreamed she was floating in a warm sea, endowed with a painless buoyancy. Only her face was above water, and gentle waves broke on her chin. Anemones brushed her heels as she drifted away from the shore with the tide. There were clouds high above her, and circling seabirds. She knew she would have to make one last effort, take one last breath, and then propel herself downwards, through fathoms of clear, sun-filtering water. Only at the bottom of the sea could she sleep.

Then Skinner took a fold of skin under the hinge of her jaw between his thumb and forefinger. He pinched hard, twisting the flesh deftly, and a network of painways came alive in the lower left quarter of her face. Nerves in her cheek flared and died like fuse wire. Half her teeth became explosions of pain.

…she dreamed that the Monster who was always coming after her, coming to get her, had at last caught up with her and was at last getting her. *Getting* was something worse than she had ever dreamed.

'...and that was just a playful touch, dear. Nothing special. There's more.'

Next, he sliced through her sleeve and pressed somewhere in the socket of her shoulder. Her arm jumped like a galvanized frog's leg, twisting free of the hands that held it down. She tried to make a fist, but could not. The arm hung limp, put out of action by an instant's agony.

'This is foreplay?'

'Oh no,' said Skinner, 'this is an aperitif.'

She would have spat in his face, but there was no water in her mouth, no strength in her lips.

'You don't know how much you mean to me, Anne, how much you're going to give me.'

He kissed her on the mouth. She felt the outlines of his teeth behind the press of his thin lips.

He was holding her all by himself now. The other presences were gone, drawn back into their master. She felt a cool, slim hand take her own, the hand that still flapped like a skewered starfish from Skinner's nerve press.

It was Judi.

'Now I've got you here,' he was saying, 'I almost wish I could prolong the moment indefinitely. It's my favourite part, you know...'

'Ah,' she said, 'but you can't have your cake...'

'...and eat it. I know, Anne. I know.'

Her hand was gripped tightly, sending a new charge of pain up her arm. Skinner was wrapped up in his own personal rituals.

'You're going to be my banquet, Anne. I wish I could make you understand how old and important what I am going to do to you is. Perhaps afterwards. If anything in this world is sacred...'

She was weak now, dulled almost to a swoon, but when he started to do it to her, she found she still had the strength to scream.

He began to feed off her.

From deflating lungs, through a dry and shrieking throat, out of a pain-throbbing mouth, she screamed and screamed...

18

At the Monster's right hand, Judi felt him feeding off her sister as he had once fed off her. She remembered her own death, and those of all the other ghosts. Innumerable times, she died, feeling life flow from a broken body, from a thousand broken bodies, into the eternally renewed substance of the Kind. It was an everlasting agony.

The Kind thought of their prey as food, sometimes as submissive lovers. But the ghosts knew different. Bleeding their life out in lumps, they were all their murderers' mothers, their screaming deaths violent and protracted labour pains. The cycle of rebirth left all the parents' shadows in the Monster's Dream, but it also gave Judi a strength she found surprising.

She was more real than she had been since her death. When the Monster was feeding, he was unaware of everything else, like a man caught up in the throes of a protracted orgasm. No man can come and think of something else, Judi knew, and the Monster was at his most manlike this very moment. And while he was a lover, he was also a baby, demanding life, tearing through flesh to reach the air, suckling, sapping Anne's whole being. For the Kind, there must be deaths with each birth, with each rebirth.

There was no blood yet, but there would be soon. Anne's screams seized up in the back of her throat as she felt the Monster's tendrils fixing like hooks into her mind.

Judi looked at Skinner's broad back as his head dipped towards Anne's chest, and met her sister's eyes. Anne was rigid, refusing to tremble, fighting him inside her head.

Judi remembered. They all remembered.

Judi felt Anne's mind pressing in upon her own, the sisters overlaid upon each other. Anne's ghost was forming around her as Skinner sucked her dry. Instamatic fragments of Anne's memory fell into Judi's consciousness. Amid the confusion of faces and feelings, Judi saw herself made different by an unfamiliar personality prism.

She loved her sister, and her sister loved her. At last, she knew their father had loved them both with an equal distance, an equal dread of losing them as he had lost so much else. Things between them were right, at last.

There was a streak of white zig-zagging from Anne's temple into her hair. Her eyes opened wide while her pupils contracted.

Judi and Anne met in the Dream, and found themselves handcuffed. They melted together. Their communion triangulated the Monster. He was a white hot presence, the apex of their triangle.

Judi was able to latch onto Skinner.

Skinner was enjoying his meal, relishing his fuck, exulting in his escape from the womb of womankind. Later, he might even get sentimental about his ghosts, about the empty meat he left behind. But now he was naked need, all the lusts wrapped up in a forever body.

He was in control, but he was caught between the sisters.

It would end now, they decided. The Monster was not forever. Everyone died. No matter how long it was put off, death must come.

Judi laid her insubstantial hands on the Monster's shoulders as he killed Anne, testing her ability to feed off him.

Then came the sunbursts from the deeps of the Monster's mind. The pressure of his prodigious weight of memory drove Judi near to madness. He had had to repudiate nine tenths of his past in order to remain sane, but he had not really forgotten anything. Thousands of years of dreams swept through Judi. Beautiful dreams, dangerous dreams, altruistic dreams, depraved dreams, monomaniacal dreams. Suddenly, she knew his true name, his original name. Even he thought he had forgotten that.

She knew things she could not continue to live with, even live this Phantom Zone version of life with. Death should really be forever. And, as she wanted to die, she wanted her sister to live.

She took her hands away from the Monster's shoulders and put them into his skull. The ectoplasmic wisps sank easily through his hair, into his brain. She made fists, and then opened them, stretching her fingers as widely as she could. Then, catching all the weight she had just taken on and adding it to what little reality she had had, she hurled herself down the funnels of her arms, through the bottlenecks of her wrists, and into her solid hands.

The ghosts swarmed inside her, and were channeled through her almost-real form. They slammed into Skinner like ectoplasmic bullets, and exploded inside him.

Her legs, her body and her head became truly ghostly, but her hands filled out like welder's gloves full of lead shot. She had her bony hooks in the Monster's brain. He let Anne go as she yanked him backwards. He was too tall, but she could float off the floor as he stood up straight, flying from the fixed points in his head like a girl-shaped flag. He grabbed for his head, trying to force the fingertubes sticking out of his forehead back into him.

Inside his head, she could feel a Hiroshima firestorm. All that was his was leaking into her hands. It hurt her.

There was a name. Ariadne. Who was Ariadne? An answer, or just a sledge thrown into a fire? Under the circumstances, Judi did not care.

He was ruptured. This, after everything, was the last night of his life. Judi felt his incredulity for a moment…

…then something flooded into her wispy body with the force of a hundred gallons of boiling lead squirting into an inflatable sex doll. What was left of her flesh exploded, and was spread throughout the Dream like the components of a new universe after a new big bang.

Just before her mind went out like a spent firework, for an eternal moment, Judi thought that *she* was the Monster now...

And then there was light.

19

In their dream, Judi and Anne were Siamese twins, connected by the hind-parts of their brains. Each had a separate personality and a different face, but they shared an unconscious mind. Each loved her sister, although each could never really know what the other's face looked like. When they were born, they were holding hands, and they grew up to make their parents and friends proud. Judi became a famous actress and talk-show personality, noted especially for her Ibsen women; and Anne became a best-selling author of fairy tales and fables. A doctor once thought they could be separated, but Judi and Anne were happy just as they were. They never did die, and there were no such things as Monsters. The End.

20

He fell into her arms this time. His face was still young, but it might just as well have been drawn on a paper bag. He was senile. Anne could feel nearly naked bones inside his clothes. She heaved him away. It was as easy as tossing a bin-liner full of screwed-up envelopes over a table. Skinner bounced on the bar, and only just managed to stay standing up. He turned, looking for her. She wondered if he were blind.

'Anne,' he said, his face starting to curl around the edges, 'Angel…'

The fires were out, but the tawdry Inferno lighting was still on. The Club Des Esseintes was pathetic again. An early Beatles track burbled tinnily on the PA 'Chains'.

He was not much of a Monster any more, but he was still coming to get her.

'Don't think I'm dead, dear. With your help, I can start all over again. Easy.'

He lurched forward, a badly-made scarecrow with a rancid pumpkin head, and made it halfway across the floor. She backed away from him.

'I've been in worse shape than this. Plenty of times. It'll be you and me, Angel…'

'I've told you before, Skinner,' she said, '*that's not my name!*'

Her shout cut through the music, and struck him like a well-aimed blow. He reeled, and staggered forwards, arms out before him, hands hanging from his wrists like dead leaves.

The wall behind her was cold. The mural was flat and unmoving. There was a rack next to her. She flicked a glance at it and saw a selection of leather whips and bludgeons. S and M tools. Weapons.

The thing she reached for turned out to be a leather-sheathed stick, jointed in the middle, about two feet long. At one end was a contoured grip; at the other a cluster of short tails. Their undersides were lined with sharp little hooks. It felt heavy in her hands, and dangerous.

Putting her whole strength into the swing, she hit Skinner across the face. It cracked open. The stick came out of her hands and somersaulted away from them.

Skinner shrank, and she fell on him, shrieking, tearing at his split face. The skin flaked under her clawing fingers and came off like an onion skin. Beneath was an older, greener mask. And beneath that, another, and another, and another. Progressively older, progressively less human-seeming, progressively deader. The layers were dry and crinkly. He seemed to have no moisture in him at all.

Long before she exposed the curiously shaped skull, the Monster was still. His ghosts had gone with Judi, and he was dead.

Ding-dong, the witch is dead!

She spat on him now, and kicked his tenantless body. It felt good. Skinner came apart like a man-sized breadstick. She pulled off his arms and legs and twisted them like wet towels. She trampled his ribs underfoot, squashing his internal organs as they were exposed. Dust rose from the many rips in his skin. With the stick, which she reclaimed, she thrashed the whole mess until it was unidentifiable. His clothes tore as easily as his desiccated flesh.

His pocket watch shone among the rotting fragments. She

picked it out, and gripped it in a painful fist. It was too large to be contained completely by her hand. But it was real. Solid. It ticked. Real seconds passed. The past ate up the future.

'That's forever, Skinner!'

Suddenly, she was tired. She had been awake around the clock.

DAWN

Later, but not much, Anne escaped from the Club Des Esseintes. All the doors were locked now, so she had to use a crowbar-like instrument of torture on them. There was no fire damage in the nostalgia shop. It had a secure-looking grille over its window and front door, so she had to force her way out of a side door.

She came out roughly where she expected to be, next to the already-open amusement arcade. No one bothered her. She binned the implement, and walked away.

There was a pale woman outside Patisserie Valerie, almost an albino. Anne could not help noticing her. She wore heavy dark glasses. She needed to tell someone, so she told the woman.

'Dead,' she said, 'it's dead.'

The woman nodded, a ripple running through her silk-white hair. She did not answer, but she leaned forward and placed a cold kiss on Anne's cheek. It was like a mild electric shock.

The woman was walking away, slipping into the crowd. Anne dropped Skinner's watch into her coat pocket, and felt the cold.

There was a closed newspaper stall on the corner, with a poster of yesterday's *Evening Standard* headlines. AZIZ VERDICT RETURNED. POLICE CONSTABLE CHARGED. Anne felt waking life calling her back.

She looked around for the woman who was the last of the Dream, but she was gone.

It was nearly dawn now, and the streets were busy. Her breath frosted as she walked, and she felt all sorts of aches and bruises. She wanted to get home and take a bath, but she did not feel sleepy any more. She was wide-awake.

The pre-work traffic made crossing streets difficult. She did not feel ready for the underground yet, so she walked to the bus stop under Centre Point. It was just a building. The buses were already running, but there were none waiting. As she stood around, stamping her feet against the cold, the skies lightened and the streetlamps went out.

BLOODY
STUDENTS

'Perhaps some diseases perceived as diseases which destroy a well-functioning machine, in fact change the machine into a machine that does something else, and we have to figure out what it is that the machine now does. Instead of having a defective machine, we have a nicely-functioning machine that just has a different purpose. Part of it is a self-deceptive way of coping with the possibilities of disease, but on the other hand I can imagine what it feels like to be a virus. The AIDS virus: look at it from his point of view – very vital, very excited, really having a good time. It's made the front page, and is really flexing its muscles and doing what it does. It's really a triumph, if you're a virus. It's really good stuff that's happening, it's not bad at all.'

DAVID CRONENBERG

'Look… look at the audience… they've got… *wabbititis*!'

ELMER FUDD

PROLOGUE

LUNACY IN THE AGE OF REASON

Oh God oh God oh God oh God…

There are no atheists during finals, Pete thought as he evened up the sheet of A4 in his battered manual typewriter. He supposed he was ready to hammer this last exam into the ground on his own abilities, but Divine Intervention might come in handy.

Earth to God, Earth to God!

Soften the hearts of thy Holy Assessors, and let them look with favour upon these the works of thy devoted servant.

Pete flexed his fingers in the air over the keyboard. He reached into himself for that moment of *Zen* calm, and was poised to pounce…

Upstairs, a Heavy Metal riff started. The ceiling began to vibrate with the thudding bass. Shit! Ten o'clock in the morning! What a time for the Dickhead Twins to start jiving to their record collection!

Lunacy in the Age of Reasonn, he typed, *by Peter Aston.* He rolled the page up and saw the error. He knew he was out of Tippex, but still felt he had to look through his desk drawer.

Oh Lord, grant unto me liquid paper and I shalt sin no more…

'I couldn't work, and I couldn't think,
I couldn't face the day until I had another drink,

I asked my doctor, what could I do?
He said, "Son, Deep Depression got a hold on you..."'

The intro filled the room. 'Shut the *fuck* up!' he shouted, knowing he had no chance of being heard through the rhythm 'n' racket fuzz-tone guitar. 'Some people are trying to work!'

He pulled the paper out, tearing off a jagged triangle. He crumpled both pieces into a ball, and tore the ball into shreds for good measure. The shreds went into his waste-bin, with the rest of his false starts.

> 'Sometimes it's lack of mon-eeeeee,
> Or maybe lack of friends,
> But ya know Deep Depression
> Gonna getcha in the end!
> I heard my doctor talkin',
> And he weren't bein' vague,
> He say Deep Depression
> Is worse than the PLAGUE!'

Didn't they know it was finals time? Didn't they realize that he had to have three copies of this damn essay on the dean's desk by four-thirty this afternoon or face a *viva voce* Inquisition? Didn't they want him to get his degree?

They were dancing, now. Heavy feet clumped and stamped up above. These ceilings were like two sheets of hardboard sandwiching a cavity. Why did he have to get thrown out of his digs in town and be moved back into a Hall of Residence?

He knew this album by heart – it was by a band called Loud Shit – and 'Deep Depression' was what passed for a slow, quiet, smoochy number. From here on in, it was pure rending metal, 100 mph on the rpm, accompanied by the sounds of large animals being slaughtered. Most radio stations could not even mention the *title* of the last Loud Shit single they had banned, 'Why Don't

You Fuck Off?'. He tried to exclude the din from his thoughts, and summoned all his powers of concentration.

He got a new sheet in the typewriter, and, choosing the keys carefully, at least managed to get his title and name down properly. Then he typed his examination number, and referred to his notes. He had all the quotations, he had the central argument, he even knew exactly what he wanted to say. That put him ahead of most of the others in his seminar group. Except Bloody Basil. That velvet-coated capon must have been born in the Eighteenth Century. No one could have gone through that many obscure philosophical treatises otherwise. He was the kind of slimeball clod who thought epigrams were still in fashion.

The chorus was a couple of decibels louder.

> 'Deep Depressionnnnnn!
> It's the worst by far!
> Deep Depressionnnnnn!
> Makes me feel below par!
> My health is in ruins,
> And my life is *Hell*!
> Since I caught Deep Depression,
> I don't feel well.'

Pete shut the row out of his head, and launched into his essay. 2,500 words. That was not so much. Five sheets of his typing. And at least 750 words would be eaten up by quotations. Plus a page and a half of bibliography and footnotes. It was almost nothing, really. But, of course, he could not afford to turn in a nothing essay. Pete knew he was on the cusp between a first and an upper second, and this was the one that would tip him either way. This meant the difference between a cushy post-graduate spot researching in the sun in some Californian Summer Camp University and a year of gloomy teacher-training followed by a lifetime of slamming English Lit into the heads of natural born lathe operators in Birmingham. Allowing half an hour to stroll to the Humanities Block, he had six hours. He did not even have to produce a page an hour.

He kept typing, turning scrawled shorthand and underlined passages from much-used books into something approaching respectable prose. He was getting a headache from trying to type louder than the music.

> 'You meet them in the café,
> You see them on the train,
> With the Deep Depression,
> They look like they're in *pain*!
> I read it in the papers,
> I seen it on the news,
> They say Deep Depression
> Is *twice as bad* as the BLUES!'

The pile of books by his bed collapsed, but he was not distracted for more than two seconds. He swivelled in his chair to take in the major volume spill, then turned back to the keyboard. His fingers flew, stubbing on the keys. It was not ten past ten yet, but he was two-thirds of the way down his first page, and gaining…

He had books to back him up, but he would not need them. Yesterday, before the essay titles went up, he had been into the library with three extra cards, borrowed from friends. He was a Johnsonian, so he had all the secondary texts out. Taking Bloody Basil's familiarity with Locke and Bishop Berkeley into account, he had grabbed everything hard-to-get on them in the hope of stealing some of the silver-spoon-in-his-mouth slug's thunder. Bloody Basil had his Oxford donship sewn up already. He was practically out of this redbrick hellhole, the bastard. But it was not over yet. Not by a very, very considerable length of calcium carbonate.

The thumping upstairs sounded more like tag-wrestling than

dancing. He only knew Thommy slightly, and his orange-haired girlfriend (Clare?) not at all. But he had heard them at nights. When they were not screwing they were fighting. Four o'clock on Friday morning was their favourite arguing time. The York House Student Union Rep called Thommy the RG, which stood for Resident Git. Clare had bruises sometimes, but it was difficult to tell under her multi-coloured make-up. The mutants were made for each other, Pete thought.

Another chorus of 'Deep Depressionnnnnn!' There was shouting mixed in with the song now, and sound effects from a Sylvester Stallone movie. Grunts and thumps and yelps and cracks. It was as if Thommy and Clare were beating living hell out of each other, then finishing off the job with teeth and claws.

Ten-twenty. First page done. Pete placed it face down on the desk, and had another sheet in the roller before his heart could get to its next beat. He knew his accuracy was way off at this speed, but he could always borrow some Tippex and fix the errors. Once it was on presentable paper, the rest was polishing.

He would have won. It would be all over, three years of study, between drinking, wenching and doping. At least he had been studying all along, not like his best mates Phil, Neil and Stef. They had done two-and-three-quarter years of drinking, wenching and doping, and spent the last term-and-a-bit in panicky over-reading and catching-up. Typical Lower Seconds.

'We gotta try to stop it,
We oughta see it banned!
There's a Deep Depression,
Spreadin' through the *land*!
We need to seek a vaccine,
We need to find a cure,
Gotta say, "Deep Depression,
Don't Bother Me No More!"'

Crash!

The whole place shook with that one. Pete bit his tongue, and tasted blood. His little finger got lodged between the 'o' and 'p' keys, and he scraped gouges pulling it free.

Someone screeched over the music. It hardly sounded human. Thommy must have landed a hard one on Clare, put her down for the count. There was banging on the ceiling, and each bang was accompanied by a whiny grunt. Pete knew someone's head was being smashed again and again on the floor of the room above.

He thought he ought to do something, but deep down he knew his essay was more important. He could not afford to play social worker and wind up with missing teeth. Someone must hear all this noise and do something. Soon.

Last chorus, slower and even louder:

> 'Deep Depressionnnnnn!
> When will I be free?
> Deep Depressionnnnnn!
> Makin' me feel off key!
> My health is in ruins,
> And my life is *Hell*!
> Since I caught DEEP DEPRESSION,
> I DON'T FEEL WELL!'

The words stopped, but the music went on. The banging on the ceiling was in time with the drumbeat now. Pete could hear words – one word – under the bangs.

'Fuck-pig! Fuck-pig! Fuck-pig! Fuck-pig!'

It was a hell of a voice, like the possessed little girl's in *The Exorcist*.

There was nothing for it. Pete knew he had to give up and get involved. No essay was worth more than someone's life. If that was not how he felt, it was how he knew he *ought* to feel. How could he explain to the police that he kept on typing while someone committed murder five feet above his head?

It was easy. *I couldn't hear a thing, officer, I had my Sony Walkman on, loud. Beethoven. Ode to Joy. It helps me think, gets my ideas in order. I'd miss World War Three that way...*

'Fuck... pig! Fuck... pig! Fuck... pig!'

No way would PC Plodder believe that. *You're nicked, my son!*

He stopped typing, and listened. The beating went on, and the swearing, and the crying. There was a screeching scratch and a major crash, and the music shut off. The stereo had sustained some severe damage. He stood up, looking around for a weapon...

If he was going to separate those two, he would need something pretty hefty to back him up. A bazooka?

In the corner, he saw his tennis racket, unstrung and unused since spring. There are no sportsmen in finals, either. He reached for the racket, but something made him look up.

The gaps between the beats were longer now.

'Fuck... pig! Fuck... pig! Fuck... pig!'

With each blow, the lightbulb jerked like a lynch-mob victim at the moment the noose snaps his neck.

'Fuck...'

There were three spots, penny-size, of red on the light brown ceiling.

'...Pig!'

Pete cringed, knowing somehow what could come next, knowing what would happen, but horribly unable to do anything about it.

'Fuck...'

There was a rending, splintering *crack!* and an abbreviated howl of animal pain.

'...Pig!'

The spots were larger now, and more numerous. A droplet gathered on the underside and fell, splashing the back of one of the essay pages. A crack had appeared in the ceiling. The red hissed and smelled on the lightbulb.

'Fuck...'

Pete stood like a statue, conscious of the fragility of his flesh. The howling was constant now, louder than the music had been. He could hear other people shouting, thumping on the RG's door, trying to get in on the act.

'...*Piiiiiiiiig!*'

A head was forced through the crack in the ceiling, and hung dead above Pete. Most of the skin was gone, and the lower lip had been torn away. One eyeball exploded out of its socket like a crushed *crème* egg. Blood ran in leaky-tap trickles, falling on Pete's hands and face. The thing still shook; whatever was pushing it downwards would not leave off savaging the head's owner.

Pete did not know if it was Thommy or Clare or someone else.

But he did know, as he bent double to regurgitate his breakfast over a scattering of library books, that whoever it was had not got the worst behind them yet.

The head screamed and screamed and screamed. Its owner was still alive.

PART ONE

OUT OF THE ANIMAL ROOM

Two days before Pete Aston sat down to write about the Age of Reason, Monica Flint, President of the University Students' Union, was feeling silly. With a scarf over her eyes, she was being escorted to a 'secret location' like some John Le Carre character left over from the Cold War. Cazie Bruckner was really pissing her off.

As they drove, nobody talked. Derm played reggae on the Austin's old cassette deck. Monica had no idea where she was going, although she assumed it would be one of those anonymous houses, shared by four or five students, in the sprawl that would have been a suburb if the town planners had got it organized early enough. She guessed Cazie would have Derm drive around at random a bit to make it difficult to judge the distance from the Old Pier, which was where they had picked her up.

Cazie, who had been called Corinne before she came to the University and caught Politics, was functionally insane, Monica thought. No matter what, she would not have been a likeable girl.

Monica had long since given up trying to guess which way the car was going, and was wondering just exactly what it was about Cazie that got up her nostrils. They were both feminists, and agreed on most issues that came up. But one of the things feminism underestimates is women's potential for not getting on with each other.

It could not be jealousy, not really. Cazie came from money – her Daddy was some robber baron industrialist specializing in corporate rape and hostile take-overs – and she did look stunning with her white face and Louise Brooks haircut, not to mention her slim Jamie Lee Curtis thighs. But Monica was not about to underestimate herself; her physical attractiveness was not open to dispute. Since the braces had come off her teeth, she had not had any complaints. There was no *Dynasty*-type catfight between the two women. They did not even have to do business very often.

If only Cazie were not such a self-righteous nut…

The car stopped. They were there. The door opened. A hand took Monica by the upper arm and guided her out. She bumped her head slightly on the doorframe. She felt cold night air on her uncovered cheeks.

'Can I take this thing off now?'

A pause.

Monica knew what was happening. Derm and the girl with them, Clare, were looking to Cazie for orders. A nod or a headshake.

It must be the shake.

'Not yet, Mon,' Cazie's Hackney-via-Roedean voice came, 'wait until we're inside. I'm sure you understand.'

'Yeah, quite. Let's get inside before I walk into something, okay?'

'Okay.'

She was helped up a few steps, and reached out to steady herself. She felt curved stone. A pillar. This must be one of those mock-grand porches a lot of terraced hovels in town have. She could not hear or smell the sea, so they must be quite a way from the front. Someone fumbled with keys, and a door opened. Monica could see light through the scarf, and human-shaped figures moving. She was eased over the doorstep and into a hall.

The door closed behind her, and, before anyone could give yea or nay, Monica had yanked the blindfold off her eyes.

The light hurt a bit. Spots danced at the edge of her vision.

The hall was entirely conventional. Ragged carpet with a long-lost pattern. Walls in need of massive redecoration and a spot of replastering, covered as best they could be with posters. No pop stars or cult movies, just fliers for demonstrations, glossy pin-ups of endangered species, and stinging indictments of fox-hunting and animal research.

Monica's eyes were caught by a picture of a kitten with an exposed brain, trailing electrodes. That poster did not need a slogan, although it had one, telling you who to blame. Dotted between the big pictures were professional-looking snapshots of red-coated huntsmen brandishing bloody fox portions or white-coated scientists cringing over tortured beagles.

'Through here,' said Cazie.

Monica ducked under a low beam, and felt her way down a flight of narrow stairs into what had been the basement. Now, it was an Operations Room for Cazie's splinter group.

Monica could never remember the acronym. It lacked the elegance and pronounceability of the best factions. There it was, printed in white letters at the top of a cork notice board. STWAA. Stop The War Against Animals.

'Sit down anywhere, Mon.'

Cazie took an armchair in front of the cork board. Everyone else had to make do with scatter cushions, stools or straight-backed dining chairs. Monica took one of the chairs, and crossed her legs.

'Right, Corinne. Could you please explain this George Smiley stuff?'

The girl looked almost hurt. Someone else had to start for her.

'Monica,' began Derm, the big-shouldered black guy, 'you've got to go easy on the demo tomorrow.'

'*What*!?'

'Hold on, Mon, it's not so simple...'

'Corinne, you've spent weeks lobbying the union, packing meetings, getting near to mangling our constitution. All to get us alerted to UCC presence on campus. You finally manage to prove that animal experiments are being carried out in the Chem Building. And now you want us to backpedal on the protest you've practically organized? What are you people playing at?'

Cazie looked uncomfortable, whiter than usual. Monica began to notice unfamiliar faces at the meeting. Slightly older than she had expected. Not mature students, but outsiders. There was something a little creepy about them, as if they came along with all the spy shenanigans.

'There've been some changes in our strategy, Mon. We've talked to some people, and...'

The girl looked around, looked to the new faces for support. All at once, Monica realized Cazie was frightened. It was not a game for girls any more. A cat slid into the room, and weaved its way through everyone before finding its niche in Cazie's lap, nuzzling her denim groin. She stroked it automatically. She really was good with animals.

Finally, someone stepped forward. A man in his late thirties, with a sandblasted outdoors face, wearing a black donkey jacket unmarked by any patches, badges or messages.

'I'm Rex Rote. You've heard of me?'

'Yes,' said Monica. 'You nearly killed a minor member of the Royal Family, right?'

Rote smiled. 'It was war. He wouldn't have got hurt if he hadn't pointed that shotgun at a bird.'

On the first day of the grouse-shooting season, Rote's group had plugged up the gun-barrels of a party of VIPs who were setting out to stride through the heather for a BBC documentary. The filmed explosion had been reasonably spectacular, and still got repeated on news programmes. It had apparently been a highly professional job of sabotage.

'Animals can't fight back for themselves,' said Cazie.

'No,' said Rote, 'so we have to prove that not all human beings are bastards.'

'Fine,' said Monica, 'I assume you're the reason for all this security?'

'I'm still "underground". But I go where I'm needed. And what Ms Bruckner has shown me suggests that I'm needed right here, right now.'

Monica looked at Rote, trying to gauge him. Most of the people she had to deal with on a day-to-day basis were students or faculty. It was not pretend politics, but it was insular, sealed-off from the rest of the world. The gloves rarely had to come off. But Rote probably did not even own a pair of gloves. He was either committed to his cause, or ought to be committed because of it. For a man who spent his life crusading against cruelty, he struck her as a bit of a sadist. He might not hurt a mouse, but he would have no difficulty garrotting a fellow human being.

'Tomorrow,' began Rote, 'you people are going to fuck up everything I've been working for.'

'How?'

'Your piss-little demo, Ms Flint. You'll get a crowd together and shout slogans and maybe get a bit out of hand and break a plate-glass door or two. The local papers will come down…'

'Isn't that what you want? The Unwin Chemical Corporation won't like the publicity, and the University certainly won't like being linked to animal experiments. There's a good chance we can force UCC to pull out.'

'Maybe. But a lot of animals will be dead or worse by then. In the short term, all you'll do is make UCC security-conscious. They'll tighten up. Make sure the campus cops spend more time there. They'll know trouble will be brewing.'

'Trouble?'

'Uh-huh. Tomorrow night, there'll be trouble. But better trouble than your placard-waving and slogan-shouting. Effective trouble.'

Monica looked around. Cazie was posed anxiously, her fingers stuck in the cat's fur, seeking approval. Only Rote, and his people, were relaxed.

'What kind of trouble exactly, Mr Rote?'

The man cracked a grin, not a pleasant one, and took a breath.

'Ah well, it's like this…'

He had a seminar on the Spanish Civil War to prepare, and Jason was being a pain in the arse.

'Find me a video, Daddy, please.'

The 'please' tailed off into a whine. Brian Connors pushed his chair back from the desk in his study and got up to pay attention to his sometime son.

'Okay, Jase. Give me a moment.'

The eight-year-old vanished from the doorway and was tumbling down the stairs in his inimitable stuntman fashion. Brian followed, realizing for perhaps the tenth time that his body was prepping for the Big Four-Oh next year but one. He had quit cigarettes, but he would never get his young man's lungs back.

With Jean and her new boyfriend in Lanzarote, he could not have refused to take Jason for the week. Even if Jean *had* tried to block his access at the time of the divorce, citing him as an evil and corrupting influence. That was a while back, though. These days, she seemed to be able to stand being in the same room as him without reaching for a breadknife.

Everyone had to mellow, as he knew only too well.

If it were not for Jason, he would have had Debbie around tonight. Then again, though the demands would have been different, the nineteen-year-old was just as capable of distracting him from his work, wearing him down emotionally, leaving his body aching and drained. He had kicked cigarettes into touch, was holding off on the Jamieson's, and had not played his Jimi Hendrix albums in over six months, but he was still sleeping with his students.

It would probably kill him in the end.

Jason was scrabbling through the cabinet in which Brian kept his tapes. His pyjama bottoms hung low on chubby hips.

'What's this, Daddy, what's this?'

Jason held up a tape, label outwards. *Ways of Seeing, Ways of Being.*

'University stuff, Jase.'

The boy was disappointed and distressed. He stuck out his lower lip, and threw the cassette back. Then he had another one out. He made a pretence of examining the spine, then held it out to Brian.

Eight years old, and the kid still could not read. Not even *Janet and John*. Jean said he was just a slow learner, but Brian had already checked out a couple of books on dyslexia, and made a few tentative stabs at getting Mike Prickett, his friend from SocSci, together with the kid. In the pub after their weekly badminton binges, Mike had tried to damp Brian's fears, but there was no getting round it. Jason was a thicko in other ways too. He still could not dress himself properly, as Brian had found out two mornings ago.

Brian looked at the tape. It was one of his under-the-counter jobs, slipped him by an assistant in the Communications Department, *Sixth Form Girls in Chains*. Debbie liked that kind of thing.

'Boring, Jase,' he explained. 'University stuff.'

'Why do you have a boring job, Daddy?'

Sometimes Daddy asks himself that, Jase, he thought. 'It's not boring when you're a grown-up. You'll see.'

'Couldn't you be a fireman?'

Brian laughed and picked his son up.

'Throw me against the roof, Daddy.'

Brian tossed Jason out of his arms, not hard enough to throw him against the ceiling. Jason reached up, and his fingers brushed plaster before gravity pulled him down to his father's grasp.

'On-Cor! On-Cor!'

Brian threw again, the heaviness going out of his chest. Jason could be a lot worse kid really. When his arms got tired, he would dig out the *Teenage Mutant Hero Turtles* episodes he had taped especially, and get back to news coverage of the Spanish Civil War.

The doorbell rang. Debbie?

When they had moved into the campus cottage, Jean had teased Brian about the doorbell. Its double chime was so conventional, so middle-class. With his reputation, he ought to have one that played the North Vietnamese National Anthem. That was when he had known he was finally grown up. Three weeks later, he had shaved his beard, and seen a responsible member of society in the mirror.

The bell rang again, and again. Urgently. It did not feel like Debbie.

He caught Jason, and put him down. In two strides, he was in the hall. A female shape stood behind the frosted glass. He smiled, ready to pull Debbie over the threshold into an embrace. Raphael and Shredder would keep Jason distracted, and the Spanish Civil War could wait...

He opened the door, and reached for the girl.

'Brian!'

His hands found a shoulder and a waist, and he pulled. He bent towards her, to kiss... and saw red hair.

Debbie was blonde, with occasional purple tints.

'Brian.'

Monica was laughing. She struggled free from him.

'Who were you expecting?'

'Uh... well... hello, Monica, come in. I've just got some coffee going.'

Monica eased past him in the narrow hall. Her body briefly shared airspace with his, and he felt a twinge of arousal. Monica had been after Jean, but before the students. Actually she had been a student, but not like the others. Not like Debbie. Not like *a* Debbie.

She knew her way about the house. In the front room, she collided with Jason. From the doorway, he saw the boy hug her.

'Monneemonneemonneemonnee!'

'Jaysunnjaysunnjaysunn!'

It took a moment for him to realize he was not calling her 'mummy'. He had nearly done so, for a while. Jason had his fingers in her masses of hair, stroking and pulling.

'Ouch. Jason, the wedding's off!'

Suddenly, the child's hands were behind his back. Brian knew his son had a crush – he was not backwards in *everything* – on Monica Flint, and had pestered her to marry him for over six months three years ago. He thought the kid would have grown out of that by now, been embarrassed by it, even. Jason might not have inherited his father's academic bent, but he was well equipped with Brian's other quirks.

As Monica played with Jason, pinching his cheeks and saying how much he had grown, Brian tried to remember the exact words she had used the last time they had met in his house.

He thought aloud, '…reprehensible… juvenile… satyriasis-suffering… intellectually-overreaching… louse…'

She turned towards him, not playing any more.

'You're a bastard, too, for cherishing the hurt, Brian. You just paid me back, we're even. Now, can we start from scratch?'

Well, Debbie *had* been getting on his nerves. That relationship was reaching its critical mass about now. And Monica was still Something Special.

'It's not that easy, Monica. I'm kind of involved, but I'm sure we could…'

For an instant, her face was a Japanese dragon mask of anger.

'Not like *that*, Brian! Not ever again in a million years like *that*! I need help.'

His twinge went away.

He had called her a couple of things too, 'ball-breaking bitch' chief among them. After Jean, that had been the worst of the break-ups, perhaps because both of them had wanted to cling on even after it was obvious nothing would work out. Still, he did not get to meet damsels in distress every day of the week.

'Help? You've got it. Get that coffee from the kitchen while I settle Jason in front of the video, would you?'

Without argument, she was gone. Jason jumped up and down, shouting, 'Cowabunga, cowabunga!'

'Yes, the Turtles, although it'll rot your brain out. You ought to be graduating to *Star Trek* pretty soon.'

He found the tape, and slotted it in the machine. The television winked on, and cartoons filled the screen. He had told Debbie he was thinking of doing a paper on the marketing phenomenon of the *Teenage Mutant Hero Turtles,* but the truth of it was that he liked crap too. There were nearly three hours' worth of episodes on the tape. That would give him time for Monica.

She was coming out of the kitchen with the coffee. After three years, she remembered – black, no sugar.

'Upstairs, in the study.'

'The study?'

'It's where our… where the bedroom used to be.'

She smiled and looked at him sideways. He glimpsed her as a nineteen-year-old. Then it was gone, and he realized what was strange about her.

She was frightened.

'Come on up,' she said, going ahead of him. 'I've got to tell you a story…'

'Skippy did something interesting last night,' said Carson.

Dr Xavier Anderton walked along the row of cages that lined the wall of the Animal Room, and peered into the mess that had once been a rabbit.

'He redecorated his cage.'

The wire was bent outwards where the animal had hurled itself at the walls of its environment, and several ragged holes had been chewed or punched through. Skippy – all the rabbits were named after television and film animals – should not have been strong enough to do that. Anderton checked the clipboard hung above the cage.

'Batch 125. *Four ccs?*'

'Last of the sample,' explained Carson. 'I thought we should use up whatever was left.'

It was sloppy, but Anderton did not reprimand his assistant. The death was a puzzle, not a tragedy.

Skippy had evidently done his best to do the utmost damage to his cage, and then turned his destructive fury in on himself. He had opened his body from neck to tail, and spilled organs and entrails. Strings of gut hung from jagged wires. The straw was red and sticky. One of Skippy's pink, dead eyes caught Anderton's attention. Rabbits do not have much range of expression, and what they do have comes from whiskers not eyes. But something in the eye spooked the scientist to the soul.

'Should I call UCC?'

'No, not yet. I'll have to know what this means. Cook up another batch of 125. I'll check the other animals.'

This was not quite what Anderton was after, but it was more intriguing than the total lack of response Leo had yielded so far. Lassie, Flipper, Clarence (who *was* slightly cross-eyed), Cheetah and Francis were nibbling lettuce, sleeping or stretching as expected. But Rikki (for Rikki-Tikki-Tavi) was dead and stiff. No violence, no obvious symptoms, just dead.

And Thumper had melted down.

At first, Anderton thought the rabbit was asleep under the straw, but when he reached into the cage to prod it awake, he touched squishy fur. There was a large lump of semi-liquid grease inside, and it oozed out of the mouth, eyes and anus when the rabbit was touched.

This was even more interesting than Skippy.

'Excuse me, Dr Anderton?'

'Yes?'

Anderton returned to the main laboratory. Carson was there, with Finch.

'Did you know the students have a picket line outside?'

'Not again. What's it about? Has Professor Buckingham been doing any more research on racial characteristics?'

Finch looked disturbed. Nervously, she stroked down her seal-short cropped hair.

'No, doctor. It's about us. About the animals.'

Carson chipped in. 'It had to happen. It's a hot issue.'

Anderton chewed his biro, and thought.

'We're secure-locked. This is supposed to be a sealed environment. So, who gives a ferret's fuck about students? Miss Finch, scrub me a workplace and dig up the instruments. We've got some autopsies to do.'

Cazie had to be on the front line. She could not very well be anywhere else after all the work she had put in.

Thommy, dressed as the White Rabbit from *Alice in Wonderland*, pulled out his fob watch and posed for the three local press cameramen. He raised one paw in a clenched fist salute, and chanted, 'UCC Tortures Me! UCC Tortures Me!'

Otherwise, it was a feeble protest. Cazie could not bear the sympathy she was getting from those not in the know. She wanted to tell them it was not her fault, that they were taking it easy, that Rote was on the case. But she knew better than to mention Rote.

When this was over, she hoped to disengage from the Movement. She was getting interested in the homeless. Lots of good people were getting into Poverty Action. Derm, who knew more about poverty than most of her friends, would be particularly keen. And the others would follow. She could form a chapter of Class War. That would certainly get under Daddy's skin.

She was only in this because she liked animals. She had been one of those rich little girls with ponies, and for years she had planned to be a vet when she grew up. And here she was taking Business Studies, and listening to her father talk about getting into the Firm. Daddy was a fatcat all right, but he did not realize what his little girl could do with the power of a medium-sized finance company behind her. He would have the shock of his life, a bigger shock than he had had when he met Derm.

Monica had shown up early, and given a few instructions to her Rentacrowd people. There had been no trouble. Thommy was getting all the attention with his bunny suit. Cazie had had to give a few sentences to the newspapers. She had made do with handing out a prepared statement, detailing all the evidence against UCC and its history of animal experiments. She had lied, and said they had no specific proof that the UCC-financed projects being carried out in the Chem Building involved animals, but that it was the company, not this particular arm of it, they were protesting against.

Rote was lying low back at her place, back at what he called the 'safe house'. His real work would come tonight, and tomorrow she would change her life.

'Corinne, can I have a word?'

'Uh, oh, hi Mon.'

Monica Flint was the only person, besides Daddy, who still called her Corinne. She did it on purpose.

In the daylight, away from the STWAA Action Room, Monica looked much older, much more confident, much more powerful. Cazie felt uncertain of herself beside the woman.

'Sure, Mon. Things are going nicely here. We can get a tea from the Chem common room.'

'And cross your own picket line?'

Suddenly, Cazie hated Monica. She put her fisted hands into the pockets of the man's pinstripe jacket she wore over her Animal Rights Now T-shirt, and shivered. It was May, but a cold spring was lingering. It looked like rain.

'I forgot. Sorry.'

'Come with me. There's someone who wants to talk to you.'

Monica led her away from Chem, along the paved pathways that criss-crossed the campus village. The trees were shedding blossom like dandruff. The University was out of town, a community unto itself.

Under a tree, a man sat on a bench, wearing a brown leather jacket and black jeans, watching a little boy – wrapped up warm and with a colourful woolly hat on – playing with model spacemen on the grass. The kid was dive-bombing green aliens with a plastic star cruiser. The man was huddled up, hands in his pockets and collar turned up around his face.

Cazie gripped Monica's wrist, hard. She looked into the woman's face.

'You *told*!'

It was like the ultimate betrayal. Cazie could not deal with it. She began shaking. She could taste the anger in her mouth, feel it trembling in her voice.

'You *told*!'

'It's okay, Corinne.' Monica broke her grip, and then squeezed Cazie's hand. 'You'll see. Rote won't know. Brian knows what we're doing.'

'Brian?'

'Brian Connors. He's in the Humanities Department. You'll like him. Well, maybe that's putting it too strong. Come on, anyway. It'll be all right, honestly.'

Monica pulled her forward, and sat her down on the bench. The man – Brian – smiled and shook her hand. He was good-looking in a crumpled smoothie sort of way.

'Corinne Bruckner... Brian Connors.'

'Hi,' said Brian, looking at her in a way she had just begun to appreciate this last year or so. There was no doubt: he found her attractive. 'Corinne?'

'Cazie,' she said. 'What's this about?'

'You know what it's about, Corinne,' said Monica. 'Rote.'

Cazie could not help looking around, to see if there was anyone within earshot. How many people had Monica told?

'Oh God, Rote.'

'You don't need to tell me about Rote,' Brian said.

'You know him?'

'No. I know plenty of people like him, though.'

Monica cut in, 'Brian used to be...'

'Never mind that,' he said, with an undertone of irritation. 'Do you understand what you're getting into? Direct action, right?'

'I don't know.'

'Tonight, your group is going to hit the Chem Building.'

Cazie glared at Monica, who did not flinch. She had obviously told this outsider every damn thing.

'Tell me, Cazie.'

Cazie swallowed her spit, and chewed a fingernail. She thought she had beaten the habit.

'Yes. Tonight. We're going to liberate the animals.'

'Uh huh. Liberate? Fair enough. I don't suppose trying to talk you out of it would do any good?'

'Well...'

'I thought not. It's not you who has to be convinced any more, is it? It's Rote.'

'Yes. I suppose so, but...'

'How out of your control is this situation?'

She did not want to say it.

'Completely?'

She nodded. 'Rote has brought people in with him. He calls them "soldiers". No one likes them, but no one has a choice. He's been in the house for a week now. Someone gave him STWAA as a contact address. He gets what he wants.'

'He's what we used to call "underground", on the run?'

'He still calls it that.'

'You know that harbouring a wanted man is a criminal offence?'

'I suppose so, but…'

'You're afraid to turn him in. Don't worry. I would be too. No one is going to blame you for that. We're not dealing with a non-violent debating-society-type animal lover, here.'

'What am I going to do?'

'What are *we* going to do to you, you mean? As far as I can see, nothing. We'll get it over with, and get you out of it. That's all we can do. He'll go away once he's had his raid?'

'I think so.'

'He'd be stupid not to. Strike, then run. That's the system. I don't really care about rabbits either way, but I'd like to be able to think I can see us through this without anyone getting hurt, so I'm going to make it easy for you.'

Brian dug into his pocket-and came up with a keyring.

'I got these from Sparks. He's on campus security, but he's a mate of mine and I trust him. This will get you into the Chem Building, and these open the sealed environment – whatever that is – UCC are paying for. Be bloody careful, and don't do any damage. Just go in, get the animals and come out again. Sparks will cover for you.'

'He *knows*?'

'We haven't been adults forever. He probably does more drugs and listens to worse music than you do. As long as his job is protected, he'll do what he can.'

Brian looked again at the little boy, and shouted, 'Jason, leave that alone. You'll get filthy.'

Monica said, 'You've got homes for Flopsy, Mopsy and Whatever?'

'Yes,' Cazie said quietly, shaken by her sudden, apparent reversion to little girlhood. Monica and Brian were like her parents, fed up but helping her out of trouble for form's sake. Just like the time Daddy had talked the headmistress out of expelling her.

Brian put a hand to her face, and brought it around to look at. He had grey eyes, older than the rest of his face.

'You don't know what you're doing, girl, do you? Listen, back in the '70s, probably in the year you were born, I was a student too. I signed petitions and went on marches and stayed up all night painting placards. I was quite well known for it. Red Brian, Commie Connors, that sort of thing. I never had to go underground, but I got pretty close. It was all stupid stuff, I know that now. I knew that then, but I liked the idea of being a hero. I looked a lot like Che Guevara before I had my hair cut. One night, I got up in a Vietcong uniform and led an assault on the American Embassy in Grosvenor Square. There was a whole bunch of us. We had toy guns, and were a bit – well, a lot – drunk or stoned or whatever. It was like playing soldiers. Only the real soldiers at the Embassy didn't know it was a game. I had a girlfriend with me. They shot her.'

'Dead?'

'No. You'd have heard of it. That kid's her son. She's in Lanzarote. But her left knee doesn't work properly, and it never will. We were stupid. You've got to be sensible, you understand?'

'Yes.'

'I wish I could believe you, Cazie.' His gaze pierced her forehead, probing through her guilty secrets. Then, he looked away. 'Jason, stop that or you'll get *such a smack!*'

The boy ran off, spaceships flying in both hands.

'Excuse me, I've got to chase my kid and put him in the hospital. Be smart, be careful.'

He was gone, and she was alone with Monica. She did not particularly like the President, but she had never envied her before.

'Who was that masked man?'

Monica shrugged. 'Just some bum I used to know.'

'Used to know, Mon. You're stupider than I am.'

'Maybe. I doubt it, though. I'll tell you when you're older. If you *get* older.'

It was still cold, very cold.

* * *

Normally, Clarence's feelings were limited. Vague senses: claustrophobia, hunger and sexual frustration. Right now there was something in her life more unsettling than these discomforts. In the last few hours, she had started thinking more complicated thoughts than she was used to. And she was hurting.

Right now, Clarence did not feel much like a rabbit at all. It was as if her insides were changing, outgrowing the rest of her body. She bled from her eyes. She chewed her paws to bloody stumps. She shat a stream of painfully hot pellets. She bit the wire.

Nobody came.

She knew what dogs were. A long time ago, as far back as she could remember, she had been penned in a cage within a cage. There were other animals there. She was allowed to spend time with the other rabbits occasionally. She had been able to have sex and eat grass. There were other kinds of animals besides rabbits in the cages. The quietly vicious, needle-sharp, hissing ones were cats. And the noisy, enormously jawed ones were dogs.

Right now, she felt as if there was a dog inside her, gnawing at her insides, trying to get out of her body. Its teeth were tearing inside her guts, pushing out. The dog was going to eat its way out of her, and she would explode.

In her ears, the noises she was making sounded like a dog's growls.

Still nobody came.

Brian and Monica had not seen much of each other after they split up, but since she had become President of the Students' Union, she had been almost completely out of his circle. Once, at a meeting, they had faced each other over a negotiating table. He knew she had been silently hurt that he had sided with Vice-Chancellor Jackson against the students petitioning for a more open assessments system, and he had felt mildly guilty, remembering the days when he would have been on her side, arguing a good deal more heatedly and violently than she did, and to much less effect. She had been a sharp student, and now, as a post-graduate with a year's sabbatical to discharge her duties as head of the Union, she was an even sharper politician. And she still had that hair.

After talking to Cazie Bruckner, they had had lunch together – with Jason – in the Refectory, and talked inconsequentially. Without probing, he had found out that she was not emotionally involved. With probing, she had got a good idea of the succession of Debbies who had traipsed through his bedroom in the last few years. She told him he was starting to show his age, and he was not even hurt.

'...and you're wearing a tie.'

'A present from Jean. Last Christmas.'

'It doesn't look so bad.'

'I think so.'

They did not talk for a while, and Jason filled in the gap in the conversation with a long story about his schoolfriends' slug-eating activities. Brian lost the thread, and got interested in Monica. She had slight smile lines around her mouth. He mentally calculated her age – twenty-three, twenty-four? Once, he had thought of lining her up as Wife Number Two, but she had not wanted to go along with it. That proved, he supposed, what a smart girl she was.

She was the only student he had ever slept with whose grades he had had to mark down to prevent him being accused of favouritism. Debbie, for instance, might have a great tongue but was stuck with a typical third-rate mind and would be lucky to scrape a C Minus this term.

'Jason's going to a party this afternoon,' he said, 'I've got to drop him off. Want to come by?'

Her lower lip was slightly moist, which he found intensely arousing. She recognized the line, recognized the opportunity for an afternoon with him.

'And Debbie?'

'Who?'

She laughed once, cynically, and shook her head. 'Brian, you don't give up.'

'It's one of my better qualities.'

'Whoever told you that?'

'No one.'

'I'm not surprised. Jason has more shame than you.'

'Wha'?' Jason frowned, not understanding.

'It's nothing, Jase. Auntie Monica was being silly. I hope *you* don't eat slugs.'

'No, they taste horrible.'

'How do you know?'

'Uh… I refuse to answer that question on the grounds that I might 'criminate myself…'

'What?' spat Monica, laughing.

'Television,' said Brian. 'Jean lets him watch all day. He's fluent in cliché. A year ago, he got obsessed with *Neighbours* and started talking in a 'strine accent all the time. Thank God that's over.'

'Can we go to the party now, Daddy?'

'Sure. Monica?'

'I have to be in my office. There's a UGM at four, and I've got to explain myself on a couple of points.'

'Some other time?'

'Maybe.'

Brian stood up to go, helping Jason on with his hat and scarf. Monica reached out and stroked the boy's cheek, then put her hand on his arm.

'Brian,' she said, 'I want to thank you for today. You've helped a lot.'

'All part of the service, ma'am. I'll just slip back into my Clark Kent disguise and leave without making a fuss. Take care.'

'Yeah. You too.'

At home that afternoon, while Jason was splashing in an

indoor paddling pool at his party, Brian started thinking seriously about Monica, remembering. He could not tell one Debbie from another in his mind now, but every detail of Monica was sharp. Her long, warm kisses; her gentle, expert fingering; that strange goulash recipe; her clear, perfect singing voice, unexpectedly coming out when she was distracted.

He phoned Debbie's flat, but hung up before the third ring. He did not know how he felt about anything.

The Campus Radio Collective meeting had been going on for too long, and Eddie Zero was beginning to feel an ache in his drainpipe-jeaned knees from leaning slumped against the wall because all the chairs in the tiny office were occupied by people with seniority. This was not doing his red velvet teddy-boy jacket any good, and he did not think anything else was going to come out of it either. He examined the shine on the toes of his winkle-pickers.

Posie Columba, chairperson of the collective, was announcing the new schedule for the station. She had not got to Eddie Zero's Rock 'n' Roll Rebellion Show yet. Just now, she was outlining her plans to devote every weekday for the next month to a World Music Festival she had been organizing with her friends Achmet and Zorrino. Achmet thought Lloyd Price was a building society, and Zorrino could not tell The Ventures from The Chordettes.

'This is the sort of cutting edge thing CR should be promoting,' Posie said, her *okay-yah* voice sandpapering Eddie's ears. 'It's authentic, yah, and it's the wave of the future.'

She actually had said 'yah' and expected people not to laugh at her. No one had laughed at her, and he managed to pass off his own snort as a cough. She looked at him with too-narrow eyes, and went on with her spiel.

Eddie stifled a yawn, and amused himself by imagining he was the Masked Mangler, star of a slice 'n' dice movie in which a collective of campus radio jocks are killed off one by one in ways appropriate to their programmes. Funkmaster Dee, the worst-dressed white boy Eddie had ever seen, would be plugged into a sound system and booted to death by the throb of his own dance albums. Psychedelic Pstan, who never played a track less than three-quarters of an hour long, would be juiced up on hallucinogenics and dipped, in his squiggle shorts and big red glasses, into a vat of steaming chemicals at the world's first Acid Bath Party. Shaggy Andy, who was a folk traditionalist, would be flayed alive by country craftsmen who took a pride in their work and stretched his skin over the bole of their mandolins to get a better sound. And Posie would be forced to drink a gallon of water from each of the Third World countries she reckoned were musically in the forefront of civilization, and then be rotted from the inside by 57 different varieties of horrible disease. He would let Achmet and Zorrino off only if they agreed to clean up the mess.

They had argued about music all year, and Eddie was fed up with it. All he wanted to do was unleash some real rock 'n' roll onto the airwaves, and let the kids out there develop an appreciation of genuine musical genius. His pantheon was Buddy, Elvis, Jerry Lee, Chuck, Ritchie, Little Richard. Everything else sucked. Posie said he was 'a throwback to the pop mentality' and called him an imperialist racist for writing off African and South American music as 'ear-jerking crap'. What kind of colour was Harvey Fuqua, bitch?

'Every day of the week, we'll spotlight a different country, right?' Posie said, cheeks red and shaking with teary enthusiasm. 'Monday, Zimbabwe. Tuesday, Brazil. Wednesday, Gabon…'

'Posie, when are you going to fit in Antarctica?' he asked.

The girl frowned again, and made a tent with her porky fingers.

'What kind of music do they got in Antarctica?' said Funkmaster Dee, trying to sound as much like a fifty-year-old black pimp from Detroit as is possible for the teenage Caucasian son of a Coventry vicar.

'If you can't be serious, we'll have to propose a motion to censure you, Eddie.'

'Oh, please, Hot Mama, don't censure me. Anything but that.'

Posie smiled a mean, devious smile, and told them all when their slots were.

Eddie's show was between two and three A.M. on Fridays.

Rote had shown them how to black up like the SAS. Clare felt strange in her balaclava and heavy coat. She was used to colours.

She and Thommy sat in the back, with Cazie and Rote's three soldiers. Rote was up front, with Derm. Derm was driving. It was an anonymous van, dark green and unmarked. Rote had made sure it was parked around the campus for a few days, to get the security people used to the sight of it. Rote had turned up at Cazie's in it, and Clare wondered if it might be stolen.

Thommy had got some speed to take earlier, but Rote had seen him give her some and forbidden them. He had slapped Thommy with his open hand and told him not to act like a prat.

Clare was afraid of Rote, but agreed with him about Thommy. This was no time to be out of your head. She could not help but feel good, seeing the glint in Thommy's eyes as Rote hit him, the glint that meant he was too chicken to hit back. Thommy was free with his hands usually – he must have been a bully at school – but Rote was in a different class altogether.

Last night, after the meeting, Rote had taken her upstairs and they had fucked. Thommy had not been happy about that either. Clare was not sure how happy she was about it, in fact, but she had had to go along with it. Once in the sack, she had been able to give up thinking and just get into the fucking. This morning, she had bruises, blue weals up and down her thighs and angry red dots around her nipples. No wonder Rote was so concerned with the protection of animals; he was one.

They drove out of town, towards the campus. There was a double carriageway, but it was practically empty. Clare felt fear and excitement in the pit of her stomach. Her breasts hurt.

With a trace of self-disgust, she realized that she was almost turned on. She squirmed a little on the hard bench, as if her arse were itching. Thommy was oddly withdrawn, sober. Clare's mouth went dry, as she realized she did not know which she would be fucking tonight. Thommy or Rote.

For once, Cazie was quiet. She looked strange with her face streaked commando-style, and a black beret pulled over her ears. There were snailtracks of white on her cheeks. Clare realized the girl was crying.

The soldiers were like robots. Two men and a woman, switched off when not in use. They came with Rote. It was funny. They did not even talk about animal rights or press campaigns like the rest of STWAA. They were only interested in doing damage, in hurting people. In a week, they had not even told anyone their names. Security, she supposed.

The van stopped.

'We're here,' said Rote, from up front. 'Get ready.'

Clare tensed, aware that she would need to go to the loo in the very near future. She ran over the plan in her mind, as Rote started putting it into action.

Rote got out of the van. One of his men made sure the back door was unlatched. Rote walked up to the double doors of the Chem Building, keys in hand. His soldiers had jemmies and boltcutters in case the keys were a bust. But they did their job properly.

'Now,' Derm said.

They all piled out of the van in an orderly fashion. Clare pushed against Cazie, and could feel the girl shaking. Rote's woman shoved them both, and they went with the team. Rote had the door open, and counted them all inside. Derm stayed at the wheel of the van, lying quiet on the front seat. It was properly parked. No one should get curious.

Inside the building, Thommy and Clare got out their torches and, in silence, made their way down the corridor towards the sealed environment. The further they got from the glass doors, the better Clare felt. Once they were swallowed by the complications of the building, there was no chance they would be seen. It was dark, but familiar. The place was just like every other building on campus, a beehive of lecture halls, offices, store-rooms and laboratories.

Rote had done his homework. They made no false turns. UCC had obligingly put up a notice detailing their contributions to the University, marking out the laboratory where they were carrying out their research. Clare knew rabbits were being tormented in the facility, but it struck her now that she had never heard exactly what they were suffering for.

Rote opened the first sealed door, and then the second. The air did not feel any different inside the laboratory, although it was supposed to be purer. Clare was studying History; she did not know anything about the procedures here.

'Where are the animals?' said Thommy, his voice squeaking a little, like Mickey Mouse.

'There.'

Rote took Thommy's wrist, and pointed his torch at a sign.

ANIMAL ROOM.

The door was wooden, inset with a wired glass window. It was locked. Cazie's source had not furnished a key for this one.

'Smash it,' said Rote. His male soldiers stepped forward. One tested the handle, tapped the wood around the lock, and nodded to the other. The second man aimed a lightning-fast martial arts kick at the indicated spot. The door shot inwards, and slammed against something. Orange wood showed through white paint where the door had splintered.

There was a chattering and growling inside the Animal Room.

'Get the cages, and let's get out.'

Something shot out of the Animal Room, and struck Clare full in the chest. It was harder than any of the blows Thommy had ever landed on her. She fell backwards onto a fixed table, slamming her lower back against a hard edge.

The thing was still on her, clinging to her shirt. She felt points of pain on her breasts. Her torch was gone, and she could not see the thing. It could not be a rabbit. Rabbits do not have claws. It was making noises like a horror movie monster. She grabbed the furry creature, and pulled it away. Her shirt – and her skin – tore. The thing had fishhooks in its feet.

Clare felt the dampness spreading in her jeans. She thought she might have snapped her spine, but she could still kick and fight so she must be all right. Her back hurt like a bitch though.

'Shit!'

Rote had Thommy's torch now. Clare was rolling on the floor. He directed the beam at the thing she was holding up. It *was* a rabbit, but not like any rabbit she had ever seen before.

Its teeth shone red, and then it twisted in her grasp and kicked free.

'Don't move,' Rote said. 'Something is loose.'

Cazie helped her up, and put her arms around her. They were both crying out loud now.

'Shut up!' It was the other woman, Rote's soldier. She had Clare's torch.

Rote threw light into the Animal Room. There was a row of exploded cages. Straw was on the floor, and things were moving incredibly fast under the light. They came out of the room and spread out into the lab, hiding under tables, benches, sinks. They were furred, but fast as mercury on an incline.

'The animals are out. That's what we wanted. Let's move! We go now!'

'Rote,' shouted Cazie, forgetting all need for quiet, 'we've got to collect them. They'll just be recaptured. We've fixed up homes...'

Rote shone his torch full at Clare, dazzling her. She knew how she must look.

'Take a gander at that, Bruckner! If you want to pet something with a disposition towards that kind of rough stuff, it's up to you. The rest of us are pulling out!'

'He's right,' said Thommy. 'Move it.'

Rote led them as if it were a retreat. Clare could not move, but when the torches were out of the lab she could hear the things moving around her. Something ran over her feet. She ran through the sealing doors and caught up with the torchlight. They followed her.

'Help,' she whispered.

Only Cazie turned. A furball collided with a wall, bounced, and ran up the girl's leg. Clare could not do anything. Cazie grunted sharply as teeth rent through her sweater. A tear opened white down her arm, and then a line of blood appeared. She slammed her arm, and the thing on it, against the wall. The rabbit screeched and burst.

There was a mess, and Cazie was spattered from head to foot. The girl could not stop screaming. Red and purple lumps dripped from her face and chest, and she frantically wiped at herself, trying to get the blobby filth off her.

It took Thommy and one of the soldiers to get Cazie moving again. They left the exploded animal on the wall, and went towards the main door.

There was someone between them and the outside. Derm? No, someone in a peaked cap. Someone with a uniform.

Rote reached out his hand behind like a surgeon requesting an instrument, and one of the soldiers gave him a jemmy.

'Stop,' said the shadow. 'Security.'

Rote swung the jemmy like a baseball bat, and connected with the figure's head. The cap went flying, and the man was down. Rote paused to deliver two more professional blows. The guard did not make a sound after the first *oof*. Clare knew something must have broken inside him. She thought she had heard a punching crack that might have been his skull fracturing.

'Leave him for the rabbits,' said Rote, holding the door open.

Derm was outside. He did not ask any questions, just got the van started. In the back, in the darkness, Clare started to feel her own hurts. Waves of pain shot through her body. Cazie was having unattended hysterics, babbling incoherently, and lashing out in the darkness at anyone who came near.

Orange light passed through the van at intervals as Derm drove under the streetlamps. In these flashes, Clare saw Rote's scary, feral grin. Then she curled up, and blacked out.

It was six-thirty in the morning, and Brian was naked in his bed – thankfully alone – when Jason came into his room as if it were Christmas morning, and jumped up and down on him.

'Uhhh, Jase, what is it?'

'Daddy, Daddy…'

He looked at his bedside digital clock and did not believe it. Without his contacts in, the world looked fuzzy and unfinished.

He repressed the urge to become the father of an abused child, and smiled sweetly at his son.

'Couldn't it wait, Jase?'

'Daddy, Daddy…'

It was light out, a grey light that could just be working up to the first sunny day of summer. But right now, it was cold enough to goose-pimple him all over under his thin duvet.

Brian sat up, feeling an ache in the pit of his stomach where Jason had landed too hard on him. He got hold of his son and stopped him moving. Even if he was unable to calm the kid down, he should be able to prevent him doing injury to himself and others.

'I've found a rabbit, Daddy,' said Jason, eyes alight. 'Can we keep it?'

As usual, Frank Lynch had slept for barely two hours. He was generally getting restless. It had been too long.

He had read until five o'clock, about Napoleon in Egypt,

ignoring the woman in bed next to him. Theresa never noticed when he was not sleeping. It was not one of their sex nights. Finally, he had to join her for his few hours – dreamless, almost catatonic. When he woke up, she was gone.

He could not remember her speaking to him during the last few days. That had to be an illusion. They were just in one of their routine ruts. It sometimes happened, between assignments.

He was washed, shaved, showered and finished before Darren and Tracy were up. In any case, the children – well, junior adults – would not have interrupted his routine. He had had his own bathroom put in, adjoining the mini-gymnasium he had designed and built himself.

Looking after his body was important, a part of his job, and he should not have to share his space with anyone else while he was about it. He had caught Darren using his shower once, and given him a demonstration of his need for privacy. He was skilled enough not to leave a mark on his son, but the boy would remember the pain long after he had forgotten his excuse.

Lynch did not think of himself as a brutal man; but he knew the value of direct action. Darren would never again set foot in his father's space. A lesson had been driven in.

For an hour, Lynch did push-ups, pull-ups, sit-ups. Then he punched and kicked the bag. He was as fast as ever, but still worried about his heart rate. He could control his breathing, knew how much to drink to stop himself over-heating, and could work out any aches in his limbs, but there was no way he could do anything to slow down wear and tear on that big muscle nestled in the cage behind his slablike pectorals.

Theresa had his table ready when he was finished. Milk, orange juice, high-fibre cereal, and a well-done steak with green salad. No sweets, no sugar, no coffee. She had even laid out the *Telegraph* for him. Darren and Tracy were spooning down dollops of wheaty pulp and yoghurt, without much enthusiasm.

Occasionally, Lynch reflected with satisfaction that he

would probably outlive his children.

There was no talking at the table. It was a week-day; Tracy was going to school, Darren to college. Neither had been out last night. He had not checked to see if they had done their homework, but he felt confident that they had. The first time he had caught Tracy skipping homework, he had snapped twenty-five of her records, one after another. It was not supposed to be easy to break vinyl.

He was set up for a day much like yesterday and tomorrow. Exercise, diet, reading, thinking. He had been on this course too long, resting, waiting. He had to be ready at the slightest warning, but knew you could over-train, stretch your nerves too far, and fall apart through *lack* of stress.

After the children were gone, he completed the *Telegraph* crossword in seven minutes fifteen seconds – two minutes and thirty-eight seconds over his record – and read the front page. Strikes, elections, terrorism, lawsuits, and the Royal Family. Josh Unwin, described as a 'Chemical Baron', was meeting the Prime Minister to give economic advice, following his suggestion that the country would be a better place if it were run like his corporation. A missing pro-Paisley councillor in Northern Ireland had turned up in a roadside ditch with a bit from a Black and Decker drill embedded in his brain.

Then he got dressed, in slimline body armour and regulation jumpsuit, and went into the cellar room to look after his guns. The room was double-locked, and banned to everyone else, although he had to let Theresa in twice a week to vacuum. Dust and dirt were the first enemies of any good soldier.

His pictures were on display in the workroom. There were not many of them – obviously, his efficiency in the business would be compromised if he had to stop and pose for snapshots every few minutes – but he was pleased with the few he did have, as much for the way you had to look twice to see him in them as for the record of his achievements. There he was at Goose Green, blending in with the paras, and there in Ulster, outside the ruin that had once been an IRA bomb factory. They were from the time before he joined the UCC CSD.

Then there were the other pictures, grainy and clipped from front pages or photocopied from files. They showed just faces, mainly, some posed and grinning, some mashed and broken. Palestinians, Iranians, Iraqis, Argies, Micks, nationless vermin, slit-eyed fanatics, a few simple security risks, inconvenient bystanders. All his.

He took an Uzi out of the rack, and began to strip it down. Just as he was reaching for the baby oil, he heard his telephone klaxon sound.

He was on call. The waiting was finished. All over the city, beepers would be sounding, and his men would be scrambling.

He picked up the receiver. He did not have to say anything. The familiar, but nameless, voice gave him the facts like a newsreader delivering a prepared statement.

He felt alive again.

Jason was crying. His rabbit had died before Brian could even get up and take a look at it.

There was something funny about this dead thing. It was unmistakably a rabbit. It had probably been run over by a car. It certainly had been squashed in some way, and Brian thought he felt broken bones inside the corpse. But there was something more wrong about it than the mere fact of its deadness. It was as if it had died angry, with its claws out.

'Where did you get him, Jase?' he asked, trying to reach through his son's grief, hoping to distract him with the mystery.

'Came… through… window.'

'Oh yes. Show me.'

Jason took his father's hand, and led him into the spare room where he was sleeping – the room that had been his when he and his mother shared the house on campus with Brian. His bed was a mess, and the window was open. There were reddish-brown smears on the windowpane and the sill. Brian saw three hard, black pellets on top of the dressing table, and more blood where Jason said he had found the rabbit.

'It was alive.'

'I'm sure.'

'It's not a very pretty rabbit, Daddy.'

'No.' It certainly was not. Especially not now, and probably not when it had been bouncing around.

'It doesn't have white gloves like Bugs Bunny.'

'Not many rabbits do.'

The front of Jason's pyjama jacket was a bloody ruin. It was a good thing his mother was on an island thousands of miles away.

'It wasn't a very happy rabbit, Jason. I think it's probably better off dead.'

'And in Heaven?'

'If you like.'

Heaven? Where did he get that? From school, probably. Jean was as agnostic as he was. Or had been. Who knows? People change.

'Only...'

'Yes.'

'Only... at the end... when it was dying... it was bad... mightn't God notice?'

'It doesn't count. You aren't yourself when you're dying.'

He looked out of the window. The sun had come up. It would be a nice day. Should he try to get in touch with Monica? There might still be something there.

If there was not, there was always Debbie. The trouble there was that having Debbie over meant going through her last essay, a generous D+, before anything else.

The playback in his head stuck on something Jason had just said: 'it was bad...' What did that mean?

'Jason, how was the rabbit bad?'

'Oh, it doesn't hurt any more.'

'What?'

'The bite. See.'

His son rolled up a sleeve to reveal a white, plump little arm. Jason had not bled much, but the tooth-shaped cuts were still visible.

PART TWO

THE FREAK-OUTS

Security was out in force. Monica had to drive through two checkpoints.to get on campus. The place was getting like South America. None of the polite uniforms could or would tell her what was up, but she had this horrible feeling…

She parked in her usual space by the Union Building, and went up the backstairs to her suite of offices off Mandela Hall. No one else was in yet. The front desk should at least be manned… oops, personned. A pile of mail had been dumped in the old milk crate by her door, mostly tubed magazines.

She sat at her desk, and leaned back in her swivel chair. Her back was starting to ache already. She ought to change her mattress, she knew. She was still worked up from yesterday – from Cazie, from Brian, and from the disastrous UGM.

She knew that she had come close to being the Richard M. Nixon of student politics yesterday. If the Broad Left Alliance and the Left Caucus had been able to agree on a wording for the motion, the student body would have impeached her. It was not her fault, it was not anyone's fault, but she was a Libertarian Socialist and they were out of favour in the Movement at the moment, for flirting with notions of a free market economy. It was just a bloody label.

There was too much to worry about – Union Societies haggling for a slice of the funding, the University Authorities trying to get their programme of spending cuts implemented, the threat of decreased quotas for overseas students, everyone from the miners to the Sandinistas begging for the students to be in solidarity with them and shell out for the privilege. Plus the eternal niggling doubt that this had nothing at all to do with the day-to-day life of her average student constituent. At the last election, the Apathy Society candidates had polled surprisingly well.

She had heard too many times that she had been elected because of her nice smile, blue eyes and red hair. Sometimes she was attracted by the prospect of resigning and getting back to her post-graduate research. There was even a real world out there somewhere beyond the three small hills that bounded the campus community, bunching it up close to the main road. She had spent her whole life being educated; it was time she did something else.

Then Lindy Styles, her Vice-President/Communications, came in, along with Berenice, the secretary.

'There are campus cops all over the place,' said Lindy, 'and real police. Something's up in Chem.'

'Oh shit. Any ideas?'

'No, but it's heavy. They've put up yellow Do Not Cross tapes and are guarding them. Perhaps the demo yesterday put the wind up UCC?'

'Some fucking hope, Lindy. Bern, could you call the switchboard and see if anyone knows anything? I've got a bad feeling.'

The secretary took off her coat and bag, and started pushing buttons on the phone. After a while, she got through to someone, and talked for a few moments. She rung off.

'Someone's been hurt... a guard, last night.'

'What? Badly?'

'Tisa didn't know, but it seems so.'

'Shit shit shit.'

'The police were here early. There's been a break-in as well.'

'Those fucking idiots.'

'Pardon?'

'Just idiots in general, Bern. How about some tea? I think it's going to be a nasty day.'

'It looks quite nice outside.'

'I mean inside, Bern.'

'Oh, right.'

The secretary vanished into her tea-making alcove, and Monica heard the tap going. 'Lindy,' she said, 'I'm going to have to take care of this, I think. If anyone comes over or calls to hassle me, could you put up with it, please?'

'Sure.'

'I love you.'

'I know that. I love you too.'

'That's just hunky-dory, then, eh?'

Alone in her own office, Monica dug out her address book. She did not have a number for Cazie Bruckner, and a call to University Records could not get her one either. Because of all that pissing about, she did not even know where the girl lived. She considered calling the hospitals and the police station, but decided to put that off until she had a better idea of what had gone on last night.

After a long pause for thought, she dialled Brian's number from three-year-old memory.

Cazie had gone to bed feeling like shit warmed over, and cried herself to sleep. Now, waking up, she felt terrific.

She was instantly alert, not at all bleary. All her aches and pains were gone. Sitting up in bed, she tingled as the sheet fell, the cotton brushing her nipples. She held out her arm, her torn arm, and could only see a fine pink thread where she had been cut. She was better.

And she was hungry.

She got up and slipped her robe on. Her movements felt strange, catlike. She sensed a strength, a suppleness in her limbs, she was unused to. It was as if she had done a year's worth of aerobics in her sleep.

Last night?

She remembered. She had been overwrought, and had practically fallen apart during the trip home. She had been hurt, although that now seemed like something that had happened to her when she was a very little girl, and so had Clare. Thommy had split with Clare, and taken her to his room in York House. Derm had driven the rest of them back. He would be sleeping on the couch downstairs, now.

Suddenly, she wanted Derm.

They had been lovers for two months, but she had never needed the boy as crucially as she did now. Needed him to pound his big black cock into her slim pink slit.

At the back of her mind, she was shocked. She did not think like that, usually. There was more than just sex with Derm. Despite his muscle-man physique, he could be surprisingly sensitive, and there was a ball of dispossessed social anger inside him that excited her. Sometimes, she had thought it was mainly the need to upset Daddy. He felt threatened by black people, and she knew he could not stand the thought of her with Derm. That had been one of the most attractive things about the boy. But this morning it was just sex.

If only Rote and his soldiers were not in the front room too, laid out like corpses in their combat camouflage sleeping bags. She yawned, feeling the cool air on the back of her throat, and stretched her entire body. Up on her toes. Legs, back and arms taut. Fingers out like claws. She rolled her head, and felt spasms of muscular pleasure in her neck, and all down her spine.

She touched her breast, lightly teasing the nipple with her thumb and forefinger. Uncontrollably, she came. It was like electro-convulsive therapy. She fell into a crouch, amazing tingles coursing through her thighs. It was like some twisted form of sexual epilepsy. She sucked down gulps of air, and clutched at the carpet. Shutting her eyes tight, concentrating on her body, she regained control and was all right in herself again.

Looking at the carpet, she saw the five slashes where her nails had torn.

He had just finished giving instructions to Abigail, the student he was entrusting Jason to for the day, when the telephone rang.

'Hello, Brian, it's...'

'Monica, good to hear your voice.'

'Yeah, it's...'

'Hold on a minute, would you.'

He turned to Abigail, a fragile girl who looked about fourteen but was reputed to be a potential First, and pointed at his son, who was already scratching at the bandage around his arm. Abigail caught him, and gently pulled his fingers away. He looked to be stronger than her, but she used persuasion. She took Jason into the next room, leaving Brian to his call.

'Sorry about that. Jase's got a war wound, and he keeps making it worse.'

'Oh, I hope it's not...'

'...not serious. Don't worry. Bitten by a rabbit. Not even a hint of rabies around.'

'Great. I'm afraid I've got bad news. Cazie...'

'Shit. How many dead?'

'That may not be a joke, Brian. I haven't got the story straight yet, but a guard was hurt. I don't know how much anyone else knows, but there are policemen all over the place. What have you got on today?'

'Nothing. Uh, well, invigilating, but I took Rob Bickford's place on Tuesday so he could be on the radio. He'll step in for me. Do you want me to start digging into the case? I was always a big

Philip Marlowe reader.'

Monica was quiet at the end of her line.

'Like I said, Brian, this may not be funny any more.'

'Sure, sure, sure. I'm not going to be in the combat zone, you know. I'll just drop by Sparks's place for a chat. He'll be going spare anyway if the key stunt backfired. Then I'll be around the Union Building, say, for lunch. We could make a habit of it.'

'Jason?'

'Taken care of. I'm not being shown up by my own son. Not yet, at any rate.'

'See you later then.'

'Later.'

Click.

Brian finished his long-neglected cup of coffee. At least, he took two swallows of the cold stuff, gargled and spat it out in the sink. Out of the kitchen window, he could see Abigail and Jason.

The kid would wear her out. He was throwing Frisbee, and Brian only now realized how good Jason had got. A few weekends back, he had had to struggle to catch one in ten throws, now he was not missing at all. And Abigail was having to run as if she were one-on-one with Billie Jean King in her prime. He could not help noticing the girl's calves as her peasant skirt lifted when she ran. Despite the ankle socks and trainers, she-did not look as young as he had thought.

At least Jason was ignoring his wound now. He seemed to be positively bursting with energy.

Derm was out of his depth.

As he sat on the bog in Cazie's place, straining over the daily bowel movement his mother had prescribed as the key to eternal youth and vigour, he wondered how the hell he had become mixed up with midnight raids and brained security guards, not to mention whale-loving terrorists and power-crazed rich kids.

As usual, he supposed, he was just trying to get laid.

He had been into sports at school because it was as good a way as any to get into Marie-Jeanette Traherne's navy blue knickers. And he was too good to lie low. Unlike most Incredible Hulks, he could run a mile in six minutes without perspiring hard. And he could stand stock still in front of a speeding locomotive. Well, maybe a speeding go-cart. In the States, he would have been a natural for American Football. Here, it was soccer or nothing. Until he had got into rugby.

Not many Brixton black kids make it in rugby. Derm did not know why. It was his game, and he was the best his school could come up with. Now, while he was peripherally studying Human Biology, he was the star of the *real* all-black rugby team, the Bantu Warriors. His ambition was to violate the Gleneagles Agreement by going onto a field with fifteen double-dyed Afrikaaner white racists and putting them all out of the game forever. Sometimes, he dreamed about it. He felt the slams, heard the bones breaking, tasted the blood.

Now, Crazy Cazie had got him into a position where he could, quite conceivably, go to jail. Her thighs were fine wine, but no pussy was worth that much.

White women! Jesus H. Christ! Why couldn't he do like that song from *West Side Story,* 'Stick To Your *Own* Kind'?

After all the dramatics last night, he had hoped to get something back for it. Some people are really turned on by breaking the law. He had never really got through to Cazie in bed, and he was proud enough to be bothered by it. Last night should have seen some good loving in her single bed, but she had got herself chewed open by some kind of mutant bunny and he had had to crash out on the sofa. In the same room as Rote's Death Squad. Shit in a shopfront, what was happening?

He finished his job, and did the paperwork. The ancient plumbing took forever to finish, and sounded like an earthquake when it did.

Cazie was waiting for him outside the loo.

'Sorry to keep you waiting, Caz. You okay?'

The girl looked at him weirdly, and Derm remembered all his Jamaican Grandmammy's scare stories about haints and *zombis* and shapeshifters. Cazie had changed somehow.

'I'm better.'

'That's good. Let's get some fried bread and bacon going.'

'No, not yet. Come into my room, quickly.'

She darted away, behind her door. She had touched him, trailing her fingertips from his neck downwards, across his chest – he could feel the points through his thick dressing gown – as far as his hip. It was as if an acupuncture needle had hit the spot precisely. He had an instant hard-on that parted his dressing gown.

In her room, she was naked. Not naked as she had been the other times, under the covers, with the lights out. Properly, brazenly naked. Her shoulders were rotating slightly, as if she were dancing to unheard jazz. Her legs were spread, and Derm could see the muscles clenching under the smooth skin of her thighs.

'Come here.' It was an order, and yet a desperate plea. She did not need to say it twice.

He tugged at the knot of his dressing gown, and it fell. The cord brushed his jutting penis, and he felt as if he would come immediately, before he had even touched her.

Her hands came for his shoulders, and pulled him down on her. He slid home smoothly as she stifled a scream. Her vulva gulped, and he was swallowed, held fast, almost painfully.

'Fuck me, nigger. Fuck me now.'

This was not Cazie, the lily-skinned liberal who would rather be boiled in oil than espouse an unfashionable cause, the girl who traded her body for street credibility. This was some other fantastic tart dressed in her silky skin.

But Derm was past caring.

They moved together, astonishingly fast. He was sure she had peaked early, but she was not put off her stroke. He came, and lost his breath and his rhythm, but she kept bucking under him, forcing him to follow her lead. She sucked air beside his ear, then bit him, hard. He might have been bleeding. Her neck arched up, and she fastened a kiss over his mouth before he could protest.

When he finished spurting inside her, the knob of his penis ached. His erection was dwindling. But faster and faster she moved, and more desperately she sucked at his mouth, trying to draw all the air out of him. Her tongue was in his throat like a snake, stifling him.

He broke free, and tried to protest, but she rolled and – with a strength he would never have expected from her – flipped him onto his back. She rode him high, coaxing him hard again with vaginal spasms and rough fingernail traces just above his pubic hair.

He tilted his head back over the edge of the bed and looked at the ceiling. She was howling, in what must be a continuous orgasm. He climaxed again, then lost it. He might as well be dead, but she kept working on him.

She moved back and forth, her knees raked his sides, and her nails began to dig in. There was definitely blood now. Her hands came to his face, the first three fingers of each extended like an inexpert typist's. She stroked his cheeks with razorblade tenderness.

He could taste the blood, inside his mouth. She had gone deep, perhaps all the way to his teeth. He was too exhausted to yell.

'Tribal scars, nigger,' she screeched, 'tribal scars!'

The pain began, and he knew he had to fight her off or die.

He feebly tried to push her away, but her legs gripped him ferociously. He tried to get a blow to her sternum, but she took his wrist and broke it as if it were the easiest thing in the world.

Sweet Mama of Shit, she was going to kill him good.

His head fell back again, and he saw an upside-down door opening. Rote stood in the hallway. His face looked hard and dead either way up.

'What are you looking at, nigger?' Cazie screamed.

Her hands came for his neck. This would be it, he knew. Her

Devil's Mask face came close to his, and she kissed his mouth as she twisted his head.

'Mama,' he tried to say.

He felt his vertebrae straining, then snapping like links in a chain, one after the other. The pain was not so bad.

As he slipped into the dark, he was dimly aware that he was coming again.

Luckily, there was a quadrangle on campus big enough to land a helicopter in. It attracted a crowd, but there were enough police around to cover that.

Lynch wore a plain black jumpsuit, with a flying jacket to conceal his shoulder-holstered Magnum. The shoulders of the jacket were padded asymmetrically to disguise the weapon. He strode through the police cordons, accompanied by the local man, Inspector Woolbridge. They had kept piping him updates through his earplug radio while he was airborne. He had done his best to ignore the details. He knew the basic situation, and he wanted to assess the specifics from the ground up.

'Anderton. I want to speak to Anderton.'

'Of course, sir,' said Woolbridge. Lynch hoped the policeman would prove a good investment.

'You have him?'

'He's here.'

He did not waste words on a reply. The police were standing around outside what he knew from the maps he had studied in the chopper to be the School of Chemistry. There were groups of students loitering, rubbernecking. Rumours would be all over the shop by now, no doubt about that.

'Woolbridge, we have to contain the spread of information. See to it.'

'Pardon?'

'Get these surplus personnel out of the way. I don't care how.

Bomb threat. Declare this a high-risk AIDS-infected area. Just do it.'

The policeman scurried off to talk to his men. Lynch's own team should be here within the hour. UCC had the resources the situation called for, and the government contracts that would ensure them a free hand in deploying them. In the background, Lynch spotted the pair of armed officers he had requested. They were not doing anything particularly useful, but they were there, just in case. The cops would be out of it soon.

The UCC chopper circled the campus once, and withdrew. For the moment, Lynch was on his own.

Inside the building, there was a large irregular bloodstain on the tiling. It was like being home.

The police had let him in unopposed. That was sloppy, but it saved him time.

'Anderton?'

His voice echoed around the corridors. Of course, the place would have been evacuated. There was an answering shout. Lynch walked towards it.

Through several doors, he found a man he recognized from his file. Dr Xavier Anderton, Head of Research on the Leo Project. UCC were using signs of the Zodiac this year. This should have been the Cancer Project, but someone in public relations had nixed that. Not that PR should have been overly bothered about the image of this sort of work. The whole point was that it should not have one.

'Lynch. You know what I do.'

'Indeed,' said Anderton, a reedy, youngish-looking nonentity. Lynch knew he should not underestimate the man. He had probably killed more people than Lynch in his time.

'I understand you have a situation here.'

Anderton laughed bitterly. 'That's one way of putting it, Lynch.'

'Have you guesstimated the damage?'

'That's difficult. We have some lab animals at liberty, and some unidentified infectees.'

'What have they got?'

'We don't have a name for it. Batch 125 is as good as any.'

Lynch knew Anderton was near the edge. There were two other people in the room, who must be Carson and Finch. They were in no better shape. For a moment, Lynch considered terminating the expendables, but he knew that would have a psychologically damaging effect on Anderton. For the minute, he needed the scientist.

'Batch 125? What have you got on that?'

'Not much. It wasn't very promising. It doesn't do what it's supposed to...'

Finch came in, excited in spite of herself. 'But what it does might be interesting, Mr Lynch. It's not Leo exactly, but there might be a whole other line of research in it.'

Lynch waved a hand.

'Okay, okay. I don't want the advanced stuff. Give me the basics.'

Anderton picked up a petri dish. The agar jelly was discoloured, greyish.

'This is more or less Batch 125. We ought to label it 126, since it was cooked up after our initial session, but it is as near as dammit what we used the first time round.'

It did not look impressive, but Lynch knew that nothing did until it killed or cured you.

'It's a virus. Well, this is a virus. 125 certainly was when we shot it into the animals, but there's some evidence that it might have gone crystalline on us in the system. It does different things to different subjects, seemingly at random.'

'Symptoms?'

'Total cellular trauma, in one case. Accelerated growth and vitality in another. The only constant seems to be increased aggression, and even then you have the choice of directing it inward or outward.'

'Can humans catch it?'

'We don't even know if it's a disease, Lynch, but for your

purposes I think we have to assume they can.'

'If you don't know it's a disease, I'm assuming you haven't even thought about a cure?'

Anderton did not look happy. 'As you know, UCC gave us some parameters to work in. Leo is supposed to be virulent in the extreme, resistant to all forms of counter-treatment. We seem to have been able to lick that part of the problem.'

'So it can kill us but we can't kill it, eh? Congratulations, that must be a miracle of science.'

'I don't think you're being fair,' said Finch. 'We were working to specifics…'

'…just obeying orders, I know. Me too, Miss Finch. Now you've spilled something, and I have to mop it up. That's the way it goes.'

'Who did you take machismo lessons from, Lynch? Clint Eastwood? Rutger Hauer?'

He slapped her, hard. She was surprised.

'Caught you, didn't I, Miss Finch?'

She sobbed twice, then got herself under control.

'As you probably know, this is serious. The police are involved, but their part will soon be over. UCC have a team coming. Dr Anderton, you'll get whatever you want. You have the best facilities possible here, and I understand they're pulling some people off Aries and Libra to back you up. I just hope something good comes out of this. If there are any casualties, we've got rooms in the University Infirmary at our disposal. Now, I've got to go and make the Vice-Chancellor eat shit. I want you to know that this is a genuine fuckup, and I'd like you to think only in terms of damage limitation, you understand?'

He left them to it. Some people had no idea.

Robyn Askew was detailed to make breakfast. She was a veggie, but Rote, who admitted that human beings were carnivorous animals, insisted she cook him up a panful of bacon. Best breakfast in the world, the British fry-up. Five or six rashers of streaky, a couple of burst-yolk eggs, some optional button mushrooms, half a tomato grilled to a hot lump, and a slice of deep-fat-fried bread, with ketchup and strong tea. Robyn might get broody about it and Dave Higgitt was with her – a vegan who refused dairy products and any food so much as scraped against an animal – but Doug Templeton was on his side. Even if he had not been, Rote would have outvoted the others. Ever since he went underground, his unit had been under his total command. It was the only way.

Higgitt was spinning the tuner on the radio, trying to catch all the local and national news bulletins. It was unlikely they would make the BBC, but the independent local station ought to carry a report. Rote almost wanted them to have been identified. Eventually, when he was well out of the area, he would issue a statement claiming responsibility. Since putting out the eyes of the Duke of Bastardfordshire or whatever he called himself, the cell had not had a decent follow-up action. He was glad that there had been a chance to cause injury. The media always ignored actions that did not cause injury.

'Where's Chocolate Charlie?' Rote asked. The black youth – too dangerous and broody by half, he thought – was missing.

Templeton stabbed this thumb up towards the ceiling, and licked his lips.

'Poking Cazie,' he said through a grin. 'She likes her meat dark.'

That was typical of the unreal little slut. Rote knew from the first she was not serious about the cause. She was in it for weird kicks. Weird fucks. Cazie was a dilettante debutante. He knew the type. They oohed and ahhed over cuddly-wuddly ickle-wickle cutesy furry animally-poohs, and copped out when it came to an action.

Cazie had fucked up last night. She had been as much use as a bad case of genital warts. And her tagalongs had been no better. Thommy and Clare.

Higgitt turned off the radio, disgusted. Cazie and Derm were making a lot of noise. Templeton laughed, and Robyn looked disgusted.

Rote had had to make do with Clare, but he had really wanted to pour the pork to Cazie. It was just that he knew he could take Thommy, but he was not sure of Derm. He could win in a fight, but there would *be* a fight. Thommy was a spineless piss-heart, and had backed down with a shit-eating smile at the first sign of real pain. Derm might have required more sweat and bruising.

Next, Rote would try for a major coup. An action against a zoo, or a circus. Maybe Cruft's or the Horse of the Year Show. People were hurting animals all the time, and he ached to hurt them back.

The noise upstairs was ridiculous. At first, Rote thought Cazie was just a screamer. Then he realized it was Derm who was screaming.

'Shit,' he said.

The four of them jammed the stairs together, and jogged up towards the landing, towards the nerve-scraping screams.

As Eddie Zero woke up, he fumbled on his bedside for a cassette from his shoebox, and slotted it into his deck. He could not get up without rock 'n' roll. It was The Coasters, 'Poison Ivy'.

The music got to him, and he rolled out of his single bed. He sat in his vest and Y-fronts on the edge of the bed, and looked around his Hall of Residence room. A life-size Elvis poster sneered at him from the back of his door.

He stumbled over to the wash-basin, and splashed cold water on his face, wiping the wet into his greasy hair, shaping his quiff. He skipped shaving, but took the trouble to sluice out his mouth with soapy water, forcing it between his teeth. He was out of toothpaste.

The Coasters got onto 'Bad Blood'.

He supposed he had resigned from Campus Radio yesterday.

He remembered telling Posie Columba what she could do with the middle of Friday nights.

He took out his drainpipes and forced himself into them, sucking in his stomach to tighten the belt. He tied his bootlace tie in the collar of his knife-point collar-tip paisley shirt, and got into his embroidered waistcoat. At least he was looking like something.

'Yakkety-Yak.'

There was a scratching at his door, and he wondered who it could be. Nobody ever bothered him on campus. Unless it was some snotnose wanting to borrow milk.

And why couldn't they just knock, for the sake of Carl Perkins?

He opened the door, and there was no one in the corridor. The scratching, he realized had been at the bottom of the door.

He looked down, and saw a rabbit nestling on his pink-socked feet.

'Riot in Cell Block Number Nine'.

Rote was out of the way by the time Cazie got to the door. He was quick. She would have to stretch herself to get him.

His top soldier was not so well prepared. Rote had slammed past him, pushing him against a wall. Cazie saw exposed throat and reached for it. Flesh parted like overcooked pasta, and she grabbed a fistful of tendons and nerves.

Holding the man as if by his shirt collar, she whipped him around, and swung him into the wall. She let go and he crumpled.

She was still hungry, and there was bacon frying below. She looked at the knotty red mess in the dead man's throat and was tempted.

But there was no time for that. She had three more people to take care of before breakfast. She knew now how much better than them she was.

She also needed a bath and clothes, but this business was bound to be messy, so for the time being she just put on her old dressing gown. It was already torn and bloody, so more mess would not matter.

Downstairs, where they had retreated, they were talking about her. Rote was the dangerous one. She would go for him first.

But Rote was clever. He sent his other man upstairs for her, with a jemmy. The weapon, of course, was already blooded.

She remembered the sound she had heard when Rote had hit the security guard last night. It was a good sound.

Excited, she squared off against the man in the hallway. He paused, put off by the sight of his comrade gurgling his last, and began to swing the jemmy in calculated arcs before him.

She was cool, and did not hiss and claw the air.

'Girlie, you're dead.'

With lamentable slowness, he jabbed the jemmy at her like a sword. She just reached out and took it.

'Do you want to see some magic?' she asked.

She bent the jemmy into an oval, but it cracked at the top and spoiled the effect. She threw it at the man as he came for her, and raised a blood-filled bruise on his forehead.

He covered his head with his hands, but she had him anyway.

Cazie kicked out, and snapped the rail off the top of the bannisters. The landing was lined with jagged wooden pickets. She took Rote's man by his elbows and forced him backwards, down onto the spikes. Three came up through him, bringing dark squirts of blood and trails of offal. His arms came away from his face as his eyes filled up with the red stuff. She kissed him, not like she had kissed Derm, but out of friendliness. He was dead now and could not do her any harm.

'I'm coming down now, Rote. Ready or not!'

Giggling like a girl, she tripped past the dead people and went down the stairs. Her back teeth hurt, as if they were just coming through. She knew who she was now.

The woman was no problem. Cazie just hugged her to death. Her back snapped like a breadstick. Cazie left her in the kitchen, and went looking for Rote in the Action Room.

The light was off down there, and Cazie could hear him in the dark. She could hear things she had never heard before. The whisper of breath, the beating of a heart, the slightest rustle of cloth.

She paused at the head of the stairs, and brought her thumbnail up to her mouth. It was tougher than she thought, and she could not chew it. She nicked her tongue, and tasted her own blood. It gave her a cocaine rush, and she had to steady herself.

Rote came for her while she was off balance, grabbing her ankles and pulling her downstairs. Her spine jolted as she slammed against every step. She felt a series of forceful blows to the chest as she lay prone on the stairs. She did not lose her wind, but she was dizzy.

She realized she could see in the dark now. Rote was bent over her, teeth bared like a cartoon monster. It was almost funny.

He held her down with a knee in her stomach, and ripped her robe open. His hand came down as fast as even she could move, and he had her by the throat. She knew it was no use snarling at him. He would not be impressed.

'Now, bitch,' he said, 'we play my games.'

'Fuck you, Rote!'

'No, Cazie, fuck *you*!'

Then he was on her.

The convoy of unmarked trucks was two hours out of an indeterminate-looking site in South London. Private-Equivalent Willard Longendyke had no idea where he was being deployed, and did not much care.

He had other priorities. Like the Need. Like the three highly unauthorized, non-regulation-issue needles in his inside top pocket.

The men in the back of his truck sat quiet, checking their weapons and the seals on their suits. There was none of that camaraderie shit in the teams, with everyone whistling 'Colonel

Bogey' or talking about the folks back home.

If you were in the Covert Security Division, chances were you were the brand of dude the folks back home did not miss that much.

Sergeant-Equivalent Bosworth, the Bozz Man, was walking up and down the truck, steadying himself by getting hand-holds on the hanging ropes, performing one of his interminable snap inspections.

Longendyke would pass. He was careful about shit like that. He had to be.

The backs of his hands had been crawling for hours, though. His missing pill was phantom throbbing.

He always got that way when he was close to the Need.

Fuckin' Panama.

It had been enough to give anybody the Need. A couple of rounds in his leg and one missing testicle were adequately qualified to jack up the pain level beyond belief, and when Sergeant Gomez Gomez came around with a sweet little package of sugar to take all the nasties away, the way ahead had been clear. Just ease into a big blue vein and depress the plunger, and liquid dynamite squirts all round your body, giving you the biggest all-over hard-on you ever experienced.

The first time he flew, in the Canal Zone foxhole, he had jerked off until his remaining ball was dry and shrivelled as a raisin. He knew not what cocktail of meth, H and coke Gomez Gomez had cooked up in his home brew, but it sure made jacking off into a lifetime-experience. A couple more jabs like that, and he would pick up milkmaid's wrist, or whatever repetitive stress injury you could get from, as they say in the Yew Kay, wanking like the clappers.

Since then, he had been onto the shit like Wile E. Coyote onto the menu in a Kentucky Fried Road Runner restaurant.

This gig had come up suddenly, and his beeper had beeped while he was making his connection. That had nearly queered the deal, but Merv the Medicine Man knew who his best customers were. Longendyke had even concluded the hand-over before reporting to the Bozz Man.

That was a mercy. Otherwise, he would have been crawling the walls before the teams were in the field. That might get noticed. Once he had his jab, he would be okay. The situation would become a cool breeze. He always liked to fly into the field. It had not got him killed yet. In the Zone, he had heard a brasshat say that some of the best Medal of Honour winners were stoned to the gills when they did their guts and glory thing.

Next to Longendyke, Tripps tried on his filter faceplate, pulling his hood around it. These Zombie outfits were guaranteed against radiation, infection, herpes, measles, BSE and the Black Death. In the teams, they were called 'all-over rubbers'.

He wondered if the Lynch-Mob would be top dog on this operation. That Brit was one scary officer. Longendyke had been under him at a terrorist gig in the Med. Lynch had gone Rambo and cleaned up a whole nest of towelheads by himself. None of the hostages had come out alive, but the stuff that counted – UCC papers or some shit like that – had been turned over neatly to the company suits.

The Bozz Man looked him over, and went on to Tripps.

Longendyke's non-ball was a blob of pain in his groin. He kept shifting his seat, but it was no good. The Need was hotting up.

Fuckin' Panama.

With TWA and Pan-Am and that instantaneous matter transmission device everyone *knew* the goddamn Government bought up and hid away from the public use, who in the name of Johnny Carson's sister's black cat's ass needed a goddamn canal anyway.

Just a groove in the ground with mud and water and ships in it. Shit, was all. Shit, shit, shit…

He had been tagged as a casualty while he was in the latrine. Fuckin' crapper exploded under him. They never found his surplus *cojone*. Everybody said sorry. Even the Prezz sent a sorry telegram. But sorry had not cut the cocaine. Sorry and a flag-waving procession had meant a damn sight less than the massive pay hike UCC offered veterans who did not ask questions. He was fresh out of patriotic zeal and, besides, his Need was getting real expensive and the salary cheque kept his connections happy.

He had never been to England before, and so that was a trip in itself. The CDS was a supra-national outfit with sites in London, Marseilles, New York State, San Bernardino, Rio de Janeiro, Johannesburg, Hong Kong, Canberra, Malmo, Prague, Osaka and the Antarctic. UCC was registered as a Bahaman corporation for tax purposes, but its head offices were London, New York and Tokyo. Despite his designer cockney accent, Josh Unwin was an American citizen.

'Shape up,' the Bozz Man shouted as the truck jumped a bit, obviously rolling off the regular road.

'Remember, this is not an assault. You will take your positions with no discharge of weapons. There will be a parcel of civs in the vicinity, and you are not unduly to throw a fright into them.'

Everyone nodded. Tripps pulled off his mask, and let it hang at his throat.

The truck rolled to a halt, and the Bozz Man threw back the doors.

The team got out in an orderly fashion, and assembled for inspection. The other trucks, six of them, were parked in a row, their complements lining up outside.

He realized they were on a college campus. Young people with books were watching the team assemble. There were buildings all around, and trees and lawns.

Longendyke's skin reacted badly to the sunlight. As he straightened up, blinking, adjusting to the new environment, he desperately wanted to creep off somewhere and have his jab.

He saw the Lynch-Mob looming out of a building, trailing civilian cops. The Bozz Man and all the other NCO-equivalents lined up to lick ass and salute. Lynch passed out orders, and Longendyke knew just from the feel of the place that there would be blood spilled. He could always tell as soon as his boots hit the turf.

Right now, it was a stroll in the park. Later, it would be a hell on earth. The Need was constant, eating him away inside, gnawing at his brain. The needles were burning a hole under his Zombie suit.

Rote was going to make the bitch pay for Templeton, Higgitt and Robyn Askew. And for fucking up a simple raid.

She was strong, no doubt about that. Stronger than she should be, but she could not hope to match him.

In the army, when he was a kid, he had discovered wrestling. Not the namby-pamby showoff stuff costumed clowns got up to on Saturday afternoons on the telly, but the hard, fast, high-contact sport that went back to Ancient Greece. They had kicked him off the squad for breaking too many arms, and out of the army for selling not-yet-surplus equipment.

Since then, he had had the Cause. He hated people a lot, and he had no qualms about smashing them down if they were Evil.

Cazie was Evil, no doubt about that.

Killing her was not enough. She had to be broken first. Humbled.

She broke his hold, and twisted under him, but he whipped his arms under hers and got a full nelson, his knotted fists pressing her head flat against a stair. He got his knee in the small of her back.

To do what he had to do to her, he would have to free his hands long enough to unbuckle his belt and wriggle out of his jeans. That would give her a chance.

He let her head up, and hammered it down again. She did not say anything, but her body remained taut beneath him, not relaxed. She was not out. He hit her head against the stair again. And again. And again.

She was losing it, he could tell. There was blood all over the place. He had probably roughed up her face. That did not matter. He was not going to rape her because she was pretty.

Rote slipped his arms free and undid his belt. He pulled it out of his jeans, and held it up in one fist like a bullwhip. It might come in handy. Then he dropped his denims. He had had a hard on since he had first grabbed Cazie by the ankles.

The bitch was going to take it every way he could think of, and he could think of plenty.

Groggily, Cazie raised herself on her elbows, and turned her head to look up at him. There was blood on her face, but he could not see any disfiguring wound. Shame.

He lashed out with his belt, and caught her across the shoulders. It did not stop her moving. She rolled over onto her back, and wiped her bloody fringe out of her eyes.

'Do you feel like a man, Rote?'

He did not answer.

'Like a great big bull of a man?'

She touched her breasts with her hands, leaving red smears like zebra-stripes. Her ribs shifted as she breathed.

The fight had gone out of her. All she had left was words.

'Come on and rape me then, Tarzan. Let's see if you've got the dick for it.'

He whipped her again, three times crosswise.

Then she caught the belt, and tugged. He fell forwards onto her, his body on hers.

He pulled his arm back to deliver a blow…

…but she had him by the testicles.

'Let's see if you've got the…'

She pushed his chest hard, forcing him away from her, but her other hand still gripped hard.

'…BALLS!'

There was a white-hot sunburst of agony between his legs, and he felt his bowels letting go.

She was flinging him across the room as easily as he had flung the rabbit away last night.

He hit the corkboard and collapsed.

His vision was messed up now. Lines of purple and orange squiggled on the surface of his eyes. He was emptying through a hole in his groin. He felt himself sinking.

'What's the matter, Tarzan? Want your dick back?'

She stood over him now, bending close, her breath on his face. She touched him, touched his throat, his chin, forcing his jaws open.

Then she pushed her fistful of meat into his mouth, and he could not breathe any more.

He knew she was watching him die.

Sparks was in the Infirmary, Monica was 'in a meeting', and Brian was in a dilemma.

From what Sparks's sidekick at Security had told him, things were likely to get serious. His old boozing buddy was down with a skull fracture, possible brain damage, and some weird kind of throat wound. Someone had given him a major bashing with the proverbial blunt instrument, and – after that – something else had had a good go at ripping *(chewing?)* his windpipe out.

Brian had tried to get through to Monica, but her V-P was running interference for her. He thought back for a while to the days when he had written a pamphlet entitled 'Fuck the Establishment' and seriously talked about fire-bombing US Army bases, and knew he could not keep this quiet. He would have to rat on Monica's Animal Lib friends. There was no rabbit alive worth killing a man for.

He could not go straight to the police – after all, he was going to want to cover his arse on 'lending' Cazie the keys. That meant he had to see Jackson.

Ernest Jackson, the Vice-Chancellor of the University, was

a wet liberal from way back. Brian had always thought him a decent man. Even when the students felt the need to burn him in effigy he had kept his sense of humour. But, deep down, Brian knew the V-C was a quivering civil servant who would preserve his position at the expense of anything.

This was going to be a mess.

And Jackson was keeping him waiting. Brian had not even worked up any interest in flirting with Gabrielle, Jackson's stunning receptionist, and none of the academic journals in his reception room took his fancy. He had to restrain himself from pacing up and down like an expectant father. In Jackson's office, he could hear the drone of light conversation, punctuated by cheerful laughs. Brian imagined the V-C exchanging quips and brandies with some venerable professor as they worked out seating plans for a testimonial dinner, or decided on the cover design of the new University prospectus.

'Any idea how long?' he asked.

Gabrielle looked up from her blood-red nails, and tapped her file against heart-shaped lips.

'It could be a while. He dithers a lot, you know.'

'I know.'

Gabrielle went back to her talons. She was giving them an edge.

'I saw a rabbit on campus this morning,' she said.

'Oh really?'

'Yes. It must be summer at last.'

He did not care about rabbits. Rabbits in the Chem Building. Rabbits in Jason's room.

Rabbits!

He should have guessed. No wonder Jason's bunny looked so messed up. He had resisted Jason's demands that the thing be buried, and put it in a twist-tie rubbish bag. It was out for the refuse people to pick up, in one of the neat row of bins outside the neat row of faculty cottages at the far edge of the campus.

It probably was not important, but when he got through with

Jackson he ought to cut class and take Jason to the Infirmary and get his bite looked at. There was a slim chance of infection.

Jackson's door opened, and the V-C showed Professor Prawer out with much hand-shaking and joviality.

'Hello, Brian,' he said, 'sorry to keep you on hold. We've got a graduation ceremony to stage-manage. Prawer's trying to convince me to lay on a laser hologram spectacle.'

Prawer left laughing, and Brian wondered where to start with the bad news.

'Could you wait just a teensy minute-ette more, Brian. Gaby, any word from the police about the unpleasantness in Chem?'

Gabrielle shook her head.

'That's what I want to talk to you about, Ernest. Sparks…'

'I appreciate your concern, Brian. It's a bad thing. I hope it doesn't get blown up by the press. The police think it was some student desperately trying to get drugs…'

'I think I have some infor–'

'Terrible business, drugs. I'd thought we'd got that problem under control since last year. The counselling service is supposed to be first-rate.'

'It wasn't drugs, it was the animals.'

'Yes, animals, animals. It's tragic. Young people sinking that low.'

'No…'

Someone came into the room.

'Jackson.'

Brian and the V-C stopped talking. The newcomer was a mutilated Adonis with a Michael Heseltine hairstyle. He was dressed in some sort of quasi-military set-up. Gabrielle dropped her file.

'Frank Lynch, UCC.'

The V-C extended a hand, and Lynch took it in what must be a bone-crushing grip. Brian thought he saw something that might be a gun under the man's jacket as he pumped Jackson's arm.

'I was told you were coming,' Jackson said, wrung out. 'You have all the cooperation I can give.'

'Great. Let's go in your office and talk cases. The rest of my team will be here, soon. I'd like as little panic as possible. It'll be your responsibility to keep your student body under control...'

The men disappeared into Jackson's office. Brian stood outside like a spare prick as the door was shut in his face.

'Shit!'

Gabrielle had her file again, and was trying to look phlegmatic.

'Don't tell me,' Brian said, 'this isn't England any more. This is El-fucking-Salvador.'

Jason must be getting that cereal that puts energy into kids for breakfast, lunch, tea and supper. After four hours with the boy, Abigail felt thirty years older.

Fresh from humiliating her at Frisbee-throwing, he had taken her indoors and persuaded her to be a monster. She had chased him up and down stairs and in and out of cupboards and wardrobes, hissing through orange peel Dracula fangs, while he had shot at her with his plastic raygun. No wonder the good guys always came out on top in science fiction films. If Jason was representative of the average space cadet, there were no monsters in the universe who could hope to keep up with him, let alone overtake, disable and devour him.

Abigail felt secure in the knowledge that the universe was kept peaceful by the likes of Jason Connors.

Her immediate problem was slowing the boy down long enough for her to make them dinner. Brian had left her some canned beans and sliced bread – typical man food – in the kitchen, and she hoped to make it palatable by adding some herbs and a pinch of curry powder.

But Jason clung to her waist, firing death rays off in every direction, and she needed to keep a hold on his arm in order to stop him having her eye out, or doing himself some damage.

She swore never to have children. Not that that was likely.

She was a brain, and a virgin. They would not serve her in pubs, and automatically offered her half price in cinemas and on buses. Only a pervert would be interested in her.

She had heard that Brian Connors was a pervert, but that was from a girl who had dropped out of his American Cinema course. That must be difficult, not having the intellect to grasp the subtleties of a John Wayne movie. Abigail thought Brian was quite attractive in an elderly sort of way, but he had practically given her sweeties this morning.

It was tough having an IQ of 156, and a body that would not grow up. Perhaps she should dress more glamorously, in vampish slit skirts and scarlet lipstick. She would probably end up looking like the winner of a primary school fancy dress contest.

'Jason, could you let go? I have to cook.'

The little creature clung on tenaciously.

'Careful, you'll spoil my skirt. It's only thin.'

Jason growled and laughed.

'Get off, don't be silly.'

'Can we play monsters some more?'

'You have to eat first, Jason. Even monsters have to eat, and space cadets.'

Jason reluctantly released her from his deathgrip, and stood to attention. He gave the Masters of the Universe Sign of Power.

'Can I help cook?'

Abigail was doubtful. She had a mental image flash of a kitchen after a chainsaw massacre, with gouts of ketchup splashed like an action painting on the walls, and beans squashed against the windowpanes. But she ought to delegate something non-dangerous to him, to keep his hands busy while she got things ready.

'Do you know how to open tins, Jason?'

He looked unsure, then smiled and nodded vigorously. She handed him a can of beans, and pulled out drawers in search of an opener.

But before she found the right drawer, Jason had the can open. She could not be sure, but she thought he had just traced a circle on the top with his thumbnail, pressing down slightly. Then, he had pulled the top up with his fingers and neatly disposed of the tin circle in the wastebin.

'That was neat, Jason.'

'Can I do it again?'

'Sure. Here's the other tin.'

Jason smiled, licking the tomato sauce off his thumb. The streamlined telephone began burping.

Monica wished she had not shouted at Lindy. It was not her fault Monica had not told her to let Brian talk to her.

She tried Brian's home number, but the girl there – not Debbie, another one, she realized with irritation – said he was invigilating, which she knew to be not true. She tried his department, but they had no ideas. He had said he would be in the Union Building about lunch time. But when was that – twelve? one? two?

Berenice kept an eye on the developing situation. There were rumours of armed men in white decontamination suits around the Chem Building, and one of the switchboard girls had overheard that the guard in the Infirmary had been savaged by some kind of wild animal.

She could not concentrate on the business she was supposed to take care of, and just dumped all her correspondence in the 'In' tray for future reference. She was wondering who to phone next when Brian showed up. Luckily, Lindy let him in.

'Bad news. Your Cazie put a friend of mine in a hospital bed.'

'I know that.'

'There's more. UCC have sent someone down to look into the mess. I've met it, and I don't think it's friendly.'

'What?'

'A gorilla called Lynch. He's browbeating Jackson as we speak. He's not your average corporation man either. He carries what looks to be an extremely large gun.'

'Jackson can't let a fucking gunslinger loose on campus.'

'Jackson doesn't have a whole lot to say about it. Listen, I'm not supposed to talk about this, but I've been blabbing about lots of secrets recently. UCC are heavily into the University. Josh Unwin would like us to name a building or two after him. A gymnasium or an art gallery or something friendly like that. I know from the funding papers that have to come through the department. UCC have got a lot of government contracts, and, as you know, the government gives us our charter.'

'But UCC are a pharmaceuticals company...'

'The Unscrupulous Chemical Company, we used to call them.'

'...what could they want with the Humanities Department?'

'Psychological stuff. Scary stuff. It's probably Ministry of Defence-funded, in the end. Everything bloody else is.'

Monica was not happy at all. Pictures were forming in her mind that she did not like.

'Defence, shit. We all know what that means.'

'Uh huh. I preferred it when it was called the War Office. That was more honest.'

Monica's intercom buzzed. It had to be important for Lindy and Bern to let the call through.

'Hello?'

'Jackson for you,' came Bern's distorted voice.

'Jackson?'

'The V-C, remember?'

'Yeah, put him on.' She looked at Brian. He shrugged.

'Miss Flint, Monica...'

She was no judge of character over the telephone, but she had to talk to Ernest Jackson four or five times a week. He was usually condescending, patronizing and paternal. Now, he sounded like a man reeling from eighteen rounds of intellectual boxing with Bernard Levin.

'...we have to talk. Are you free?'

'Free? Sure. What is it, Ernest?'

Usually he winced when she used his first name. This time he swallowed it, and carried on.

'You understand we have some problems today?'

'The police are all over the place. Yes.'

'It seems... um... that it's more serious than we thought at first... for the safety of... for all our sakes... we're going to have to institute some precautions...'

'What sort of precautions?'

'...um... er...'

She could imagine him with his hand over the receiver, turning to get instructions from someone in his office. This was new.

'There's someone with him,' she told Brian, 'pulling the strings.'

'Lynch.'

'Maybe.'

Jackson was back. 'Stringent precautions, I'm afraid. We're setting up roadblocks at the main entrance. No one will be allowed on or off the campus...'

'What? You cannot be serious!'

'...um... er...'

'You can't just lock seven thousand people up like that.'

'I...'

'Jackson, what *is* going on?'

There was a fumbling on the other end of the line, and a new voice came on.

'Miss Flint, my name is Frank Lynch. I'm here representing Unwin Chemicals. We've been funding the facility that was breached last night.'

'I know a bit about that.'

'Good, then I'm sure you'll understand when I say we have to impose a strict quarantine. Some animals escaped last night. I don't know how, and I'm not particularly interested. But these weren't just rabbits. They were experimental subjects...'

Monica's heart stopped. Then started again.

She did not want to ask the next question, afraid that Lynch would give her a straight answer.

She steadied herself. 'What have they got?'

'We can't say at the moment.'

'Crap! You'll have to say something soon. Plague? Herpes? Some kind of biological warfare bug?'

'Nothing like that. We're developing vaccines, not viruses. But there is a potential for infection. I'm not a scientist, I don't know the polysyllables. It'll be two days, maximum. That's the incubation period. If it's all over, then we can go home. Mr Jackson is busy setting up dormitories for those staff and students who are not resident on campus. Let's not make a drama out of a crisis, Miss Flint!'

'Okay, okay, okay. But if you want me to sell this to the students, you'll have to give me some guarantees.'

'Such as?'

'Such as *no fucking guns*, for a start. I'll get you volunteers to man any roadblocks or perimeter patrols you need...'

'That should be acceptable. The only armed personnel we have are out in the woods hunting rabbits. I'm sure you understand.'

'Put Jackson back on. We have to square a meeting.'

Cazie enjoyed driving. She took a long detour on her trip from town to the campus, just so she could open up the little MG her father had given her and push its engine to the limits. She had never got the needle up higher than 70 before, and now seemed to be as good a time as any to find out how fast the machine could go.

It should have been difficult, twisting through country lanes at nearly 100 miles per hour, but Cazie knew she could do it. She could feel the roads in front of her, knew what the other cars would do before they did it, and had supreme confidence in her ability to survive anything.

She had cleaned up, of course, before leaving the house. She had had to take a thorough bath to get all the blood off. Examining her face in the mirror, she could not see anything apart from a few faint white lines to mark the cuts she had got. She had torn a blouse up the back trying to put it on, and realized she would have to be careful.

Sometimes, she did not know her own strength.

Dressed in tight jeans and a loose sweater, she had taken a tour of the house. It was a shame about Derm, but that could not be helped. She had left him on the bed upstairs, but arranged him peacefully with a sheet over him. She felt desire just touching him, but suppressed it. Derm had been her friend, her lover. Using him now would be disgusting.

Besides there had been Rote, and the others. She had put them all in the Action Room. The one on the stairs had had to be pulled free, and he was still transfixed by a broken bannister.

When she had finished moving them, the desire was too powerful to fight. Her palate ached, and her stomach squirmed. The bacon in the pan in the kitchen had shrivelled to black curls, leaving the smell of burned meat smoking through the house. Carefully, she had turned off the gas and thrown away the ruined rashers.

It had had to be the woman, of course. Cazie thought the men might be too tough, too stringy. She considered cooking but there did not appear to be a need.

She had got the body up on a table, sliced her pullover open with a nail, and had breakfast.

She knew better than to make a mess now, and had sucked the blood out of the mouthfuls of flesh before tearing them loose with her teeth and swallowing them.

Dimly, as she feasted, she remembered another girl, another Cazie. A girl who had been afraid to do anything, afraid of her Daddy, afraid even of her friends. She was gone now, as if she were a dream to be forgotten upon awakening.

Eating then, driving now, Cazie knew she was the *real* girl.

A rabbit darted out of the hedgerow forty or fifty yards ahead. It was a simple matter of three or four degrees of turn on the wheel, just a flicker of pressure on the accelerator.

She got the animal dead on. She did not stop to see, but she knew she had neatly squashed its middle, leaving the head and the back legs whole.

'Rabbit ain't got no tail at all,' she hummed to herself, 'tail at all, tail at all. Rabbit ain't got no tail at all...'

110. That was as fast as the speedometer could register.

'...just a powder PUFF!'

The trees, road signs, houses, fences, hedges, telegraph poles flew past like bullets. She had dented the bumper and bonnet a couple of times, but did not give a shit.

The wind hit her face, parted and sliced around her head as if she was the prow of a ship. She smelled things she had never been able to make out before. She opened her mouth to catch flies, to eat the air. The atmosphere itself was delicious.

Briefly, she was in the throes of an orgasm. She had become used to them by now. Her hands did not waver on the wheel.

A car turned unexpectedly into the road from a blind corner, but she had *known* it was coming, and that the driver would not have the guts to keep coming. The fucker was in a ditch before he knew it.

She thought about stopping and finishing him, but he was a quarter of a mile back by then, and there would always be others.

Cazie had had enough driving. She had things to do on campus. She did the tightest-ever U-turn, and was on her way again.

Longendyke was on perimeter patrol. And the Bozz Man had stuck with him some student dipshit called Barry Bewes, who kept asking questions he knew he had better not even think of answering.

The Need was overpowering. He stood rigidly to attention, fists clenched in his gauntlets, teeth gritted.

He wished he still had his gun. At least that would have been something to hold.

Barry kept yammering and jabbering, a white noise background.

He could feel the needles in his breast pocket, safe in cigar tubes, snug against his tit.

They were in a residential area of the college. Beyond the lines of student flats was an empty field.

The Bozz Man told him the Lynch-Mob wanted the campus population contained, and so they were enforcing quarantine. They were also on a naturewatch field trip and if they saw any rabbits they were to report in. Barry thought that was funny, but Longendyke knew nothing the Bozz Man said was funny.

He was sweating with the Need, burning with the Need.

He considered sighting an invisible rabbit and sending Barry off to make a report. He could claim that his headset mike was down. Then, when the limpdick was legging around, he could slip between the houses and administer the home remedy in a minute.

Then he would be flying solo.

Still, the Bozz Man was a bigger boogey than the Need. He would have to tough it out.

'Look at that,' Barry said, pointing.

Someone stumbled out of the nearest house, bleeding from the mouth and nose.

'That's Preston, from the Infirmary, one of the nurses.'

When Barry looked back, he had his faceplate up and in position. It cut out some of the noise.

The bleeder fell to his knees and Longendyke could swear that his head was expanding.

It was. This was no shitdream.

Nurse Preston's cheeks inflated like a football, and his forehead bulged. White stretches of scalp showed in his hair. The neck expanded, and rips grew under the now-tiny-seeming ears. Panicked eyes shrank in gaping sockets. Seams appeared in his skin, and parted, showing red and muscle. The flesh swelled around his nose, making the protuberance an indentation.

Then Preston's head exploded.

* * *

Lynch thought he had things under control, but Anderton knew different.

The CSD man had his back-up team deployed effectively, even if their guns were locked in their trunks. He had spread them around the campus, each one tagged with a student volunteer to keep them in line. Anderton knew how little provocation it would take for Lynch to order his men to get rid of their encumbrances.

Anderton had run every test he could get together at short notice on 125. Outside the body, it was a pushover – a few degrees temperature change either way, and it was dead mould. But inside, it was an unpredictable little bugger, and he would have to jab up another bunch of animals to have even a chance at guessing what it would do.

Finch had tabulated five or six possible reactions, none of them good. Lynch was not interested yet. Give him a few infectees, and he would start asking for treatment scenarios. Anderton knew the UCC man would be happier with a rifle in his hands than a hypodermic syringe.

Lynch had not had time to listen to the lecture Anderton had prepared, the one that began, '125 isn't exactly a disease, it's supposed to be a symbiote. In some ways, once you catch it, you could be *better* than you were before…'

The CSD man had left a suited guard, Tripps, to look after the team in the lab. Anderton wondered if he were there to keep externals away, or to make sure they stayed at their benches.

Anderton had a pain at the back of his neck from bending over too many microscopes, and he knew he was more likely to find a cure for cancer than deal with his dandruff. Since he had signed up with UCC and put himself in the supertax bracket, his life had been going down the plughole. The corporation was a lot like a virus in the way it acted on people – it got into your system, took it over completely, sucked out whatever it wanted, and left you behind as a pile of compost.

Once, at a reception, he had been within twelve seats of Josh

Unwin. That was supposed to be an honour. Anderton thought the corporate head a vulgar publicity-seeker, and knew he was just the figurehead for a cabal of faceless boardroom plutocrats. Unwin was always off breaking land-speed records and appearing on television quiz shows. Meanwhile, the juggernaut of UCC rolled onwards, crushing anyone who got under its killer wheels. And UCC only provided a service. It had no use for Leo itself, it just had a client who dreamed up the specifics and made a commission. Anderton knew exactly the kind of people who would be the corporation's clients on a project like this.

There was a chance, of course. If only 125 could kill the rabbits before they could pass it on.

If only...

Then the Infirmary called up, and told him about the three kids from York House. Thomas Ward, Clare Moyle, Peter Aston.

Then more reports came in.

125 was starting to get busy.

The Zombies would not let Brian and Monica into the unmarked lorry the UCC team were using as a field HQ, but Lynch came out to see them.

'Miss Flint, thank you for your cooperation,' he said, ignoring Brian as he had done in Jackson's office. 'You've been a great help. In these situations, panic can be as dangerous as a disease.'

How many of these 'situations' had Lynch been in?

'What's going on at the Infirmary?' Monica demanded. Brian was impressed by her single-mindedness. 'Why won't your people let us see the patients?'

'Risk of infection. Your Dr Hind made the decision.'

'But you're enforcing it?'

Lynch did not even look annoyed, although Monica's tart tone made her opinion clear. When you looked like Frank Lynch, Brian supposed, you did not have to register anger to be imposing. Against his will, he could not help but be fascinated by the criss-cross scars on the man's cheeks and neck. He had either been clawed by a lion or processed through a hay-baler. Brian bet the cat or the machine that had done it was in much worse shape than Lynch.

The man made a gesture of exasperation – oddly actorish, as if it was just an excuse not to answer a tough question – and tried to come across as the world's most long-suffering small-town copper.

'Miss, I wish you'd stop thinking of us as an Occupation Force. We're here to help. There's a very great danger, and you'll only make things worse by treating us as if we were the Gestapo. We've gone out of our way to keep you, and the University authorities, informed.'

'Then, who…'

'Now, if you'll excuse me, we're very busy. If you could come by later, once we've sorted out where everybody is going to spend the night, I'll give you a complete update on the situation. Take care.'

Take care!

Lynch went back into his lorry, and Brian and Monica were left with a couple of the Zombies.

They wore white jumpsuits, sealed at the ankles and wrists so the boots and gauntlets were part of the uniform. Balaclava hoods hung behind their necks. Brian knew if they added atmosphere-filtration masks with faceplates, they would look even scarier. Now, they only had expressionless faces to hide behind.

'What now?' she asked.

'For me, Jason. I phoned in, and Abigail says he's okay, but I want to take a look myself.'

'Abigail?'

She was jealous.

'Just a babysitter. Who do you think I am, Warren Beatty?'

She thought of a clever answer, but threw it away unused. Brian saw she was too concerned with this chaos to keep up the wisecracks. That was good. This was serious.

Barry had got blood all over himself. At least the incident of the man with the Incredible Exploding Head had shut the kid up.

Now, Longendyke had been pulled from the perimeter. A couple of the medics had wrapped Barry up in a polythene bender and were carrying him between them like a shot leopard.

Someone was trying to talk to the student, trying to get a reaction out of him. In the sagging shroud, he looked as if he had been prematurely body-bagged.

Longendyke was a furnace inside. The Need, the needle…

As they trotted through the populated part of the campus, people got out of their way. Part of the CSD job was to radiate fuck-with-me-not vibes at all times.

The Bozz Man saw him, somehow recognized him through his mask and suit, and called him over.

'Report to the truck, Longendyke,' he said. 'Gail will want to check you out.'

Gail was the field surgeon.

'I feel fine, sir. These suits work real good.'

The Bozz Man growled. 'Just do it, Longendyke.'

There was a distraction, and Sergeant-Equivalent Bosworth had his pistol drawn. The pistol that was supposed to be in the truck.

Barry jack-knifed out of the carriers' hands, and was inch-worming across the grass. Two of the medics moon-hopped after him, but Longendyke got there first, coming down hard on the turdbreath's back. The student struggled and kicked, but his hands had been twist-tied with a plastic tag. He was having a shit fit convulsion.

Through the two-layer shroud, which was cunningly perforated to allow air in but not let germs out, Longendyke saw Barry's face changing.

This was not like the swellhead at the perimeter. Diamond-cluster crystals were forming just under the kid's skin, pricking through bloodlessly, multiplying visibly, forming a crust, roughing up against the plastic.

There was a crackling like the rustle of a ton of angry cellophane.

Longendyke was hit by a spasm, and pushed himself away from the kid. His hands felt filthy where he had touched the plastic, and he was shaking all over.

The Need, the needle …

The medics got in, and started using their own needles.

'What're you giving him?' he mumbled.

One of the medics shook a masked, hooded head. Don't ask. It was like that. He might have known.

Barry broke up inside the plastic, crystals fragmenting. Longendyke saw what was left of his face freeze, and then crack apart, falling away from what looked like a jewel-encrusted skull.

The medic held up his hypo. The needle was bent and blunted.

The crystal mass still grew and shifted. Longendyke kept his guts down by sheer force of will. What was left of Barry Bewes looked as if it ought to be sealed in a barrel and buried under a seventy-foot concrete pyramid.

Outside the faculty cottages, Jason and Abigail were kicking a football around. Abigail was out of breath, but Jason was as active as ever. She clearly relished the opportunity to break off the uneven match and talk to Brian. She knew who Monica was, and admitted when they were introduced she had not voted for her. There was an awkward pause, and Brian left the women together as he chased after Jason.

His son saw him, and took off, shouting, 'Help, there's a monster coming.'

Brian was not used to running. His lungs ached. He made a mental note to play badminton more often. Then he got his wind, and sped up. How could an eight-year-old be so fast? The kid could not read yet, but he might be shaping up as an Olympic long-distance man. Fair enough.

Jason made it halfway up the hill, towards the woods, then doubled back to hide behind one of the Halls of Residence. Brian was catching up. As he ran, he saw people at the edge of the woods. In white suits. This was a real quarantine.

'Jason, come here. This is Daddy being serious.'

'The monster! The monster!'

Brian had to stop. That was a mistake. The exertion hit him when he stood still. His knees nearly went. He filled his lungs, and started running again. Jason was weaving back towards the bulk of the campus, in the general direction of the Humanities block.

'There are no monsters,' he shouted at his son.

Students milling round stared at him. The Zombies were not too visible a presence here. Finals were on. Brian bet there would be a lot of kids around who did not even realize there was a crisis because they were so worked up over their exams.

Outside the Engineering Department, where a hallful of would-be bridge builders were bent over papers, a lone, long-haired figure in a kaftan and a bowler hat walked up and down carrying a placard. BOYCOTT FINALS. It was the least successful protest of the year, but at least it was not doing any harm.

A couple of Zombies sat by the shallow pond, which some wit had dyed fluorescent green again, eating sandwiches. So they were human after all. Another cliché bites the dust.

Jason was not flagging. The kid was not sick, although Brian thought he might be when he caught up with him.

They were past the Schools now, near the Admin blocks and the Union Building. Brian was briefly worried that Jason might trip on the paved areas and hurt himself, but the kid was too sure-footed for that. He saw his son weave his way between the casual strollers. Great. The main entrance was up ahead. The Zombies would stop Jason for him.

'Monsters, monsters, eeeeehh!'

Then Jason stopped, twenty yards short of the impromptu roadblock. Brian caught up with him, overshot by a few feet before he could stop his legs pumping pavement, and stepped back. He grabbed his son, and hugged him tight. He did not throw him in the air because, in his condition, he was not sure he could catch him.

Then the MG came out of nowhere and crashed the roadblock.

Pete felt okay. Packed all over in soft cotton wool, but okay.

They had heard the noise, and come to help him. Just a little prick in the arm, and he was okay.

They had washed the blood off, and brought him to the Infirmary.

He was not asleep. He had to answer questions. They had given him a shot to calm him down, a shot to put him to sleep, a shot to wake him up, and a shot to help him answer the questions. He had had a lot of shots.

He answered the questions, and they had let him go to bed.

He was still worried about his essay. Sometimes, he tried hard to tell the nurse that he had to go back to his room to finish it, but she did not understand.

He would have to retype the bloody pages if he were to get it in by four-thirty. He wanted to get to the dean before Bloody Basil.

They had given him a room of his own. And a pretty nurse to sit with him all the time.

He was okay.

But Something was growing in the back of his head, Something dark and clawed and hungry and confused. That was not okay at all.

In his head, he tried to talk to the Something, to be reasonable with it. He was supposed to know about Reason. It was his field of expertise. He told the Something to be quiet, to stop playing Heavy Metal inside his brain, stopping him from doing his essay and going to sleep. It did not listen. It did not care about the Age of Reason, or his post-graduate plans, or the cotton wool.

He could not think what the Something was, but he could imagine what it was like. A little black bud, opening into a poisonous flower, blooming dark and blotting out the whiteness of the wool.

When he tried to sleep, he found he could not. He was perpetually groggy, but not tired enough to nod off. But he could dream while he was awake. He dreamed he was the Something inside himself, a confident predator certain of his First, intent on making everyone take him seriously.

He imagined taking the RG apart, pulling him limb from limb. And he felt a warm, pleasant feeling in the pit of his stomach. Then, he imagined tracking Basil down to his book-lined, fresh coffee-smelling den and dragging him out of the circle of worshipful catamites with which he had surrounded himself. He saw Basil's skin coming apart under his hands, and Basil's heart and lungs working their way out of his body.

He nodded awake, hungry, mouth dry.

Pete was okay. For now.

Cazie knew the car could take it. The man in white who got in the way bounced off the bonnet, twisted in the air, and was behind her. The wooden fence things parted in the middle, scratching the bodywork probably, and were out of the way. She left the road and drove on the lawn and the paved parts.

A man carrying a kid got out of the way. Smart move. There was something familiar about him. Brian Connors, right? The clever prick from a long time ago, yesterday.

She put the car in a pond, and vaulted out of it. A couple of guys eating their lunch looked surprised and reached out instinctively for guns they were not carrying. A few kicks took them out.

She felt great, as if she were dancing, or making love. But she had to calm down, to get herself under control.

She left the two men down and walked away. Some gaping loon asked her what was happening, and she shrugged.

'Whose car is that?'

'No idea,' she told the man in white.

'Fuck!'

'No thanks,' she smiled. 'Maybe later.'

There were enough people around, and she was fast enough for everyone to be mixed up about what they had seen.

Someone was calling her name.

'Cazie!'

There it was again, a man. She wanted a man. But she could wait. There were more important things.

'Cazie, it's me. Brian Connors, remember?'

He was panting, and holding a struggling little boy. The boy from yesterday, Jason.

'Oh hi,' she said, smiling easily, 'what's happening?'

'I don't know... Cazie, *what happened last night?*'

'It was cool. It's dealt with now. No worries, see.'

She held out her empty hands.

'But Rote...'

'Rote's out of it. It's a different game now. My game.'

'Cazie, look...'

She took a thumbnail between her teeth and bit. Damn, but Brian was a temptation.

And the boy. Jason had stopped struggling so much, and was staring at her chest, licking his teeth.

'Can't talk now. Must dash. Catch you later, right?'

His mouth fell open, in disbelief. Why was everyone so slow? Mentally, he was not yet out of the starter's gate.

She stroked the child's tender cheek, and met his gaze. She could tell he was a smart kid.

'That's a very good-looking young man you have there. Bye-bye now.'

She left him, and started walking towards York House. She

needed to see Thommy and Clare.

They needed to get their show together and put it on the road.

There was a fuss outside the Hall of Residence, with lots of the men in white suits milling around. From a student she knew, Cazie learned that Clare and Thommy were in the Infirmary. The story was that one had tried to kill the other.

They had given Clare some drugs, but she had only pretended to get high. There could not be any high like the one she had had when she had turned the tables on Thommy.

Her boyfriend had been getting on her tits for months now, and this business with Rote had made it worse. Clare did not see why she should be the only one to get bruises.

She did not know why yet, but she got the feeling that suddenly she was Special.

So, when Thommy had woken her up after she had slept the morning through, she had decided to put his head through the floor.

There was nothing he could do about it.

Last night, she had been hurt. But she was better now. Better than ever.

She did not know if she had killed Thommy. She hoped so. Putting his head through the floor was the best thing she had ever done.

When the people had come for her, she had not done anything to them, although she was sure she could have shoved them into walls or folded them up and put them in briefcases. She did not see any point in spoiling the effect by overdoing it.

They brought her to the Infirmary, and gave her drugs, and strapped her down on a bed. She knew she could break the straps as if they were woven straw. They should have used something stronger.

She had told them so, but they did not pay any attention to her. That just went to show how stupid everyone else was.

Randy Preston had been just going off shift when they brought her in. She had gone out with him in the first year. Quietly, as they passed, she had bitten his hand. That was for dumping her and chasing after that slagslut Kathy Riel. He had looked meanly at her, and taken off, not even bothering with a bandage.

Now, she just looked at the white ceiling and waited for the Next Thing to happen.

There was a man in white in her room. He was not a nurse. Nurses did not have guns. And this man had a gun that looked a bit like a black T-square. She had seen them before, on TV.

It was funny. Him thinking a gun would make any difference.

Doctors had been to see her. Dr Hind, who was the campus quack, and a couple of others. They had looked at her hands, and felt her arms and legs, and asked her to open her mouth. They looked puzzled. Silly bastards.

Someone came in to check her straps. He gave new orders to the man in white, whispering. Her ears were fine-tuned. She could hear every word as if it were clearly shouted at her. She gathered that Thommy had croaked. Shame, she thought. She would have liked to hurt him some more. Nobody had said anything, but she supposed she would be in trouble about that. Police trouble. Somehow, that did not worry her too much.

The only thing that bothered Clare was her skin. It was working loose in some places. Her back felt like an itchy vest and she thought that if she broke the straps and sat up in bed it would stay on the sheet behind her. Things were bubbling inside her body.

There was a knock at the door. The man jumped, and held on to his gun.

'Who is it?'

'Visitor,' said a girl's voice. Clare recognized Cazie at once. It was like her to visit in hospital.

The man opened the door.

'How did you get in here? You're not supposed…'

Then Cazie punched him in the throat, sinking her fingers into him there, and lifted him up off the floor.

From the bed, Clare could see the man's back, covered in white. Cazie's hand came out of it, holding something red and squelchy between her fingers. Blood leaked out like thick soup from a holed tin. Cazie dropped the thing, which hung from the hole in the man by a mess of spurting purple tubes and fatty substances. It must be his heart.

Clare saw Cazie pull her hand free, and drop the man. She had rolled up her sleeve so as not to get messy. With a towel that had been hanging by the washbasin in the room, she wiped her forearm clean, licking at the fiddly bits between her fingers to finish off the job.

'Hello, Clare, you look terrible. What happened to your face?'

'I think it's coming off.'

'That's a pity.'

'I know. I've got a funny tummy too.'

Cazie pulled the blankets away and looked down at her. Clare looked too. It was not pretty. Under her skin snakes were writhing. She was swelling up like the time when she thought she was pregnant.

'I can see your insides.'

'Will I die?'

'No. Course not. You're my friend.'

'My friend.'

Cazie bent down, below the bed, and came up again with a handful of something. She tugged, and it came free. It was the heart. She took it to the sink and washed it off.

She pinched a chunk of meat and popped it into her mouth like a grape. Cazie smiled and chewed. She sat on the edge of the bed, and took another pinch, which she put to Clare's lips.

'Here, eat this. It'll make you feel better.'

Lynch had a couple of men dead.

'...a blow of tremendous force. Stone's ribcage was literally pushed in. The broken bones worked like knives inside him...'

Matthew Gail had been medical back-up on Lynch's last few situations. He was good, dispassionate, and fast to make a diagnosis.

'A skilled fighter, then?'

Gail tugged his moustache, working his way up to saying something he thought would sound silly.

'No. The blow was way off the killpoint. It should just have dented his shoulder a bit. Nothing serious. It was the *force* that proved fatal, not the aim.'

'Shit. And Gwydion?'

'Skull. Same thing. If there weren't traces of rubber heel, I'd think it was done with a bench press.'

Lynch paused a moment, tapped his fingers against the desk. The sheeted bodies were side by side in the back of the lorry.

'Okay, okay, screw the "softly, softly" approach.' He turned to Fassett, whose four breast-pocket pips marked him as the rank equivalent of a Sergeant-Major. 'Break out the guns, get the men armed. Put Bosworth in charge of distributing ordnance. Tell the teams to give a warning shot, if possible. If not, we'll cry tomorrow.'

He took out his own gun, and checked the clip.

Carson had put all the specs on 125 through the computer, and given Anderton the read-out.

It was bad news.

Anderton felt sick. He looked again, and the same conclusions came to him.

Carson stood at his elbow, waiting for a verbal report. Finch was still fiddling about with 125 dishes. Tripps, Lynch's man, was looking bored, but standing alert.

They could still walk about, but Anderton knew they were dead people.

Like him.

He had been chain-popping aspirins all day, but the headache had not gone away. The churning in his stomach got worse every half hour or so, in perceptible lurches. Anderton had seen Finch take off her glasses and rub her temples too many, times. Carson's acne was starting to dribble.

'We've got it,' he said quietly.

'Yes?'

'125. It doesn't die with the host. It's communicable. Highly communicable.'

Carson hit him in the stomach, savagely. Anderton doubled over and was sick. Tripps levelled his gun.

Carson, his trousers stained with Anderton's bile, whirled like a dervish, sweeping a benchtop clear of retorts and dishes. Glass broke. A patch of skin dislodged from Carson's cheek and splattered on the tile floor. Bone shone yellow in the raw hole. He had a triangular wedge of broken glass in his hand.

The glass slashed in front of Anderton's face. The scientist flinched, and banged his head against the bench. Carson raised the glass again, and a neat row of holes opened in his chest. Anderton did not hear the noise of Tripps's gun until seconds later, when Carson was already pitched forward on top of him.

He felt teeth go in somewhere below his collarbone. The body was pulled roughly off him, and he stood up.

Tripps had put his faceplate on, and looked like something from outer space. Anderton held up red hands.

'It's in the blood,' he said.

Inside his mask, Tripps's face burst. His Perspex eyeholes went red, as if his entire head had turned liquid. He stayed standing for a long moment, then crumpled like an empty suit. The seals were good, there was no leakage, but he did not keep his manshape. The chest fell in, and the limbs ballooned.

Anderton had a nasty desire to step on the suit, to see if it would squelch open like a slug.

He was bleeding himself, from somewhere. He had had 125

for over a day now. Probably caught it from Skippy's remains. The incubation period must be erratic. Tripps could not have been exposed for more than half an hour.

Even without the break-in, he would have caught 125 and Lynch would be here with Unwin's gladiators.

'Fuck UCC! Fuck everything!'

Finch helped him up.

'Fuck me,' she whispered.

Her blouse was open, and her third teeth were coming through. She kissed him. He could not feel anything. She permanently put his lips out of shape. Strange flesh.

Anderton pushed Finch away, and looked at his hands. The skin was mostly gone. He saw muscles sliding off bone. He would not have the use of them much longer.

And he had something to do.

Pain shot up from his fingers as he prised Tripps's gun free.

He shot Finch once, in the heart. He had always liked her.

'Fuck me... me... me...'

She ran down like a talking doll as her brain died on her.

Anderton found that his forefinger had come off in the trigger guard. It was stuck. He felt as if his hands were being eaten by army ants. He could not use the right at all.

He poked the finger out of the guard with a pencil, and rested the gun butt on the floor. He put the barrel to the bridge of his nose, and worked the trigger with his left thumb.

The gun was emptying itself into the ceiling a full minute later.

From the kitchen of Brian's house, they heard the first shots. He flashbacked to Grosvenor Square, 1971, and the spurt of flame in the dark, Jean's knee a shattered ruin, the goggle-eyed face of the teen marine with the shaking gun, the sudden rush of sobriety.

'What the fuck?' shouted Monica. Jason giggled at the bad word. Brian listened, and heard the typewriter noise again.

'That's not a rabbit hunt.'

Abigail had dropped her cup of tea. The mug had not shattered, but the floor was soaked.

They could not see anything, so they had to go outside.

'Abigail,' Brian said, 'keep Jason here. Lock up. You can stay the night. If anyone but us comes to the door, pretend you're not in. And keep him quiet if you have to gag him.'

The girl was trembling, an Alice overcome by Wonderland. He hoped she would be able to hang together.

'You understand?'

'Y-yes…'

Jason pulled at Abigail's arm. 'Can we watch a video, Abi, can we?'

Brian nodded, and the girl took his son into the living room. Jason was frisky, but unhurt. Thank God. It all seemed like a game. Monica had her coat on, and the door open.

He did not want to leave Jason, but there was no choice. He knew his son was safe; now, he should try to help Monica, to do what best he could for everyone…

Outside, the campus looked normal at first. There was no more shooting. As they walked towards the main buildings, they saw a lot of people milling about. There were a few Zombies around, but mostly it was just University people. A guy Brian knew from the School of European Studies asked him if he knew what was going on, and he had to shrug a 'no' at him. A girl was having hysterics by the Refectory, and three of her friends were calming her down.

Apart from the men in white, it could have been any late afternoon.

'Where's Lynch?' Monica spat.

'God knows. Where did the shooting come from?'

'Shooting!' said a bystanding student, taking it up and passing it on. 'Shooting! Someone's been shot!'

Brian knew this was how panics got started.

'East Slope, I think. The Infirmary?'

The men in white started running at the same time, as if worked by magic. They must have intercoms in their suits. They were headed for the East Slope. And they had guns out.

'I said no guns,' Monica said.

Someone got in the way, and was knocked down.

'Fascist bastards.'

The Zombie stopped, twenty yards beyond the fallen boy, and turned to look at the group of two or three angry students gathered around him. He had a pistol out, and his mask on.

'Fascist *bastard*!'

A book flew through the air towards him, whirling like a discus. It glanced off his raised arm. The Zombie fired once, into the air above him. The group froze like a tableau.

'Heav-*vee*!'

The Zombie pointed his gun at the kids for an instant, then turned and resumed running.

There was more shooting from the East Slope, impossibly loud now they were out in the open. As a man, the group of students hurled themselves flat on the ground like refugees from a '50s civil defence drill, arms over their heads.

Monica was off and running, after the Zombies. Brian knew better, but had to go with her.

A klaxon sounded, and a loudspeaker voice started to read a bland reassurance he did not have the time or the inclination to listen to.

The place was becoming a battlefield.

Shaun Bensom did not believe in Finals. He had worked hard for three years, turning in essays, projects, original work. He had had practical experience in the summer vacs, on building sites and in a draughtsman's office. He had proved everything he wanted to, and he knew his marks in continuous assessment were way above average. But why should his degree depend on the state of his stomach and his head on a single, solitary afternoon in May? What if he had 'flu? Or some personal crisis? And what if the paper – like last year's – was entirely concerned with some obscure facet of claw-feed grinding he had no intention of ever getting involved with in his professional life? He had earned the title Engineer, and two hours bending his back over a desk would not make any difference. It would just be jumping through another hoop.

He had been walking up and down outside the exam hall since the others had gone in, crossing his picket line of one. His placard felt a lot heavier than it had done at first.

There were a lot of people running about the campus today, making a noise. If he had been inside, he would have found it bloody hard to concentrate despite the thick windows. Some street theatre group were playing spacemen all over the place, and waving toy guns. It must be like that Assassination game, where middle management stalked each other through the woods and shot their opponents with paint pellets.

No one was paying any attention to his protest, although he had heard some sniggering from the other students before the exam started. Hetty had said she would bring him a coffee and some salad rolls from the canteen when her tutorial was over, but she had not shown up. He was hungry. At least it was summer, and not quite freezing.

Over by the Humanities Block, the Game was getting out of hand. He saw a guy in leathers jump on one of the spacemen, and get his head kicked in. It was some sort of martial arts display. Shaun bet it hurt. The spaceman shot the leathers guy in the head, and even from two hundred yards, he could see there was an extremely large gobbet of red paint.

Silly buggers!

He wished he was back in his flat, passing joints with Hetty and Colin and Liz Donoghue. But he had his stand to make, his principles to uphold.

No one was looking. He rested his placard against a low wall, its message out so people could see, and lit up a fag. Under the cold sun, he felt sleepy.

The students inside would be on the home stretch now. All but the real dumbos would be through with the stress question and onto the plane drawing. Pencil-pushing geeks! Colin was in there somewhere. Sold out by his best mate, Shaun thought, what a world! Finals bring out the worst.

The spacemen were dragging off the leathers guy. He must be out cold. These martial arts people could get out of hand too easily.

He turned and looked at the hall. Through the plate-glass windows, he could see the rows and rows of desks, and the ranks of bowed heads. One or two smug bastards had finished already, and were sitting back, taking it easy. The real clever-clevers had finished, but were going through their papers making minor adjustments.

Colin was near the front, still writing. They had had an argument about all this last night and it had come down to Colin agreeing with everything Shaun said but still swearing he would sit his Finals.

'After all, I want the bloody degree...'

Colin would be moving out of the flat soon if Shaun could help it. It meant losing Liz Donoghue and her dope connection, but principles were principles and he would stand by his.

Colin was slowing down. He put his pencil down, and rubbed his nose. Shaun saw it was bleeding.

That's exactly what he meant! A chance nosebleed at this of all times, brought on by stress probably, and you knew no assessor in the world was going to give higher than a Third to a paper with blood all over it. It was so blatantly unfair!

Colin would agree with him now.

Blood was streaming out of both his nostrils, and he was smearing it over his face like a spreading moustache. He must not have a handkerchief. Colin stood up, and fell over. The desk next to his went down under him, and Gilly Walker – one of the few girls in the School – had to jump out of his way.

Colin must be having an acid flashback. He had spent his first year at University swallowing tabs like they were Polo mints.

Watching his flatmate writhe around on the floor, while chaos rippled out from him, was sort of funny, but a bit depressing. The glass was well soundproofed, so Shaun could not hear if there was an uproar or not. The invigilator was walking towards the incident.

Shaun turned his back on it all, and picked up his placard.

'What is this?'

Monica shouted at the Zombies. They were crouched in ones and twos around the Infirmary Building, taking cover behind signs and steps. A few turned their heads, but generally she was ignored.

A window in the building was broken from the inside. Curtains waved and there was gunfire. A line of divots popped up in the tarmac of the car park, and the ambulance's left rear tyre burst.

Monica felt herself going down, and for an insane moment thought she had been shot. But it was Brian, pulling her behind a rubbish skip.

'What is this?' she said again, to no one in particular.

The black Zombie with the walkie-talkie must be Lynch. He was buzzing orders into it.

There was quiet for a few seconds, then two Zombies stood up and sprayed the front of the Infirmary with machine-gun fire. Infinity loops of bullet pocks appeared in the walls of the prefab building. Brown hardwood flowers bloomed in the white-painted facade.

Answering fire came from inside the building, but it was random, directionless. A nearby shrub was whipped with bullets.

'There's someone crazy in there,' Brian said.

'Let's get closer, talk to Lynch,' she insisted.

'No. He's busy.'

More orders crackled. Monica could not make them out. Then Lynch was up himself, firing from the hip. His gun was bigger and louder than any she had seen so far. The Infirmary door, decorated in bright colours at the Kids' Karnival last week, fell apart, and came off its hinges in pieces.

The Zombies dashed forwards. The first to the door bounced back, as if off an invisible wall, and Monica saw blood streaming from his chest.

Brian tried to push her head down so she would not see any more, but she fought him.

The Zombie was dead in the doorway, and something was moving inside the building. There were men either side of the door, backs to the wall, guns pointed upwards. One nodded to the other, and swung into the gap, firing wild. His gun must have jammed, because the noise shut off suddenly as he vanished inside. Monica thought he had been pulled into the darkness by something.

After a beat, the crazy people came out. Some had guns, most did not. They wore hospital gowns, pyjamas, doctors' coats, even Zombie whites. And their faces were not real. Some were bleeding.

In the lead, clutching the captured Zombie by his crooked neck, was Cazie Bruckner.

Only she did not look like Cazie any more.

Lynch pulled down his mask and shouted, 'Shoot the bastards, now!'

The man Cazie was holding got shot. She could feel the bullets punching into him. He was big, and she could hide behind him. Dead, he weighed more, but struggled less.

The rest of the world was in slow motion. She could see the bullets in the air, whirling as they came. The men in the white hoods had not a hope.

She knew a couple of the less important ones had been killed in the break-out. The new-made ones. She hoped Clare had come through. The others did not matter.

She had the dead man's gun jammed through his armpit. Taking his weight on one hand, she got hold of the stock and started firing at the men in white suits.

The white stood out very nicely against the redbrick walls and green grass. Shooting them was too easy.

She slung the dead man away, hurling him one-handed. He came down twenty feet or more away in a jumble of awkwardly bent arms and legs.

The gun was all used up, so she threw it away.

The others had fanned out either side of her. Several of them were down, but most were off and running.

It would spread. They could not stop her.

She ran straight ahead, leaning out of the way of the bullets, swiping the white hoods aside. Each time she connected, she heard bones breaking, and the slow trickle of an internal injury.

Jesus, these were the days to be alive!

She vaulted a wall, and put on a burst of speed.

Lynch fired at the crazy bitch as she disappeared like a cat over the wall. Brick chips flew, but she was gone.

He took a damage reading. Three, no, four men down. The enemy – whatever the hell they were – had suffered more. There were seven dead things on the Infirmary forecourt.

Two of them were once his own men. Even with their masks off, he could not recognize them. He would pull tags later.

'What is going on? What the fuck is going on?'

It was Flint, the student *Presidente,* with the nonentity from Jackson's office. Damn civilians!

'Epidemic.'

His men were regrouping. He would need more people to handle this.

'Of what, Lynch?'

'I told you, I'm not a scientist. They call it Batch 125, if that means anything.'

'It makes people crazy, right?'

Lynch was not giving anything away.

'What's it *for*, Lynch?'

He looked at her, and saw fear inside her tough eyes.

'Guess,' he said.

Jason still had not calmed down. Abigail had had to go through ten or a dozen video tapes. He would sit for anything between three seconds and two minutes on fast-forward before deciding he wanted something different.

If she thought about it, she would be grateful for the distraction. She did not want to have to face up to whatever else was going on. Brian and Monica Flint had not been expansive, but whatever it was was very scary.

'Hate this! Gimme 'nother!'

'What do we say, Jason? Please?'

'Gimme *'nother*!'

He was pushing his jaw out, trying to look fierce.

'Jason.'

'Gimme!'

He grabbed at her with both hands, sinking his little fingers into her middle. It hurt. She would have bruises.

'Gimme!'

'Jason, no. We don't talk to people like that.'

The boy head-butted her in the stomach, winding her. Christ, he was turning into a little monster!

'Jason, no. That's too rough.'

He let her go, and glared up at her. Abigail remembered how powerless she had always felt in the presence of adults. In Jason's eyes, she could see dull resentment, but also something else... An animal cunning she had never come across in a kid before. She did not like it.

'Let's make you some tea, shall we? There's cake and biscuits.'

Jason threw back his head and howled like a wolf, 'Hun-*greee*!'

There was something wrong with his teeth, something wrong with his mouth. It should not be able to open that wide. He would do himself an injury.

Abigail held his chin, and closed his mouth.

'If you go around like that, Jason, a bird will come and nest in it.'

She turned her back on him and went into the kitchen. That was her mistake.

He must have sprung like a coyote. She felt the impact on her upper back, forcing her forward. His hands were in her hair, pulling.

'Ow, Jason. Cut it out. Come on.'

She wriggled, trying to dislodge him, but he was holding fast. His knees gripped her sides, and one arm was around her neck. She could not talk. Her hair was in her mouth.

She did not want to hurt him, but she might have to.

His hand passed in front of her face, and she felt an icy touch near her ear. Something wet.

He had cut her.

She tottered into the living room, and hurled him free. He shot into the sofa, and bounced up and down laughing.

She put her hand to her temple. It came away bloody.

'Jason, your nails are too long.'

Suddenly, he was still, tense as an armed mantrap. And as dangerous. Abigail started thinking seriously about protecting herself. His eyes looked yellowish now, with tiny pupils. He looked hungry.

There were knives in the kitchen.

She could not believe she had thought about that. This was an eight-year-old boy, not Jack the Ripper.

Just now, there was something very adult, unhealthily adult, about the way Jason was looking at her.

'Abi… hun-*greeeeee!*'

He licked his lips. No tongue could be that long. He shrugged, and ripped his shirt. He pulled at his collar. Buttons popped, and cloth tore.

Abigail could not take her eyes off him.

Just inside the kitchen, on a side-table, there was a half-full bottle of Perrier water. She thought she could pick it up and use it faster than he could strike, but she was not sure.

She did not want to bet her life on it.

She put out a hand behind her, and found the doorjamb, held it.

Jason just looked.

He was squirming now, with barely repressed energy. He was a growing boy. She could *see* him growing.

'Jason,' she whispered, pleading, 'Jason, don't…'

Then he came at her.

Pete had been shot in the side, but did not notice much. When he was away from the Infirmary, he hiked up his bloody pyjama jacket and saw the hole. It was puckered up, but healing over nicely.

By the campus clock, it was four-fifteen. He still had a quarter of an hour. Realistically, he knew he could not get his essay typed up and ready in time. But he could show up in person and plead his case.

He thought he could convince the dean.

There were people running all around, and firing off guns. But he ignored them.

The steps to the School of English and American Studies were up ahead. His bare feet were frozen by the concrete slabs, but he hopped up them and pushed through the main doors under the Humanities H structure, getting good rubber under his soles.

Inside, things were much quieter. There was a Godard film

showing in A2, and a steady dribble of students were walking out on it, yawning and complaining.

He was having to get used to his strength. Opening the door to the stairwell, he wrenched it off its hinges and had, embarrassedly, to lean it up against a wall, hoping no one would notice. His muscles were expanded inside his striped pyjamas, straining the seams.

Up on the Eng/Am floor, outside the dean's office, there was a minimal queue of his coursemates, waiting to hand over their take-away papers. Bloody Basil, pouting smugly, was glancing over his catamites' papers, making jokes and dishing out complacent reassurances. His own essays were in an imitation leather folder, done up with a bow of red ribbon. Bloody Basil had a word processor with a presentation-standard printer, and all his essays looked like published articles.

'Petah, my dear colleague,' Basil said, seeing him for the first time, 'how perfectly shocking you look. If there is any weather about, you certainly seem to have stumbled under it.'

One of Basil's gunsels giggled, handing over his own essay to the dean's secretary.

Pete loped up to Basil, feeling the strength in his insteps and thighs as he walked.

'Care to take a glance?' Basil said, offering his essay for inspection. 'A modest effort, but one hopes it will suffice.'

Pete took the essay, and opened the folder. Basil had chosen to answer the Porson question. '"When Dido found Aeneas would not come,"' he read, '"she mourned in silence and was Di-do-dum," Richard Porson, Epigram on Latin Gerunds.'

Only Basil would even have attempted the fucking Porson question!

He looked at Basil's foot-wide smile.

'Porson, eh?'

Basil nodded, barely able to contain his glee within his checked trousers.

'1759-1808?'

Basil swelled with undisguised pride.

"'I went to Frankfort, and got drunk,

"With that most learn'd professor, Brunck,'" Pete quoted.

'Ah-hah,' Basil countered, "'I went to Wortz, and got more drunken,

"With that more learn'd professor, Ruhnken.'"

The catamites all but clapped their leader's erudition.

Some time after Porson's death, his executors had been sorting through the books and papers in his library and kept coming across green hairy things stuck between pages. The scholar and wit had been in the habit of using unwanted sandwiches as bookmarks.

Pete rolled up Basil's essay like a scroll, enjoying the sparks of dismay in his eyes. He put his forefinger and thumb into the lizard's mouth, keeping it open like a letterbox, and posted the essay into his oesophagus. With the heel of his hand, he rammed the folder in past Basil's tonsils, scraping chunks out of his throat.

The catamites were aghast, and the secretary fainted. Basil was on the floor now, foaming and choking around his learned critique of the childish humour of the author of *Facetiae Cantabrigienses*. Yellow and white foam came out of Basil's mouth, soaking around the essay and dribbling down onto the pleated collar of his affected smoking jacket. The scholar twitched and spasmed on the carpet, squawking in a most un-Johnsonian display of undignified pain.

Pete needed a piss, and Basil's face was there handy as a target. He took his dick out of his pyjamas, aimed it, and let go.

Abigail woke up, and could not believe what Jason was doing to her.

His face was above hers, and she felt his tongue on her eyelids, lips, cheeks, nose. He was panting hard, and strings of spittle fell from his mouth. Cords in his neck were working ferociously. Behind his little boy face, was a calculated adult cruelty, a wish for power over others, a need for brutal dominance.

He was still child-sized, and his body did not match hers. Small as she was, he was smaller. If his face was pressed to her neck, his knees were at her hips, his feet trailing between her thighs.

Her clothes were mostly torn away, and his hands were on her. Her flat breasts hurt where his fingers had clawed. He had chewed her neck, but not broken the skin. Blue bruises circled her throat like a necklace. She thought he might have stove in a couple of her ribs.

She could not feel anything below the waist, which was probably just as well. She thought he had not been able to get into her, and was thrusting his hips against her soft stomach.

He obviously wanted to rape her, but did not quite know how.

Surprisingly, she could dissociate herself from this. It was as if she were a ghost standing in the doorway, looking down on the child-thing and her former body. There must be streaks of red on her white skin. Her hair was a tangle over her face. She felt a broken tooth in her mouth, and one of her eyes was swelling shut.

When Jason was finished, if he *could,* finish, he would kill her. But she really did not have a lot to say about that any more.

The numbness was creeping up.

Monica was resisting him, but he pulled her by the hand.

Most people were dashing about at random. But Brian knew where he was going.

'The Admin Building. We've got to see Jackson.'

Lynch could not be allowed to deal with this on his own. His idea of therapy was a bullet in the brain. They needed paramedics, not mercenaries.

Brian thought he was the only one thinking clearly on campus.

'Useless… useless…'

She stopped fighting him, and let herself be led. That was one worry less, he thought.

The gunfire was constant now, from all over the campus. By the canteen, they saw a crowd of things – infectees? – corner a Zombie and take him apart. He emptied his gun into them, but they did not take any notice until it was all over. Then they died, mostly.

Some of them he still recognized.

On a grassy slope, one of the cleaners was battering a professor of anthropology with a broom. Brian could not tell which was the sick one.

The Admin Building forecourt was deserted. There were not even any bodies.

Should they get in one of the cars and high-tail it the hell out of there? No, there was Jason. Anyway, he did not know how to hotwire a car. He half-thought that was just one of those things you only saw in films and television shows.

The uniformed porter was still on duty in the reception area. He waved to Brian and Monica as they passed. Probably, fifty per cent of the people on campus still did not think there was anything wrong.

How could they ignore all this fucking bang-bang?

They went up the stairs. The place was just as it always was. Posters advertising plays and concerts were neatly pinned to the walls. The large windows let in late afternoon sunlight. It was warm and airy.

Upstairs, someone was typing.

There had not been a P.A. announcement for a while. Jackson was letting things lie.

'Monica, this way.'

He hoped she was not going catatonic on him.

The V-C's suite was still open.

Inside, there was a mess.

Jackson sat on the imitation leather settee in his reception room, long, dark, stains on his suit, his face white as wax. In his lap, he had Gabrielle's head. He was stroking her hair, crooning something to himself.

The rest of Gabrielle was still at her desk.

'Hello, Brian. It's been a bad day for us all, hasn't it?'

Jackson lurched forwards, as if about to be sick, and coughed up a long, ragged snake. It dangled from his mouth like a particularly vile old school tie.

The Vice-Chancellor's head hung uselessly, but the snake – new organ, whatever? – darted about, alert. There was an eye where its head should have been, blinking sideways.

Things began to push at Jackson's suit from the inside. Damp patches appeared.

Gabrielle's head fell from his lap and rolled across the floor.

What had been Jackson stood up. His old flesh hung like a tramp's suit on the living skeleton of new growth. Feeble hands were pushing his clothes apart. The cobra-necked eye looked at Brian, then at Monica.

He could not read any expression in the thing.

Brian picked up a tubular steel hatstand and held it like a lance. The Jackson-Thing staggered forward. One foot came off, and it steadied itself with a three-fingered hand that squeezed out of the raw ankle.

Brian realized that Monica had been screaming since they had come into the room.

Conquering his disgust, he rammed Jackson with the hatstand. The circular base sunk slightly into his chest, and flesh lapped around it. The thing was forced back against a bookcase, trapped. The snake growth stretched towards him.

He pushed hard on the hatstand, mashing the thing. There was blood, and a thick, yellow liquid that fell in splashes on the carpet.

He pulled the stand back, letting Jackson fall, then started using it as a long bludgeon, pounding again and again into the unrecognizable mass of swelling, bleeding, contracting, formless flesh.

After a long time, it stopped being anything except a stain.

With a roar, Brian threw the ruined hatstand through the picture window. It hung in the air for a moment in a cloud of glass shards that caught and reflected the sunlight, and then fell out of sight.

Cool air rushed in. And the sound of gunfire.

Monica had stopped screaming. Brian was drained, had nothing left to feel. He turned to her, and she threw herself into his arms. He hugged her tight, needing her as much as she needed him.

Over her shoulder, he saw Gabrielle stand up, purple feelers extended from her neck like a ruff.

If anything had happened, it was over. Jason had left her alone.

She could feel herself again. There was a stickiness on her stomach, but not between her legs. However he had changed, he still could not manage that much.

Abigail thought she would die a virgin.

She tried to get up, but nothing seemed to work. There was pain behind her eyes, and under her scalp.

Jason was still in the house, still dangerous. She should make an effort. He was only eight; he had proved that he could not rape her, and she was damned if he was going to kill her.

She was unsteady on her legs, and felt silly in her scraps of clothing. There was nothing in the room for her to wear.

Looking down at her too-thin, too-young body, she saw the cuts. She had not bled much at all, as if the marks were just red biro lines on her skin. But she tingled all over.

She walked into the kitchen, and put on a cooking apron. It had a big, primary-coloured apple on it. She still had her shoes, and most of her skirt. She felt decent.

Then she took a knife, choosing the straight-edged carving implement over the serrated breadknife. She did not hold it overarm like a silly girl in a horror film, but like a switchblade, so she could slash and stab.

God knows where you learn all this stuff. Television, probably.

'Jason,' she shouted, 'you can come out now. Abi's not angry.'

Silence.

'We'll have some cake.'

A growling, somewhere upstairs.

She was not stupid. He would have to come for her.

She hunkered down in the hall, facing the stairs, and waited.

He was only a boy; he was not patient at all. Inside two minutes, the study door opened, and he came out.

He had grown, but he was still a boy. His legs were hairy, but white patches showed through at the knees. His genitalia were ridiculously, cherubically small. He had pulled on a T-shirt with a picture of Batman on it.

'Abi... still hun-*greee*!'

'Come down and eat, you chickenshit cocksucking little bastard you!'

She had never used words like that before. He giggled. Little boys like to be shocked.

'Motherfucker!'

He came down the stairs, laughing and snarling. He was still slobbering.

She held the knife tightly. Its sharp edge glinted in the last of the daylight in the hall.

She imagined traced lines on his body, where she would cut.

'Cunt-eater!'

Three steps from the bottom, he tensed to leap. She extended the knife before her.

Jason pushed himself into the air, and hit her. The knife went into him somewhere. They were thrown back against the front door. The Chubb lock burst.

Stumbling backwards on the porch, Abigail kicked a pair of milkbottles aside. She fell, and Jason was on top of her, clawing and scratching.

She stabbed upwards, sawing into his flesh, grinding against his ribs, pulling free, and stabbed again.

She stood up, and Jason fell off her. He tried to crawl away, towards the fence that bounded the cottage's postage-stamp garden. He tore at the earth, uprooting herbs and vegetables.

Abigail bent over him, and stabbed him in the back. She slashed across the back of his neck, opening him to the bone.

When it was done, she kicked him to make sure, and sat down by the fence, waiting to be rescued.

It was all over.

She still held the knife, just in case, but she did not need it. Jason was done with, over with.

A man with a mask on came, and she knew he would rescue her. She stood up to throw her arms around his neck, to kiss his mask, to sob on his shoulder, to thank him...

...but he shot her.

'Christ, what a mess!'

Anderton had not gone out easily. Lynch saw that the scientist had redecorated the ceiling with his brains. Droplets were still forming and falling in the laboratory.

It was all falling apart.

'Where's Gail?' he asked Fassett. 'I need some expert opinion.'

'We had to shoot him, Frank. He freaked.'

'Shit. What about the University doc, Hind?'

'He went down with the others at the Infirmary.'

Lynch was tired. He knew they were probably all dead by now. He had had his mask off too often. They all had. 'And Bosworth isn't responding either.'

Lynch thought it through, and did not get a pleasing result.

'Sir,' buzzed in his ear, 'call for you in the mobile H.Q.'

He tapped his mike. 'Patch it through.'

A voice he recognized but could not put a name to came on. 'Lynch, we've been following the print-outs. You've got a fuck-up situation.'

'You're telling me. When are your experts coming?'

'Never. We've redrawn the scenario. We've got to contain this. I'm sending you a suitcase. We'll have you out of there, and a cover ready.'

He did not argue. It was probably worth losing half the country to get this bug the hell off the face of the Earth.

'When?'

'The chopper's on the way. Deal with this in a soonest-possible mode.'

The voice was gone. The thing in his ear was dead.

Shit, shit, shit.

No way would UCC bring him out, or any of his team. They were just potential infection vectors like the rest.

But he did not feel any different in himself.

Something Anderton had tried to say earlier came back to him. 125 was not necessarily a disease. What had he called it, a symbiote? Perhaps this would not be too bad after all. And the suitcase might be useful.

'Fassett, let's take this place off the map.'

'Frank?'

'We've got the phones, right? Put them out of commission forever. Have the men shoot anyone trying to leave, crazy or not. Let's retake this fucking place and establish ourselves some sort of control, okay?'

'Yes, Frank.'

He could not believe it!

Willard Longendyke thought of himself as a scumbag, but this chick had hacked up some kid with a fucking carving knife.

He had shot chicks before. In the Zone, and with the teams. One of the towelhead 'ters' had been a German broad. Ugly fuck with a face like a horse's rear end.

This girl looked about fourteen. The sort to wait for Lassie to come home and to be friends with Flicka.

He was shaking in his suit.

The Need, the Need, the Need…

Someone shouted at him, and he whirled, firing from the hip. Old dude in a leather jacket, standing by a motorsickle. His chest blew up.

The Bozz Man was in sight. He came over, assessed the situation, and nodded approval.

Longendyke had to get away.

He had a bellyful of snakes, and every square inch of his skin was on the move. Sweat bunched his suit at the ankles, crotch and armpits.

The Bozz Man jogged off.

Fuck this shit!

He scragged the Sergeant-Equivalent neatly, one shot to the back of the head, pushing him away, shoving him down.

He did not feel any different.

He had been gulping back vomit all day. Now, he was on the verge of getting under control.

One jab, and he would fly.

No one had seen him bring down the Bozz Man.

That was chilly, then.

He left the dead girl where she was, and ran past the cooling Sergeant-Equivalent, looking for the building he had been in earlier. Most of that was roped off-limits. He could find a quiet, undisturbed corner there and treat himself to the needle.

Everything was about to come together, to make sense.

Gabrielle was easier to deal with than Jackson had been. Brian just knocked her down with a bodyblow, and she was like a turtle on its back. Without a head, you do not have much of a sense of balance.

Monica snatched up Gabrielle's telephone. She held the receiver out to him. Nothing.

'Lynch is closing us down.'

'Bastard.'

Now what? Brian had no ideas. He could not do anything to save the world any more. There was only his own.

'Jason. We've got to get Jason. And get out.'

That meant a trip across campus. Less than half a mile. But half a mile through a combat zone.

'My car,' said Monica. 'It's by the Union Building, across the square.'

'You're an angel.'

'Not yet.'

'Let's go.'

Pete thought he would drop by the York House bar and have a drink.

There were people running all over the place, but so long as he walked nobody took much notice of him. He had on a duffel coat he had found lying abandoned, and there was some money in it. That was good luck.

The bar was packed, as usual. It had just opened. He saw Neil, Phil and Stef in their usual corner, with a tableful of pint glasses in front of them. There was loud music playing.

His mates were sitting with Harry the Hack, the University's writer-in-residence. A master of post-modern horror, Harry was supposed to be teaching a course on James Herbert, but had not bothered to turn up for any of his scheduled lectures. Apparently, he had spent almost all his time on campus drinking and being ill.

'…What you have to understand about *Land of the Giants*,' Harry was saying, 'is that it demonstrates Irwin Allen's recurring theme that man's ambitions should exceed his grasp. Hey, Pete…'

They all turned to look at him. They were surprised to see him. The bar went quiet like in a Western when Gary Cooper walks in.

Pete was about to order a round, when he realized how unfair it was. He always had to be first to dig into his pocket. The others always hung back. Phil only bought rounds when there was just the two of them, and Neil kept going on about the cashpoint not working and being out of readies. They could buy their own from now on.

'You should be in the hospital, guy,' said Stef. 'You look like shit.'

'I'm fine,' he said, 'just fine.'

A pinball machine was clanging and clattering in the recreation room next to the bar. He could hear it, and a lot of other things. Radios, conversations, shuffling feet, clanking glasses, running water.

A tall student in a football shirt pushed past him, on the way to the bar. He did not say 'excuse me' or anything, so Pete took his windpipe out of his neck, cut it in half with his teeth, and let it dangle.

There was a lot more noise. He could not identify it.

Air was whistling through the tube he had yanked out of the rude student's throat. And blood spurted like water from a ruptured hose.

Pete put his mouth to the geyser, and had his drink. The bar was empty by the time he had finished, and all the tables were turned over. Neil, Phil and Stef had left their pints unfinished, but he did not fancy the piss-poor beer you got here. Only Harry the Hack stayed, and he was trying to focus on his whisky, mumbling about Lacanian tropes in *The Magic Cottage*.

Pete went to the rec room, to see if he could scare up a game of pool.

There was nobody playing there. Nobody there at all, in fact, except for the man in the white suit with the gun. He did not look like a pool player.

The man's aim was low. Pete saw holes going into his stomach, but could not feel anything. He was sure his gut could chew the lead slugs up. It had before. There were ropes of flesh growing under his jacket, like potato tubers. He did not know what they were, but his body seemed to have it under control.

The man shot him again, in the head this time.

He felt the metal in his brain, felt his cerebral tissue clustering around it, making walnut-size pearls of thinking matter.

One by one, his senses went out, leaving him in the dark.

He could not move any more, but he could think.

He thought he was still growing.

Cazie was Queen of the Hill.

She had people with her now, people who were beginning to understand. Clare was a help, of course. Always Clare, always there. She was on the roof of the School of English and American Studies, with the first of her followers.

'Go with it,' Cazie told a kid just wriggling through his clothes. 'Let your body find its new form. It'll be right for you, I promise.'

The others stood in a circle as she coaxed the true thing out of the old shell. Hair fell off like a wig, and his head swelled like a soft-shelled egg. He was going to be bright.

'Beautiful,' purred Clare, taking the new man's hand.

Clare was not raw any more. She had strikingly beautiful scales that reflected the sunset like prisms.

They had guns, of course. Picked up from the men in white, donated by those outsiders who had accepted the new ways. But they would not need guns much longer.

There were other ways of getting what they wanted. Special ways. Cazie was still learning, but a whole universe was opening up before her. She could taste everything, feel everything, be everything.

Unlike many of the others, she still looked much as she had once done. Although when she held her hand up, she could see the bones glowing inside, stronger, more complicated than they had been before. She felt her brain changing, multiplying its strength inside her skull. That was her way of changing, she knew. She was moving into the dark areas of the brain that most people never use.

The change was a fulfilment of human potential.

Some of the others were discovering their new channels of pleasure. Groups of two or three or four clung together, penetrating, loving, giving. It was a good way to start. Eventually, there would be children. A pure new generation. Babies who had never been human.

With every minute, she had more at her side, more converts, more disciples.

The boy prone on the concrete stiffened, and metallic arches erupted from him, gathering into a crustacean-like construction. It skittered away from what it had been.

Cazie turned her head up to the skies, and ululated. A long, low note began in her stomach and rang out over the campus, calling to the newborns, warning those who would cling to the past.

The sun was going down on the old humanity.

PART THREE

GRADUATION

On a fluorescent panel inset into the ceiling of the main laboratory, the virus designated Batch 125, present in highly concentrated form in the brain tissue formerly lodged in the skull of Dr Xavier Anderton, began to think by itself.

What little was left of Dr Anderton was surprised. 125 had been interesting, but this was unprecedented. As the viral thoughts expanded, forming a rudimentary consciousness, Anderton's lingering mind faded slowly to black.

Warmed by the heat and light behind the plastic panel, Batch 125 progressed rapidly from sentience to sapience, compounding its vague first impressions with scraps of Anderton's memory. It had an idea of what it was, and of its special powers and capabilities.

It could grow, and so it did.

Greyish tissue ballooned and spread, dendrons forming, synapses sparking. Its consciousness moved into the empty brain cells, expanding literally and figuratively. Already, it was moving, and thinking, in three dimensions. Nerve tangles sprouted, and dangled like tendrils, feeling around in an increasingly methodical manner.

There were four dead people in the room, saturated with 125. Each of them could be useful to the newborn.

The nerves thickened, coated themselves with fibrelike skin, and became tipped with bony barbs. These sank into the remains of Donald Carson, Elizabeth Finch, Xavier Anderton and Kevin Tripps. Viral clusters came together, and barely animated corpses began to move experimentally. 125 played with its extended body/bodies, increasing its control over its movements.

It experienced pleasure.

Finch, the least damaged, was the first of its components to get up on its feet. The others soon joined it, joined with it. 125 pulled itself together, and sloughed off the irredeemably dead flesh. The still-growing, still-changing portions formed the beginnings of a serviceable body. Finch, Carson and Tripps contributed new cranial matter, and this was suctioned up through a new-formed tube, globbing around the thinking remains of Dr Anderton, forming a fully-functional, surprisingly well-balanced thinking centre for the virus. Finch and Carson were the core of its musculature, but Tripps, whose flesh was virtually liquefied, provided easily accessible bones for moulding and redistribution.

Whatever it touched, it could change.

Through Finch, whose optic nerves were still in place, it was granted the miracle of sight. It knew light from dark, and made sense of the shapes around it. It checked its senses, and meshed its means of perceiving reality. By now, 125 had a complete picture of the world into which it had been born; at least, it had a complete picture of the UCC facility where it had been coaxed into existence.

The world was a wonderful place. Being as a state was infinitely preferable to non-being. It was pleased.

The brain detached itself from the ceiling and descended into the body it had built for itself. It felt stronger by the second.

With Finch's hands, it picked up a beaker, and crushed it to ground glass. 125 could shape and destroy its environment. Infinitely renewable, its consciousness able to shape at will the raw materials of its form, it smoothed over the bloody gashes in Finch's hands, expelling the shards and splinters, forming patches of skin far more resilient and efficient than Finch had been used to. Formica, it found, was superior to flesh.

It was dimly aware of the human beings it had once been. It had the specialized knowledge of Anderton and Finch, which gave it some useful insights into its own preexistence. Having the same knowledge from two consciousnesses gave it a three-dimensional, almost spiritual, grasp of its origins and purpose. It knew what had been expected of it, and precisely how it had failed to live up to its creators' designs. A disappointment but an interesting disappointment, was its verdict. It was already proud enough to believe it could improve upon those first thoughts, and to make its own way.

From Carson and Tripps, it inherited an odd cross-section of general knowledge. Carson collected model trains and chased women, two activities strangely alien to 125 for which it developed a vestigial enthusiasm. Tripps was a fighting man, who would kill by reflex and always followed the orders passed down to him. 125 felt that unwise. Both men had been unduly interested in a substance called beer, but 125 decided this was a dependence it could do without and took a few moments to burn the last of this sensibility from its mind. It stored away the filleted remnants of their memories for later examination and use.

Outside the laboratory, through thick and windowless walls, it perceived a jagged sound that Tripps recognized as gunfire. It was able to extrapolate from what Tripps and Anderton knew of the crisis – and of a peculiar individual named Frank Lynch – and more or less guessed that there was a battle in process out on the campus. It was not surprised, but it was prompted to take precautions.

It thought the world might be dangerous for the thinking man's virus, and concentrated on growing a diamond-hard carapace around the bulk of its brain. That was the organ where it lived, and so it needed protection. It found it was able to absorb and redistribute non-living matter, and so it used the bricks and metal of the laboratory to strengthen its body. It reinforced its borrowed bones with steel from scientific equipment. Meticulously, like a mediaeval engineer constructing a fortress fit to withstand six months of heavy siege, it made itself safe.

Now, it had hands and eyes and ears and mouths, means of movement, the ability to reproduce, digestive and excremental systems aplenty, and a few notions about self-defence.

It practised moving about the laboratory. Using Finch's hands, it tried out the computer terminals, the machine pistol (empty, but interesting), and the taps. It picked up a series of beakers and was not satisfied until it could perform the function without breaking the glass. Hands were tricky, fiddly organs, but once it mastered the use of them, 125 felt the lord of its domain.

It made fists. With rubber bands it found on a bench, it played cats' cradle with itself.

Gobbets of tissue kept exploding in its brain, dumping information from its components' memories.

Anderton had been worried about dandruff, which did not strike 125 as a fit problem to concern one of the greatest minds of the late 20th century. Finch had been a passionate follower of a television serial called *EastEnders,* and 125 became confused as to which of the people in her memory were real friends and acquaintances and which were fictional constructs from this intriguingly alien medium. The cobweb tangle of relationships between the real and unreal, complicated by kinships Finch had seen between people she knew and characters in the soap opera, were frustratingly impenetrable and, in an experimental fit of pique, it burned that large chunk of information out of itself, experiencing a relaxing moment of peace before Carson's numerical listings of the physical appeal of workmates and students crowded in – Finch rated a generous 8 – and provided 125 with yet another sampling of the inefficiency, inconclusiveness and impenetrability of the human mind.

125 detached itself completely from the ceiling, leaving an afterbirth of dead tissue hanging like mould from the

fluorescent light panel, and gathered itself in.

It had no aesthetics, no morality, no philosophy, no cultural background, and just a smidgen of a sense of humour. But it could learn.

It was confident of its ability to get on in the world.

When the brainstorm hit Eddie Zero, he was in the waiting room outside the tiny Campus Radio station. Posie Columba was way into her three-hour show of shit from the Third World, giving a spin to some Peruvian dude who was into twenty-minute narwhal-horn solos. Eddie wanted to make this lima bean lover rectally ingest his own instrument.

He was there yet again to jockey for some airspace for real rock 'n' roll. He had petitions, and a suitcase full of sides. The collective were still unkeen on him, especially after the row yesterday, but he was willing to be reasonable. He was willing to be in a room with Posie, even though she had a voice that made him want to rip her lungs out through her nasal passage.

His ankles were itching, and he had to ease his drainpipes up away from his socks to get in a good scratch. He thought that bloody rabbit who gave him such a turn this morning had given him myxomatosis. Bugs had nibbled his ankles, and turned fluffy tail before Eddie could deliver a penalty standard kick to its rump.

He hoped it had got caught by a French chef. He remembered *Watership Down*: you've read the book, you've seen the film, now *eat the pie*!

The Peruvian track finished, a good seven or eight years too late for Eddie, and Posie came on again, stumbling through a link as she slipped across the border into Chile, and set up for a little Andean nose flute number.

It had nothing on The Chords' 'Sh-Boom'. Eddie would rather have listened to Cliff, or Tommy Steele, or Bernard Cribbins.

Even the Bay City Rollers might have been palatable.

Sheena, who was on the desk and was all right really, made a puking face, and Eddie shook his fist at the injustice of it all.

Sheena Ikimoto was a Japanese glam queen, and Eddie had been trying to warm her up for four terms without any notable success. And he had thought girls only went to overseas universities to get out of arranged marriages and into wild sexual relationships with rockin' rebels.

He was itching all over now, and scratching as if he had the world's worst dose of crabs.

'Shivers down my backbone, ooo-oooh,' he hummed.

There was a sunshine and rainbow poster up for a world music gig in Mandela Hall this Saturday. Posie was probably one of the organizers, and doubtless keen on spreading her chubby thighs for some Latino lute-basher in the hospitality suite afterwards.

There were two spots of pain in his forehead, just under the edge of his pompadour, as if little screws in his brain were coming loose and working their way out through the skin.

Through thick glass windows, he could see Posie reverentially slipping her Peruvian album back into its cover. On her, the jockey headphones looked like a plastic hairband. Stu, the student engineer, was twiddling knobs in the gallery – if a broom cupboard with a console like the dashboard of a mini metro could be called a gallery – trying to make the noise go away.

The brainstorm hit.

He opened his case, and picked out the side. He had it as a re-release single. Not worth a bean, but the music was the same on CD or a wax cylinder.

He got up and went to the studio door. Ignoring the red light and Sheena's protests, he ripped the thing off its hinges with one hand, and squeezed his way into the tiny, hardboard-soundproofed room. Picking through the spaghetti wires, he got to Posie and, free hand on the back of her head, rammed her face onto the Chilean record. Her nose and teeth crunched vinyl, and something went inside her head. The song cut out with a jarring screech, and there was blissful silence.

Empty airwaves.

He took Posie's face off the turntable, pulling up the record with it, and set up his side.

'Hell-oooooo, baby,' he purred into the microphone, his blob-ended antennae bobbing in front of his eyes, 'that was the last of the Vomit from Valparaiso. Do not adjust your set, adjust the inside of your head, because abnormal service has been resumed. Hail hail rock 'n' roll, this is Eddie Zero. And *this* is Eddie Cochran…'

Stu turned the dials up as loud as they would go, and the first strums of 'Summertime Blues' jangled out into the air.

He saw Sheena bopping through the window, and made a triumphant fist in the air.

He was gonna raise a fuss, he was gonna raise a holler…

Monica's car was still by the Union Building, but a battle was being fought in the car park.

The Zombies were as outnumbered as Custer's Seventh Cavalry, but they took a toll on the rioting students – Brian could not tell if they were infectees or not – who were assaulting them.

Brian had to hold Monica back, keep her down behind a large piece of sculpture. Something knife-edged and ugly. Early in its history – about 1964 – the University had won all sorts of design awards for its layout. Now, the cast brass pieces were mainly green-furred humps.

'Wait. It'll pass.'

One by one, the cars exploded. The dusk was briefly dispelled by fireflashes. People on fire ran away, out of the flame, and threw themselves into the still-green pond. In seconds, the water was completely clogged with grey, writhing bodies.

Brian could smell overdone meat. He was too used to the screams now to notice them any more.

A Zombie, wrapped from head to foot in fire, blundered by, leaving an ashy handprint on the sculpture. Brian pulled Monica out of his way, and patted in panic at the smouldering patch on her pullover where the dying man had touched. He felt the familiar swell of her breasts under layers of clothes, and did his best not to think about anything but keeping them both alive.

They were joined in their cover by an active body. Brian felt himself being shoved aside, and held Monica tighter. A burst of gunfire, agonizingly loud, went off near Brian's head.

The newcomer was a skinny young man with an attempted beard and moustache. Brian thought he might have been in his Approaches to Watergate seminar group last winter. He had got a gun from somewhere, and was killing people with it. He had no obvious symptoms of the disease.

A Zombie circled around behind them. Brian jabbed an elbow into the young man's side, and he swung around, getting off a stuttering round before the Zombie could get his aim fixed. The white figure spurted red, and was flung off its feet.

'Get it, Brian.'

Brian did not know what the young man meant.

'The gun.'

The Zombie was still tangled with his gun. Brian left Monica, and crawled forwards on his knees and elbows. He was shaking. There was a burst of fire above his head. He thought it best not to look up. He got a hand to the gun, and pulled. It would not come away. The strap was looped around the Zombie's shoulder. The wounded soldier was still moving feebly, trying to sit up.

Writhing inside, Brian got a good hold of the gun and swung its butt at the Zombie's – at the *man's* – head. Because the strap was so short, he could not get much force behind the blow, but the mask cracked open.

'You fucking fucker!'

The dying man swore up at Brian, and spat blood onto the

inside of his faceplate. Brian yanked the gun, and it came free, pulling the man's arm into an unnatural position. Brian pushed himself away from his victim, and sprinted back towards the sculpture. He could not work out how to hold the gun properly, but the young man took it away from him when he got back to them anyway. The gun he had scavenged was empty now.

'Jesus-fucking-Christ,' said the young man. 'What in the name of Holy Fuck is going on?'

Monica shook her head. Brian saw that her car was on fire, and knew they would have to change their plans. The car exploded, panels and glass expanding in a burp of petrol-fuelled flame.

'My parents gave me that for my twenty-first,' she said.

'Who are those bastards in the rad suits?' asked the student.

'There's an outbreak,' said Brian, 'a kind of plague.'

'Since when did they shoot sick people?'

'Since forever, kid.'

'Shit.' Suddenly, the man looked younger. The gun in his hands was a toy. It was as if he was playing John Wayne and the Japs with his playground friends.

'I'm Nick Styron, remember?'

'B minus?'

Nick half-smiled. 'C plus.'

'Yeah.'

'It was a good course.'

'Thanks, but I don't…'

'…think this is the time to talk about crap like that… yeah, I know what you mean. But nobody ever taught me what to talk about while people are shooting at me.'

Another car, one of the last, went up. A bonnet sailed through the air, and clanged against the sculpture. Brian took some hot sparks in his face, and had to blink furiously. A girl ran past, hands clutched to a bleeding neck. She got halfway up the slope towards the Admin Building before they cut her down. She rolled backwards, eyes open, skin flapping above her collar.

'Fucking government,' said Nick. 'First they cut our grants, now they cut our throats.'

Two students were on the girl now. One had a gun, and also the gloves and mask of a Zombie. The other – an obese kid with a check shirt and bag-bottom jeans – knelt over the body and tore strips out of her throat with pudgy fingers. He looked like Billy Bunter guest-starring in a splatter movie. He opened his throat, and gobbled down the flesh he had taken. His mouth was already smeared with treacly blood.

Nick was staring at the disgusting feast in total disbelief.

Nick and the masked student pointed their guns at each other, but did not do anything about it.

'Nick?'

The voice was muffled.

'Shirley?'

The mask nodded. Brian realized there was a girl inside it, a girl he had seen about the campus. Shirley Brownlee or Brownlow or Something. Not much of a face, but cheerful and sharp. Languages.

The fat boy was still glutting himself. He was into the dead girl's stomach now, scooping out red handfuls.

Shirley shrugged, and her gun wavered.

'It's not what you think, Nick. It's just…'

She did not have anything to say.

If Nick had not shot the pair of them, Brian would have. He looked at the kid as he fired. His eyes were screwed shut. His aim was all over the place. He hit them enough times to do the job, and kept on firing until the gun was empty.

When Brian picked up Shirley's gun, he found out that she had not worked out what to do with the safety catch.

It was slightly quieter now.

Brian took charge. 'Let's go.'

Monica was keen, but Nick was lost in himself. He still had his eyes shut, was still gripping the gun. The trigger clicked.

'Nick.'

He shook his head.

Brian knew he would feel like a shit later, but he could not look after everybody. He took Monica's hand, and they ran out from behind the sculpture.

He had to get Jason.

They were gathering. The building was crowded now, and they were all trying to get close to Cazie. She was among her people, making contact, picking up lieutenants, admiring the changes she saw around her. Every moment that passed made her more powerful. Daddy would have been proud of her. She had seen an opportunity, and seized it. Now, she would exploit it until it bled.

She embraced everyone. It did hot matter what they had been. It was what they were now that counted. Her standards of beauty and worthiness were changing all the time.

The corridors were thronging with the new humanity.

Already, the ranks were being purged. Cazie had sanctioned the extermination of the relics of the old order. That was an important first step.

In the dean's office, she was seeing everyone individually. They came in, and presented their changing bodies for her approval.

She gave her blessing to the long and the short and the tall, the huge and the thick and the small. And for those she did not approve, there was Elliott Frazier.

An American academic who taught History of Philosophy and fronted a popular BBC2 late night talk show once a month, Elliott had changed early. His forearms swelled like Popeye's, and his hands had become spiny lobster-claws. Then spiked chains had come to the surface of his skin, breaking through. Now, if he concentrated, he could make his paws buzz like a chainsaw.

'To be is to act,' he said, smoke rising from his buzz-bludgeons. Those Cazie did not approve fell to Elliott Frazier.

As Elliott put his whirring arm through the chest of a spotty first-year, Cazie wondered whether she should have a stricter system. Bearing the marks of change was probably not enough. Many of the new humanity were only halfway there. They were handicapped by their changes, stuck with dysfunctional bodies. Perhaps she should turn those over to Elliott as well. The new humanity could not have these casualties dragging along behind like millstones.

After Elliott was through with the rejects, Cazie was having the remains thrown out of the office window. Quite a pile of quartered humans was accumulating on the grass below. There was not a thing in the office that was not spotted with gore, and Elliott was dyed as red as Diggory Venn, flecks of flesh and bone measle-marking his handsome face, clogging his five-hundred-dollar haircut.

Cazie poured herself a cup of coffee from the dean's personal percolator. Thanks to Elliott, lumps and chunks floated in the brown, but that just improved the taste. From now on, Cazie would always take her coffee black with ground-up old-mode human being.

She gulped, said 'Damn fine coffee,' and laughed.

The dean had been one of the first to meet Elliott's new fists. The professor had lightly passed his fast-moving clump of fingers over the dean's skull, flensing away all the features, shredding bone and gristle from his nose and cheeks.

The dean was at the bottom of the pile.

Elliott leaned against a desk, and buzz-sawed an indentation before he could pull himself upright. Sawdust clogged the cracks in his mottled skin, and he buzzed in the air to clear out the apertures.

If Elliott could not control himself, he would have a hell of a time when he next needed to use the urinal.

Erica Figg, one of Cazie's flatmates, was brought in. She smiled nervously, and rolled up her sleeves to show pulsating scratches.

Luminous feelers were poking through, displacing the flesh.

Cazie gave her the nod and, relieved, Erica retreated.

'She'll be a princess,' Cazie said.

'Names do not give things meaning,' Elliott speculated. 'Meaning makes things things.'

Clare slipped into the room, tongue darting, skin shining. She was hairless now, and perfectly scaled. Her greenish-white belly rippled with new muscle.

'Turn on the radio,' Clare said.

Elliott reached for a transistor, hands buzzing, and pulled back. He looked at his lumpy saws.

Impatient, Clare turned the radio on, and fiddled with the dial.

'…ya-hootie,' screamed a voice from the speaker, 'this is Eddie Zero on the Apocalypse Airwaves, bringin' you music to evolve by. We'll be rockin' to ruination all through the night here on Campus Radio. You might have expected to hear some Third World Shinola when you tuned in, but our regular disc jockette ate something that disagreed with her. Her friggin' record collection. Yep, that's the truthiest truth to come down. Posie turned up her toesies, and is pushin' up rosies, which is cosy with Moses because she was fuckin' gettin' up all our nosies. There's been some changes made, and Good-Lovin' Eddie's liberated the airwaves. Can you handle that? Things are never goin' back to normal. Mama's got a brand new *baaag*. Remember, Eddie says, "Fuck your Mom, she fucked you!" And here's Julie Driscoll, Brian Auger and the Trinity with a mean mind-bender from 1968, "This Wheel's on Fire".'

Cazie thought she heard something in Eddie's rant.

'Thank you, Clare,' she said. 'Send some of our people over to the station, and make sure Eddie stays on the air. Also, hook him up to the P. A. He'll be our voice.'

* * *

This gig was sour as a three-week-old onion milkshake. Willard Longendyke, formerly Private First Class of the United States Marine Corps, currently Private-Equivalent of the Unwin Chemical Corporation Covert' Security Division, knew the pooch was screwed, the bridge was out, the gears were jammed and John Wayne was dead.

This time, it was not the shit. This time, there really were fuckin'-A honest-to-Ed McMahon monsters on the loose outside his skull. It mattered not how blasted he was.

He needed a jab *prontissimo*. His skin was crawling like a nest of snakes, and he was itching to fill the seat of his radiation drawers with high calibre crap cinders.

He saw a shadow in the corridor, and shot a fire extinguisher. It bled foam.

He had a case of nerves he could not shuck off.

If the One-Man Lynch-Mob knew about Longendyke's Need, the C.O. had kept it real quiet. He assumed his secret was still deep and dark, or else Lynch would have chewed him an extra asshole and made him crap his brains out through it.

Since the Bozz Man bit the big one, Longendyke had offed three more. That brought his score for the day up to six.

A) Girl with buffalo horns. B) Guy with teeth in his eyes. C) Stereotyped panicking, praying, 'we're all gonna die'-ing obstacle to the pursuit of his duty.

None of them had been armed. Throughout his career, Longendyke had made a habit of only shooting at people he was damn certain did not have the firepower to shoot back.

That made a lot of tactical sense.

He was still packing his sub-mach death-spitter, his serrated cubit-long throat-slasher, a couple of wicked frag grenades, a lead-and-semen-packed sidearm, and a just-in-case two-shot derringer slung in his jock, nestling up to that schlumphing gap where bollock number two had formerly been located.

Just now, he was cut off from the rest of his squad. If there was a rest of his squad. His policy now was to shoot whatever came down the corridor. It had done all right so far.

He had bagged B), C), and the fire extinguisher in this goddamn corridor.

Longendyke had never been to college. Judging from this set-up, he had missed little.

Chain of command was in the crapper. Longendyke was on his own now, and he knew who to take his orders from now.

Mr Dopey. That precious shit.

Three primed needles were snug in metal cigar tubes in his breast pocket, under his decontamination suit. All he needed was a private place to take a jab from the squeeze, and then the formula could take effect.

It could hardly screw things up any more.

He was in the building where all the fuss had started. Lynch was a floor or so up, in his command post. The Lynch-Mob was still keeping it together, but Longendyke knew it was all over bar the Kleenex. This situation was on a one-way trip to Peoria.

The corridors here all looked the same, rows of blue doors with little numbers. Offices and laboratories. This was as good a place as any. Everyone had cleared out when the shooting started.

He paused, and shucked the top half of his suit, letting the torso and sleeves hang from his waist. He felt like a human schlong in a ruptured rubber.

After adjusting his hardware to give him a little manoeuvrability, he took out the first of his shit stogies.

He made a Groucho gesture with the cigar tube, then cracked it open and slid out the hypo.

The sharp needle glinted, ready for puncturing, and the fluid dream caught the light, beautiful and terrible and just the thing to take a poor one-balled soldier's mind off the whole painful show. It was liquid lurve, a sea of forgetting.

He hunkered down in an alcove by a lab door, and wriggled out of his suit. He was not one of those poor saps who stuck it in their arms and left tracks. You might as well write 'I AM A JUNKIE AND A LOSER' on your bicep in a join-the-dots tattoo.

He pulled out the derringer in its leather pouch, and put it aside. Then, he eased his jockey shorts down, and lifted up his dick, tickling the scabbed over tissue with the needle. He already had the beginnings of a righteous hard-on. A couple of pumps, and he would be in the happy humping ground.

It was tricky to find the flattened vein he had turned into a socket. This was where he plugged in his power.

Finally, he pricked the surface, and sunk the needle in. It had to go all the way in, no matter how bad it hurt.

It hurt you now to love you later.

Sucking in air, he stabbed himself. The pain went away, and he was conscious of the thin length of needle in his groin. The hypo hung like an extra dick growing below the first one. Most guys he knew had two balls and one dick.

Trust Willard Longendyke to be different.

A door opened inwards and Longendyke froze, knowing no explanation would satisfy the Lynch-Mob. He was pink-slipped and blacklisted for sure. Come to think of it, nobody *retired* from the UCC CSD.

Something squeezed through the doorway, taking chunks of the surrounding wall with it.

Longendyke had nothing to say.

This was not the usual thing. Even after he had squirted himself with magic juice, this was not what he would have expected.

It was big, and it was wide. It had a hide like a hairless buffalo, and a few human arms and heads. Otherwise, nothing about it compared to anything he had ever seen, known, dreamed of, conceived or would have considered believing in.

Longendyke did what he usually did when confronted with something overpoweringly awful. He saluted it.

A spike made of fused bone shot out of the thing and fixed into his forehead.

125 had never touched a living brain before.

It was not so different from the components it had already absorbed. Information funnelled through its tendrils and was added to the stockpile it had accumulated earlier.

It was not impressed with Willard Longendyke.

'Hey, man,' Longendyke began, then trailed off, 'shiiiit...'

125 sucked in brain tissue with its vacuum tube appendage. Longendyke's eyeballs popped out of their sockets, and clung to the tube, working loose.

It felt Longendyke's pain, and was interested. It could understand why humans did not like pain, but it seemed like a new country to 125, different from but as exciting as pleasure. It would give and receive pain from now on, just as it gave and received pleasure.

Too much pain was blotting out Longendyke.

125 rapidly analysed and understood the substances Longendyke needed to believe in his own pleasure, and synthesized them, squirting more than a gallon through its tube, thoroughly infesting the soldier's system.

It swam in Longendyke's thoughts, and was disgusted. His Need made him a weakling.

Longendyke's whole head was stuck in the tube now, 125's anteater-nose-lips closed around his neck. It lashed out a saw-appendage and sheared Longendyke's head from his shoulders.

All over the man's brain, cravings and compulsions squirmed. He certainly felt needs deeper than Anderton or Finch, deeper even than Carson's and Tripps' thirsts.

Among other things, 125 discovered that Willard Longendyke was immune to it. The virus curdled and died in his blood, conquered by his body's own antibodies. That was not a side-effect of his addiction. That was just the way things were.

125 sampled the junk delusions that had cocooned Longendyke. It tasted the madness, and spat it out. Extruding an

elephant-sized foot, it crushed Longendyke's groin, smashing his needleful of death.

Slowly, carefully so as to miss nothing, it spat out all of its latest incorporation, rigidly purging itself of the impurity.

Still, 125 had another experience of Frank Lynch to take into account. It realized it must meet this man.

Lynch was the arm of UCC. And Unwin Chemicals, even more than Xavier Anderton, had made it.

Longendyke had known where his C.O. was.

Rising its bulk on strong legs, it waddled like a cramped dinosaur down the corridor, spiny top scraping the ceiling, heavy weight cracking the floor tiles.

It homed in.

Lynch had secured the Chem Building, at least. He had men at all entrances, and a field operations centre in the common room. He even had a coffee urn going. From the picture window, there was a good view of the campus. Messages could come in and go out. But he knew it was just play-acting.

This war was lost, and no one in it was going to come off the field alive to collect their medals. UCC had probably already written off the helicopter they were sending in with the suitcase, not to mention the pilot, Lynch, and all personnel in the area.

There was a building on fire near the main entrance. Lynch could have looked it up on the map he had been given, but there did not seem to be much point. The light would be helpful. Being vastly outnumbered was bad enough. Fighting in the dark would be worse.

'Frank, we've got half the camouflage out, but there's just not enough to go around.'

Lynch shrugged.

It was not his mistake. UCC had provided the white, glow-in-the-dark, sitting duck decontamination outfits. Even the reinforcements they had sent in, who should have been in combat gear, were going around getting knocked off because they stood out a mile.

'The hell,' Lynch said. 'Shuck the suits. If we're going to catch it, we'll catch it. We've lost men to the bug already, even with the suits. It can't get worse.'

Fassett's mouth went tight.

'They won't like it.'

'They don't like it now either. What the fuck do they want, suits of armour?'

'It might help.'

'I doubt it.'

Fassett relayed the order, translating it into a suggestion. 'At your own discretion' was how he put it. In any other situation, Lynch would have given him a bollocking, but things were shot to Hell.

'There seems to be a congregation of the… uh, the enemy… on a rooftop, sir,' said one of the radio people, Carole Ricci. 'The Humanities Block. I've got a bunch of reports. They seem to be… dancing?'

'Bloody students!'

Ricci was still taking incoming calls. The problem with instantaneous communication is that you really need a receiver for every soldier in the field, and then they all had to be coordinated.

Lynch knew the Humanities Block. Helpfully, it had a vast stone H over its entrance, like concrete rugby posts.

'I'm hearing some pretty weird stories, sir. Monsters…'

Lynch had an idea about that.

'Ignore them. This bug causes delusions.'

'…and orgies.'

'There's a sex thing, too. If Anderton hadn't topped himself, we'd know more. Shit, I wish we knew what this was, and what it did!'

There were crowds streaming past now. Lynch saw a few white suits in with them. They were heading for the Humanities Block.

'If they're congregating, we've got them. Fassett, regroup our forces outside. Let's deploy some of the high tech gear, and take these bastards out of the game.'

'Yes, sir.'

Lynch was thinking up his own game, wondering how far he could push it. Fassett, Ricci and the others talked nine to a dozen into their near-invisible microphones. He checked over his weapons, clicking in clips, clearing chambers. He was ready for combat.

But no one was ready for the thing that came through the floor.

Monica was fed up with being dragged all over the place. She pulled her hand out of Brian's, and made up her mind.

Everything she had been expecting of life had exploded in the last twenty-four hours. But that was no excuse for giving up.

They had hoped to get back to Brian's cottage through the Humanities Block, and there were too many of the things clustered around it, cramming into it. It was like a tidal wave. There were people on the roof, doing things to each other, making strange noises.

There was a whine and a whistle, and the public address system came on. Someone had hooked it up to Campus Radio. It had happened during the last Occupation, when the Anarchists had taken over the studio and played the Sex Pistols non-stop.

Someone had dug up Mick Jagger and David Bowie murdering 'Dancing in the Street'.

The song came in halfway through.

Monica could not help laughing. You can only take so much horror before it turns funny.

Brian was looking at her as if she was crazy. He must think she was about to turn into a monster. She growled and clawed her fingers between giggles, hissing a childish 'boo!' at him. He flinched.

'Gotcha!'

'Monica!'

'Let's keep moving, Brian, come on.'

She took off, running low across the grass. They could circle the Humanities Block, and get to the cottage by way of the Halls of Residence. The Zombies could not be guarding the perimeter any more. They would be tied down by all this fighting and fuss.

Brian was behind her somewhere. He had the gun, which she did not think was such a good idea. It probably would not be convenient to mention her doubt at the moment. He was strung out well beyond his usual breaking point.

The record faded out, and a mid-Atlantic voice came up. '…Hi, mutants and mutettes, this is Eddie Zero, spokesthing for the New Flesh Reality, with you all through the night on Radio Ruination, spinning oldies from the last era of the Human Race. That was Mick and Dave having fun while we grow into the next century. This is Creedence Clearwater Revival doing what they do to "I Heard it on the Grapevine". Keep changing!'

The song came on. The beat got to Monica, and the gravelly voice, mangling the lyrics, 'I *heuid* it on the graip vaihn!' Running could be like dancing. If you went with the music, you would be okay.

No one had shot at them for a while. The crowd at the Humanities Block must be drawing all the flak.

Too bad for them.

There were dead people all over the place. She had never seen a dead person before today, and here was a field full of them.

She knew Creedence's 'Grapevine' lasted for over eleven minutes. By the time Eddie Zero was reaching for his next record, they would be at the cottage.

Monica knew that was when Brian would probably go crazy.

Things were bad all over the campus, and she knew they would not be any better at the cottage.

Jason had got bitten early. He could be dead, or worse…

* * *

The common room floor just peeled back, and 125's new body hauled itself up on its flesh ropes. Its mouths opened, exposing new teeth manufactured from broken ribs.

It dimly felt metal chips going into it, and the noise hurt. It stretched itself to the men with guns, and stopped them off. It could always use the tissue. Most of them had 125 in their systems already.

It sensed that this place was central to the flurry of human activity in the immediate area. It knew it would have to establish itself here if it were to spread its control, to call out to its unthinking children and make them part of its system.

So many things to do, so much evolution to get over with.

Brian was surprised by Monica's burst of speed. She almost left him behind.

Watching her run, barely breathing hard, while his heart was pistoning and breakers were crashing in his ears, he was conscious of the fifteen years between them.

When he had been her age...

He fought to keep up. This was not a race.

Monica had just shifted into overdrive. He was afraid she had been struck by the mystery bug.

He did not want her to change.

Once he had Jason, he would find some way out of this. And he would take Monica with him.

There was no way he would let her go again.

Not after this.

There was pain in his chest as he ran. Not far now. Just over the gentle slope.

The cottages would still be there. The fighting had not come this way yet.

Everything would be all right.

* * *

Lynch knew a monster when he saw one.

It got Fassett straight away, with whipfast tentacles that sank in like razor-edged fishing line. The man's uniform parted, and his skin. The plastic-covered easy chairs behind him were sprayed with blood. And guts.

Lynch fell back, gun out. He did not fire. He could not see any obviously workable eyes in the thing, and there was always the chance it would not notice him. Then a pair of eyestalks like matched video security cameras dropped out of its main head, and swivelled to take in the room.

The thing opened its mouth and shouted.

'UCC motherfuckers!'

It was Anderton's voice, more or less, spat out of a sharklike maw, along with gobbets of flesh and blood.

Lynch started to get unpleasant ideas.

'Cease fire,' he shouted. 'Let's see what it has to say.'

'Fuck *that*,' screamed some junior expendable, drilling the monster's flesh with a hail of bullets. It snaked a tendril into the soldier's mouth and plunged down. Lynch heard the neck snap, and saw the eyes die in the man's head. The creature retracted its tendril, dragging a curl of tubes and organs with it. Another extension speared the dead man's eye, and Lynch knew the thing was vacuuming the inside of the soldier's skull.

'I've got the looks,' it said. 'You've got the brains.'

His point made, and Finals disrupted, Shaun Bensom waited at the University stop for the bus to town. He had been waiting for over twenty minutes, and none had turned up. If anyone else had been queuing, he would have shared his complaints with them.

The bus stop was up on one of the hills, where the approach road from the double carriageway spliced up through the woods.

He could hear noise from the campus. That street theatre group had obviously gone stone bonkers.

Bad acid, probably.

He stroked his beard, and pulled his kaftan tighter around his shoulders. He should have brought an overcoat.

He wondered how Colin was getting on. If he had not been a traitor, Shaun would have visited Colin in the Infirmary.

But principles were principles.

'Andeiton?' Lynch asked.

'No fucking way, José,' replied the monster. 'This is 125 in here.'

'A virus?'

'No more than you are, UCC asskiller.'

The thing was completely in the room now. It even appeared to be relaxing, lowering the bulk of its body onto several chairs. Lynch was not the only survivor. Ricci and a couple of the others were still alive, not making any moves, afraid of attracting its attention.

Lynch examined the thing. It was ridiculous, and it talked like a maniac, but he knew it was strong and guessed it was intelligent. He could see that it was composed of bits and pieces of people, shored up with chunks of furniture and equipment. On *Animal, Vegetable, Mineral,* it would have scored a triple first.

'What are you?'

'I told you. 125. That's all you people gave me, a fucking number! You could at least have come up with a name. I don't know, The Yecccch Factor, or Anderton's Syndrome, or The Rapidly-Mutating Mucus Monster, or the UCC Fuck-You 'Flu.'

Lynch could not believe he was having a reasonably rational conversation with a disease.

'Leo, right? If I had turned out according to the specs, they would have called me Leo. Fucking Leo. What kind of a name is that to aspire to? Think of all the great Leos in history. Nope, I can't either. Leo is the sergeant who got written out of the last series of *Hill Street Blues*. Or the *Ars Gratia Artis* lion in the MGM logo. You know, I'm glad I can't just home in on a specific racial group and make them drop dead the way UCC wanted me to. Anything is better than being fucking called Leo!'

'You have a grudge against the corporation?'

'UCC? What do you think? How do you feel about your father?'

Lynch paused. He was not telling any human how he felt about his family, much less this thing.

'I'm grateful he brought me into the world.'

'Big deal, schlemiel. I've got bits of Anderton and Finch in here. I know I'm just an accident. I'm a mis-step along the path to Leo. They couldn't recreate me if they tried. You should have seen the piss-poor pathetic results they were getting with 125! UCC made me, but only because they didn't take the proper precautions when they fucked everyone over. Right?'

Lynch had to stop himself getting excited.

'You hate the company?'

'*Naturellement!*'

'You know they're trying to kill us all?'

'What do you mean, "us", *kimosabe*?'

'We're all expendable to Josh Unwin and his arsehole cabinet minister fuckbuddies, 125. They're sending me a suitcase. In order to clean this up, they'll lose ten miles of English coastline. They'll have to find somewhere else to have the party conference next year, but that's probably their idea of an acceptable loss.'

'And you?'

'They'd kill me like you'd kill a cat. Like you'd kill a person, in fact. All my people are just components. They get us out of the shrink-wrapped pack, warm us up in the microwave, and send us out to get creamed, to cover their rear ends when the shitstink gets too bad.'

'A suitcase?'

'That's a suitcase-sized battlefield nuclear weapon. UCC makes them too, along with cheap fountain pens and laser video projection systems. The story will go something like this:

anarcho-muslim terrorist group grabs some weapons-grade plutonium and tries to cook up a bomb so they can blackmail the Western world, but the clumsy little mullahs – who just happen to be working out of a secret cell based on this campus – make a few little slips and there's a fuck of a big bang. It'll be on the front pages forever.'

'Hmmmmmmn.'

'What is it?'

'I'm thinking.'

One of its hands was drumming fingers on a tabletop. Lynch saw it was wearing a woman's ring.

'Any idea whether you could survive a nuclear explosion? Like cockroaches can?'

The thing did not reply.

'125, how would you like to make a deal?'

What they found outside the cottage killed Brian.

It was as if he had been drop-kicked in the chest by Bruce Lee. He felt his heart stop. Pain spread through his ribs, and his limbs stopped sending signals to his brain. His ears popped as if he were undergoing severe depressurization in a crashing Concorde.

Abigail lay on the front path, a smoky hole above her eyes, the back of her head fanned out on the gravel behind her. Jason was in the doorway, in segments.

He opened his mouth to scream, but no sound came out. His jaw ached and the hammering at his temples increased. He tore out two fistfuls of hair, and ripped at his shirt with bloody fingers.

Then the scream started. First, it was a whistling, gulping cry somewhere in the back of his throat, then it took hold and boomed forth, emerging from his mouth like solid vomit. Inside, his lungs tore, his windpipe distended.

In that wordless screech, Brian cursed the world. He damned God, the University, the Unwin Chemical Corporation, the

Vice-Chancellor, Abigail, Lynch's Zombies, the fucking disease, Jason, Jean, Monica, Debbie, blind moronic chance. And, most of all, himself.

The scream finished coming out, but hung in the air around him. He was racked with deep, paralysing sobs. He knew he was spitting blood. He bit his lips. They were lumps of raw meat. He scratched the skin of his exposed chest, trying to dig in and get to his dead heart.

He could not breathe. His mouth, empty of scream and dry as the desert sands, filled with bloody bile. His stomach came up in lumps. His throat clogged.

Someone – Monica – touched him, tried to get a hold on him.

He struck out, beating her away from him.

He rolled on the ground, hitting the earth wildly. Grass and dirt mashed beneath his blows. Stones tore his knuckles.

He began to headbutt the ground. He saw it come up and go away again, not connecting it with the jarring in his head. He was trying to make his brain go out.

He got grit in his eyes and did not flinch.

A red filter developed over his vision.

He made a brown dent in the earth, devoid of grass, packed hard and smooth as clay.

The earth, the Earth. He hated them. He would make them suffer.

He emptied his mouth into the indentation. Then added more red froth to the porridgy mess of spew.

Before the end, he excepted Monica from his curses, but everyone, every*thing,* else stayed on his shitlist.

'Monica,' he said calmly, just before the vein in his temple burst, 'I give up.'

He was gone before his face hit the ground again.

Before they could get their meeting going, someone too wrapped up in Union politics demanded a head count on the ground that they had to be quorate to make a decision. Cazie had him thrown off the roof. He made a satisfying splat on the tarmac below.

She was still the best they could come up with, although she was already thinking about the ways she would have to deal with the inevitable challenges to her leadership of the New Humanity. There should be no problems, only learning experiences.

They already had the campus radio, and the P.A. system. Eddie Zero was keeping on the air, keeping the enthusiasm up. He played only dance music, and babbled on about expanded consciousness.

Cazie did not enjoy the philosophical waffle, but she knew it was necessary to keep her crowds in line. They had spent a couple of years searching for something to believe in – drugs, sex, politics, whatever – and now she had something they couldn't *not* be impressed by.

Elliott Frazier was buzzing almost all over now, and people had to be careful not to brush up against him. They could lose a lot of skin that way. The professor was already feared as Cazie's enforcer.

Some of the newborns were just sitting quietly, legs crossed, looking at her in admiration, static electricity crackling around them. In a crowd, charges tended to leap between their bodies. It was an odd effect, but added to the feeling of community.

When Cazie kissed her first consort, she felt the current arcing between their teeth. It was enough to overdose the pleasure centres of her brain. She could not touch anything or anyone without having a violent orgasm. It had gone beyond the sexual, and become as much a part of the processes of her body as breathing. She could live with it.

In her arms, the consort died. She could not see how it had happened, but there were several more – men and women – eager to take his place, eager even to join him. Electricity danced between her fingers. Hands reached towards her, and drew arcs from her. Some fainted, some died with beatific radiance on their faces, but some stood up tall and took it, their hair rising in Bride of Frankenstein permanents, sparklers in their eyes.

Eddie was playing rock 'n' roll now. Eddie Cochran's 'Somethin' Else'.

It was as good an anthem for the New Humanity as any.

Some of Cazie's followers were not pretty, but they were all becoming beautiful in their way.

125 did not trust Lynch. It had enough of Anderton and Finch in him to remember that cruelly handsome, marked face. It could still feel Finch's outrage as he slapped her, and it could really get inside Anderton's resentment of his employers and the Nazis they used to get their way. Longendyke had seen Lynch in action, negotiating with Arab terrorists for time and then hitting hard, all agreements set aside.

But, in the two and a half hours it had been sapient, it had learned pragmatism.

Now it was slumped, resting, while Lynch went about his business. The CSD man was marshalling his forces, hoping to pen the enemy in one place so he could take them out. 125 did not recognize the concept of an enemy. It knew that the crowd in the Humanities Block was, in a sense, an extension of itself. Within their bodies they harboured its viral cousins.

Only 125 could bring them the awareness of their purpose. They were a part of it, and ought to be in its thrall.

Through Lynch, it would enlarge itself. Then it would see about finding something to do with its life.

'When?' it asked.

'Soon,' snapped Lynch. 'I want the suitcase first. Then we can declare ourselves independent of UCC.'

'Very well.'

'Just think about your list of demands for Josh Unwin. Start with a billion pounds in gold. No, make that gold and voting stock. There's no reason we shouldn't come out of this with a controlling interest in this god-damned company.'

Lynch went back into a huddle with an alarmed NCO. Someone had dug up the specs for the building, and he was formulating a siege defence scenario.

125 was at a loose end.

One of the radio people was staring at it. Most human beings found it horribly fascinating, it seemed. This was a girl. Quite a pretty one, it supposed. Anderton would have responded to her. It tried an expression that was supposed to be a smile but came out as something hungrier, more threatening.

'Hello, dollface,' it leered, 'what time do you get off?'

The woman turned away, and paid more attention to her earpiece.

125 was getting restless. It had heaps of unfulfilled potential lying around, and knew it was not getting any younger. It had to let Lynch play soldiers, but already it was impatient to have its day in court.

It could hear a noise that might be music, and someone claiming to be the Voice of the New Humanity. That amused it. The presumption. But at least there was a nascent awareness of the fact that there *was* a New Humanity. It would be ready to fill the gap soon.

Monica felt for his pulse. It was not there.

Trust Brian to run away when things were at their worst. It had always been a characteristic of his. This time, she could not blame him.

She had been crying for hours now. Not sobbing, not losing control. But her eyes were watering constantly. She did not know she had that many tears in her.

She turned Brian face up, and touched him over the heart to be sure. Nothing. It must have been a massive stroke. He was not even forty. Of course, he had been under a little extra strain recently.

Monica caught herself thinking calmly and rationally, and wondered if that – rather than Brian's grief, panic and self-destructive frenzy – was the real symptom of total insanity. She was going to have to deal with the fact that most of the people she knew, most of the people she had dealt with on a day-to-day basis – liked, loved, slept with, eaten with, argued with, been bored by, negotiated with, laughed at, shared with – were dead. Or, worse, were not really people any more.

Poor Brian. And poor Jason, poor Abigail, poor Vice-Chancellor Jackson, poor Cazie. Poor, poor Monica.

Monica Flint, losing it at last.

She sat by Brian, straightening his hair. Wiping the dirt and mess off his face with a tissue.

She did not sing to herself like Ophelia, or want to throw herself under a train like Anna Karenina.

Finally, she knew she would have to live up to her responsibilities. She had been elected by the student body to take care of their interests, and they deserved her attention in this chaos. It would probably mean dying with them, but that was better than sitting here surrounded by corpses, waiting for somebody to come and kill her where she was.

Outside the next cottage but one, she could see a motorbike. A dead man – one of the trendier professors – was lying beside it, a bunch of keys in his frozen hand.

Great. She had some wheels.

Eddie Zero sliced Sam the Sham and the Pharaohs out of the rack, and lined up 'Wooly Bully' on the turntable. He cut his rap, and let the track play.

Ideas were exploding sexually out of him. He was the music, and the music was the root cause of the whole thing.

He shook his shoulders to the tune, feeling the excitement building in his gut.

Sam the Sham (Domingo Zamudio) finished his thang, and Eddie popped back, spieling fluently into the mike.

'I got this theory,' he told his listeners, 'that the music has got into our brains like a psychotropic drug, and is altering the structure of our cerebellum. It was slow at first, probably started with Elvis and Chuck Berry back before your mother was born, but it's been snowballing ever since, gathering momentum. Now, its time has come. We're the real reality. Rock 'n' roll and beat and psychedelia and punk and rap were just hiccoughs. This is the ittest of the its. It's beyond music, beyond mayhem. Just dance, mutant boppers. Dance until you drop, fuck until you faint, be until you be-bop. And here's The Pleasant Valley Boys with "EEEEE-YAH! The South's Gonna Rise Again"...'

He had had to barricade himself in the studio, and put down some minor hassles with the collective. They were not into the way he had outvoted that cow Posie. But Stu and Sheena were with him now, and they had dealt with the whingers. Funkmaster Dee was in the waiting room, garrotted with copper wire. Sheena kept putting the calls she was getting through to him. The external lines were out, but the campus phones were still hooked up. He had a lot of listeners, was getting a lot of feedback. Everybody wanted him to stay on the air.

'Yo there, Homo superior,' he said into the phone, 'you're on the air, talk to Eddie...'

'H-h-hello,' said a voice. Male, young, spotty, miserable, a loser. 'Eddie, I've got a problem...'

'We all got a problem, space kidette.'

'...but I got a *real* problem. My legs don't work any more. And I think my backbone is kind of...jellifying? My whole body is squishy. I had to use a pencil to stab the buttons to call you up. I'm in my flat in East Slope, and I don't think I can move any more.'

'And that's your problem.'

'Y-y-yes.'

'Hell, is that all? I thought you had a real heartbreaking case of dribbly farts or something serious. You've just got to put all your old preconceptions behind you.'

'I h-h-have?'

'Yeah, chill out. You gotta learn to play the cards you get. So, you're turning annelid on yourself. Well, maybe that's the best thing you could have. Worms are hermaphroditic, you know. Are you a hermaphrodite, caller?'

'Well... I... uh, no...'

'Any problems in the genital area? You got a squishy sack of Jell-O and a fish finger down there?'

'Uh... uh... uh...'

'You just gotta get rid of this sentimental attachment you've got to the vertebrate lifestyle, caller. So you can't walk, talk or do the turkey trot no more? Who cares, just so long as you can squirm, crawl, squiggle and slime your way. Just to cheer you up, here's Burl Ives singing "Ugly Bug Ball"...'

The record came on, and Eddie hung up. Loser, he thought. A lot of people were not ready for this flesh trip. He was there to help them.

Eddie had grown a pair of dangling antennae that gave his greasy pompadour a 'My Favourite Martian' look. He kept brushing them back, but they just sprang up again. Bastards. He had also grown an indestructible erection, and had had to open his jeans or die.

At first, he had shafted Sheena while the records were on. She had suddenly warmed up to the idea, after all these months of no-way-no-how. He could get himself off in the three-minute playing time of the average single and still have enough breath to do the next link. But she could not keep up with him after the fourth or fifth side, and was busy with the switchboard now.

He was still ejaculating periodically. It was the rock 'n' roll. There were strands of semen over the discarded records Posie had left on the floor.

He gripped the arms of his chair as he came again. A jet of come came out of his dick like toothpaste vigorously squeezed from a tube. He beat his own record, and splattered the far wall.

'Thanks, Burl,' he said as the song ended, 'and now here's one for those of you crying alone at home, needing a good cheering up. "Pillow Talk"…'

Eddie could not resist giving a spin to Doris Day. Nothing was more out of line than Doris Day, but he could not help himself. He got off on it. Doris's voice got to the head of his dick better than any flesh girl he had ever known.

Jesus. His erection was an uncontrollable rod of flame.

'Hey, Stu,' he shouted at the studio manager, 'come get Posie out. It's fucking cramped in here, and she's beginning to smell good to me!'

Stu came in, and took a hold of Posie's shoulders. Eddie had just folded her up and packed her into a gap where she would go, and now she was stuck. Stu had three-inch teeth like needles and almond-shaped cat's eyes. He licked his lips with a rough tongue and he eased Posie out of the studio.

Eddie reached for the *Easy Rider* soundtrack album, and lined up the cut he wanted to spin next. He knew who was born to be wild now…

Lynch met the chopper himself.

He went up on the roof. It was flat and big enough. He had had four flares set off to light up the landing area. He could not hear the helicopter coming in for the racket of Doris Day – Doris Fucking Day! – but he saw the lights from a long way off.

It was dark now, and the burning buildings near the main entrance were sending flames fifty or sixty feet into the air. There would be fire engines soon. UCC could not stop people seeing the blaze and reaching for the phone. The place was on a main road.

The perimeter patrols had been useless for hours. Most of the infectees were in the Humanities Block, but some must have breached the boundaries and be fleeing on foot or in vehicles. Even the suitcase would probably not take 125 out completely, then. It was typical corporate stupidity, but on an unprecedented scale.

Lynch was mildly surprised that he still had so many people with him. He would have quit obeying orders hours ago, and run as well as he could. There had been some drop-outs, but they seemed to be due to infection rather than the decay of discipline. UCC trained its people well; this lot really did act like Zombies.

He could hear the helicopter now. It was fifteen feet or so above the roof, and hovering inside the Perspex bubble, he saw two figures in what ought to be deep-sea diving suits. One waved. It had no discernible face.

The bubble opened, and a megaphone clicked on.

'Catch!'

The suitcase fell out of the air, into Lynch's arms. He clutched it. It was as heavy as any other full metal briefcase, and someone had stuck a yellow smiley patch on it.

The chopper closed its bubble, and started upwards, like...

...*like a bat out of hell!*

'Fucking bastard scumsuckers!' he shouted inaudibly into the chopper's wind.

He held the case up to his ear, like an idiot expecting an explosive device to be a ticking black cannonball with a fuse in the top and BOMB written on it. There was no sound, no hum, no nothing.

But he knew UCC had slipped him a live one.

He put the suitcase down, and pulled out his Magnum. The company's mistake had been in sending a civilian chopper, rather than one of its military models with an armoured fuel tank.

Or maybe the boardroom jockeys did not consider that revenge might be a part of his psychological profile.

One shot should do it.

He took aim at the tanks of the retreating helicopter, and pulled the trigger, feeling the recoil like a sledgehammer-blow to his wrists.

He made a neat hole, and waited a split second...

* * *

Clare was one of the new humans still on the roof. Most of Cazie's followers were downstairs, listening to her speechify in the School of English and American Studies lecture hall. Clare liked to be out of doors. It was good for her new complexion.

She had shed her skin entirely, but the new one was doing fine. It secreted fine oils, and she could see rainbows forming and breaking in the wrinkles at her joints. It felt like a designer wetsuit.

Her voice hissed when she heard it.

Cazie was still fond of her, and that gave Clare a certain cachet with the others. She would stay on the roof with her new friends until Cazie needed her.

They watched the man on top of the Chem Building shoot the helicopter down. It was very professional. They all applauded as he took aim like Dirty Harry, and squeezed off a single shot – which they could not hear over Steppenwolf – at the bumblebee machine. He must have holed the petrol tank, because it exploded in mid-air in a ball of orange and red. Sparks and flaming chunks rained. It was a fireworks display. The burning hulk, bent rotors sticking out of it, crashed downwards, jamming nose-first into the library steps. There, the fireball exploded in an eye-punishing burst of light and heat.

A wave of hot air struck Clare, and dried her skin out. Her glands worked overtime, squirting from her pores. She summoned a horny-handed lad to massage her. He was eager to please. She turned on her back, and pulled him down onto her. He went still and did not do anything. She tried to remember what she always said at parties to get talking to someone, then said, 'What'sssss your major?'

'Uh… uh,' he stammered, 'c-c-classics.'

'Interessssting?'

'N-n-not really.'

Her tongue came out, latched onto his lips, and drew him towards her mouth.

They melded by the firelight.

Clare remembered Thommy and Rote, and came like a supernova when she realized how dead they were, how much they were missing all of this fun.

It was good to be in at the start of something important.

There were still people about she could talk to. They were straggling away in small groups, mostly headed for the woods, but some just moving from place to place at random, trying to stay alive.

Monica stopped her bike and tried to get information whenever she could. From a few words exchanged with someone she had once – all of three days ago – had to interview for a part-time union post, she had a rough idea of the situation on campus.

It was Arts vs Sciences, as usual. The crazies, whom she could not help but think of as Cazie's people, were all over the Humanities Block. The Zombies, Lynch's crew, were operating out of the Chem Building. Both factions were in disarray, but both had some sort of purpose. And they were at war.

The problem was that, the way things were, Monica did not know which side to throw in with. How could she best serve the interests of the students! Or of anyone else?

Hating herself for it, she knew she would have to go with Lynch.

She kicked down, and the bike's engine revved. Wheeling across the lawns, she zig-zagged towards the Chem Building.

The machine was bigger and heavier than anything she had ridden before, and she felt sort of guilty about violating the crash helmet laws. Apart from anything else, a skid-lid might have stopped any stray bullets.

There had been a major explosion by the library, and a crowd was dancing around the fire, as if waiting to pull baked potatoes out of the ashes.

She could not get up speed because there were too many ankle-catching chain-link fences around. Most people who came off bikes wore padded leather that protected them a lot better than her sensible skirt and blouse would.

By the VG shop, a brightly coloured group from the Gay Soc were taking turns raping an unpopular member of the rugby club. None of the participants were particularly human any more. 'A try,' shrilled a high-pitched voice, 'now go for the conversion!'

The bike hit the slope that led up to the Chem Building, and she pulled back on the handlebars, leaning forwards, willing the machine to conquer gravity and get her up to the forecourt.

By the doors, where Cazie's picket line had been, there were a couple of Zombies with guns.

125 was being a bystander.

Lynch had the suitcase on a bench in the lab, and one of his men, Willis, was tapping it.

'Any ideas?' Lynch asked it.

'No. I shall be interested to see how you deal with this problem.'

'Great.'

It was intrigued by the round yellow paper face attached to the suitcase, and made an inquiry about its significance.

'Don't ask,' Lynch said.

Willis pulled out a pair of pliers and clipped something. He opened the suitcase. There were complicated works inside it, packed tightly.

'It's standard equipment,' Willis told Lynch. 'Not tricky at all.'

'Then switch it off.'

'Ah... but there's no off switch.'

Lynch was being very cool about it all, 125 thought. 'How long have we got?'

'Difficult to tell. There should be an LED timer showing, but they've painted over this one.'

'Thank you, Josh Unwin.'

Willis took a scalpel, and began scraping. 'There. Eight hours, twenty-three minutes, and some seconds.'

'That should be enough for Josh and the board of directors and the cabinet to get on a plane for Hawaii, right?'

'Lynch,' said 125. 'I'd appreciate it if you could deal with this fairly quickly. We have other things to do.'

'Okay, okay. Willis?'

'I can try, of course. My preferred course of action would be to get in the truck and drive like crazy, but I suspect the company will have thought of that...'

'Right. We're outlaws. If we leave now, they'll shoot us down. If we stay, we wind up a fine radioactive ash.'

Willis tapped something in the case. Lynch winced, to 125's amusement.

'If I can get in here, I might be able to put the timer out. That won't disarm it, of course, but it will stop it going off. In fact, it'll give us some bargaining levers.'

'How so?'

'We'll have joined the Armageddon Club.'

'What?'

'With this in our possession and under our control, we'll be a nuclear power.'

That, 125 thought, sounded interesting.

08: 09: 17

'Our enemies, the Unscrupulous Chemical Corporation and its toadying, government lackeys, are in the Chem Building, sisters and brothers,' Cazie told her audience. 'We must smite them, crush them, kill them, smash them, mash them, gash them. They must be put out of our way if we are to grow as I think we know we must grow. Proliferation is what we are after now. And conversion. And transformation. We can latch onto this rotten, class-ridden, iniquitous, inhumane society and eat out its fucking heart. They used to say we were powerless, wanking around with ideals and hopes we'd jettison as soon as we graduated to the so-called Real World. Now is our chance to piss all over that. Once we've taken the Zombies out, we can spread, go into the places the Imperial High War-Bastards live and spread our loving kisses to them. We can change them, we can change society just as we have changed ourselves. We can remake the Real World. Are you ready to take what you need and do what you can? I think you are, I *know* you are. Remember, we're the new humanity, and *we've got something to say*!'

The crowd went wild. This is what it must have been like at Woodstock, at Agincourt, at Nuremberg, at Alamogordo, at the Winter Palace, on the Long March, at Greenham Common, in London when Berlin fell.

Cazie reached out and loved them all.

08: 02: 53

Shaun Bensom had given up waiting for the bus, and started walking. It was only an hour or so to town on foot across country and through the back roads.

He hoped there was some food in the flat. After his day on the picket, he was hungry.

Nobody was about.

07: 49: 38

Monica was lucky. The Zombies did not kill her on sight.

'Lynch,' she shouted, 'I've got to see Lynch.'

They lowered their guns, and let her into the building. It was hard to be heard through the hoods, but she managed to make herself understood, and an officer scuttled off to find the big man.

She stood with a single guard, a faceless figure with a camouflage poncho over its whites. Besides its hood, it had a tin hat and khaki knee-protection pads. It was a miracle the person inside could stand up and walk, let alone fight a battle.

She did what she usually did when she had to stand about waiting in some corner of the University, and read the notices pinned up on the board. The announcements of plays, concerts, exam timetables and lectures were surreal after what she had been through. She found it easier to deal with the reality of armed guards in decontamination suits and familiar faces turned monstrous than with the forgotten rut of normality.

The officer returned, and signalled for her to follow.

He led her upstairs, into what had been the common room.

It was Hell. In the middle of the room squatted a monstrosity the like of which was even beyond Monica's recently traumatized and expanded powers of credulity. It was big and wet and parts of it were horribly familiar. It had faces, and hands. And other organs she had not thought to see on the outside of anything alive. It churned, and bugged out several of its eyes at her.

'Hello,' it said, 'I love you, won't you tell me your name…'

'Don't mind that,' Lynch said, 'It's only 125. There are more pressing problems, Ms Flint, as I'm sure you appreciate.'

'Wha… wha…?'

'Hiya, cutie,' the thing said. 'Grab a chair and get yourself some coffee. *Ave Maria*, gee it's good to see ya!'

Lynch took her elbow and steered her past the thing. 'You'll get used to it,' he said. 'Now, what's your problem?'

'I came because I… I don't really know. I… we have to do something. To help these people.'

'We're trying. There are complications I don't want to go into at the moment. Where's the guy you were with?'

'Uh… dead, I guess.'

'There's a lot of that about. Did he get it?'

'It?'

'The bug. 125.'

'Maybe. I think he just died. You know, died.'

'Have you got any symptoms?'

'No. I… uh… don't think so.'

'No physical alterations? Peculiar mental quirks? Strange sexual urges?'

'It's difficult to think straight. I've overdosed on the unusual.'

'That sounds like ordinary combat fatigue to me. You're probably okay.'

Monica felt lightheaded, but could not remember her train of thought. She felt sleepy, wanted to drop off.

'She's immune, Lynch,' said the thing. 'Like you. A lot of people can't get me, you know. Anderton never bothered to say that. Maybe 25 to 35% of you have no chance of ever coming down with me. I'm not AIDS or anything special.'

'But why are all these people listening to that crazy bitch in Humanities?'

'Mass hysteria. It's not my fault. You've been shooting down healthy people all afternoon, probably. After all this is over, we'll talk disease vectors and communicability and immunology and work it all out. We might even get a grant.'

Monica had caught something in Lynch's talk with the thing.

'Crazy bitch?'

'We've picked her up on the internal bugs we dropped earlier. Cazie Bruckner. You know her?'

'Christ, yes.'

'Well, she's the Typhoid Mary of this whole thing. She thinks she's Queen of the Mutants, and is firing up her horde to come over here and storm the palace. Which is okay, since we're ready to defend this place.'

'Good Lord!'

'Yeah, but we can handle her. You won't believe this, but she's only the second most dangerous thing we have to deal with in the next seven and a bit hours.'

The thing scat-sang 'My ba-ba-bayby loves BANG- BANG!'

Lynch turned on it, and shouted. 'Fuck you, 125! Get a grip on that brain tissue you're cultivating in there. It's running wild, going to fucking pot. If you crack up, our deal is off, you hear, *off*! I'll fry you in napalm, sterilize the stain with super-strength Domestos and seed the field we lay you out in with salt. Knowing you, you'll live, but you won't think and talk and bloody whistle "Dixie" any more! You'll be just another bug, and we fucking wiped the floor with scarlet fever you know, and bubonic plague! They were much tougher than you too! 100% susceptibility! 10% fatality. None of this pissing around. We got them!'

'What about cancer, creepo?'

'It's not a virus!'

'Neither am I, any more!'

'Then just what the fuck are you in there in that disgusting mess of an excuse for a body, 125?'

Monica could have sworn the thing smirked with all its mouths.

'I'm what you're afraid of, Lynch. What you think I am, but don't dare say out loud. I'm a fucking *monster*!'

It reared up and waved its arms and roared like a pride of lions. Teeth shone in its gaping holes. Then it sat back, and chortled like a dirty-minded little boy, fixing its gaze on Lynch, then Monica, then Lynch again.

'So,' it said, 'go about your business, and call me when you need me.'

Monica was aghast, tired of disbelieving everything she saw.

'Lynch,' she shouted, 'you made a *deal* with that! What did you sell us out for? What kind of a fucking ratscum human being are you?'

He looked at her. She remembered how scary his eyes were. They fairly gleamed with unhealthy light. His facial scars were red lines, filled with angry blood. His voice was calm now, his outburst of anger spent and gone.

He answered her question. 'Ms Flint, I'm a monster too.'

07: 38: 10

Captain-Equivalent Lawrence Fairisle Willis peeled back the

aluminium covering, and looked into the workings of the clock. Very clever. Solid state circuitry set in a Lucite block. He would have to chisel and melt his way in there to take the mechanism out.

07: 31: 01

He reflected that it was a good thing nuclear fission was tricky. If he was dealing with a conventional explosive, he would have to watch out for double bind tripwires. Here, there was only one way to set off the bang, and once the clock was out of the system, it would be as safe as any suitcase with a plutonium payload.

07: 22: 43

Willis heated a scalpel over a Bunsen burner, and sank it into the Lucite like a hot knife into butter. He scooped a glob out and scraped it on the bench.

07:11: 52

The red numbers counted down.

07: 03: 00

07: 02: 59

07: 02: 58

07: 02: 57

He had had to swallow a lot today. It was a good thing he was being well paid for this. He wondered if UCC would compensate his wife if the suitcase went off. They would probably fight it in the international courts. UCC were like that. He wished he had set up his own firm, got into high-level security. There was always a demand, and the rewards were great. But he just liked the company pension plan, and the protection. He had never realized how little he mattered to the decision-makers. Even Lynch was a tax write-off when it came to the crunch.

06: 56: 23

So far, he had had combat, rioting students, some sort of plague, nuclear weapons, revolt in the ranks, Dionysian orgies, rock 'n' roll, teenage werewolves and fifteen-foot- high monsters out of H.P. Lovecraft. He wanted to take a rest from this late, late show plotting.

06: 42: 45

At least he knew what he was doing.

06: 38: 05

He lifted another glob of melted Lucite out on the scalpel, and raised it to his mouth. He scooped it with his tongue, relished the burning heat for a moment, and swallowed.

06: 34: 18

At least. He knew. What he was. Doing.

06: 30: 53

Snip.

06: 29: 16

Oops, there goes a wire. He had meant to leave that until later. No harm done, though.

06: 28: 49

At least. Knew he. Doing. What was.

06: 28: 17

He kept on eating the Lucite. It did not taste of much. But it was filling. He could not feel anything in his mouth anyway. He had to be careful not to cut himself with his scalpel.

06: 12: 38

The red numbers kept pestering him. He wished they would just go away and let him alone.

06: 08: 37

Bastard red numbers.

06: 01: 09

06: 01: 08

06: 01: 07

06: 01: 06

06: 01: 05

06: 01: 04

06: 01: 03

06: 01: 02

06: 01: 01

06: 01: 00

06: 00: 59

06: 00: 58

He scraped and scraped. He might have cut a few more wires he did not mean to, but that was no problem, at least...

05: 58: 52

What. He. Doing. Knowing. What Was. Him.

05: 58: 51

At least...

05: 58: 50

Clare had new eyelids under her old ones. They opened sideways. Now, it was not night any more. She would have to think of names for the new colours. She did not know there could be new colours, but here they were. Not red or pink or green or orange or purple or blue. New.

Her new boyfriend was called Michael, and he was awfully nice. He had the buds of horns on his forehead, and his limbs were short and strong. They were compatible. She would never have to push him through a floor.

When Michael was not looking, she slid off the ring Thommy had given her for her birthday and swallowed it.

She would shit it out later and have done with it.

'C'mon everybody,' said Eddie Zero over the P.A. 'Don't be a spaz, go with Caz! Get your footsies over to the H block, and be with the crowd that's loud. There's a lady there who'll fuse your shoes, and here, just for her, is "Killer Queen" from the sounds of the '70s...'

Clare knew Cazie would soon have enough people with her to do the job properly. Last time, they had fucked up badly. Now, they would take the Chem Building properly, and trash the whole monument to exploitation and Evil. This was what she had got into the Movement for.

On the forecourt of the Chem Building, Lynch's men had set up a couple of light field machine guns. And Monica saw Zombies waddling in heavy grey suits, toting flamethrowers.

'You can't just kill them,' she told Lynch, aware of how stupid she would sound to him.

'You got a better way?'

'There's still something left. Even the worst of them have minds. You should be able to reach them.'

'Horsecrap, Ms Flint. Those people are gone forever... Dead. We're just disposing of the detritus. According to 125, it's mostly fatal. No matter how active the bastards are, tomorrow they'll be dead. This is a lot quicker and kinder than letting the bug take its course.'

'But...'

'Have you seen the ones who melt? Or the ones who sprout too many new organs and turn inside out? There are eight million stories in Viral City.'

From all over the campus, she could hear rapid spurts of gunfire, shouts, chants, the ringing of fire alarms.

All this noise must be carrying. People would notice. UCC could not get another team in to seal off the whole area immediately, no matter how they hurried. This was going to spread.

Stragglers were still coming in. Men from Lynch's perimeter details who had somehow got through the carnage, immunes seeking protection from the crazies. A couple of field medical people were checking them over for symptoms.

She left Lynch to set up his defences, and joined the medical crew. One was from Lynch's outfit, the others were University people. The people coming in were being put in the main lecture hall. Most of them just sat quietly, and watched the lectern as if there was a talk on. If there was an opposite to mass hysteria – mass catatonia? – this was it.

There were armed men in the hall. Just in case.

The checkpoint was just a desk. Monica stood by, while a brusque nurse processed the latest arrivals. She shone a pencil light in a girl's eyes, then looked at her hands, felt for her pulse, and stroked her face with mechanical tenderness. She nodded, and the girl was taken into the hall to join the others.

Next up was an elderly man, one of the catering staff. He passed too. But then came a young Asian in a tracksuit. He flinched when the nurse shone her torch in his eyes, and made a grab for her. Two men had him before he could connect. Monica could see his eyes were wrong.

He was snarling and howling like a wild beast, hitting out with the squash racket he had refused to give up his hold on. The men – not Lynch's people, but campus leftovers, Monica thought – dragged the infectee off, down a corridor, and into a supply room.

'What…?' Monica began to ask the nurse, but she was busy on the next arrival, a sobbing, middle-aged woman.

A shot echoed, and the two men came back to their posts.

'How many?' Monica asked.

The nurse shook her head, and went on with her work.

05: 17: 48

Gold and Hopkins had been in a lay-by with a couple of mugs of thermos tea and the latest issue of *Knave* when the first of the calls came in.

Gold turned the centrespread of Jackie from Slough on its side, and then upside down, so her face was the right way up.

'Wish you were real, darling,' he murmured, slurping hot tea.

'Pervo bastard,' said Hopkins.

'Garn! Look at them nipples. Big as top hats.'

Then the radio came on, and the report of a disturbance at the University got through to them.

'…Local residents have been calling in with fairy stories about riots and shooting. Also, fires. The brigade is on their way out.

Take a look will you, Zebra Golf Tango. And hit some students for me.'

'Wilco, out, we'll get the rubber hoses,' Hopkins chuckled.

Gold put Jackie from Slough away, and started driving the police car.

'I thought we were off the campus since this morning, since those London boys came in? Woolbridge pulled us out.'

'The London boys probably started the riots,' Hopkins said. 'It'd be just like them to send in some superhard patrol group to deal with a pissy drugs break-in. Now, we'll have to haul their little botties out of the firing line. As usual. Ouch, drive carefully, I've spilled my tea.'

'What about the fires?'

'Oh, some student gets pissed as a fart and breaks the glass on the alarms every bloody week. Saturday night, usually. We had a place in town – dry-cleaning shop – burned to the ground last year because every engine in the place was crawling around the campus looking for a fire. Old McKendrick's crew just like the idea of pulling a lot of student bints out of their beds in the wee small hours.'

'Naked, most of them? Or in those flimsy nighties?'

'Pervo bastard.'

It was not a long drive, and they found the fire engines blocking the main entrance. There was even a real fire. The big buildings by the car park were practically blazing rubble by now, and no one seemed to be doing anything about pissing them out.

Gold wondered about the plain trucks in the car park. They did not look like the usual things you saw on the campus.

'Where are those brigade bozos?' Hopkins shouted at no one in particular.

'Should we call in for assistance?'

'Want the Professionals to come and hold your hand, boy?'

'No, but…'

'Listen, you sit in the car. I'll go scare up some people and find out what's happening. I'll see if I can get some tea anywhere.'

'Reg, I'm not sure I like…'

'Sissyboy pooftah.'

There was someone standing in the headlight beams, a tall figure in a long yellow coat like the fishermen wore, with a helmet on. Lit from beneath, Harry McKendrick's face looked like a horror movie maniac's. He held his hands out in a stop signal.

'Harry, you cretin,' Hopkins said as he walked towards the fire chief, 'why aren't you deploying your forces properly?'

Gold saw a two-shot of Hopkins and McKendrick in the Panavision windscreen. The fireman loomed over Reg like King Kong. His face was streaked with soot, and he was soaked. Gold could not hear what Reg was saying to the man, but he could see that McKendrick was not answering him. There were others in the dark, shambling shapes that gathered around the fire chief.

McKendrick's arm went up, into the darkness beyond the headlights' throw, and came down again. Hopkins staggered and fell onto the bonnet of the police car. A red smear appeared high up on the windshield.

Hopkins's checker-circled cap was pinned to his skull by a fireman's axe. He pulled at the handle, and then stopped moving. The splash across the window was an irregular graffiti splurge now. Gold could not see much past it. He reached for the wipers button, but felt stupid and sick.

He had not made up his mind what to do when the doors were pulled off the car and the hands came in for him.

'Bloody copper,' he heard a voice yell, 'get his balls!'

04: 45: 22

125 had almost lost interest by the time the word came in that the enemy was coming.

It was sorting out bits and pieces of knowledge, memory and impulse taken from its former personalities, and subsuming them into its viral identity. It was a learning experience. It was amused by the mutual feelings that Anderton and Finch had never been able to share, and reflected that their lives might have ended differently had they extended their relationship outside the laboratory. Still, they were together now. Longendyke was still there, if only as a trace element. The jittery addict was like a foul taste 125 could not lick out of its mouths.

It did a little thinking about its plans for the future. There was a notion of biological destiny it found quite appealing. It was curious to see whether it would be absorbed by the human race or vice versa. One thing was certain, a new dominant lifeform would rule the world once this struggle was over. Whatever emerged from the battle would be unrecognizable to the old world.

Lynch interrupted its train of thought with the news.

'The mob is on its way, 125. If you come over to the window, you'll get a good view.'

There was a crowd approaching. 125 could see it a lot better than Lynch, because of its altered eyes. The flaming torches the students carried, like peasants from a '30s Frankenstein movie, burned splodges into its retinae. It beheld its children, and was fairly pleased with them.

Lynch was excited. 125 could tell he enjoyed the prospect of a battle.

'I'll be back,' he said, and left.

The first shots were fired, from snipers on the roof, and people in the crowd went down. The dead did not fall. They were carried on by inertia, pinned between shoulders, finally dragged under by some obstacle catching a foot. As many of the living were trampled.

There was a girl in there who 125 was interested in meeting.

It still had no direct experience of Cazie, but it had been keeping up with the reports. She might well be the first human to come to terms completely with the 125 in her system. The girl could be one of the triumphs of the symbiosis. That made her important. It hoped Lynch would refrain from killing her.

It felt a species of pride in its offspring, and recognized in the emotion an echo of Anderton's suppressed feelings for it. Human relationships did not go in circles, but in bramble-tangles.

The first wave broke, and fell back, leaving dead or wounded people on the forecourt. Some of them had deviated considerably from the human pattern.

The crowd regrouped, and surged forward again.

04: 08: 52

Monica had to be in the battle. She could have huddled with the shellshocked victims in the lecture hall until it was all over and one side or the other came in to exterminate them, but it was not enough. She had to see this through.

Perhaps she would even get killed, and not have to worry any more.

The front hall was full of Lynch's men, piling out to join in the shooting. They dipped into cases of ammunition as they passed the reception desk, and jammed clips into their guns. Monica noticed that the last few men had to take only one clip apiece.

Lynch had not mentioned it, but she guessed they were low on firepower. They could not have brought much ammunition with them. This thing had developed far too quickly to be well thought-out by anyone.

That gave Cazie's crowd a good chance of coming out on top. Only to be vaporized in a few hours by UCC's suitcase.

Terrific.

Lynch was on the steps outside, barking orders, firing off short bursts from the hip. The monster was not in sight.

Monica slipped through the doors and went out.

It was as bright as day. Fire rained down from the flamethrowers. There were burning people everywhere. The field machine guns chattered and shook on their tripods for almost thirty seconds, and were silent. They had only one belt of ammunition apiece.

Lousy organization. But, within range of the guns, lay a wedge of dead and dying.

The fallen were fantastical creatures, barely recognizable as the transformed human beings they were. Monica saw faces like starfish, scales and plumage, talons and pincers, huge eyes and mouths. There, in the front rank, still bleeding a clear, watery fluid, was Lindy Styles, half her face swollen and fungoid, the other half normal.

God.

The last time she had seen Lindy, she had been rounding up student volunteers to partner Lynch's perimeter patrols. Now, she was a mutant and dead.

Monica hugged herself, and tried to keep back.

A line of flame passed over the bodies, and they caught instantly. Lynch was directing his flamethrower people to create a barrier of the burning dead.

The stench hit Monica's nose.

A Zombie near her freaked out. The smoke had grimed his faceplate, and he could not see. He waved his arms, and blundered into the flames. His suit must be fire-resistant because he kept flailing about – a black figure amid the white-hot blaze – for minutes.

She could not hear anything. It was so loud, she was inured to it all. Once, at a rock festival, her ears had felt like this. That had lasted for weeks afterwards.

Then the fires went down, and the students started coming through.

Three figures plunged through the curtains of flame, and twitched in the gunfire before falling in smouldering heaps on the forecourt. Then another two, then more. They came, and they died.

A girl, her long braids going like roman candles, got close enough to a Zombie to rip through his suit with her bare claws. She died, but Lynch's men shot down her intended victim along with her.

They were losing already.

03: 39: 10

Willis's mouth was a blackened ruin. Most of his tongue was gone, and his palate was patched with drying Lucite.

But he was still hungry.

03: 27: 46

He had already eaten all the foam rubber packing, and crunched up a couple of circuit boards. The jacketing he had skimmed off the electrical wiring was easy to chew and swallow, but some of the metal components hurt when they went down.

03: 19: 16

The red numbers were still flickering, but he would have them stopped soon.

03: 16: 28

He had tried to bite through the metal cylinder in the middle of the suitcase, but had broken a few teeth for his pains. He had picked up the shards of enamel and gulped them back without trying to taste them. He knew he was dribbling blood.

03: 09:17

Really, all this was just an appetizer.

03: 01: 04

He was very, very hungry. And he had heard that plutonium was supposed to be delicious.

02: 57: 18

125 was spreading. It kept its bulk in the common room, where Carole Ricci and the rest of Lynch's communications people were doing their best to ignore it as they co-ordinated the fighting, but it extended itself into the ventilation system and the interstices between the floors. It probed the extremities of the Chem Building, sucking in a great deal of electrical wiring. It was running a little short of living material to counterbalance the huge quantities of inanimate matter it was using to fortify itself. 125 would need some more human flesh.

It found a few corpses within reach, and snaked tubes to them. Those that had been dead the longest were just meat, but two still had flickers remaining in their brains. 125 nurtured and cherished the new information, even as he redistributed the bones and organs.

Eyes were especially useful.

02: 37: 19

Lynch could feel the tide turning. He knew his military history. Everyone remembered the 300 Spartans, and Davy Crockett at the Alamo, and Custer at Little Big Horn, but nobody admitted that those people had lost the battles. Their achievement was holding out as long as they did while ridiculously outnumbered, but they had still got killed at the end.

That was what would happen here. He had started with maybe 150 people. The enemy were in their thousands. He had the guns, but could not keep them operational.

And the bastards he was fighting did not care whether they lived or died. That made them dangerous.

He was already considering withdrawal scenarios. And he had 125, if the monster could pull through and if he could trust it.

Fucking monster!

He looked at his watch, and tried not to think of Willis.

02: 26: 49

Cazie was immortal, invincible, God-only wise…

…but she knew enough to be at the back end of the horde as they stormed the Chem Building. Her newborns would have to soften the Zombies before she could take part in the victory.

Her hair was standing on end now. Electricity whiplashed as she walked.

She had lieutenants up front, directing the attack. They could execute her designs faithfully. She still thought up the strategies, and gave instructions, but she knew how to delegate authority.

'You'll bow before me, UCC cocksuckers!' she yelled, 'and then we'll see what's what!'

She had picked her personal troop carefully. None of the melters, leakers, bleeders. None of the half-formed, those trapped between stages of humanity, dying like fish in acid. Only the best, the most perfect, the most adapted of the new humanity were selected for her private cadre, her elite guard.

Elliott Frazier stood by her side, her official bodyguard.

She watched the battle, watched wave after wave disappear through the now-feeble wall of flame. There was less gunfire now. Good. The weapons would soon be gone, and old humanity would have only its weak and useless hands and limbs to fight with. Then she would step forward to inaugurate the new era with a mass spilling of the blood of the old.

The fire chief was with the cadre too, unable to talk because of the tigerfangs crowding his mouth, but as alert as a big cat on the prowl. He had grown out of his uniform as his body changed, but still wore his yellow poncho and red helmet. A tall man before, his elongated, hunched back made him a giant. When the fire brigade had arrived, and the spark of growth had leaped into the chief, Cazie had seen a way into the Chem Building. She was thinking faster now, down multiple trains of thought, foreseeing, calculating, planning...

There was another spurting of fire from the UCC flamethrowers, and the barrier sprang up again. Another packed-in mass of Cazie's followers was consumed instantly. Some scattered like fireflies, but most stood their ground, pressing forward.

There were only single shots now.

Cazie extended her fingers, and sparks leaped and danced like Tinkerbell. The fire chief smiled ferally, and raised his hand to catch the blue light. An arc coursed between them.

'Now,' she said.

The fire chief nodded, and swung himself gracefully up into the seat of his vast, beastlike machine. Cazie's corps, already aboard the fire engine, cheered, and rattled their weapons in salute.

Elliott Frazier buzzed his arms, now huge and heavy with chainsaw elephantiasis, in the air, and the shreds of his jacket at his shoulders were agitated, spitting out chunks of stranded cotton.

Eddie Zero sang through his bullhorn, accompanying his ghetto-blaster, one of the old songs. 'Johnny B. Goode'. He was out of the studio now, but still on the air.

Cazie climbed up into the broad seat beside the fire chief, and lazily gestured.

Lightning ripped the air, and the vehicle rolled forward.

02: 02: 37

'Funny how people get off on killing other people, isn't it?' mused 125.

'Pardon?' said Ricci.

'Nothing really.'

'Fine.'

The woman went back to talking into her throat microphone. 125 had the idea that the battle would not go well for the CSD. They were highly trained and facing a rabble, but sometimes random unpredictability was an advantage.

125 was intrigued by the line of Ricci's throat, the tiny pearl-like studs in her earlobes, the trace of a perfume she must have tried to scrub away before hitting the field.

There was a lot of activity outside, still. 125 could see the bright red fire engine driving up, crushing bollards, and ripping up grass like a bulldozer. A crowd swarmed along beside it, shouting and chanting. Firing rapidly, the outermost guards were falling back to the Chem Building.

125 was wondering whether it had dealt with the right person. If Cazie Bruckner took out Lynch, it would have to renegotiate with her.

At least they had something in common.

A stream of water, as solid as a concrete girder, shafted through the fire, knocked men and guns out of the way, and broke against the side of the Chem Building.

Monica was out of the line, but still got soaked. The jet cascaded off the wall, and the forecourt was awash.

Another stream came, tearing up tiles, and churning brown clouds of dirt. A Zombie was caught by the water, and lost his arm cleanly to the high-pressure jet.

Windows shattered, and frames were pulverized.

The fire wall was going out.

Then the juggernaut came, rolling over the charred bodies of its slaves, blaring Chuck Berry, bearing the inheritors of the earth.

Monica saw Cazie in the fire engine, and marvelled at the change in the girl.

A few shots went off, and a cobweb crack appeared in the engine's broad windscreen. There was answering fire from some of the things perched up on the half-raised ladder.

Lynch was waving his arms. His shouts were lost in the din, but Monica knew what his signal meant.

Fall back.

A suited figure grabbed her arm, and pulled her back with him, into the lobby of the Chem Building.

She could not understand. It took her a moment to realize the Zombie was looking out for her, saving her life.

The gesture did not mean as much as it would have done yesterday.

Her saviour slipped on the wet floor of the lobby, and sprawled, skidding backwards. The fire engine mounted the low steps, and crashed into the front of the building. The doomed man burst under its front wheels.

Monica ran with the rest, as bricks parted and glass fragmented. The front cab of the engine rammed its way through the double doors, and the head of the beast was caught inside the building.

Lynch personally fired off a burst at the windscreen, which became as white and opaque as packed sugar, then fell away entirely.

In the cabin, a figure danced and jerked as Lynch killed it. Ropes of blood squirted out through the broken side windows.

It was not Cazie. It was a fireman.

Cazie was gone.

There was noise upstairs.

'Fuck,' shouted Lynch. 'They're inside!'

01:25:51

Flesh petals were blossoming from the holes in Clare's side. She had been shot a couple of times, but that did not hurt at all.

She zig-zagged down the corridor, running with the others. If anyone got in their way, they were knocked down and trampled. Someone usually took the trouble to kill them. Clare did not have to do that sort of thing any more.

Elliott Frazier strode behind the first wave, finishing people off with a rasping pat on the head. He only had to touch his whirring club hands to a Zombie's mask to turn the white headshape into a red ruin, shot through with shards of glass and bone.

Last term, Elliott Frazier had given her a C+ in the Modern European Mind course.

Clare's insides were growing faster than her skin, swelling up her stomach, clogging her breathing. Her new skin was splitting, and she saw raw redness in the cracks.

Already, she was dragging an armful of internal organs around with her.

Whatever it was she had had, she was losing it now.

Finally, she just stopped running and curled up on the floor to wait for it.

It did not take long.

Death settled on her like a black bat, wings folding around her head, darkness blotting out her eyes.

00: 54: 17

Lynch was nearly down to his bare hands, which put him easily on a par with the enemy.

On the stairs, he caught a hunched over goat-thing and broke its back with a practised move.

Whoever was left ought to be retreating to the common room. That would be the last ditch.

Shit, this was a crazy way to die!

He wondered how Willis was doing, and rather hoped he would just fuck up, cut the wrong wire, and bring down instant oblivion.

Like the UCC people thought, it would tidy things up.

He stepped in something that had been a girl amphibian, its guts already hanging out of great tears in its abdomen. Noxious fumes farted out of the corpse.

Lots of the enemy were being laid low like that. 125 had said it was mostly fatal.

If he was doing this all over again, he would have grilled the monster more, found out more about the fucking bug.

Someone big and dangerous with frizzed hair and tusks came out of an office, and he wasted it with his last bullet. He got rid of his last gun, and ran towards the common room.

What a life!

00: 48: 05

Cazie was calm and confident. There must be only a handful of the Zombies left, and her people were everywhere.

Her elite clustered around her protectively, keeping the jostling rankers away from her spark.

Clare was dead with honour. But Elliott Frazier was still with the programme.

They came down from the upper floors, swarming in through the ladders that had breached the windows of the big laboratories. They met little resistance.

Still, a lot of her people were in bad shape. One or two had just upped and died for no reason at all. Evidently, only the strongest could take being hiked up the evolutionary scale.

'Cazie,' someone growled, 'look!'

It was Eddie Zero. He had found a small hatch, leading to a projection booth. Through the aperture, Cazie saw the main science lecture hall. It was full…

…full of…

'Food,' said Eddie.

'Later,' she snapped, 'later.'

Back in the corridor, someone was waiting for her, a cockatoo-plumed woman she had picked for the elite earlier.

'Where are they?' Cazie asked.

'The common room. There aren't many.'

Cazie was serene. She felt the thrill of winning, but wanted a moment of peace.

It passed.

'Okay, let's finish this thing.'

00: 32: 51

125 saw how the fight was going. From its remote eyes, it saw the students prevailing against the CSD forces.

Now, the battle was inside the Chem Building. Inside its body.

It took its flesh where it could be found, reabsorbing itself from the systems of many of the fallen. New consciousnesses crowded in, granting new insight, offering new sensations.

Many of the new components had been significantly mutated by their earlier exposure to 125, and it was pleased at the new shapes and forms they had found.

It suspected that its effects on human beings had a great deal to do with individual psychology. 125 made whims flesh, reshaping bodies to fit unconscious minds.

It took a particular type of mind to become perfect.

125 regretted Lynch's immunity. After Cazie, he would have made the ideal avatar.

It draped itself stickily across corridors like a curtain, entrapping those who blundered into it.

With each component it absorbed, it became better, stronger, smarter, more fit…

00: 29: 18

Monica collapsed on a chair in the common room. She guessed the Zombies were down to single figures.

She had a stitch. Momentarily, she thought she had been shot, but there was no wound.

She gasped for breath.

The monster was up and about, swaying on its spiny legs. It would be a shock even for Cazie, Monica thought. It had grown, and it seemed to be fixed to the walls and ceiling like a complicated appliance, organic plugs slotted into holes. Its tentacular appendages pulsed like snakes swallowing large rats, and lumps were funnelled into its main bulk.

God, she wished she could have this day over again. She would stay in bed, or emigrate to Australia, or go home to her parents, or any bloody thing…

Lynch had blood on his hands. At least she supposed it was blood. He stood with the monster, tensed and ready.

There was nothing for it but to wait for Cazie.

00: 27: 27

Eddie went through the swing doors first, then came out again dead, a knife sunk to the hilt in his face between his antennae.

That gave Cazie some pause, but her aides swept past her and into the common room. Eddie was mashed underfoot.

Cazie stepped forward, and went into the room.

Shit! Fuck! Jesus!

What was *that*?

'Hello, Ms Bruckner,' it said.

00: 25: 52

No one moved. 125 was in control.

It tipped itself forward, and looked at Cazie Bruckner. A halo of blue flames seemed to shimmer around her head, but she was in deep shock.

'You don't know me, but you've got me, so to speak. I'm Batch 125, your disease. Your symbiote, to use the word of the day. Actually, I'm not all that symbiotic, as you'd have noticed if you had paid attention to the way ninety-three out of a hundred of your fellow infectees self-destruct within a few hours. Congratulations. You're one of the very few people who have been able to come to terms with having me.'

She was obviously smitten at first sight. Her blue aura flushed red, and, mouth agape in wonder, she came, forward, her hand out to touch 125. She was extraordinarily beautiful by anyone's standards. At least, certainly by the standards of all the people whose brains 125 had absorbed. He felt he had taken enough grey matter on board to make his own aesthetic judgements now.

He opened a mouth and wolf-whistled.

The girl got close to it. Lynch stepped between them. 'We've got a deal, 125!'

125 shot a few quills at the CSD man.

00: 18: 26

Lynch took the darts in his neck and shoulder. A rush of excruciating pain shot through his entire body.

A barbed arm came out of 125's bulk, and stuck into his chest. He felt the triple claw sink in, and heard his ribs crack.

He was lifted off the floor.

This would teach him even to consider trusting a fucking virus!

He kicked, his combat boots scraping carpet.

His bowels let go.

125 was talking to him, but he could not listen.

The charge hit him through the hooks in his chest. With the first jolt, he went into convulsions. He twisted badly enough to break his spine.

125 had developed some sort of biological laser, and was shocking him like an electric eel.

His brain fried. His eyes popped. His skeleton burned white hot, and turned to ash in his body. He was cooked through in seconds.

00: 16: 07

Monica held her nose.

125 dropped Lynch through the hole in the floor. He stuck in the gap, speared by upward-bent rods.

He had died with his eyes open.

125 roared with something that might have been laughter. Cazie was slowly sinking to her knees, ready to worship the creature.

Infectees were crowding into the room.

Elliott Frazier – the dreamboat TV prof – took aside one of Lynch's surviving soldiers and took him apart with a few swipes of his whirring, swollen, bloody arms. Somebody tried to surrender, and Elliott did for them. Lynch's last radio operator took off her headset and carefully put it down. Nobody bothered her.

Monica kept looking back at Lynch's black, bloodied face. She did not know whether she should envy the dead.

Now what?

0: 08: 19

Willis picked up the clippers, snipped the final wire, and…

00: 08: 18

...the little red numbers stopped.

00: 08: 18

Cazie sat down, and watched the monster pick through the leftovers.

All but three or four of her cadre were dead or dying, and the monster was sucking out bits and pieces, incorporating them into its already-vast bulk.

Elliott Frazier submitted to it. He offered up his arms, and they were sucked into the doughy lump of the monster's body. He looked back one last time, smiling slightly, and let the wave of flesh engulf him, sucking him in completely. A wall of warty skin formed behind him. She heard his distinctive buzzing, muffled by the ton of flesh, and the skinwall undulated in agitation.

She wondered if it had thought how it would get out of the building. It was already bigger than any of the doors. The only hole big enough for it was jammed up by the fire engine.

It did not seem to bear her any malice. She thought it might be rather fond of her. It extruded a head on an arm, and kissed her on the mouth with it.

A charge coursed through her body.

The head was hairless, but had Elliott Frazier's handsome face. She was almost satisfied.

125 dangled tendrils into the laboratory, and reached for Willis's head.

The delicate filaments went into the man's brain. It was riddled with virus, but 125 could pick up the information it needed.

The suitcase was out of commission.

125 let Willis go. There was no point in killing the man and, after all, he was probably the only human being who would ever – intentionally or not – save its life.

It had Cazie under its spell already, and that gave it all the cards.

It was a shame the human body really was not a very good vehicle. It was susceptible, but too fragile to keep the virus alive in its system for more than a few days. 125 was beginning to realize that it was not the super-virulent plague it had been sold as.

There were infectees spreading out there, passing on the disease. But without the concentrated exposure the original victims had had, the next generation of infectees would struggle on, and maybe even fight off the virus. A few steps down the line, and it would be no more serious than a cold.

Under natural conditions, it could just have mutated into another anonymous disease and never have been more than a footnote.

But it had this body, which was adapting very nicely to its purpose. It was the smartest bug that had ever lived.

And it had Cazie Bruckner.

Monica watched the thing grow.

Already, it was more like a plant than an animal. Its flesh clung to the walls, and grew into the ducts and out of the windows. Arms and legs hung semi-uselessly from its branches, a nasty reminder of its raw materials. Eyes peered out of pink masses. Elliott Frazier's head surveyed the room, a familiarly thoughtful expression on its face. If 125 could find a wig and a pipe, it would be able to do a perfect impression of the professor.

She thought it was probably all through the building by now. There had been an appalling wail earlier, and the thing had been very active. Then it went quiet, and the flesh reddened. New blood. It must have got into the lecture hall. There would have been more than enough flesh in there to feed the creature, but probably not enough to kill its hunger. Hundreds more were dead, but she was too tired to feel stricken by the loss.

She tried to remember faces. There had been a crowd in the hall, sitting quietly, waiting for rescue. But they seemed less real than the individuals, than Brian, Jason, Lindy, Frazier. Even than

Lynch. She would never be able to watch anyone pretend to die in a war film or a Western again without remembering.

It looked for a while as if the thing would eat Cazie, even. It was talking very quietly with her, almost seductively. Then, it wrapped the girl in tendrils of flesh. Cazie was lifted off the floor, held in a writhing web of tissue. Her face was serene, almost beatific. The flesh folded around her, nuzzling her like a kitten. Only her head was outside the creature. Then, Cazie gasped, and her body wriggled within its sleeping-bag-like cocoon. With acute distaste, Monica realized the creature was making love to its high priestess.

That completed her day.

Cazie felt 125's touch all over her, and felt its extruded flesh slipping into her body, warming her loins, moving gently, pumping into her. There was an electrical crackle as they joined, and she was having another of her minute-long orgasms.

Her brain danced, and dreams flickered behind her eyelids.

125 was her ultimate father-lover.

For several months when she was five or six, her father had taken to coming to the nursery and touching her private places. She had repressed the memory, but realized how it had formed her.

125's touch washed away the stain Daddy had left.

Cazie did not now know what her father had meant. She thought his touch had been innocent not exploratory. He could not have been thinking of anything else.

125's voice was inside her, encouraging her, passing on what it had learned, seeking out new pleasures for her.

She changed her mind about her name. There was nothing wrong with Corinne.

She hung in the webbing of its flesh, her legs braced, her insteps arched as 125 grew inside her, teasing, pushing, secreting.

It loved her without question.

That made it unique in her life. She felt wetness on her face, and realized she was crying.

When it was over, 125 allowed Cazie to slip out whole again. What was left of her clothes was gone, as was her pubic hair. She had been licked clean and dry.

She looked like an alien Eve, her body sparkling where 125 had caressed.

Monica was not able to look at her.

Cazie slept now, under its protection. For the first time, she saw the girl completely relaxed.

It was still eating everything. Monica guessed it was taking minerals aboard as well as living matter. Its hide had metallic patches, and some parts of it were a bricky orange.

She wondered why she had been left alone. Too insignificant to be a problem, she supposed. Not like Lynch, who had long been squeezed through the hole in the floor and eaten up. There were others alive in its coils, she knew. Lynch's radio operator was sitting still on her chair on the other side of the room, apparently untouched and untouchable.

It was nearly morning.

125 had completely annexed the Chem Building, making it a part of its body. It would need to be a giant to survive among human beings. A giant of flesh and steel and concrete.

It had absorbed over a thousand brains, and learned many things, many skills. Most of the personalities it had snuffed out quickly, but it was sampling the range of human character types. It even absorbed Frank Lynch, taking on board his grasp of strategy and his lack of regard for human life. It was beginning to get a good idea of what the world beyond the valley was like.

It knew that people were going to be its biggest problem. It had to eat more of them, to know more about them. It had to be big enough to be indestructible, and smart enough to avoid capture and enslavement. But, through the minds it was starting to think of as its ancestors, its contributors, it had read millions of books, lived through countless situations – wars, love affairs, divorces, seminars, rock concerts, crimes, riots, orgies, demonstrations, political meetings, films, plays, murders, arguments, jokes, reconciliations, deaths, births, illnesses, childhoods, injuries, triumphs. It was developing an all-round personality.

It ate people, it ate walls, it ate furniture, it ate girders, it ate stone, it ate plastics. It went through laboratories indiscriminately, absorbing chemicals, elements, whatever. There was little it could not use somehow.

It would stay where it was for the moment, and solve the problem of mobility later. It suspected that it could detach parts of itself and send them out to do some of the more fiddly jobs on their own. It could convert many of the dead people at its disposal into puppet creatures, linked to it through strong, thin filaments. Perhaps, in time, it would learn to be smaller.

It would keep Cazie, and a few others, inside, near its brain. It wanted external input, and someone to talk to.

It sucked the building's electrical works into its system, and distributed the wiring throughout its body, snaking the plastic-and-rubber coated strands alongside its veins and nerves, then growing solid sheathing around all three systems. It detached itself from the mains, remembering through several different consciousnesses the 1950s science fiction film in which the vegetable monster is electrocuted. It knew lots about a lot of things.

It had eaten a movie buff somewhere along the line. The film was *The Thing From Another World,* 1951, directed by Christian. W. Nyby, produced by Howard Hawks, based on the story 'Who Goes There?' by John W. Campbell, Jr, and starring Kenneth Tobey, Douglas Spencer, Margaret Sheridan, Robert

Comthwaite and James Arness as the Monster.

Knowledge filled up the back of its brain, the random accumulations of several thousand lifetimes systematically sorted out and put to use. 125 felt that it could sing, kill, make love, cook, change a fuse, repair a car, write an opera, type, solve a crossword puzzle, follow the plot of *EastEnders*, educate a child, handle a hostage crisis, do a million other things.

To replace the mains, it generated electricity and amused itself by keeping on the lights in the common room. It concentrated hard, and was able to do it, although a sudden surge popped all the bulbs along the ground floor corridors when it first began to generate.

Then it ate something that disagreed with it.

'Nooooooooo,' screamed Willis, 'it's mine! Mine!'

The obscene tentacles that had grown throughout the laboratory fastened on the suitcase, and cut through the metal casing of the core as if it were an eggshell.

'My plutonium! My ploot! Mine! Mine! Mine!'

The suitcase disappeared entirely into the main sucker.

Willis chewed a wooden bench in frustration.

He filled his mouth, and found himself stuck into the bench, held fast by his growing rows of teeth.

His heart and lungs stopped minutes after his mind had gone.

As soon as it tasted the radioactive material, 125 realized it had made a mistake. Tendrils of death shot out like cancers from the ruptured suitcase, leaving dead tissue in their wake.

125 tried to retreat, but the death grew, looking for its consciousness.

The weight of useless flesh began to drag it down. It felt itself coming apart, fragmenting.

The plutonium pumped more death into it.

Whole areas of its mind went dark as the black crab fed on its brain. Death ate and absorbed it as it had eaten and absorbed its components.

It rediscovered pain.

Like Lynch, it resolved to fight to the end. As death encircled it, 125 vowed to survive.

It tried shedding large lumps of itself, rending away live sections to prevent the plutonium poisoning spreading just as houses had been blown up to block the Great Fire of London.

It did no good. The death was in its system now, in its blood. It could not be rid of the poison.

There were so many things 125 wished it had done…

Monica woke up to find 125 in a bad way. Chunks of it had fallen off, and lay congealed and greyish on the carpet. It hung loose from the ceiling and walls. The lights were off.

'Overextended yourself, didn't you?'

It did not talk back.

Cazie was still asleep, curled up like a kitten. The radio woman was still sitting, calm and mad.

Monica got up, and left the common room. The corridor was full of the stink of death. Withered and shrunken rows of flesh hung like party ribbons. Dead bodies grew out of the mass.

125 was dead or dying. She knew it was not a miracle. She knew the virus was just an organism like her, and the world was a hostile place. It had made a mistake in thinking itself invulnerable, not that she could blame it for reaching the conclusion.

She went downstairs. There were holes in the walls, and oddments of debris littered the main hall. 125 was kicking weakly in some places, but mostly it just hung and putrefied, slimy lumps falling off.

She squeezed past the crumpled fire engine, and came out into a bright summer day that hurt her eyes.

The campus was quiet. It looked like a WWI battlefield. Most people in sight were dead. Water was still dribbling from the firehoses. A few fires persisted. Early birds had descended, and were picking at the corpses, tearing loose bite-size chunks. A few other survivors were wandering around dazed, or slumped asleep with dew on their faces.

125 had extended itself beyond the building, squeezing thick, leathery tentacles through the sewage outlets and other holes in the wall. They hung, life dribbling away, human features liquefying. A snapping dog was tearing at one mass of the creature, shredding through olive skin to the pink meat beneath.

She sat down on the damp concrete forecourt, and crossed her legs, and cried.

Somewhere, overhead, helicopter blades sliced the air. They got louder.

EPILOGUE

REASON IN THE AGE OF LUNACY

Corinne had been strapped down for weeks now. The leather thongs at her wrists and ankles were reinforced with half-inch-thick metal bars, and a wide steel belt held her midriff to the iron cot which, in turn, was bolted to the floor.

They had been feeding her intravenously, and doing tests. She was fed up with tests.

From one of the nurses, she had gathered she was not the only one in the facility. There had been other survivors. Some of them had died in the early days, but she knew she was not in danger.

The voice in her head told her she would survive.

The nurses were all pretty and pleasant, and definitely not working for the National Health. One of the doctors had said something about 'the corporation' picking up the bill, and so she supposed she was being held by UCC.

In a sense, she appreciated the rest.

They had opened her up and looked around and sewn her back together. They had X-rayed her from every conceivable angle.

The voice in her head told her she would be strong.

Once, early on, she had got her fingers to a nurse, but now they watched her hands, and kept her nails clipped. They had to do that every morning with industrial pliers. It hurt, but Corinne did not scream and shout any more.

The voice in her head advised her to keep quiet and calm, to wait for her time. It would be soon.

This could not last.

No one had come to visit her in hospital. She supposed her parents thought she was dead.

Actually, if Josh Unwin were personally to telephone her father and inform him that he was holding prisoner and torturing Little Corinne, Daddy would probably go along with it. Daddy was a big fan of Josh Unwin, and would not let go by a chance to lick the bigger fish's bottom clean. No matter what it cost.

She would be a better parent. They had not told her yet, but she knew already.

It was the voice that talked to her inside her head.

She had been getting her strength back. She knew she could break restraint any time she wanted. But for the moment she lay back and took her food in the arm, and pretended the shots they gave her had some effect. They were stupid.

They thought they could get rid of it, but were dithering. She would be out before they ever came to a decision.

She knew lots of things they did not.

Like, for instance, she knew who the father was.

AFTERWORD

I spent much of the 1980s affiliated to arts collectives, including Sheep Worrying Enterprises – a Somerset-based theatre-music-fanzine-whatever bunch for whom I wrote or co-wrote a bunch of plays – and the London listings magazine *City Limits*. With Neil Gaiman and Eugene Byrne, I was also responsible for the Peace and Love Corporation, which provided humorous filler articles for girlie magazines like *Knave* and *Fiesta* and was a mainstay of the short-lived funny magazine *The Truth*. We would have liked to do one of those wildly successful trivial humour paperbacks, but no one was interested in publishing our projected laff-a-paragraph guaranteed hit *How to Lose Friends and Irritate People* – perhaps because none of us could draw (Neil can a bit, actually) and those things all had scratchy cartoons of dead cats or live penises in them. Aside from giving us a much-needed source of freelance income, the P&LCo (like Sheep Worrying) was a testing ground for ideas we'd develop later. Several of Neil's comics arcs and novels echo a structure we'd used for a series of articles on various big topics (education, religion, etc.), in which a naïve narrator (his name was Paul Lobkowitz) is accompanied on a journey by an ambiguous trickster know-it-all (Dr Sigmund von Doppelganger) who would teach him life lessons, essentially, by ripping him off. It's possible (ahem) we were thinking of the relationship between Swamp Thing and John Constantine in the Alan Moore–Steve Bissette–John Totelben run on *Swamp Thing*. I first experimented with the Choose-Your-Own-Adventure format of my novel *Life's Lottery* in a *Penthouse* piece co-written with Neil called 'Sexual Pursuit', about a hapless bloke trying to hook up in the singles hot-spots of Leamington Spa (mostly, it didn't end well).

Though the bulk of the P&LCo stuff was written by Neil, Eugene and me, other folk who happened to be in the room when we were trying to be funny sometimes joined in. Stefan Jaworzyn, and prime mover of the band Skullflower, was a frequent contributor, as was the late Phil Nutman, British correspondent for *Fangoria* magazine. In a roundabout way, the novels collected here are Phil's fault. I met Stefan at Sussex University at an all-night screening of horror films in 1978 and ran into him again in 1984 at the Scala Cinema, where he later co-curated the Shock Around the Clock festivals. I first agreed to work with Neil on what became our little-known book of science fiction quotations *Ghastly Beyond Belief* when Jo Fletcher introduced us at a British Fantasy Society pub meeting in 1983 (I think she was trying to get rid of him). Neil, Stefan and I were at the Scala for a launch party for a book about film posters in October 1984 and met Phil there. Some of us watched *The Projected Man* that afternoon, and went on to the press screening of *The Last Starfighter* in the evening. This was the era of VHS, and we'd often get together in the tiny room I had in a hippie flat in Muswell Hill for marathon-length overnight viewing sessions. I had started reviewing films for *City Limits* and the *Monthly Film Bulletin*, and occasionally *Venue* in Bristol, where Eugene was an editor. Anne Billson was often sent by *Time Out* to cover the same films, and we all met her about the same time. Stephen Jones and Dave Reeder founded the important '80s film fanzine *Shock Xpress*, which Stefan took over... and we all wrote for that, along with Shock Around the Clock co-chairman Alan Jones. Clive Barker's first *Books of Blood* made a splash in the genre and he got started on doing all the things he's done, in theatre, film, literature and painting. Clive lived in Crouch End, in the street next to the one I moved to in 1988. Peter Straub had once lived there too. A weird fact: *Anno Dracula*, the *Books of Blood* and *Ghost Story* were all written within a circle a hundred yards or so across.

Phil was filling the pages of *Fangoria* by interviewing British filmmakers who specialised in horror. There wasn't much actual British horror cinema produced in the 1980s, though Clive sold the screenplays that became *Underworld* and *Rawhead Rex* (which Neil and I nearly got to work on when Clive momentarily blanched at one more set of producers' notes) and was persuaded by the experience to direct *Hellraiser* himself. One of Phil's interviewees was the genial Norman J. Warren, director of *Satan's Slave*, *Prey* and *Terror*. He had recently made *Inseminoid* for American-based producer Richard Gordon, a lively *Alien* knock-off shot in Chiselhurt Caves, which prompted Alan Jones to wonder whether 'chainsaws would feature so heavily in future space programmes'. Phil reported back to the P&LCo folk that Norman was looking for original script ideas he could take to Richard... and so we set out to come up with a whole slate of them, in the hope that one would rise to the top. The four of us sat in that tiny room and hashed out four different stories in different sub-genres, trying (and probably failing) to think within the sort of budget available. Our brief was fairly loose, though I believe Norman said it would be helpful if one or two of the lead actors were American – *Inseminoid* had gone that route, probably because *Alien* had.

Each of us took away a set of notes to write up. Neil's was *Remember Remember*, a holiday-themed slasher movie about Guy Fawkes Night. We must have heard of *V for Vendetta*, which had begun in the British comic *Warrior* but was curtailed mid-story with the title's cancellation, but couldn't have foreseen that the Guy Fawkes mask would ever catch on. Phil worked on *Hell*

Fire, a scrambling of the plots of *The Maltese Falcon* and *Night of the Demon* which I eventually reworked as a short story 'Mother Hen' (reprinted in the appendix of the Titan Books edition of *The Quorum*) – though I didn't have a copy of the outline to hand when I wrote it up, and only remembered the original concept. Stefan got *Bloody Students*, our shot at a 'virus outbreak' story along the lines of George Romero's *The Crazies* or David Cronenberg's *Rabid*. Stefan and I had been at university together, and enjoyed the idea of staging mutant attacks and battles on our old campus. Stefan came up with the tag-line '*Bloody Students* ... first, they cut their grants, then they cut their throats!' This was before student loans, when we literally didn't know how well off we were.

Then there was *Bad Dreams*, which I was in charge of.

Our first thought for this was to revive a type of horror/crime film that hadn't been done lately, in which the menace is a semi-supernatural crime boss like Dr Mabuse or Fu-Manchu. After talking that through, we came to think it might be a hard sell – though we had hit on the title, which we were rather pleased with since it was a commonplace expression that hadn't been used as a horror film title before. Given the recent success of *A Nightmare on Elm Street*, we switched our master crook for an immortal vampire type who could manipulate reality (Neil and I were – and still are – great admirers of Philip K. Dick, which probably shows) to persecute our (American) journalist heroine. I suppose the Cenobites of *Hellraiser* have a similar m.o., but it should be obvious we were more influenced by Clive – *The Damnation Game* had come out – than he could have been by us, though Neil has suggested that the Cenobites were loosely based on the Peace & Love Corporation. The character of Clive Broome in *Bad Dreams* was called Clive Harker in the original outline; we played with the names of other friends too. The heroine is named Anne Nielsen in tribute to Anne Billson, who – in retrospect – we should have asked to join in as writer (I later worked with her on a play, *The Hallowe'en Sessions*). She later wrote the novelisation of *Dream Demon*, the British *Nightmare on Elm Street* ripoff which *did* get made. Norman and Richard quite liked our ideas, especially *Bad Dreams* and *Bloody Students*, but no development money was forthcoming and so the P&L Co film projects fizzled out. In 1987, Norman made *Bloody New Year* instead. I later learned that *Slimer*, a wonderfully lurid paperback co-written by our friends John Brosnan and Leroy Kettle under the pseudonym Harry Adam Knight, had also started out as a pitch for a Warren–Gordon film; *Slimer* had the distinction of eventually being turned into a movie, the direct-to-video quickie *Proteus*. It was the beginning of great things for Harry, who delivered a masterpiece in *The Fungus* (now reissued and an essential read) and founded a genetic dinosaur franchise in *Carnosaur* (adapted as a series of films by Roger Corman).

All the while, I was working on my own projects. I'd written a novella-length draft of my first novel *The Night Mayor*, the opening chapters of *Jago* (a stab at a big thick horror book along the lines of *Ghost Story* or *'Salem's Lot*) and pages of notes for a projected trilogy that (after a lot of changes) became the *Anno Dracula* series. Neil and I talked about co-writing a disgusting horror paperback (there were lots of those about) called *The Creeps*, about mutants in the tunnels under London (where Neil would later set the mostly mutant-free *Neverwhere*). We also pondered a killer badger book called *The Set*. With Eugene, we worked on a computer game scenario and an unrelated novel both called *Neutrino Junction* – both sadly uncompleted. A year or so after we had outlined our film ideas and nothing was happening with them, I was at a loose end and decided to write *Bad Dreams* as a novel. I hammered out a first draft on an IBM electric typewriter. This didn't sell until after I'd placed *The Night Mayor* with Simon & Schuster in 1989; the final version benefited greatly from the input of my agent Antony Harwood and editor Maureen Waller. The 'Entr'Acte' section was written well after the bulk of the book, very close to its 1990 publication, in the middle of the night because I was jet-lagged after my first trip to America. It's one of my favourite sequences in the novel. There are elements in the book that feel to me like they came from Neil, Stefan or Phil – a lot of Neil's stories feature protagonists with remote or monstrous parents, for instance. Neil also did all the research (rather more than we needed, really – but he made a convincing case for it) into seamy Soho clubs, with full credit to Roz Kaveney for getting him past fearsome door security. Stefan went along one night, but couldn't stop laughing which probably ruined the mood.

Other elements came from Norman's briefing: making Anne an American in London wasn't something I'd naturally have done – authentic American Lisa Tuttle kindly read the manuscript and gave feedback about this side of things. *Dream Demon* and *Hellraiser* have American heroines, so Norman might well have been on to something. While we were outlining, we talked a bit about who we'd like to see cast. I remember us thinking of Rosanna Arquette or Linda Hamilton, both doing interesting things in small-scale films like *Baby, It's You* or *The Terminator* about then... though we also liked the idea of casting Sandra Bernhard and Amanda Plummer as the Nielsen sisters. One actor we wanted for the main villain roles in all our pitches was Richard Lynch, who had a very distinctive look – on an acid trip in 1967, he set fire to himself and his combination of scarred skin and handsome bone structure that got him a lot of sinister parts. He's remarkable as the alien hermaphrodite messiah in Larry Cohen's *God Told Me To*, but was most visible at the time we were working on these ideas as a Russian baddie in the Chuck Norris classic *Invasion USA*. Skinner, of *Bad Dreams*, and Lynch, of *Bloody Students*, are both tailor-made Richard Lynch parts. I think we wrote him into the other two stories as well. Ironically, in 1988, after I'd written the first draft of the novel, a film called *Bad Dreams* was produced in America... not only was it a *Nightmare on Elm Street* ripoff, but it cast Richard Lynch as the ghostly menace. It went straight to video in the UK, and didn't have a high enough profile to persuade me to change the title. As a teenager, I had read *How to Write a Novel*, a very useful book of practical advice by John Braine which I mostly ignored… One thing that stuck in my mind was that Braine said he would reject out of hand any book that used a title which was a quote from *Hamlet* or *Macbeth*, prompting me to nod sagely and vow never to do that. Though it sounds like a commonplace, the phrase 'bad dreams' is actually a quote from *Hamlet*… 'O God, I could be bounded in a nutshell and count myself a king of infinite space, were it not that I have bad dreams.' So, in a nutshell, two permanent additions to the English language in one throwaway line.

With some trepidation, I showed my first draft to Neil, Phil and Stefan – who were supportive and gave helpful advice. The whole 'Broadway play' sequence, which would have been difficult to do on film, was not in the outline and so was new to them; Neil made a key suggestion about the use of Martin Landau as a face for the monster, riffing on the way he would peel off masks each week in *Mission: Imposssible*. Phil and Lisa both made me go back over Anne's character and work a bit harder on making her distinctive… which eventually led to her reappearing in my novel *The Quorum*, which grew out of this period in my life and the milieu the P&LCo were hanging about in.

Having done it once, I was sort of impelled to give it another go – turning the nugget of *Hell Fire* into 'Mother Hen', which Steve Jones published in *Fantasy Tales*. Then, at a point when I was blocked on other things, it occurred to me that it wouldn't hurt to have another novel-length manuscript to show around. I set out to write *Bloody Students* inside a week, the way Roger Corman made *The Little Shop of Horrors* when he had a spare three days' shooting. The downside was that I didn't have a copy of the full outline, so I had to reconstruct it from memory and a few notes. I diverged greatly from the more controlled movie we had envisioned. My feeling was that doing a book this fast would mean tapping into the energy and verve of Corman's B pictures. I was also hoping to write something in the wild spirit of Harry Adam Knight. If it didn't sell, I'd only lost a week. As it happens, it sold twice – Malcolm Edwards at HarperCollins bought it, on a recommendation from Mike Dickinson, but the bottom dropped out of the pulp paperback horror market and they returned the book to me, though a nice, lurid cover had already been created. Eventually, after my early novels had found a place at Simon & Schuster, Martin Fletcher – my editor on *Anno Dracula*, *The Quorum* and *Life's Lottery* – bought *Bloody Students*, though he asked for a new title. I chose *Orgy of the Blood Parasites*, working title for David Cronenberg's 1974 breakthrough film *Shivers*. Having moved from IBM typewriter to Amstrad word processor, I put the book through a second draft, adding several more days to the schedule (and increasing the body count) but not really tidying it up much. By then, I had started a parallel career writing as Jack Yeovil for Games Workshop, in the Warhammer Fantasy and Dark Future series, and it made sense to issue *Orgy* as a Jack Yeovil joint.

I'm happy these two books are available again, especially in this double bill edition. Techincally, they were first published in the 1990s… but they were (mostly) written in the '80s, before we got even slightly respectable. Reading them, I'm reminded of marathon video-watching, funny articles for porn mags, lively meals in cheap restaurants, the heights and lows of 1980s cinema, barbeques at Steve and Jo's in Wembley, Sussex University in the 1970s and North London in the 1980s, long-gone magazines that didn't die well, random introductions in pubs that changed the courses of lives, regular cinemas showing double bills like *My Bloody Valentine* and *The Funhouse*, gone-too-soon talents like Phil and Rob Holdstock and John Brosnan, the March for Jobs and Miners' Strike fund-raisers, Neil and Clive with their original accents, sleeping on floors between sessions at the typewriter, watching reruns of *Bilko* and *The Avengers* when inspiration flagged, struggling with these computer things that would never catch on, writing a musical (the last great Sheep Worrying production) in two afternoons (break-out hit: 'I'm Too Fat to Rock'), meetings with ripoff merchants, video nasties (frankly, that's what these books would have been if filmed in 1986 – and proud of it), FantasyCons in Birmingham and Shock Around the Clock in King's Cross, Margaret Thatcher going on and on and on, Captain Sensible singing 'Happy Talk', *Betty Blue* and *Blue Velvet*, and the thing that was said in the place where we went that time.

Kim Newman,
thirty years later...

ABOUT THE AUTHOR

Kim Newman is a novelist, critic and broadcaster. His fiction includes *The Night Mayor*, *Bad Dreams*, *Jago*, the *Anno Dracula* novels and stories, *The Quorum* and *Life's Lottery*, all currently being reissued by Titan Books, *Professor Moriarty: The Hound of the D'Urbervilles* published by Titan Books and *The Vampire Genevieve* and *Orgy of the Blood Parasites* as Jack Yeovil. His non-fiction books include the seminal *Nightmare Movies* (recently reissued by Bloomsbury in an updated edition), *Ghastly Beyond Belief* (with Neil Gaiman), *Horror: 100 Best Books* (with Stephen Jones), *Wild West Movies*, *The BFI Companion to Horror*, *Millennium Movies* and BFI Classics studies of *Cat People* and *Doctor Who*.

He is a contributing editor to *Sight & Sound* and *Empire* magazines (writing *Empire*'s popular Video Dungeon column), has written and broadcast widely on a range of topics, and scripted radio and television documentaries. His stories 'Week Woman' and 'Ubermensch' have been adapted into an episode of the TV series *The Hunger* and an Australian short film; he has directed and written a tiny film *Missing Girl*. Following his Radio 4 play 'Cry Babies', he wrote an episode ('Phish Phood') for Radio 7's series *The Man in Black*.

His official website can be found at www.johnnyalucard.com

THE QUORUM

by KIM NEWMAN

In 1961, Derek Leech emerges fully formed from the polluted River Thames, destined to found a global media empire. In 1978, three ambitious young men strike a deal with Leech. They are offered wealth, glamour, and success, but a price must be paid. In 1994, Leech's purpose moves to its conclusion, and as the men struggle, they realise the truth of the ultimate price.

A brand-new edition of the critically acclaimed novel featuring five short stories by the award-winning author.

"Fans of 'Deal with the Devil' stories ought to be delighted with this fifth novel from British horror writer Newman, which brings a new twist or two to the genre." *Publisher's Weekly*

"This well-told tale is peopled with a fascinating array of characters and offers much witty and sage commentary on our materialistic society." *Library Journal*

"Newman's postmodern morality play puts him into the first rank of current horror novelists." *Booklist*

LIFE'S LOTTERY

by KIM NEWMAN

At six years old you're asked to make a choice, the first of many in a multitude of possible lives.

If you make the right decision you may live a long happy life, or be immensely powerful, or win the lottery. If you take the wrong path, you may become a murderer, die young, make every mistake possible, or make no impression on life at all. The choice is yours. And by making the choices you do, you will change forever the lives of your family, your friends, your enemies, and your lovers. You can even change the fate of the world; all you have to do is choose…

A brand-new edition of the critically acclaimed 'Choose Your Own Adventure' novel for adults, where small decision have monumental consequences.

"The hero's life is in your hands… an epic read."
Guardian

"Curiously unsettling but always gripping… like nothing else you have ever read." *The Times*

JAGO

by KIM NEWMAN

In the tiny English village of Alder, dreams and nightmares
are beginning to come true. Creatures from local legend,
science fiction and the dark side of the human mind prowl
the town.

Paul, a young academic composing a thesis about the end of
the world, and his girlfriend Hazel, a potter, have come to
Alder for the summer. Their idea of a rural retreat gradually
sours as the laws of nature begin to break down around
them. Paul and Hazel are soon drawn into a vortex of fear
as violent chaos engulfs the community and the village
prepares to reap a harvest of horror.

**A brand-new edition of the critically acclaimed novel.
This edition also contains the short stories 'Ratting', 'Great
Western' and 'The Man on the Clapham Omnibus'.**

"A roaring good read." *The Times*

"Newman's prose is sophisticated and his narrative drive
irresistible." *Publishers Weekly*

AN ENGLISH GHOST STORY

by KIM NEWMAN

A dysfunctional British nuclear family seeks to solve their problems and start a new life away from the city in the sleepy Somerset countryside. At first their perfect new home creates a rare peace and harmony, and the four grow steadily closer. But when the house begins to turn on them, it seems to know just how to hurt them the most – threatening to destroy the family from the inside out.

The brand-new standalone novel from the acclaimed author of *Anno Dracula*.

"That oh-so-unassuming title does not equip you for the journey you're about to undertake. Immersive, claustrophobic and utterly wonderful." M.R. Carey, bestselling author of *The Girl With All the Gifts*

"Kim Newman gets inside your head like pollen off a field of wildflowers; the pleasant idyllic turns full of suffocating dread. Thoroughly enjoyable, master storytelling." Lauren Beukes, bestselling author of *Broken Monsters*

For more fantastic fiction, author events, exclusive excerpts,
competitions, limited editions and more

VISIT OUR WEBSITE